MW01107597

GROWING UP *Mennonite*

Broken Horses

BAILEY LARROQUETTE

Growing Up Mennonite

This is a work of fiction loosely based on a true story, all names of people and places (other than three provinces) have been changed to protect the personal identities of those who may resemble a character in this book. The novel was not written to accurately depict any particular person.

tellwell

Tellwell Talent
www.tellwell.ca

ISBN
978-0-2288-7666-3 (Paperback)

TABLE OF CONTENTS

CHAPTER 1

The Phone Call

BRENDA-JANE GRIPPED her cellphone tightly, wishing it was his throat. Years after the mechanical decision at a church alter call to forgive her father, new annoyance threatened to undo her hard work.

"And don't hit your kids whatever you do," he had said quietly. Silent tension—was there ever another kind?—filled the space between them. Her emotions teetered between anger and pain but came to rest on exhaustion. The laundry was piled on the table, and she still had bologna sandwiches to make for the kids for school tomorrow.

"I am not ready for parenting advice from you, Dad," Brenda managed at last. "You of all people."

More silence. She waited for the customary explosion between them whenever this topic was discussed. Usually it wasn't.

"Besides, I don't hit them, I spank them," BJ snapped. "Last time I checked; spanking was still legal in this country."

"Yeah but it doesn't work," Father argued.

"You're telling me," she threw back at him. Memories of vicious whippings he had delivered along with demands for complete silence resurfaced.

"You didn't spank us, Dad. You beat us. I have scars that never quite healed. So, you're a fine one to preach to me, aren't you?"

"Well, that's the treatment I got. So, don't hit her anymore."

"Okay then. As long as you had a good excuse. Be sure to write that book on parenting sometime soon." Was it her imagination or did he chuckle? They said their "auf wiedersehens" and concluded the confrontation almost pleasantly, a mammoth step for their once volatile relationship.

She tapped the red button on her phone to hang up, suddenly nostalgic for the days when one could actually slam a receiver back onto its cradle with a resounding crack.

BJ poured herself a cup of chamomile tea and sank down onto her goodwill chesterfield, watching the lights flicker and dance across her Christmas tree. Had she just received one of those authentic gifts only God could deliver? She felt better about her relationship with her father than she had in years. Not that things hadn't constantly improved over time—counselling sessions and healing seminars—but a candid conversation on ghosts from the past was new. And the anger had disappeared as quickly as it transpired.

The child in conversation was Brenda's eleven-year-old firstborn, Riley. She was as rough on her mother's fragile parenting skills as her sibling was angelic. The girls were from different men who were as identical in nature and habit as they were opposites in color and culture.

Abusers. Emotional batterers. Males had picked up where her abusive childhood left off, and two more were created in the process. In summary.

It had never been her intention to repeat her father's parental habits, and she was pretty sure she hadn't nor had Brenda copied her mother's, other than an occasional swat to a behind and some yelling. No, this was a cake walk at a Saint Patrick's parade compared to the childhood she hailed from and was haunted by.

Riley, however, had discovered a 1-800 number and an overly dramatic school counsellor. The child knew nothing of abuse, BJ mused. When one grew up on an isolated farm in Northernmost Alberta where the spirit of a horse and child were broken alike in the name of training and discipline, that was abuse.

And then the flashback. "SHUT YOUR MOUTH!" He stood towering above her; willow stick still raised in his fist. "You shut up or you'll get more!" Not even tears were allowed when one's backside was lit a fire with wild lashes of the sapling rod. Or his belt. A piece of plumbing pipe. Or whatever he could get his hands on.

So, Brenda had learned to cry on the inside, and she had the digestive problems that coincided. "Classic IRRITABLE Bowel Syndrome," the doctor called it. A gentle title for an enraged colon in need of anger management therapy, she thought ruefully. And then there was the deep depression caused by years of repressed anger, said her therapist.

There were many good memories, BJ changed the gears between her ears, still watching the lights sequencing and chasing on the five-dollar Christmas tree she had bought from the second-hand store.

Perhaps ruminating of better times is what kept her connected to her parents now in friendship, not viewing herself as a helpless kitten in a rainstorm with no one to help. She was no longer a victim, or a "Very Insecure Child Trapped in Muck."

Before the girls were due home from school in all their bickering glory, BJ slid into a reclined position and reminisced about her childhood Christmas memories-carefully setting her tea down on the scratched coffee table. Even the holidays were celebrated very differently from how her little family commemorated special occasions now.

In 1979, Fieldarp, Alberta, was a county few had ever heard of nor spotted on a map. It lay thirty snowy miles from the little town called Hatchet Prairie with only a grocery store, post office, Sears's outlet, and grain elevator. Back then, you could easily snowshoe the perimeter in a day, but her mind, as usual, was more up for cartwheels than careful footsteps. Her favorite memory twinkled now as it had twenty-seven years ago in the neighbors' treed yard.

Father had taken Brenda along for an evening walk despite mother's protests of the cold. At the end of the Gardener driveway, a half-mile straight east, the Henry's outdoor Christmas tree glowed through the falling snow and distance

Back then—she was starting to feel older than her thirty-three years—there wasn't a church on every block like there was now. There were four branches of Mennonite denomination from the strictest to the elaborate Evangelical Mennonites. Where your membership was inscribed determined your lifestyle.

Brenda's parents belonged to the second most strict congregation—the Old Order Mennonite Church. They forbid any worldly activities such as decorating the house for Christmas, having a television set, or expressing emotions.

Mother and her two sisters wore dresses all year, and at "Weihnachten" (Christmastime) God decked the outdoor trees with real snow.

Instead of stockings, everyone had their assigned place at the table they occupied at mealtimes where an empty mixing bowl was set to hold assorted nuts and hard candy. The bowls were set out and filled the same day—on Christmas Eve.

That Christmas, four-year-old Brenda-Jane and her two- and nine-year-old sisters all stood in line by their mother at the kitchen sink and waited for a bowl. Mother explained how she chose a container according to each family member's size and appetite. Father got the biggest cookie-dough bowl since he was the oldest and the largest by far. To his right at the table placement was Mother's moss green mixing dish. Baby Marlene reached up to push her stainless-steel receptacle into place and then climbed up on her stool to wait for a meal. Everyone had a good chuckle. The children then left Mother in the kitchen—no easy feat in a three-room basement on Christmas Eve.

Eventually, Dad joined her after the chores were completed to help place gifts beside the filled bowls while the girls waited in their bedroom. The sack-cloth drapes Mother had hung in betwixt the front room and sleeping quarters barely contained their excitement and curiosity. The gifts were unwrapped, since wrapping paper was a worldly thing, and simply plunked by each setting at the table. Bowls brimmed with peanuts, mixed nuts, a single orange, hard candy, and usually small trinkets like pencils, sharpeners, erasers, and small toys.

When they finished setting up, they called the children to the table.

The following Christmas, the family had moved upstairs where Mother's cards strung up on red baler twine looked even more festive above the new birch cupboards.

Brenda-Jane remembered her father taking her for the crisp walk every year to walk to the end of the driveway to peer at the neighbors' Tannenbaum. In falling snow, the swirling flakes seemed to transform each pastel bulb into a misty circle.

A commotion at the door brought Brenda back to the present. Both girls were giggling and scrambling in competition with each other.

"You squished me!" Rachel accused Riley laughingly. "You squashed my vital organs!"

"RACHEL," Riley snapped, dropping her backpack in midstride, mid-entrance. "If your organs were crushed, you would be dying."

"Mom, you promised to take us sliding." Rachel opened the fridge door and leaned over to peer in in search of a snack. "So, can we go today? And will you go to the food bank soon?"

Wearily, BJ agreed. She was still preoccupied with the, past as the three trudged on foot to the nearest hill just a few blocks away. For the umpteenth time, she wished she had a car.

Watching her giggling daughters descend down the well-packed hill, she thanked God for them again. They were her personal angels; Rachel even resembled a fairy-tale version with her blue-green eyes and curly blonde hair. A single large freckle dotted her upturned nose. Brenda loved tapping it playfully to get a rise out of her little spitfire.

Riley had inherited the brooding, melancholy side of Brenda and her father's aboriginal coloring. Her eyes were large and dark, framed in long eyelashes and rarely missing anything going on in her world. Long straight black hair often drew the nickname "Pocahontas" from her schoolmates.

Dusk clouded the winter sky rapidly, and Brenda announced their upcoming departure.

After a bout of soccer in the living room with Rachel and the customary battle of wits with Riley, the long day ended. The thick gray blanket covering Brenda's life remained stationary.

Looking at the two sleeping faces, colored so opposite and featured alike, Brenda wondered what was wrong with herself to be so blessed and feel so little thereof.

That night, BJ had a nightmare—not anything unusual; most of her waking life had already been one. Instead of fictional horror and outlandish creatures haunting her slumber, the dreams were usually a replay of the past. Other times, flashbacks would drag her backward in daylight through a knothole, often at the most inopportune moment.

CHAPTER 2

The Nightmare

BRENDA WAS selected to accompany her parents to Hazel's Crossing with a load of wheat they were hoping to sell. It would be an hour-long drive in a noisy, rumbling grain truck seated in between Mother and Father with the gear shift stick right in front of her. Father took the three girls to "da folks," as he referred to his parents, who lived just a half mile east of them, to drop Margaret and Marlene off.

Grandpa Gardener always lit up when he saw his three granddaughters, his blue eyes twinkling at them.

"Hello, boys," he'd drawl as they entered the old farmhouse without knocking.

"Come in! Come in!" Grandma shrilled, wiping her hands on her bibbed apron. It was usually the same print as her dress or close to it. The kitchen always smelled of fresh bread, lye soap, and wood heat.

Father didn't make much small talk, and soon, BJ was wedged on an overturned pail between the two bucket seats of the grain truck hurtling down the gravel road.

Mother was as chatty as father was aloof, and she prattled on and on while he grunted infrequently and shifted gears. Eventually, BJ was lulled to sleepiness by the regular sway of the machine and let her head fall against her mother's left arm. Immediately, Mother sprang forward to scrutinize the passing landscape as if she had lost a beloved dog. The move caused Brenda-Jane's head to fall between the seat and her mother's ribs. She leaned back as abruptly as she had lurched forward, pinching Brenda's head and appearing not to notice. The child repositioned herself and tried again. The adult leaned away again, studying her rear-view mirror intently. Over and over it went until Brenda finally gave up and let her head fall forward toward her chest. An awful feeling of dread crawled over her, like she had something terribly wrong with her. So, wrong her own mother didn't want to touch her. She felt like the dirt bouncing around on the floor of the truck—dirty, despicable, and unacceptable. An ugly, insignificant clod.

There wasn't enough quality time on the farm; work always took precedence over leisure and fun. Sometimes, the adults would sit down with a coloring book beside a child, usually in the wintertime, when work demanded less of them and snow hid the fields and garden.

On one such a night, the coloring books and wax crayons from the previous Christmas were brought out and set up around the table.

Mother took Brenda's side, and they chose a set of pages.

They had just begun rubbing the blunted tips of the crayons over Mickey Mouse and Donald Duck when Brenda's hand slipped and enlarged the beak.

"Don't color past the lines! See? Do little circles like I do," she scolded and demonstrated dainty little nudges with the crayon. Brenda tried, but at four years old, she soon lost interest in the slight progress and resumed her broader strokes. Father paced the kitchen-living-dining room, chewing sunflower seeds and spitting them on the floor.

"Who's going to clean that up?" his wife queried.

"We have girls." He motioned his head toward Margaret and Brenda.

Marg sat coloring a Disney-themed book also but with pencil crayons. Marlene lay sleeping in Mother and Father's room in her crib. Brenda and Margaret's bedroom lay directly off the main area, and it served as the hallway to the master bedroom.

The bathroom—more like a toilet and sink crammed under the stairs—had no bathtub. The painted wooden stairs would lead to the main floor of the unfinished house one day. For bathing, Mother melted snow on the woodstove and poured the hot water into a large galvanized tub beside the oven.

This only happened once a week on Friday night.

"There! Look there! You did it again!" Mother scolded. "You're making a mess of it!"

Suddenly, anger boiled up inside Brenda. She grasped her crayon and slashed it across the page so hard it tore through the picture and broke the orange crayon.

"I wish you would do something about THAT kid," Brenda heard mother direct at her father.

He swooped down, grabbed her by the arm and lifted her off her feet, carrying her dangling like that to the base of the stairway. He ripped the leather belt out of his pants and stuck her across the back of her calves, buttocks, lower back—everywhere it seemed. Her entire body seemed to be on fire. She screamed and he struck harder.

"SHUT YOUR MOUTH OR I WILL SHUT IT FOR YOU," he growled, breathing heavily.

"You shut up, hear?"

Work was impressed upon the young as soon as they could toddle. In the wintertime a lot of the work conditioning took place beside the living room quarters of the basement that held the wood furnace. Chopped wood was dropped in from an opening in the wall by Father and Margaret until a pile hid the cement floor. Then the piece of rough plywood was slid back over the hole and levers at each end rotated to hold it in place. Next, Brenda and Mother stacked the wood against the three walls.

The furnace and wood cook stove walled the wood room in, sitting staunchly side by each. Behind them and to the right was the bathless washroom, its sparse lightbulb dangling from a wire and the switch hanging from it as a string. Everything seemed to be moss green in the little, basement near Hatchet Prairie. From the U-Haul toilet to the bowl perched on a stool for washing hands. Lord help you if Mother thought the wash water had been thrown out before its expiry. A dingy hand towel you could spit through hung from a six-inch nail on the wall. There was no mirror; the church didn't approve of a worldly thing like a looking glass.

The front room floor was clad in a light green linoleum Mother had glued down when Father brought it home from the auction. Mint and white diamond faux tiles ran together up to the duct taped molding and where the linoleum met the cement.

From the two-by-four framed, curtained doorway of the washroom facing out, the basement opened into a spacious rectangle that housed the enormous deep freeze and water tank. Off this area, behind a dark walnut wood door mother had a cold storage room where she kept carrots fresh all year by burying them in a chest full of sawdust.

Finally, a heavy steel door lead to a concrete staircase up to the outdoors.

Mother had done her absolute best to make the abode pretty. She had wallpapered the top half of the room in an ivy-pattern on an ivory background. On the bottom half, she had applied paper that looked like gray bricks with ivy growing all over it. Over the two windows higher than eye level, she had strung white cotton curtains also patterned with greenery, on baler twine.

Between the beams hung more baling twine for dry-hanging clothes after they were washed in the round-barreled washing machine. Brenda held fascination with the twin rollers that circled inward to wring the water out of each garment mother fed them. They looked like two rolling pins suspended one above the other, forming a bridge over the suds below.

She and Marlene fought over a baby doll with a ceramic head named Helen one night. She looked so real, and they both wanted to hold her at same time.

"Stop it!" Mother yelled, banging lids of steaming pots and checking bread inside. They each pulled, one on Helen's tiny feet and the other, the head. Quickly, Mother snatched up the toy and flung it into the woodstove they had been playing in front of. The doll ignited before she slammed the wrought iron door shut. Both children had been crying, but now, they cried more, aggravating Mother further. She grabbed them one at a time, stomped into the kitchen, and sat them down on the floor, hard. Brenda didn't understand what had happened at first except that she could not breathe.

Beside her, Marlene hiccupped and snuffled. Everything started spinning around her, and she grasped wildly as if oxygen was a discarded toy laying nearby just out of reach. She would have grasped anything that would give her air.

It felt like forever until she could breathe normally again. Brenda wriggled to a sitting position where she could see Marlene better. Mother came in and lovingly picked up her baby, consoling her tenderly. Even after oxygen was restored to her, Brenda felt as if everything around her was surreal.

CHAPTER 3

Confrontations

AN INDIGNANT yell from the barn sent everyone scurrying to the porch door window.

"Duh bizzette schween!" (You evil pig!) Margaret shrieked, chasing Shadow across the yard. Behind her was her father, lunging for the dog and then rushing to the three-wheeler.

Using the machine like, a horse, Father chased the dogs as if a rodeo calf. When he got close, he veered in toward the canine, grabbed his collar, and tackled him while the tricycle lurched forward, rider less.

Gripping the dog by both ears, Father picked his head up by them and slammed it down into the ground while the Black Labrador screamed.

"Get away from the window!" Mother instructed quickly. "C'mon, let's do the dishes." She snapped Marlene's plate up and dumped the contents into the slop pail for the pigs.

"Is Dad going to kill him?" Marlene's chin wobbled.

"Pshaw! He's just giving him a spanking," Mother soothed.

The yelping continued over the sputtering of the trike. When it finally quit and the three-wheeler drove again, all parties leaned to look outside the window.

"Hey?" Mother opened the porch door and called across the yard. "What is loose?" (What is wrong?)

"That evil dog was eating an egg when I came in to feed the chickens!" Margaret shouted, still angry.

"He's been eating the eggs!" she added, still white-faced with rage.

Mother's face twisted with worry and paled.

"Shteck hunt," (darn dog) she muttered. Loudly she added, "We'll have to clean him up if he doesn't quit! Come and get the slop pail before it stinks up the whole house."

"Clean up" meant two different things on the farm. Beside housework, it meant the extermination of a pest. Coyotes, wolves, and magpies were among those that got "cleaned up" or "up-yeah-reamt" as well as any farm animal not earning its keep.

The dog hid for several days, so it was Brenda-Jane who caught sight of movement in the pasture one afternoon. A crouching red shirt and a blue one crept along the fence that surrounded the old slat barn.

Brenda-Jane felt fear raise the tiny hairs on her neck. She reached down and grabbed Marlene's hand, pulling her out of the sandbox.

"Who is that?" Marlene's eyes were enormous.

"I dunno. Let's get Mom," Brenda-Jane whispered. She found her mother by the clothesline. "Mom look." she pointed

Mother straightened her posture and squinted into the horizon. Marlene released her sister's hand and took her mother's.

"You get off my property or I'll call the police!" she yelled. The two figures froze. Brenda-Jane stepped closer to her mother.

"I mean what I say! You get off our property or I'll call the police!"

After a long pause, the two turned and ran back toward the barbed wired fence line.

"The Henry boys," Mother remarked, shielding her eyes from the sun. "Well I'll be!"

After that, a small pair of binoculars were slipped into her apron pocket and frequently used to scan the fence line.

Lunchtime was a meal of "keel cheh;" thick noodles in a buttermilk sauce with sliced cucumbers eaten cold. The children ate their soup sprinkled with parsley while their parents discussed the prowling neighbors.

"I wonder if that's where the vegetables are going," their mother mused. Father slurped his soup noisily.

"And the bales and gasoline?" Margaret eagerly interjected.

"Shaw!" her mother waved her hand to quiet her.

"We must turn the other cheek," Father finally spoke. "The Henry's are godly people; they must not know what the boys are up to."

"Well, Johan Henry owns a whip," Mother argued. "And a stone fist to work it with!"

"He works in the bush every winter like I do," Father reminded her. "And he probably does not know what his boys are up to. They are in the bad years." (Teens) Davey and Jacob Henry were the youngest left of a dozen sons who had left home.

"But surely you aren't going to allow them to sneak around here! It isn't safe for our children!" Brenda-

Jane shivered. Her father slurped his meal again, lapsing into a grim unhappy line.

Father did turn on the electric fence system and checked all the fences to ensure the current was passing through all the wire. The girls had a good time daring each other to touch it. The spark was strong enough to cause a sensation like the bones of one's index finger temporarily separating before reconnecting. Father also hung a few no trespassing signs from chains on the gates.

Almost as if ashamed of falsely believing the neighbors were responsible for the eggs disappearing, Mother packed two dozen eggs into her latest care package and delivered it to the house behind the manicured yard and a large barking Saint Bernard.

The boys were tossing a baseball back and forth when they turned into the lilac framed driveway. Davey and Jacob immediately hung their heads and crept away into the caragana bushes once they spotted mother.

The middle step was still wet from fresh paint, so Mother gingerly stepped over it with her polka dotted patent pumps.

"Oh! Hello," Mrs. Henry pushed the carved fame of the screen door open and smiled at them over her dark round bifocals. She wore a long-flowered dress on her vast physique and smelled of incense.

"I brought you some…food, mostly from my garden." Mother passed her gift to the woman of the stucco house. There were intermittent pauses in conversation like that when a German speaking Mennonite translated to English.

The two women fumbled for a moment. Mother nearly let go too soon and her receiver didn't grab a hold of it firmly enough but then did.

"Ooh, it's heavy!" The Missus exclaimed.

"A box of rocks," Mother joked, recovering.

"Good—we'll make stone soup!" the recipient chuckled, setting the box down on the chest freezer behind her.

"Did you want to stay for coffee?" she suggested.

"Oh no, I shall not keep you any longer," Mother awkwardly excused herself. "I've got soup on the stove."

Mrs. Henry thanked Mother profusely as they left, making their way back along the perfumed boulevard.

"Look!" Mother stopped on the roadway by the pond that lay at the base of the garden plot and brief parting of trees. Like all else the Henrys inhabited, it was pruned and pristine.

"Do they ever sleep?" Mother wondered aloud. "I am sure grass doesn't grow around their feet. Well, anyway, now the boys will think we spoke to their parents about their shenanigans," she declared of her psychological warfare proudly.

For an afternoon snack, they had fresh sliced tomatoes drizzled with honey. Cooked tomatoes sat in jars on the stove in mother's big black and white speckled canner.

Pickled carrots floated upside down in their overturned masons, cooling on the wooden cutting board. A load of pickled beans had already been cooled, labelled, and stored downstairs in the cold storage.

Residents of Fieldarp kept fairly close tabs on each other by proximity, relation, party line phone service, or all the above. It was how everyone knew only Mother's garden was missing produce, who was buying a bull, selling a horse, building a shed, and so on.

That's how it came as a surprise when hammering and sawing started one afternoon from behind the empty goat barn. The slat building and surrounding fence was no longer in use. The path leading past it led the cows to the creek to drink or brave the hand-hewn bridge to the back pasture.

The construction symphony was a mystery—no one was in sight, and Father was out working the fields.

"It's coming from the Penners." Margaret shielded her eyes from the sun.

Mother put up her binoculars. "No, it's coming from the trees behind the goat shanty, but I can't see anyone."

All day, there was hand sawing and hammering echoing across the Gardener farm. Someone was determined to leave his mark on the world—and on another man's property.

"I've had enough!" At suppertime, Mother lifted the axe from the chopping block near the wood pile still stained with traces of chicken blood from the latest butchering. "Let's go!"

Margaret fell behind Mother with Brenda and Marlene flanking her. They stomped the dirt trail to the abandoned shelter, the trio struggling to keep up with mother's swift step.

Once they reached the gate that now permanently sagged open, mother halted and raised her forearm to her eyes to shield them from the late afternoon sun.

"You stop whatever you're doing on our property!" She shouted. "It's illegal, and I will report you!"

Walking beside her in a half trot/march, Brenda-Jane felt excited and a little afraid.

The hammering stopped. All ruckus and racket stopped.

Once they passed the stately old coop, they caught a glimpse of several people on a ledge in the trees. Down the trail, over the sturdy bridge and to the right, the Henry boys and their henchmen were building a treehouse.

Guilty expressions flitted over freckled faces. Davey's shadow dropped with his grip and landed on the soil beside him. A weathered ladder had been propped up against the edge of the platform. A railing had been constructed around the perch, and more slabs lay strewn at the base of the trees.

Deftly, mother raised her axe and struck the bottom rung of the ladder, splintering the wood around the nails.

"How long do you figure this will last on my property?" she demanded. She struck the ladder again and again, the boys scattering like the rungs.

When the ladder was disassembled, Mother pivoted and faced them.

"You are trespassing, and not for the first time. The fence marks the beginning of our property. Cross it again to steal or sneak around here, and I will call the police. This is your last warning." Ashen faced and mute, the Henry boys gathered their comrades and retreated, defeated.

"I think you scared them, Mom!" Marlene boasted on the way back to the house.

"Umbaleadet tahckle," Mother muttered, meaning "untrained brats." But that didn't really explain the boys' behavior, having come from such staunch, upright parents.

After that, the neighborhood was quiet where prowling was concerned. The story made the Faspa headlines wherever peanut butter was spread on pickled gherkins and company was present. Of course, it was told from the vantage point that the Henry spawn ganged up on her and she had been forced to defend herself, how the Henry youths were exactly like Cornielius Timber, and how the Gardeners were just plain fed up.

Father didn't say much about Mother's story nor did he join in until he remarked, "Well, for me to see, there's nothing Christian about the Henrys as long as they don't control their children."

"But they are Mennonite," the male visitor quickly replied.

"Then there's hope. "

CHAPTER 4

Church on Sunday

EVERY SUNDAY morning, Father bellowed for the family to "get up, get up, GET UP!" for church or else. Else meaning a severe beating and a verbal cut down after the offending soul's covers were rudely jerked off their half nude slumbering body.

And of course, with Father being the head Sunday school teacher and his father Grandpa Gardener as the bishop of the congregation only added pressure to keep up with the image.

The Old Order Mennonite place of worship squatted on a piece of plain unpaved dirt and gravel along the road that led to Hatchet Prairie. If a wooden grain outbuilding could have been enlarged and had storm windows added sparsely to its perimeter, that was the church; a white-washed plywood exterior with cement steps below its two entrances; one for the men and one for the women.

The house of varnished wood and painted pews was divided in half to keep the genders separate.

"I wonder why they insist people stay married if they separate them for worship," Mother often grumbled aloud. To which father replied nothing.

In the middle of each segregation sat a single wood-burning stove; his and hers. Or in this case; theirs and ours. The pews next to them were built shorter to compensate for the space. Over the wooden benches lined up on the polished chipboard floor, a few oil lanterns hung from the ceiling on wire, ready for use in an evening meeting or wintertime services. Most of the light came from God through the windows since there existed no electricity or plumbing in His house. Too worldly.

Two unmarked outhouses at opposite corners of the church outside were the potties for males and females, stationed between the building and wheat field beyond. A boring sermon droning on guaranteed an elevated number of trips to the loo for both sexes.

Brenda-Jane sat with Margaret, Mother, and Marlene on the women's side. Sometimes, when father was off from teaching "Zinda shull" (Sunday school), he took little Marlene to sit with him. The men did that on occasion with younger offspring since it was allowed to help the many overladen ladies out.

Soon after everyone seated and right on the ten o'clock dot, a row of men in dark suits marched down the front of the church from their little room off to the women's side. Each one stepped up to the platform, climbed the steps beside the pulpit, and walked until he stood in front of his chair. Once they all stood poised to be sat, all did.

These were the song leaders. Brenda always shivered a little at the solemnness of the event, especially the part where the preachers and deacons entered. Again, they marched in, four men in dark clothes up to an invisible line and then stopped. The front runner spoke up loudly, "DIE FRIEDE DES HERRN ZI MIT UNS ALLE (The joy of the Lord be with us all)." Then they filed up the few stairs and took their places on the side of the pulpit opposite the singers. Now a song leader declared a High German song and waited for everyone to find it in their hymnbook. Then he announced again and launched into the melody. Two hymns were sung before every service and two in conclusion. At a funeral, the body was carried in by the "appalling" bearers and set on a flat backless bench after the second song. Before seating themselves, the head pallbearer would lift the lid of the peaked coffin and reveal the blanched corpse to the family, and all parked in its proximity.

Death was a big deal in Hatchet Prairie. The old-fashioned Mennonite groups believed one could never know one's eternal destiny for certain, only that it was heaven or hell. A parishioner could only follow ancient traditions, customs, and religious beliefs under the denomination's leadership and hope to gain God's favor upon expiration. Yet due to the deceased having obviously ceased sinning, they were clothed in white cotton and laid out on a white sheet in their home-hewn casket. A black ribbon ran all around the outer edges of the box, hiding the nails that held the sheet taut underneath. The black ribbon also encircled each wrist and was tied in a neat little bow. Still hands were crossed over each other in silent reverence. The body had been stripped, scrubbed, and dressed by an elite group of volunteers from the church family of the deceased. Usually, middle-aged women performed the undertaker duties and a man from the same congregation built the container.

Brenda-Jane had been four when she attended her first funeral. She had no way of knowing that, nearly two decades later, she would have the granddaughter of the deceased woman.

Mother did not sing on this particular Sunday morning, Brenda noticed. Then the preacher stood up and spoke in High German, which was really just more horking and gagging in public than Low German required, warning everyone of the upcoming end of times and to ward off all worldliness. Brenda could not understand him entirely, but she had overheard her parents' conversations about church and the general climate thereof.

Funerals were typically held within a week of the death and to return on Sunday for a second service felt strange.

When the eulogy had been read, everyone lined up and either circled around the body to gawk at it or simply rose and filed out one by one, gossiping as they exited.

"Did you want to see?" Mother had asked Brenda, grasping her by the armpits and hauling her upward above the dead. The woman had red hair slicked back off her forehead and held in place by a black kerchief. Her mouth hung slightly open, her skin a pale yellow, and her folded hands were large as a man's and work worn.

Everyone wept on the women's side of the church, including Mother. Tears were allowed at a funeral if you were female, if you didn't make too much of a scene.

"Why is she like that? Who is she, Mum?"

"Shh! I won't ever show you again if you keep asking questions!" Brenda's mother snapped.

That night, some waxy figure in a white robe chased after her all over the night-blackened family farmyard. She tripped and fell, screaming to be left alone.

"Get back to bed." The next thing Brenda felt was being jerked to her feet by her left arm by Father and pulled up back onto her bed. He left her there like that, huddling and afraid, still above the bedclothes.

Still shivering, as she pinched a corner of the quilt and gingerly pulled it over herself. Brenda squeezed her eyes shut to avoid seeing vague outlines and shadows in the dim moonlight. Gradually, her quaking body ceased, and she fell asleep again, waking up to pots clanking and a sweet falsetto singing, "I wanna go to heaven when this life is o'er…" Mother.

Brenda shook off her nightmares and washed her hands in a bowl of fairly fresh water and a mint bar of zest soap because Mother hated Grandma Gardeners homemade lye concoctions for washing.

Grandfather always sat up front on the raised podium, with the pastors facing the women's side of the church. When the sermon grew insufferable, his blues eyes twinkled at Brenda-Jane in a way she was sure was meant only for her. Mothers sat with bundled youngsters in their arms, rocking slightly to keep them pacified.

Should the Ezekiel Gardener family miss a Sunday, Grandma Gardener staunchly called and asked for an explanation.

The plank pew got harder and harder as the sermon droned on. Babies cried, and their mothers carried them out of the service to the cry room by the women's entrance. Opposite that room was a leadership room where song leaders and clergy gathered before marching out for the morning program. Should Brenda or her sisters fidget, a stormy look would cross Mother's face, and she would inform Father of their shenanigans afterwards. Well, not insomuch Marlene. And Brenda wriggled and squirmed under Mother's glare.

The wooden pews were painted a dull gray-blue color, but everything else was varnished and kept in its natural hue. The summer before this, Mother had painted the outhouse with leftover paint from Grandma and Grandpa. To her dismay, it was the same as the pews.

"Every time I go, I'll feel like I'm holding church!" she lamented.

"Well, as long as you don't get them confused for real." Father snickered.

"Imagine sitting there with my pantyhose down in plain view of die fashteh!" (The frontline or clergymen).

They both howled.

Brenda poked at her shredded wheat cereal in fresh chilled cow's milk and remembered her how Grandmothers voice always carried above the crowd.

After the funeral benediction and preacher's farewell, sunlight blinded them, glancing off the beveled windshields. The Gardeners piled into the big blue two-tone suburban left running during the service in the wintertime to keep it warm.

All the way home, Mother sat in tense silence, her neck as rigid as the starched point of her kerchief.

Finally, her husband asked something that the engine drowned out.

"I wish you would do something about those kids!" she exclaimed. "I couldn't catch anything of church with all the wriggling and cavorting beside me!"

Brenda's stomach got warm, like it always did when something bad was about to happen. Her neck hair prickled.

When they got home, Mother quickly took Marlene inside. Margaret got out of the truck from her seat behind Mother and Brenda-Jane caught the look on Father's face. He had on a strange smile. "Come here," he ordered, striding to the doorway above the cement steps leading downstairs. Meekly, the girls followed him. He took off his belt and asked, "Do you know why I must do this?" They shook their heads.

"Mom said you didn't sit still in church." With that, he reached out and grabbed Margaret's upper arm. She yelled, so he slapped her across the face. Hard. Then he struck her across the shoulders, behind, and wherever with his leather pants belt. Over and over. When he finished telling her to shut up, he let go of her and she ran inside. Brenda-Jane was next. The belt burned her flesh.

"I have to beat the bad things out of you so you can go to heaven," he explained. "Otherwise you will stay bad and burn in hell forever one day."

Brenda sobbed quietly, hiccupping all the way to the dinner table.

"Are you girls going to play dolls today?" their mother asked the two girls at the table with teary faces. She always acted really sweet to the child who had just been beaten. It both angered Brenda and made her tears want to start all over again. She shook her head no. And because she didn't respond cheerily enough—and Margaret didn't speak at all—Mother snapped.

"Do these looks like two repentant children!" she snarled at her husband.

"They need another spanking perhaps," he sneered. "We'll have to do that more often."

After dinner, the family all laid down for a Sunday afternoon nap. Those were one of two ways Sunday afternoons were spent, "napping," or socializing. Mother kept a guest book for guests to sign as a record of whose "turn" it was to host or visit. Even relationships had a system. In the summertime, when the days were long, it wasn't unusual to have afternoon company that left after faspa, a light meal comprised of snacks and served earlier than suppertime on a weekday, and then have another family over for the evening. Of course, socializing could also work in other dimensions, but that's what Sunday afternoons were for; Shpitzeerin forn (going visiting). It was code for catching up on all the latest gossip within your denomination and the greater Hatchet Prairie populace. There wasn't a pious enough local that ever had a problem with gossip. Christians don't gossip they "share," and Mennonites just plain shared.

Faspa was always delicious—all the baked goods from the labor of the week came out along with canned wuerst, homemade pickles, and white dinner rolls. During the week whilst she baked, Mother allowed the children to eat the burned and imperfect cookies. The best was always kept for Sunday.

Still, she was an excellent cook and baker—even her failures in the kitchen beat the best intentions of a few others.

CHAPTER 5

My Mother's Keeper

EVERY SPRING, Mother dug out a cardboard box of leftover seed packages to sort through in anticipation of the coming year's garden. A colorful seed supply catalogue also arrived in a brown sleeve by mail, and she pored over it like it was the Sears Christmas wish book. The girls were prodded and coaxed to choose a flower or favorite vegetable they could plant and claim the row of in Mother's vast garden. They could pick from the catalogue, seed box, or from the display of enveloped seeds in the grocery store on the weekly trip to town.

The routine of Saturday was to get up later than a school or church morning of the week, eat breakfast, and then clean the house for the company possibly coming to "shpitzeer" (visit) on Sunday. Marlene had to help with the barn chores before coming in to resume with the housework. Saturdays were stressful days; they woke up to Mother yelling about all the work to be done as she worked. Brenda-Jane learned how to clean house from the time she could walk. Her designated room, the living room, was reserved for company, like the parlor of the well to do, and all the best furniture and knickknack bric-a-bracs were stored within its wallpapered perimeter.

Elizabeth Gardener had a fetish for clean, and she tired not of vocalizing about it. God help you, however, if you dusted and mopped and carefully set things back exactly in their customary positions.

Brenda-Jane was carefully setting a glass swan down when Mother materialized to check on her work. She strode up to the china cupboard in the middle of the wall flanking the kitchen in her high heeled sandals and swept the ornaments to one side of the shelf.

"That's nothing! You have to move each one. Dust can get underneath you know. I always have to do everything myself!"

"Shecken an zelse gohn!" (Send for and end up doing it yourself) she exclaimed.

"No—" Brenda started to protest.

"Shut up! Yes, I do! Want a slap for your mouth?!"

Crestfallen and subdued, Brenda shook her head. "I have to do everything plus a few around here! Your father is off visiting his mother and Margaret is lazy—would rather work outside where she can talk to the cows instead of lifting a finger in the house. Totally useless!" She shook a rag at Brenda. "Now do a good job like I showed you."

Her heels clickety-clacked out of the room. Brenda-Jane glanced around. This was by far the most elegant space of the entire farmhouse. The brown plaid couch didn't match the black patent leather sofa, but the mottled blend of blacks, browns, and gold flecks in the leopard-like linoleum seemed to pull it all together. White and gold wallpaper set off a stark contrast between the walls and dark foreboding furniture and flooring, with the lime green vinyl curtains conflicting with the room altogether.

A console record player in a walnut wood encasement held records behind its camouflaged doors in case the church elders should ever perform a home inspection. Only Mother and Father handled the music playing, and only in the presence of company they trusted or knew had similar secrets.

Brenda loved to while away the afternoon of an empty Sunday flipping through the various albums, from Charley Pride to Jimmy Swaggert, Loretta Lynn, and Conway Twitty. There were even recordings by more modern Mennonites from other communities—The Dycks, Wiebes, and Heinrich Sisters.

Mother's large spider plant hung in one corner, drooping vines with long slender leaf clusters. Several times a year, it bloomed tiny white flowers, and visiting ladies praised her green thumb, whatever that meant. Brenda had studied her mother's large, veiny, work-worn hands, and they were red and raw from scrubbing socks on the washboard. Not green.

A black metal bookshelf full of books was hidden behind the generous spider plant tendrils. Books like *Papa's Wife* and *Papa's Daughter* which, no doubt, would be frowned on by the more devout Mennonites if they could read the titles through the greenery.

The china cupboard and hutch were another fascination of Brenda's. Behind its glass doors, one could behoove all the family treasures; Father's ceramic buffalo and horses, the Blue Willow dish set Mother refused to use, pink glass swan duo that kiss-fitted together with silk flowers protruding from their backs. There were Margaret's three glass horses, Brenda's crystal bell angel, and Marlene's pink tin piggy bank sporting gaudy bright flowers all across its body.

"Are you even moving?" A call from the kitchen startled her. "Do I have to come in there?" "N-no. Almost done, Mom," Brenda quickly reassured her.

"Well, hurry up! Bruck mole-shwunk!" (Use some effort.) You are going to have to learn how to wash those floors next!"

Quickly, she set all the finery back and closed the glass doors. One shut with a loud bang. "What did you break?"

"N-nothing."

"I HEARD something break!"

"No! Nothing!"

"Don't you lip off to me! Hear? Tell me what you broke!"

"It's just the door—the way it closed. Honest, Mom!"

"Of all the—" Heels clattered across the floor swiftly again. Mother inspected the living room, sweeping and swooping, plumping a pillow here, pinching off imaginary lint there.

"You won't amount to anything much if you keep that up." She finally finished off her raid.

After the house passed the standard came bath time. The new washroom upstairs had a white metal tub, a white toilet that flushed, and a sink sunken into the marble-look vanity top. Still, water didn't flow from a limitless supply, so the tub could only be filled to one quarter of its capacity, and Brenda-Jane and Marlene had to share a bath.

On the way to town, Mother's mood became upbeat, almost jovial. She chatted Father up, cuddled Marlene on her lap, and occasionally hummed along to the portable cassette player running on battery power.

Suddenly, she turned to Brenda-Jane, sitting behind Father, and asked, "Have you decided on a flower you want to plant yet?"

"Black Eyed Susan!" Brenda blurted happily. Her Mother's face fell, and she turned away.

"Well, that'll please your grandma."

Brenda-Jane looked to Margaret for comfort, confused at her mysterious transgression, but Margaret was glaring already. Something had upset Mother.

"You always were your grandmother's girl," Mother said in a tight voice. "Looked like her since birth, sound like her, and now this."

"But, Mom—" Brenda tried desperately to backpedal. Fix the problem, assuage Mother's hurt feelings.

"Bah!" Mother shook her head and turned to the passing fields in her window. Brenda-Jane shrank into her seat and looked out her window, wishing she hadn't spoken out of turn or chosen a proper posy. She decided to try harder to please.

Outside her window, behind Father, springtime busily turned the wintry farm scape into murky Old Testament mire and the gravel road to mud. Snow still lay thick on the fields, melted, and froze again as it did on the farmyard, forming icy puddles. If a child fell in one, she got scolded and spanked for making more laundry and hence more work for poor Mother.

CHAPTER 6

The Neighbors

THERE WERE several farms around Grandfather's big field, off the dirt road that encircled it.

Besides Ezekiel junior's farm were the Timber brothers, the oldest and the youngest in their family. Both places could be seen from the Gardeners back porch through a thin fringe and then a clearing of trees.

Cornielius, the youngest, had the small acreage between the Gardeners and his older brother. Gossip granted that his half acre lot was on loan from his brother, Bart, whose heart was in the right place but his brain was out in left field searching for it.

Anyway, Corny lived there with his wife in a tiny cabin among a plethora of dead vehicles and a few weathered and lackluster outbuildings. Grass grew as tall as the stories he told if he spoke to anyone at all. He smoked a lot and always wore the same dirty coveralls.

Hardly anyone ever saw his wife, but she was said to be as sweet, tiny, and pretty as he was big, smelly, and nasty. His long face resembled a quarter moon, a protruding forehead, deep-set beady eyes, and a pointed chin. The same dirty baseball cap sat on his dirty blonde hair whenever he was seen.

A creek divided his lot from his brother's farm, and a plank connected it again. Bartholemew was so much older he had children Corny's age. One daughter still lived at home. Colleen and Margaret were the same age and quite good chums. Sometimes, Brenda-Jane was allowed to go with Maragaret, and she loved visiting the neighbors with the beautiful home.

Colleen's parents looked as old as a pair of grandparents did, if they were even up and about. Usually, Colleen had the run of the house while her parents were out visiting their married children or napping.

Cornielius, or Chief Smells-A lot, as Margaret had dubbed him, was as mean and dishonest as he appeared to be evil. If he ever made it to church, he was late. He stole from everyone, and everyone knew it. No one did anything about it besides talk. A child or youth who behaved that way would have been taken behind the barn and horsewhipped. Yes, sirree. A great multitude of issues got resolved behind the barn; a Mennonite therapy session.

Zeke had a tank of purple gas on the farm that was always beyond his usage. Tools went missing magically whenever they were gone.

"You are going to have to do something." Mother got terse at Father's "turn the other ass cheek" approach to the thefts.

Everyone was aghast when Father hired "Smelly Cornelly" to help him build a horse barn. The other eight families in the neighborhood shunned him. Only Bart

Timber and Father had any dealings with the local adult problem child.

"Let his brother take care of him," Elizabeth Gardener snapped. "Why do you have to be his pappy? Your parents are the leaders of the church—they even avoid him. That jerk cleans out your fuel tank every month."

They were arguing in the kitchen after the kids had gone to bed. Brenda-Jane heard her father's quiet voice but couldn't make out what he was saying.

"I don't want that filthy thing in the house!" her mother snapped. "You can pack a lunch and eat with him outside."

Lord, help her if the clergy or more stout church followers heard her talk that way. Women were second in rank, and goodness, those were to be seen and unheard unless spoken to, like children.

Judging by the sound of her mother's voice, she was winning the battle. Half of it anyway. Father knew she did some of her best cooking in a good mood, and he sure loved his perogies in cream gravy. Digestively speaking, it behooved his best interests not to irk her.

As soon as the snow was gone and most of the mud dried up, the two men went to work building.

The farm did boast of a few barns; a chicken coop, a slat-sided shelter for the cows, and a small barn behind the pasture that once housed the goats. The pigs had a shed also, but the new barn would conglomerate the cows, chickens, and pigs under one roof. It would have a hay bale loft and worldly electricity like the house.

"If I was a Hutterite, the thing would be up by now," Zeke grumbled one day. Yet in spite of his long list of character defects, "Smelly" was a good worker, and the barn was built within a couple of weeks of the argument in the kitchen.

And no sooner was it built when he tried to burn it down. He walked home through the pasture as was his custom, flicked a cigarette into the dry grass, and caught the pasture on fire.

Elizabeth shouted to her husband, "Heah ass feah*!*" (Here is fire.) Father came lumbering.

"Feah!" she screamed. It spread all over the pasture and zig-zagged toward the new hip-roofed barn.

Margaret ran to the rain barrel with her milk bucket. Mother came running out to with potato sacks from the cold storage, thrust them into the rain barrel, and ran to beat the flames with Father.

"Stay with Marlene!" she yelled at Brenda over her shoulder. She found her baby sister alone in the house, playing on the floor, oblivious to the clamor around her.

Brenda-Jane ran outside, heedless of her mother's instructions. She wanted to run and cling to her parents but could not see them in the smoke. The wind pulled the hazy curtain aside for a moment and revealed their shadowy shapes bowing and rising, beating the flames with wet sacks.

Stories of hell and ever burning lakes of fire scared Brenda back into the house. Curiosity still pulled her to the living room window, and Marlene followed her.

"Look—" Brenda fibbed, pointing to the billowing smoke. "Mom and Dad are having a wiener roast."

"Weiner roast! Weiner roast!" Marlene chanted happily.

A tall stooped figure had joined the trio and was pounding the ground with a shovel.

After the fire was put out, a sooty, sweat-streaked bunch stood around the smoky pasture watching for flare ups. Father gestured to Cornielius, which meant he was talking. Mother and Margaret turned away and walked toward the house briskly. Brisk was how Mother moved, as did anyone trying to keep up with her. Fire or no fire.

"Cannot stand the man another moment." Mother was fuming out loud as they walked in. "I could box his ears off his head!"

Boxing someone's ears meant forming a box with each hand and clapping them over the victim's ears rapidly until they were disoriented, or their ears popped or both. The whole thing was meant to degrade more than cause physical pain and worked. And Mother could have been an Olympic champion in ear boxing to be sure.

"Dad should spank him like a little kid!" Ten-year-old Margie lamented, picking up her schoolbag where she had hastily dropped it.

Elizabeth started noisily making supper preparations, fury accentuating every movement.

When Father came in, sweat had soaked a "v" into his brown T-shirt, forming an arrow that pointed to his bulging stomach. He stomped into the kitchen like he always did, noisy and causing the stove burners to rattle in their tin catchers.

"Did you tell him anything?" his wife asked anxiously. He responded by pulling out a red handkerchief with white polka dots and blowing his large sunburnt nose.

"That's not what I asked you."

"I told him I did not pay overtime to put out fires he himself started, and that if he plans to keep working here, it had better not happen again."

"It figures." Mother's expression darkened. Nothing more was said, but her silence screamed louder than she did on a Saturday morning.

CHAPTER 7

Grandpa Gardener

"GROSSPABEH" (GRANDFATHER), as all the grandkids called him, had a way of embracing you with words. Piercing blue eyes twinkled at the sight of his grandchildren.

"Hello boys," he greeted the three daughters of his namesake the way he always did.

Whenever their parents had to go into town on business, the three girls were dropped off at their house without much notice. Grandmother didn't miss a step in her crazy work dance but simply invited the children along to join in whatever task she was engrossed in. There were times the trio was firmly convinced the raspberry patch existed purely to ruin their lives.

Father's younger three sisters still all lived at home, all waiting for a man to come along and marry them. They worked with Grandmother in the kitchen and garden mostly, because they were women. They also helped Grandpa with the barn chores and livestock, since all the men in the family had married and left home to farm their own. The youngest boys, Uncle Daniel and Uncle Isaiah, still came home to help with the fieldwork twice a year, cultivating and seeding in the spring and swathing and combining in the fall.

Grandfather had been known to demote the misbehaved and offending son to housework should they irritate him while outside. Usually Father and his twin-like brother, Uncle Isbrandt. Brenda could not easily picture Grosspabeh's sterner side.

The three aunts each took on a niece to tag along with them on their duties. Stout Aunt Margaret took Margaret to hill potatoes; the oldest with the oldest. Pinched and pious-faced Aunt Susanna threw Brenda Jane an apron and a pair of homemade gardening gloves. They were going to weed the garden acre. Mary, the baby, and Marlene would stay in the hot kitchen and help Grandmother bake buns.

The vast old barn usually spouted baby kittens, and Grandpa wanted them gone now that they were old enough. Farms needed mousers, but there were enough cats on staff, so he had placed a classified advertisement in the paper.

"If you pick a whole row, you can go play with the little kittens." Aunt Susanna raised her freckled brow whenever she spoke, and lines were already forming horizontally on her forehead. Reddish sandy colored hair was parted in the middle and smoothed back into a wide braid. Her brown fortrel dress with the pleated skirt reached the top of her rubber boots.

"Pick these, not those." She showed Brenda Jane the weeds versus the pea plants. She eyed her niece's attire; knit green slacks and an off-white sweatshirt.

"I don't know why your mother dresses you in man's clothes. Girls aren't supposed to wear boy's clothing. It's a sin."

"But these are girl pants!" Brenda protested. "Look at the design!" Seashells or fans were printed in off-white and purple on the green background.

"It's just for working," Brenda added, squatting to pluck a strand of grass from the row. "I can do this in a dress."

"What about Aunt Mary?" That one waddled around in tight angel-wing blue jeans whenever she had the chance or excuse.

The stern looks on Susanna's face stifled Brenda, and she continued along the row, pinching the tops of weeds and pulling them up by the roots like she had been taught by mother.

Oh, Susanna. Perfect, pious, and plain. Her dress never wrinkled nor dirty, her apron ever fresh. She hummed German hymns whilst she worked; Brenda Jane caught the tune from further down the row. "So fliehen unsre tage hin…" (How quick our days are passing by), and Brenda wondered how it was indeed that anyone could lay claim to a day and say they owned it.

Her Aunt could have been pretty were it not for her attitude and freckles. She had Grosspabeh's sparkling eyes and a full mouth.

"Were you named after the song 'Oh Susanna'?" She dared to interrupt and ask. She expected the dirty look along with the answer.

"Goodness no!" Her auburn-haired aunt exclaimed. "It's just a good German name and not a worldly one like yours." A hyphenated handle of all things—and for a girl? It was unheard of.

After her row was finished but before she could beeline into the loft to cuddle the kittens, Grandma rang the dinner bell-once-cowbell, signaling supper was ready.

After a meal of roast beef, potatoes smothered in cream gravy, and green beans came a dessert Grandma called "Pink Delight." It was homemade cottage cheese turned crimson with Jell-O powder and mixed with chunks of canned pineapple.

Grosspabeh's eyes shone with pleasure over his bowl.

"Barley," he called Brenda-Jane. "Would you pass me the toothpicks?" So, she picked up the small recycled pill bottle, fished one out, and handed it to him. Everyone was trying not to laugh out loud.

"You pass the whole thing; you don't touch anyone else's toothpick before they use it." Margaret acted all embarrassed.

He was a good sport and used the toothpick anyway.

The two dogs barked announcement of an unusual event. Both were a mixed breed between German shepherd and collie. They kept up the clamor until Grandpa got to the screen door and hushed them.

"C'mon, boys," he said sternly.

"Mam, Mary is still wearing her jeans, and her outside chores are done," Susanna whined.

"Mam, Susie is wearing that Old Colony dress 'Pabeh' (Papa) told her to ship back to them." Pleats were code for their club—ahem! Denomination.

A strange blue van had driven into the yard with an aboriginal man at the wheel. He got out and sauntered toward the gate of chicken-wire and frame fence that lined the lawn.

The women all crowded by the door at the top of the steps that led down to the vestibule to peer through its door at the intruders. Grandfather and the visitor were soon joined by a dark-skinned little boy about Brenda's age while a woman stayed in the front seat.

The three walked toward the barn.

"They've come for the kittens," Aunt Mary breathed. Sometimes, the first nations from Eagle's Creek came to Hatchet Prairie to shop the sales, and because Hatchet Prairie stores had more to offer than their meager grocery store.

A few felines were frisking in the slanted evening sunshine of the open barn. One was a favorite; he had a white belly while the rest of him was coal black like Sylvester.

"I hope Pa doesn't give him the prettiest one," Mary protested. As if on cue, Grosspabeh stopped down, picked up the cartoon kitten, and placed him in the boy's arms.

"To an Indian!" Aunt Susanna was credulous. "He gave our best kitten to an Indian."

Brenda-Jane's heart swelled with pride over Grandpa's actions. It was a trait among the locals to be prejudiced against other cultures and downright racial toward aboriginal people.

"Pa, why'd you do that?" Aunt Mary cried out when he entered the vestibule.

"Nah!" he dismissed her with the sound that simultaneously meant an objection and disapproval.

The older two aunts meekly followed him into the barn for milking time, and the remainder of the family began cleaning up supper dishes. Except for wide-eyed Marlene, who still sat poking at her food in the wooden highchair.

Grandma was built like a teapot; short and stout in her round-necked navy-blue dress and flowered navy-blue apron. Her thin gray hair was pulled back severely under a big black kerchief that hung down between her shoulders ending in a point. Just above the triangle, a cluster design of pink roses and blue forget-me-nots was stamped. For church, she wore a fringed babushka and tied it under her chins.

Suds flew when Grossmam (Grandma) washed the dishes. She was always delegating with her fine-lipped mouth. "Mary, you wipe the table. Margaret, here's the slop bucket—set it by the door. Barley, (Brenda's nickname) help your sister out of her highchair."

It proved no wonder how Grandma and Grandpa had raised a dozen children on a large farm. Everyone was fed off the land and then sent to work as soon as they could walk. Even the barn cats had an assignment, to catch and kill mice. The enormous ranch was built on unpaid child labor, and it sprawled long and wide, bustling and lucrative.

It was great fun to explore the heart of the farm, the giant barn with a full-length hayloft, tack room, and milk shanty. Aging gray timbers encircled the curious child, enveloping her into a sea of dim light until her eyes adjusted. A row of small square windows dotted each upper wall of the barn evenly spaced apart.

A concrete walkway ran the length of the barn's interior, flanked by a dung channel trough on each side under the business end of the cows once parked. The walkway intersected to allow a partitioned hallway to the milk room.

Brenda-Jane found her favorite animal in his stable—Big Red. He was an old Heinz 57 plow horse whose head nearly touched the ceiling of the barn, and he had grown fat and lazy in what Grandpa called his "retirement years."

Big Red was a big exception of the expectations of farm animals. Usually, the motto was "if it lives, it lives; if it dies, it dies—but if it doesn't earn its keep, it dies a lot faster."

"I keep meaning to put him down, but he keeps asking for one more year." Grandpa's quiet voice came from behind Brenda-Jane. Red immediately moved closer to the man and lowered his head to touch the old man's chest.

"Hello, old boy," Grandpa said softly. For a seemingly ethereal moment between man and beast, they stood together, silhouetted in the setting sun and the open barn door.

CHAPTER 8

Goats and Geese

SMELLY ACQUIRED a male goat that came to visit the female goats on the Gardener farm long before a banjo player came for Aunt Susanna.

The old slat-barn of split logs in the back of the pasture with the bark turned outward now housed a half-dozen nanny goats and their mother, "Snow White," named for the obvious. A barbed wire fence ran around a mini pasture within the electric line Father had enclosed the entire farmyard with.

Smelly's Billy goat was hot to trot for Snow, and he proved it by getting tangled in the loose barbed wire near the barn. He brayed and hollered until Father freed him with a wire cutter.

They were in competition, animal and owner, as to who stank worse. Perhaps that'd attracted them to each other, became the running joke around the neighborhood. Every time Smelly attempted to "farm" a critter, it became a nuisance to someone else. His Saint Bernard charged at vehicles and bicyclers. His chickens got into Mother's garden and ate their fill before they were discovered, and the bony Herford got stuck in the creek between the two Timber brothers' properties.

Shadow, the old black Labrador, did not seem to faze the goat one bit. He barked whenever the creature made his odorous appearance—even nipped at his hind legs.

The burly Saint Bernard had become the Henry's canine just a half-mile up the road, and the Penners had rescued the cow with a rope around its neck and pulled of their dilapidated tractor. Once the cow dragged herself the rest of the way out of the bog, they just left her attached to the bucket on the rope and took her home. Oddly, even more so was Corny's lack of protest. Maybe he planned to merely steal them back when no one looked, but evidently, his schedule was already brimming with activity.

Brenda-Jane and Marlene were playing near an empty bale trailer when the goat charged at them. They clambered up to safety, screaming at the white-rimmed eyes trying to follow them. He tried to jump up, but the trailer sat too high for him, so he contented himself to lunge upward every now and then, making that creepy nasally braying noise. The girls had stepped on the metal hitch to boost themselves, but he couldn't secure footing and slipped each time he tried.

Mother came running from the garden, brandishing the hoe over her shoulder and swung it at him. She struck him once in the flank, and he bleat-yelped before he suddenly remembered his home and dashed for it with her is pursuit.

It would have been comical in another time—Mother in her stiffly pressed dress ending in a triangle above her rubber boots waving the hoe and shouting as she chased him. He, the horny horned goat racing away from her so fast his legs were as straight forward and back as far as possible. Mother didn't let off until he reached the trail through the windbreaker that connected Corny's patch to the farm. Only then did she lower the utensil and gasp for air, flushed from the exertion and anger both.

"DO SOMETHING ABOUT THAT THING OR I WILL," she threatened over supper.

"I could talk to Bart." Father slowly stirred his coffee.

"What good would that do? It's a driveway past the problem!" she argued. "Our poor little ones crying and afraid, stranded up on the trailer. What next!"

She need not wait long to have her question answered. The creature returned the next day, ready for another round of abuse if, please oh please, he could just have a moment with Snow White...just a moment...*meh-eh-eh!*

Father lassoed a rope around his neck and tightened it none too kindly. He yarded on it to practically drag the animal home; it writhed and wriggled and grew higher pitched in his bleats, losing the battle.

"He is so strong," Mother admired from the window.

"What's for supper?" He wanted to know on his return home.

"Bah! You change out of those stinking clothes before you come in here!" So, he obliged, slipping out of his pants and T shirt and into a pair of coveralls by the rain barrel.

"What's for supper?" He one tracked.

"Goat burgers." Mother hid a sly smile.

"Mom," Marlene asked. "Why did God even make Billy goats?"

On one rare evening, the Gardeners went to see Mother's parents before they sold off their farm and moved to Saskatchewan. The farmhouse was already gone, sold, and moved off its cellar-hole. Grandpa and Gramma Gruenwald were sequestered in a one-room cabin without running water, plumbing, or electricity. The bathroom was a weathered outhouse.

Gramma wore her gray hair permed and uncovered by a kerchief. She also wore colorful dresses with bright splashes of flowers against a dark background. They reminded Brenda of the one flowered spot in Grossmam's babushka.

Grandpa Gruenwald sat at the home hewn table with the oil lantern on the table, his hand around a brown bottle and an open Bible in front of him. His eyes looked glassy behind his wire glasses as he greeted them jovially.

Father took the only other wooden chair across from his father-in-law. The girls and the women sat on the two bunk beds across from each other. Furniture quite often was built into the walls in small abodes like these, the chest of drawers between the beds, the beds, the drop-leaf table. All but the chairs the men sat on were attached to the inner walls of the cabin. This also kept furniture from moving during such times that the cabin had to be relocated.

The girls sat and listened in on the adults' conversation since it was too dark to play outside. Usually, this was not permitted, and they knew better than to speak up.

Brenda-Jane busied herself tracing the outline of the flowers where the skirt of Gramma's dress lay on the bed;

in her mind, she recited the songs Margaret boisterously sang while she went on her chores.

Sweetly sings the donkey
At the break of day
If you do not feed him
This is what he'll say
"Hee haw, hee haw."
And then he'll run away!

No famer in Fieldarp had a donkey, however. Just the usual assortment of cows, horses, chickens, pigs, dogs, and barn cats. Some had sheep and goats, and Grosspabeh even had geese, but most stuck to mainstream farm animals.

Brenda switched to "Billy Boy," still careful not to make an audible sound.

Oh-oh where have you been Billy-boy, Billy-boy, Oh-oh where have you been?
Charming Billeee…
I have been to seek a wife. She's the joy of my life She's a young thing and cannot leave her maaa-ther.
How old is she?
Billy boy, Billy boy
How old is she?
Charming Billyeee…
She is six times seven
Twenty-four and eleven
She's a young thing and cannot leave her maaa-ther.

Did she get for you a chair?
Billy boy, Billy boy
Did she get for you a chair? Charming Billeee…
Yes, she got for me a chair
But the bottom was not there She's a young thing and Cannot leave her maa-ther.
Can she bake a cherry pie?
Billy boy, Billy boy
Can she bake a cherry pie?
Charming Billeee…
Yes, she can bake a cherry pie
Quick-as-cat-can-wink-her-eye She's a young thing and
Cannot leave her maaa-ther.

The evening grew heavier on the children's eyelids, and at last, the adults said their departing farewells and packed them up to go home to bed. Margaret had to wake up and walk herself while Father slung Brenda over his shoulder and Mother carried Marlene out to the suburban.

Grosspabeh's geese got liberated of their enclosure during the children's next visit. Brenda-Jane walked by them knowing nothing about the big fowl, and one of them flapped his wings, each one expanding like an accordion. On her way back to the house, a goose or gander ran after her, wings outstretched and low.

Brenda heard a hiss before it bit into the back of her skirt and got scared of geese that instant. She started running, the bird close behind her, firmly latched on.

Around and around the house she ran, sobbing breathlessly. It seemed like forever before she glanced over her shoulder and saw it release her dress from its beak.

Still blubbering, she ran into the house.

"*Vat ass louse?*" Grandma queried. (What is loose? Meaning; what is wrong?)

The three aunts were playing keep away with a potato, and poor Susanna was the "piggy in the middle."

"The goose bit my dress and chased after me. It wouldn't let go!" A fresh batch of sobs welled up from her throat. To add to her horror, all four grownups in the kitchen laughed at her. She cried.

They howled. She ran into the living room to get away from them.

"Nicht in die growteh shtove nan gohne!" (Don't go in the great room!) Grossmam called.

Reluctantly, Brenda-Jane slid off the sofa and trotted back to the kitchen.

"Here." Grandma handed her a molasses cookie. A lot of problems were resolved with a dose of Grandma's cookies, from gingersnaps to molasses cookies. The chocolate chip especially, had healing powers.

Grandpa herded the geese back to their pen and did not so much as smile over the feathered tale.

"It's time for a goose roast," he spoke quietly like he always did when he was absolutely peeved about something. "And goat burgers!" Marlene chimed in exuberantly. That cracked everyone up.

CHAPTER 9

Flies in the Buttermilk

GRANDPA AND one of Mother's younger brothers came over one evening just before they moved. He looked bleary eyed, and his smile seemed surreal. Uncle Corky was wide eyed and spoke with a stammer. Stuttering ran in Mother's side of the family. Corky lived quite a vagabond's lifestyle the way he turned over jobs, pickup trucks, and women. Everyone said he would never settle down. His real name was Frank, but quite frankly, no one remembered. He was known as "Corky" for his drinking habits.

Brenda-Jane sat at the table with her head in her coloring book, being careful not to go over the lines listening in to the grownups' conversation. "Upshnacken", they called it. She had developed a knack for it; lower your head and pretend to be engrossed in what you are doing, and adults forget you exist.

Mother's new sewing machine sat at the end of the kitchen table, ready for use. It was electric; a step up from the black wrought iron treadle sewing machine she'd had to pump with her feet for power.

"Soon, the neighborhood will have new overalls,' Grandpa teased her. "They'll have to build more clotheslines."

"*Yo* (yes), the first dress I make will be all yours," she returned.

Father came in from the supper chores with Margaret to a noisy greeting. They washed up while Mother served coffee and leftover "pigs-in-blankets" from supper. They were pig sausage wrapped in pie dough, essentially.

"I have something for you girls in the truck." Corky's blue eyes were dancing. Marlene's eyes grew larger, but she said nothing from her perch on the high stool beside Mother.

An uncomfortable warmth spread over Brenda's midriff as always when she felt something negative lurked near about to happen.

"Go get it," Grandpa instructed. Corky obediently rose, and his boots pounded the orange linoleum floor. Father joined the group at the table, beaming. He loved people, loved company. It was an opportunity to entertain them with his barrage of funny stories and jokes.

Outside in the darkness, a truck door slammed, Shadow barked, and Corky's bow-legged gait came banging up the steps. Instead of coming right in, he closed the heavy door behind him and knelt on the mat to deposit a bundle comprised of an old wool coat. It moved and whimpered.

"C'mon, go look," Mother coaxed the girls, smiling.

The three shyly approached Corky, mesmerized. With a flick of a wrist, he exposed the head, and the coat gave birth to a puppy. He instantly wriggled free of his covering and became the hero of three adoring youngsters.

"Not on my clean floor!" Mother admonished.

He was a German shepherd, black on top, with brown markings starting with his underbelly.

Under his chin, he had a white tuft of fur. He didn't wag his tail; he wagged his entire body.

Bedtime was forgotten in awe and affection for the new playmate.

Grandfather and Corky smoked until the room turned into the color of exhaust in the wintertime. Mother kept busy running to the garbage to empty the ashtray and discreetly reached above the dish sink to open the window on one occasion.

Grandpa and Brenda-Jane had a competition for the pigs-in-blankets. Every time he ate one, she took one, and so it went. Then they got to the last one, and him being company, she knew she had to let him win the contest.

Before they left, Grandpa slid his baseball cap back onto his head and remarked to Mother, "I'd sure like to get you out of this back corner."

He meant the land. There was no civilization after Fieldarp. (Field and "darp," meaning village, combined made the name of the county).

After they were gone, Mother ruminated, "He kicked me awake if I didn't get up in time for chores, and he would have done the same had he ever caught me smoking."

Brenda-Jane listened for her father's response from under the homemade duvet. He said nothing. She wished the puppy was snuggled in beside her, but Mother would never have that. He had been stashed in the barn for the night. She could hardly wait for morning to arrive so she could play with him again.

The last thing she heard as she fell asleep was her mother singing as she cleaned up:

> "Flies in the buttermilk,
> Shoo fly shoo!
> Flies in the buttermilk,
> Shoo fly shoo!
> Flies in the buttermilk,
> Shoo fly shoo!
> Skip to the loo my darling…"

Brenda loved to visit Colleen Timber with Margaret, two farms down. Sunday afternoons, while parents took naps, the three of them would spend hours playing by the pond at the corner of the Timber property. If one considered muddy springtime runoff from the ditches nearby collecting at a low point a pond. They wound lilac flowers into loose braids and crowned each other, peering into the water for their reflection. The lavender scented flower clusters disintegrated and scattered through their hair, enhancing the feeling of beauty.

When they grew hungry, they traipsed over the enormous green lawn into the elegant white house for faspa. Colleen had made herself while Margaret and Brenda-Jane admired the rose-patterned wallpaper and faux marble linoleum. The dining room was separated from the kitchen by beer-colored glass pony walls.

"I have to go the cellar," Colleen announced, fixing her blue eyes on their gawking ones. She opened the door in the foyer, and they stepped from luxurious to rickety, brightness to darkness. Carefully, they footed the stairs and a doorway to the left. A wooden slab door creaked in its dirt embedded frame as it swung into the cold storage room.

The entire basement had been scooped from the earth and the house plopped on top of it. Both were L-shaped, but beside that, they were close in proximity only.

Colleen picked up a flashlight and expertly shone it around the dank room of shelves like a detective without a cape, fedora, and pipe.

She located a jar of pickled cucumbers and plucked it off the shelf.

"Let's get out of here," she dramatized with extra breath in her voice.

They climbed back to white ceramic fixtures and pink roses, glass chandeliers with strings of glass beads drooping between electric candles on metal loops.

The girls ate the typical meal of canned sausage, white buns, pickles, homemade jam, cheese, and peanut butter. Colleen added a jar of honey and sliced tomatoes, and once the sweetness was drizzled over a slice of the fruit, it tasted heavenly. Only one knew better than to say such a thing out loud.

"My mom could preserve a two-by-four," Colleen boasted playfully."

"My mom—the barn door," Margaret said, laughing. Soon, they had a rowdy game of name that ridiculous preserve going.

Once they cleared the table, they went out into Colleen's playhouse, painted white with a burgundy trim to match the big house. Both had false shutters flanking each window and three wooden butterflies fastened to the outer wall by the front door. All burgundy also, of course. Both had plush beige carpet that your feet sunk into slightly.

Brenda-Jane didn't ever want to leave that little playhouse with its miniature kitchen and rocking doll crib. Two small glass windows wore two ruffled pink curtains that matched the roses on the wallpaper. They played house until Margaret checked her watch and declared their time was up. Reluctantly, Brenda laid down the baby doll she'd been mothering. Time for Alice to leave Wonderland.

CHAPTER 10

Technical Difficulties

THE EARLY telephone system in Fieldarp was called party line because four neighbors shared the same phone line, each with a coded ring to differentiate between them.

The Gardeners were two long and two short, senior Gardeners had four short rings, the Penners a long ring, a short ring, and another long, and finally, the Timber calls rang long three times. The entire quadrant could pick up the phone and eavesdrop on the other's conversations, but the telltale clicks alerted those conversing. It was a good way to glean firsthand gossip and get an education on dating by listening in on awkward cousins embarking on the dating game. If the four attached numbers wanted to contact each other, the caller had to enter the numerals on the circular dial and then pull the claw-like receiver down as if to change their mind to hang up but let it spring back upward. With receiver still in hand, the phone rang the specified ring of the recipient on both ends of the line until someone at the receiving end picked up.

Soon, progress was reacquainted with the farming community, and the four-way string got divided by two. Now, only the young Gardeners were connected to the older and Grossmam's shrill voice threatened to split the receiver even when on a call to an outsider of the lines.

Within the household were three phones: a black poly resin wall hanging unit that hung from the kitchen wall, and two pretty white desktop versions. One of those sat on Father's desk in his office and-everything-else room, the other above Mother and Father's headboard.

Brenda had to get her sex education strictly from Margaret's phone calls with her friends now by picking up an extension until a near-death experience cut her off.

Skippy, the new puppy, grew like a Hutterite, and his large paws indicated more size to come. It was comical to watch him run alongside Shadow, jumping toward the Labrador's neck to try and cut him off in the race. Shadow's teeth and the whites of his eyes were yellowing with age, and although he tolerated the antics of his comrade, he didn't take much else from anybody.

One Sunday afternoon, during a backyard wiener roast, a rusty pickup truck roared into the yard and stopped in a flurry of dust. Smoke from the bonfire and dust mingled together to obscure the driver for a moment.

"Chief-Smells-A-Lot," Margaret announced." He makes his corners like that."

"Nah," her mother argued.

Quite befitting, the haze cleared to reveal an overall clad smelly-pointed chin, evil gleam in his eyes, his tail and Pitchfork in a shop somewhere. A greasy baseball cap covered his horns to be sure.

"IS IT POSSIBLE," he spluttered like his poorly maintained truck engine, "FOR YOU TO KEEP YOUR DOG OFF MY PROPERTY?!" The absurdity of his request was almost comical after what his goat pulled off.

Skippy sat behind Father's chair, tongue lolling, ears perking and relaxing with a "Who, me?" expression all over his furry complexion.

"HE'S STEALING MEAT FROM MY SHED!" Smelly hollered. "A big side of beef off my freezer!"

"Well, that's your problem then, isn't it?" Mother stood up from her seat in a lawn chair. "Meat goes IN the freezer, not on top of it."

"I ONLY LAID IT THERE FOR A MINUTE!" he sprayed. "And that's not the only thing he's stolen from me—"

"What about your stealing from us and everyone else?" Margaret shocked everyone with her explosion. "You steal gas and tools, and everyone knows it. And YOUR animals are NEVER where they are supposed to be!"

"Margaret! Get in the house. All of you!" Mother urged the children. So, they retreated to the laundry room from the front porch and observed from behind the curtain of the open window.

All the while, Father sat in his lawn chair, saying nothing. A faint uneasy smile played on his face.

From behind him, Shadow growled and showed his teeth.

A pink flush crept up Smelly's face from the soiled dew rag tied around his neck.

"You listen to me, you wet calf." Mother raised her index finger and shook it at him. "You've got no business tearing into our yard like that accusing us of your problems! Your goat couldn't stay home. Your chickens ate the lettuce out of my garden before we could. Our purple gas is emptied before we can use that much. Tools go missing from the garage!" She paused. He reddened and started backing away slowly. "Our dogs go everywhere together, so if one did it, you'd have seen them all. But you didn't, because the older one doesn't leave the yard. AND," she concluded, "this is Sunday.Shame on you for your behavior. Go shame yourself!"

Ashamed he was. He slunk away like a wounded rabbit and drove away meekly.

Mother spun around, furious. "You're supposed to be the man of the house, and you sit there like a stump at a time like this and say nothing?!" She turned to the picnic table and vigorously started clearing the dishes, her cheekbones flushed and her dark eyes smoldering.

"Well, I—"

Brenda-Jane and Marlene just knew it was time to go play on the swing set nearby.

Friday night, the girls took turns eavesdropping on the calls to Aunt Margaret, Susanna, and Mary.

"Ahem, coss du mat forn?" (Can you go for a drive?) a shaky male voice asked Susanna. That's how Mennonites dated. Boy gets license, boy borrows pap's truck or buys a beater with the earnings from a meager job at the local sawmill, boy calls his interest and asks someone to go for a drive. Or the bolder males drove around to the homes of eligible females, and if they answered, the boy asked, "Vas mat?" (Want to come along?) This process was called "going girling,"

Once seated on the passenger side next to the door of his or his family's pickup, the dating life began. Even dating had a system; Sundays were the ultimate day for first dates. Depending on how things went, either party could "quit" the other. If things went well, eventually, the girl slid over beside him in the truck and he came to see her on Wednesday and Saturday evenings also. Woohoo!

Aunt Susanna paused. Brenda covered the mouthpiece with her hand and whispered, "Nay, ack cone du nicht leaden (No, I cannot stand you)."

She kept her grip on the mouthpiece so they could not hear them giggling.

"Ah, venaya?" (Um, when?) She sounded nervous.

"Somebody schnackt up!" (Someone is eavesdropping!) He blurted out, annoyed, all shyness forgotten.

"Yo, and ack vite vaya dot ass!" (Yes, and I know who that is!) Susanna snapped. Now the newly dating had something to talk about.

"Yee vorn shacht cree-in!" (You will get a spanking!) Susanna threatened.

Carefully, Margaret hung the phone back up on the receiver as to prevent a click. A torrent of giggles erupted.

Grosspabeh was very strict about young men simply pulling into his yard presuming a date. If anyone dared venture that way, he himself answered the door and disqualified the would-be suitor before sending them away (Sometimes, young men travelled with a friend to help their nervousness at the beginning of a relationship).

Young men who brazenly drove from house to look for a prospective wife were considered lowlifes. Hence why the Derksen brothers were labelled "door-to-door Derksens."

Word was out about Grosspabeh's particulars, and Brenda could just imagine the fierce glow in his sapphire eyes when he declared someone unfit for his daughters. Thick eyebrows enshrouded nothing of the glowing embers beneath them.

So, dating meant aimlessly driving along with a young fellow and his cronies, and if he liked you, he asked you to repeat the process the following week. Soon, the new courtship was moved from the cab to each other's bedroom, but premarital sex was strictly forbidden. The Amish, a sister religion of the Mennonite faith, took the bedroom stage a step further…they placed a plank on its side in the middle of the bed and encouraged the young male and female to talk all night in preparation for marriage, sexual relations again, prohibited by plank and polyester.

Mother often told story of how she was visiting with an English lady in a doctor's clinic and the other woman had employed a Mennonite babysitter.

"She took her boyfriend right into her bedroom!" the woman had exclaimed distastefully.

At the growfash (grandparents), the girls' bedroom came with a sitting room. The boys were still subject to a sit-down with Grosspabeh before they could take the little hall to the right of the main one. After all, the girls sleeping quarters were a room just off the little parlor.

Father hired Smelly again to dig a new outhouse hole after the old one filled, and he wanted to move it from the fence line to a spot behind the house. The two parties had not spoken since the altercation between him and Mother and, somewhat, Margaret.

Day after day, the greasy red baseball cap descended further and further until that was all that showed of the tall gangly man. The girls decided it would be a really good game to throw dirt clods at it and then duck behind the greenhouse.

"You girls are not to throw dirt on Corny anymore." Their Father peered over his wire-rimmed coke bottle eyeglasses.

"How did you know?" Marlene queried, hence admitting guilt on the part of all three. Mother was trying unsuccessfully not to smile, but she failed, and even Father chuckled in between mouthfuls of sommer borscht (summer soup).

"Is it possible for you to keep your dog and your dirt clods home?" Margaret breathily mocked Smelly. Only she sounded more like Susanna's ambitious young suitor.

"Ya, hull deen hunt toes (Yes, keep your dog at home)." Mother was always an excellent mimic.

"Da trubble ass, du bass en hunt (The trouble is you are a dog)." Margaret role-played telling Smelly off. Everyone howled until Father's meaty hand slashed the air. After he left, however, the role-playing continued.

"Your dog opened my freezer and took my meat." Mother walked wide-legged steps to the sink.

"And then he smoked a cigarette and walked home with it on two legs," Margaret added.

"No way, your meat stinks too much for my dog—any dog!" Brenda inserted.

"Girls stop—" Mother struggled to catch her breath. "We have to stop, He's not worth sinning over," Mother instructed.

Father built a large vestibule over the new cistern beside the kitchen door. Mother's wooden cook stove was placed in one corner of the white and gold linoleum. A beautiful white door with a mock-slatted window was placed in the other corner of that same wall as the oven. It opened up to a veranda that looked out toward the entire back pasture. White cotton curtains hung over the two new windows and the light birch paneling glowed as nearly as gold as the designs in the floor. Everyone was so proud of the new amenities. And maybe now, they could flush urine instead of letting it sit until it became concentrated. Brenda-Jane was forever flushing," it was such a novelty.

"There will still be limits," Father and Mother warned.

Smelly came careening into the yard for work one day, and everyone heard a thud, yelp, and whimper. Then an engine idling. Margaret, Marlene, and Father were in the garage when the young dog came running in, spitting blood and crying. He drank water from a bucket of rainwater and held his head crooked, as if trying to thoughtfully process what just happened.

The girls crowded around him, petting him and examining him. Brenda-Jane caught up with everyone in the garage in time to catch the expression on Smelly's face. It was pink again but accompanied by a sly, gleeful smile.

"Are you going to do something about him?" Mother demanded of Father. Her almond-shaped brown eyes snapped, and her mouth was drawn into a thin strip. "You do more about his complaints about the kids than you've ever done about his behavior. You do more about the kids for a lot LESS than the things he does!" A sprig of brown curls escaped her kerchief and shook for emphasis.

"I don't jump that easily," he mumbled. "I just don't handle things that way."

"Hah!" she scoffed. "You're right there. You don't handle anything!"

From then on, Skippy held his head slightly tilted in a thoughtful posture, no matter what he was doing. It made him look older and wiser except all the rest of him. And definitely cuter, which no one would have thought possible.

Every man has a line, and Smelly hitting the barnyard sweetheart did it for Father. He evidently fired him, because he was not back to work or even on the Gardener farm again, visibly speaking. Padlocks appeared everywhere also…on the gas nozzle and the garage door.

They say, although who knows who "they" are, "you can turn your back on a thief because you know what he will do. But never ever turn your back on a liar." Unfortunately for "them," some people's kids are both.

CHAPTER 11

Running Away

BRENDA-JANE DREAMT they were still living in the basement. "Don't touch the sheets I put up," Mother told her. The baler twine was still suspended between the beams for drying clothes. Large sheets hung in rows to dry.

"If you touch them, they will stick to you forever!" Mother hollered down the staircase after her. It was like being told not to lick the pump handle. Then you had to.

Brenda ran into the clean fresh-smelling sheets and inhaled. Uh-oh. She felt the cotton stick to her face as tight as a skin. Through the material, silhouetted in the doorway, was an aghast Margaret.

"You'll never get it off now!" her sister whispered, horrified. "Never."

But Brenda-Jane always had to do what she was told she could not. She pulled and pulled, and at last, the sheet came off her countenance.

Margaret mouths dropped open, and she stood as if frozen to the spot, shocked.

The next morning, Brenda-Jane told her about the dream over cow's milk on cornflakes.

"It means learn to obey instead of behaving like a savage brat!" Mother snapped icily. "I have work to do." She slammed and sloshed her way through the dishes, fuming all the while.

"Your father puts Margaret to work outside, making her useless for me! Of course! He always comes first!"

Father was in the chalkboard-colored old Ford pickup when Brenda-Jane caught up with him.

"Dad, can I go? Can I go?"

"You don't even know where I am going," he teased, starting the engine.

"I don't care! Where? Can I go?"

Brenda got into the truck on the passenger side. The pickup had a door for every function it performed, a lid for every turquoise compartment. Long chrome rods reached the sides and held the oblong mirrors.

As usual, they walked into the Growfash (Grandparents') house without knocking, the wooden framed screen door banging shut behind them. Three aunts were polishing the wooden floor in the lean-to as they entered, or rather, Mary watched while Susanna instructed how to use the oil. Margaret suddenly grabbed the mop and sloshed the mixture everywhere like Donald Duck, quacking and swabbing. Even Grandma and Grandpa snickered at her antics.

"Nay, nicht zoe!" (No, not like that!) Susanna threw her head back and laughed in spite of herself.

Brenda-Jane followed her father past the trio and the scent of the warm oil and wet wood. Up the steps into the kitchen where the growfash (grandparents) sat having coffee and chocolate chip cookies.

"Good day!" She turned to greet them.

"Come, sit. Eat." Grandfather's greeting was much quieter.

After her cookie and a glass of milk, Brenda slipped out of the wooden bench from behind the long table and wandered into the "great room." It was as much a living room as could be in this house. The entire space was square; the windows were square; the furniture was square in its placement. The walls were clad in timepieces like Geppeto's workshop. A grandfather clock stood in one corner, another ticked from the paneled wall with gold Roman numerals and flowers circling through them above Grosspabeh's desk.

"Barley," Grandfather called. "Pull the shortest chain on the wall clock."

Carefully, she set one foot on the wooden armrest of the staunch and upright davenport. She rose to the height of the reduced cord of the clock. Gingerly, she reached up and pulled. The chain rattled as the clock wound up and grew longer. She hesitated; afraid she was breaking something.

"Keep pulling until you feel it pull back," Grosspabeh instructed.

Gently, she drew the chain down until her efforts felt resistance.

"Good!" he called out, praising her. "Maybe now we'll have more time."

CHAPTER 12

A Hole in the Wall

AFTER KLAUS and Ardeth Gruenwald (mother's parents) moved, the dilapidated cabin they had survived in while the sale of the property was in progress came to the Gardener farm. Father being Father, plopped it right in the back lawn without rhyme, reason, or routine.

The three girls were excited—a full-size playhouse to playhouse in. Until they looked inside. A crude demolition had taken place; everything had been stripped from the interior but the wooden frame around the only two windows. It was completely disemboweled, even the curtains were gone.

"Let's ask Mom for some stuff." Margaret brightened up. "I can sew new curtains."

"So, can I," five-year-old Brenda added. She could thread a needle and push it in and out of the wrong side of two pieces of fabric held together, turn them right-side out, and form a garmentless pocket.

Corky had acquired another dog he couldn't keep, so he dropped it off after a brief conversation with Father by the garage door. It was a big rust-colored dog with yellow eyes named “Rusty.”

Mother was furious. “I don’t want another dog! If he had talked to me, I would have said forget it! Ohhh! Trust my nuisance brother for this!”

Margaret could use the treadle sewing machine, and she got busy sewing for the cabin.

“Let me try, let me try,” Brenda-Jane pestered her until she relented. The hem of a new set of window coverings and a matching tablecloth was already folded over twice and pressed down.

Brenda-Jane placed her index finger on the line where the fabric was to be sewn in place since she had seen her mother do that.

Gold letters spelling “Singer” covered most of the iron body of the machine. Mother’s new instrument sat on the kitchen table, not that there was a dining room.

She moved her feet up and down after tugging the wheel to a start and then pushed down with her heels and then toes on the big wrought-iron pedal. After the first few pumps, it got easier, and soon, the fabric slid along under the needle nicely. Her index finger followed the fabric instead of letting it slide under it, and the needle pierced her pointer through the nail.

“Owww-hooo!” Brenda screamed as the mark grew purple and blood rose to the occasion.

“Oweee!”

“OOO-hooo,” Mother wailed, mocking her. “Oh-heee.”

“IT HURTS!” Brenda sobbed, holding her dripping digit up. Marlene stood by her, eyes large with wonder and fright. Margaret obediently laughed at mother's antics, and she, in turn, stopped to snicker at herself.

That was the way one survived in that setting; you couldn't beat your parents, so you joined them.

Kill or be killed, eat or be eaten.

"It hurts!" Brenda cried again. And cried.

"Oh, here." Mother got up from her place at the table where she'd been mending clothes. She jerked the cupboard above the moss-green fridge open and snatched the box of Band-Aids down. She fumbled with the wrapping on one and poised it, ready.

"Here! Then come here!" Mother practically snarled. Brenda held her hand out.

Mother grabbed a scrap of material off the floor and swiped at the trickle of blood.

Quickly, she pulled the tabs back from the Band-Aid and closed it around the wound. "There. You are not allowed to use the sewing machine anymore until you're older." Over supper, Mother told Father of the mishap.

"She said 'ohh-hoo and eee-haw!" She mimicked Brenda-Jane joyfully.

She wished Father would say something to get Mother to stop. He didn't. Her sisters were both giggling softly to appease Mother. Father kept his focus on his plate and ignored them all.

At bedtime, after everyone had washed their feet in the oblong "foot bowl" and gone to bed, a thud sounded.

"What was that!" Mother demanded from the kitchen.

Silence.

"Margaret Irene Gardener! You tell me what you did, and you tell me NOW!" From the third bedroom, a sheepish reply came hesitantly.

"I-I was exercising and I kind of, well, I put my butt through the wall."

"What?"

Everyone ran to the door of her bedroom. Margaret still lay with her legs over her head, broken paneling holding her nightgown clad rear hostage via splinter and spectacle.

"Can you get yourself out?" Mother was aghast.

Margaret kicked and wriggled free, a shower of sawdust sprinkling like fairy dust behind her behind.

"What were you thinking?"

"I, um, was just trying to do a somersault to exercise—" Laughter and giggles broke out.

"What will Dad say?" mother exclaimed. Brenda could guess as little as possible. He hadn't returned from the field yet.

"Do I have to be spanked?" Margaret wondered innocently while rubbing her injured site, a move that sent a new torrent of giggles through the group.

"That's up to Father." Mother gasped.

They inspected the wall opposite the perforated one in the younger girls' room, but it hadn't been broken through.

Father just laughed, turning red with the effort and rubbing his huge belly. He did not laugh out loud much; most times when he chuckled, he smiled an open-mouthed smile and wheezed or gasped infrequently.

The new dog went missing, and paw prints around the hen house and goat-barn hinted of wolves. Wolves usually had slightly bigger paws than a dog, and there were more of them together.

Father kept Shadow and Skipper chained near the house for the next few days. Then, if the wolves came that close, he'd get a sure shot at them.

"Why are they called Timber wolves?" Brenda wanted to know.

"That's just the kind of wolf they are, kind of a dull gray-beige color with big feet," her father explained. "There's also the brown wolf, red wolf, and few others."

Timber wolves were privy to remote North American areas like Fieldarp.

One night, the dogs went into a frenzy of barking and tugging on their chains. Brenda heard the window in her parent's bedroom slide open and then loud gunshots.

"Go back to bed," Mother snapped at someone.

"But! Want to—" Margaret whimpered.

"I TOLD YOU!"

The next morning, two wolves lay dead near the chicken coop, the ashen color of the wolf father had described. Mother took a photo of the deceased with her 126 camera that produced one square three-and-a-half-inch picture and two postage-stamp-sized ones of the subject once processed.

Uncle Isaiah stopped in to borrow the grain auger and study the exterminated farm pests now hanging upside down in the garage to be skinned. Isaiah was Father's youngest brother but older than the three girls at home.

He was tall and skinny, with thick wavy blonde hair like Grosspabeh in his youth, right up to the bluest eyes.

While the men stood chatting, the bull in the pasture lazily reared up and placed his front legs on the rear of the cow in front of him. He dropped back down on all fours, apparently having changed his mind.

"That's how cows and girls are alike," Uncle Isaiah said loudly, his baritone echoing across the barnyard loudly. "They both need a male in their midst."

Brenda-Jane didn't hear her father's response, but anger burned in her gut hearing such boorish jibber.

Uncle Isaiah was married and had two daughters younger than Marlene, who was three. He was very much an Old Order Mennonite and the bull of his pasture. His wife, Aunt Tina, and their toddlers all dressed in collarless dresses with long skirts and had their hair pulled back. He wore dark brown homemade trousers and shirts like Grandpa.

Brenda told her mother about the comment Isaiah had made, watching the pie crust suddenly being pinched a little harder around the edges.

"Huh." Mother snorted. "There's always bull when he shows up, period." She took her scraps pail and set it on the new veranda outside the porch.

"I thought you'd never step outside again with that newborn baby in the house," Uncle Isaiah teased from across the yard, referring to Mother's new sewing machine.

"Not for you, anyway," Mother snapped.

Brenda-Jane was secretly glad Mother had put him in his sweaty place. She watched him get in his truck, hitch up the auger, and leave.

"I wonder how Tina does it," Mother mused. "Well, she's as dry as he is." Brenda pictured her raven-haired aunt with the snapping dark eyes. She had announced at a family pig butchering that if he didn't stop clowning, he could cheerfully move into the garage and have the carcass all to himself. That said after he held up a string of entails and offered Mother a snack.

"We are not all as easily pacified as you are, Isaiah," Mother shot back. Everyone laughed, and Brenda felt warm inside—a happy, proud warmth like the stove her father had lit to heat the garage.

Father could create absolutely anything with his hands. The pot-bellied stove replica perched in the corner of the garage was merely a metal barrel turned upward with a door cut into the side and placed on hinges. He had welded the door onto the hinges and even "shustad" (made) a hook and eye handle for it. A pipe ran from it to the ceiling to let heat escape.

Back in the kitchen, Mother and Father were arguing over whose brother was more dysfunctional—Isaiah or Corky—while she prepared night lunch. Some days acquired a fourth meal, leftovers from suppertime. There would be cold buttermilk soup with thick homemade noodles and sliced cucumbers swimming in it. Mother would also be putting out canned sausage and for dessert she'd made rhubarb pie.

Lord love a duck, the plant was a rodent on roots in the garden, but it sure made good pie. Sometimes, Mother sliced up a raw stick of rhubarb and gave each of them a plate of sugar to dip the tart snack into before ingesting it.

CHAPTER 13

The New Doll

BRENDA-JANE HAD coveted a new baby-like doll since the last one had perished in the wood stove in the flare of her mother's temper. The doll she wanted was poised like a baby with its limbs bent and had moveable eyes. It had a pink cloth body and a rubber head with hair etched into the surface of the skull. So adorable she was that Brenda kept after Mother to get her the baby girl doll—it had to be a girl, she was too pretty to be a boy—but Mother declined. "It isn't Christmas or your birthday," she said.

Gifts were usually reserved for rare occasions. On trips to town, they sometimes were treated to some form of junk food or a meal in a restaurant. Marlene and Brenda's favorite order: fish and chips and root beer.

Sometimes the trip to shop for necessities ended at the Butterhorn General Store in the next county. Only fifteen or so minutes away from the farm the way Father drove, one could buy groceries, gas, and the odd bauble. Inside, there was even a post office as well as a fabric section with narrow selection.

Sometimes, the children had to stay and wait in the truck while Mother and Father shopped. They entertained themselves making faces at other children stuck in the same predicament in the parking lot. They much preferred to go inside to the toy aisle and look at the dolls, jigsaw puzzles, and games. There were dish sets and stuffed farm animals, storybooks, and a toy sewing machine. Brenda discovered her namesake, the much yearned for "Baby Brenda" among the walking dolls with plastic legs and glass eyes. Margaret and Brenda already had walking dolls with rubber bands stretched across their inner pelvis to make their legs snap forward in turn individually when you stood them up and nudged them.

Brenda carefully lifted the box the baby was in and showed it to Mother and Father,

"Can I please have it? There's only one left! Someone else will get it if we don't." Mother smiled a little and said, "We'll see." That got Margaret started on a paint-by-number set and Marlene wanting the same doll.

When they got home, there were no gifts, only groceries and swatches of fabric to make three identical new Sunday dresses with. Mother often did that—dressed the girls the same. Sometimes she even sewed the dolls a matching outfit, but not herself. She made her own clothes entirely differently and sometimes made Father a western shirt the same fabric as her dress.

"Do you like the material?" she lovingly stroked the royal blue cotton. "I got it on sale. Look." She pulled the layer aside and revealed the next one. It was a flowered roll on a royal blue background.

"I'm going to make the sleeves, collar, and bottom ruffle out of this."

"It looks like Grandma picked it." Margaret rejected it.

"Hah!" Mother snorted, beginning to get angry. "Which one?"

"Grunwald—cuz it's so flowery."

"Oh." Mother pacified; the three sisters all exchanged knowing glances. "Oh."

Brenda-Jane loved when she was able to choose the buttons from the button tin. It was kept in the linen closet with the scrap material and old clothes. There were as many buttons as people in the world, to be sure. Most were different, with a few sets of a kind still on their cardboard backing on string. Brenda choose a burgundy plastic collection that resembled beads. A lot of the flowers were that color.

It was fascinating how some of the contents of the old shortbread cookie tin reminded her of people she knew. There was a set of glittering black ball-top buttons with a needle hole at the bottom out of sight. They looked like Aunt Tina's eyes. The metal coin-sized coat buttons were a replica of her parents' financial situation—very few among the rest. A set of large black plastic basket-wove looking buttons reminded Brenda of Grosspabeh in his Sunday suit.

"Do me! Do me!" Marlene begged as Brenda-Jane laid them out on the kitchen table, telling the resemblances out loud.

A small mother-of-pearl seed button with a hook for attachment was Marlene, she decided. A big forest green disc she deemed as Father in his Sunday school teaching suit.

"That one is from his suit." Their mother picked it up. "An extra one."

Brenda pointed out a pewter rose bud. "That one is you, Mother!" She looked pleased.

"The ugliest one is you," Margaret scoffed at Brenda, so she flicked an orange disc with a yellow center at her. It sailed past the target and hit the stove.

"Girls! Do I have to bring Father in here?"

Brenda resorted to crossing her eyes and sticking out her tongue.

Father had made a sandbox out of an old truck box, welded the tailgate shut, left the white lettering saying "Ford" and set it on skids. He had plunked it beside the outhouse and filled it with sand from the local sand pit.

Father had also inflated a giant inner tire tube from his biggest tractor for the girls to jump on— the equivalent of a trampoline. From an old debilitated wagon of Grosspabeh's, he had harvested half an axle, welded it onto a huge rim for a base, and strapped four pieces of wood to the wagon wheel on top to serve as seats for the homemade merry-go-round. One had to hold on to the weathered board, running in synchronization with other riders and then on a count, all jumped on, and whirled in circles until the momentum slowed down enough to jump off and repeat the process.

"Now our cousin's merry-go-round looks like a sissy!" Marlene exclaimed. Karla and Kenneth had a hardware store ride with plastic seats and aluminum handles to pump it with.

The three were sitting on the tire tube facing the center and taking turns standing up and flopping back down as hard as they could to try and upset the other two. It was a giggling good time until Marlene and Margaret both jumped off of it at the same time, leaving Brenda alone with the rebound of their efforts. The force threw her off the tube onto the jagged corner of the partially rusty sandbox with the back of her head. Blood gushed instantly and profusely as head wounds tend to do, dribbling down Brenda's wispy pale blonde hair like the strawberry sauce on the angel food cake Mother always made for birthdays. Margaret led a screeching preschooler into the house, ashen, shaking, and wide- eyed, with Marlene close on her heels.

Brenda saw Mother's expression freeze and then blanch for a moment before she recovered enough to place cold rags on the swelling wound to soak the blood up. When it had stopped bleeding, the wound looked like a pig snout protruding from the back of her head. Mother showed Brenda how to manipulate the handheld mirror behind her head and look into the medicine cabinet door which was mirrored—a sin to be sure. Right now, inner tire tubes were a big sin, and that took precedence over others.

That night, Brenda could not sleep on her back nor for many nights to come. Some mornings, she woke up with a bloody pillow from her injury.

"We can't take her 'in,' the doctors will blame us for it, and the authorities will take her away," Mother whispered to Father. They had heard of such things.

Mother started drilling Brenda-Jane on the alphabet and numbers soon after that incident to see if she could learn. Soon, she would be attending school with Margaret near the general store; she would climb on the big orange cheese wagon and ride the one-hour school bus ride to Butterhorn Junction School.

Not that the school lay much farther away from the store, but the bus had to dipsy-doodle all over the countryside to pick up all the "chinga" (Children).

Far into the woods in the back recesses of the Butterhorn wares was a car garage where unlicensed mechanics fixed vehicles and farm machinery. They were the Humboldt brothers, orphaned in a car accident and forced to make a living at a young age.

"How old were they when it happened?" Brenda asked Mother, looking at the photograph of two mangled cars." Mennonites photographed everything; pictures were only a sin if they were put on display.

"Well, the oldest was of age, so he took over raising his younger siblings so the welfare wouldn't take them away. They did well for themselves, each one raising the younger and working on people's cars to make a living."

"Did the welfare people try to take the kids?" Brenda knew full well that social workers were a dirty word.

"They are hard to find unless one knows they are there. The land belongs to their uncle, who owns the store. The yard is really overgrown looking, and they live above the garage, so it doesn't look like anyone actually lives there."

Brenda-Jane had been to the garage with her father when he took his Suburban and Super Cab there for repairs."

"They didn't believe in public school, so the kids were home-schooled even before the accident," Mother mused.

"How long do I have to go to school for?" Brenda queried.

"Nine years at Butterhorn Junction." Mother pulled a tray of cookies out of the oven. "Dad and I quit after grade seven. We were both needed to help at home. The farm came first."

The cookies were "jam-jams," two golden halves stuck together with homemade raspberry jam.

"Can I have one?" Brenda begged.

"At school, they will make you say, 'may I'," Mother corrected her. "So, you better get used to it now."

"May I, then?"

Mother lifted up pastry pieces until she found two slightly dark for her liking. She spread a dollop of jam on one and stuck the two together and passed it to Brenda.

"Why can't I have one of the good ones?"

"I keep the best for company. God wants us to give our best away," Mother replied, surprisingly not angry with the question.

Brenda thought it must be another one of God's multiple rules, like the spanking your children into better people rule. God seemed to be a begrudging distant old man in the sky with a long white scraggly beard who hated children. He and Jesus were in cahoots against people—especially youngsters, and one had to be really trying hard to get on their good side.

"God has a book in heaven," her parents often said. "He writes down all your bad deeds and good deeds. One day, he will show you the lists and tell you if you made it into heaven or hell."

Father and Mother made an unscheduled trip to Butterhorn General Store not long after Brenda took her spill. They left the girls home in Margaret's care, and they all played house, the offending tire tube long removed from the play area.

In the cabin that the Gruenwald grandparents had lived in, Margaret had hung her new curtains on baler twine, and the red gingham brightened the drab room. They hauled non-split firewood in around an overturned wooden crate for a table to use as dining room chairs. The "meal" was an assortment of garden vegetables, mostly peas and carrots with *kohlrabi* as their "ice-cream" dessert. Once the thick green skin was pulled off the orb, the remaining white bulb resembled a scoop of ice cream, still attached to its root which they grasped it by like a cone to eat.

Mother was beaming when they returned from the impromptu shopping trip holding a cardboard package as she walked toward Brenda-Jane. She thrust the box at her, saying nothing, still smiling. A rubber head was crowning at the circular opening of the containment.

"A Baby Brenda! A Baby Brenda!"

She tore at the edges of the stiff paper and wires unsuccessfully until Father called, "Oh bring it here."

He reached into his pocket for his ever-present jack knife to release the doll while Mother explained to the other two that this would serve as Brenda's consolation present to help her heal from her head wound.

"Well, that's all fine and dandy for now," Marlene announced loudly. "But next time, I want one!"

CHAPTER 14

The Homestead

FATHER HAD a piece of land close to the Butterhorn Junction area. At the end of a dirt road, nestled against the Blueberry Hills, the land measured ten acres and was, for the most part, covered in wildflowers, wild berries, and rocks. Where the trees were cleared and dead brush piled up to be burned, there were more dead branches and scattered rocks on the rich soil. There were many rocks and roots thrown into piles, and Father couldn't keep up to the work.

The entire Ezekiel-the-second Gardener family got involved in the work on the homestead whenever there was a parcel of hours to be spared. Wherever the land was cleared and not raw forestation, they worked, picking rocks.

It happened on a rock pile that Brenda's theory of an uncaring God was challenged.

Father had just lit a brush row afire and stood back to watch the flames spread horizontally along the line.

"See all these dead branches?" he gestured around himself.

The girls nodded.

"That's what God will do with all the bad people one day. On judgment day."

"Where are the good people?" Marlene asked innocently. "Are they the rocks?" Snickers rippled through the group. Mother paused to wipe the sweat from her brow.

Margaret and Brenda-Jane were to gather rocks and throw them on the pile already made with machinery consisting of larger rocks.

"The good people are kids who were spanked until they are good," Father answered.

Margaret stood on the peak of the rock heap. "I'll bet you can't do this," she bragged to Brenda. "Bet you can't climb this high." Naturally, Brenda began navigating the rocks. Partially up, Margaret set a small boulder loose, and it came lurching and zigzagging down straight for Brenda. They both gasped. Brenda shut her eyes tight and winced. There wasn't time to pray.

Right before it would have struck Brenda's leg, it veered away and then continued falling off the mound, like an invisible hand had flicked it out of the way.

Brenda heard herself breathing again.

For supper, they had a wiener roast on the brush pile, consumed while perched on stumps. Dessert was wild strawberries—small, scarlet, sweet.

"I'll make jam if you pick enough," Mother offered. So, the girls drifted from their original task and plucked wild strawberries from the mossy hillside until they couldn't find the little gems of fruit anymore.

"On the Christ the solid rock I stand..." Father sang on the way home. "All other ground is sinking sand..."

"Please!" Mother protested. "I am trying to forget rocks right now?"

"How do you know English songs?" Brenda asked Father.

"Grossmam taught us kids when we were all still at home." He beamed. A surprising revelation being that senior Gardeners were leaders of a High German church group.

"Vist Grosspabeh dot?" (Did grandfather know?) Margaret asked.

"Oh sure," Father answered proudly. "The whole family sang the old English hymns every Saturday to get us in the mode for Sunday. We just were not allowed any instruments."

"Then how did you learn to play the guitar?"

"Secretly."

Musical instruments were deemed a sin among the many sins one could own or commit. Father had a harmonica, acoustic guitar, electric guitar, an old church organ, and a 120 bass accordion.

One day, the plan was to sell the farm and move to the homestead to the new house Father would have built on the hilltop. He wanted to build it out of logs with a real rock fireplace just like Pa Ingalls. The children wouldn't even have to change buses.

Mother wasn't so sold on the log home idea, but she marveled over how well things grew at the homestead.

"I should plant a small garden there next year," she plotted out loud. "The soil's so much better than the coyote crap I am trying to work with now!" As if she had time, overworked as she was now with cow's milk to separate and make butter from, eggs to wash and sell, a house to keep clean, meals to cook, and clothing to sew. Mother even made bed linen and bedspreads from scratch. Old clothes were taken apart at the seams and new patches for quilts cut right from the edge.

Mother's hands were worn and rough, like a man's, only much cleaner. Father's hands were calloused, and grease stained at the fingertips from often coaxing old or borrowed machinery to chug another mile.

Brenda-Jane decided that if someone like Grandpa and Grandma Gardener dabbled in English hymns, there must be something wrong with the Old Order Mennonite way of doing things.

At night, she dreamed of purple Bluebells swaying in the breezes at the homestead, accompanied by wild pink roses, wild ferns that bloomed a blueish purple, and fireweed, also called purple loosestrife. Then something bit the back of her head and jolted her awake.

The dusk of summer that darkened the house blinded Brenda for a few moments. She felt her pillow for moisture and the tender point left from when her noggin got a floggin'. Mother had said if she noticed any blood to take her pillowcase off and soak it in cold water in the bathtub instantly so the it wouldn't stain the bedding, but she felt nothing wet at the back of her head or on the pillow. Relieved, Brenda lay down on her left side, which left her facing the door of the bedroom, closed her eyes, and returned to visions of the rich life they would experience on the homestead.

Mother took sick with a cold and didn't miss a step. She couldn't very well take time off from work when home and work were one and the same. Sunday afternoons provided her with one nap for the whole week—the only time she lay down beside nighttime. That's why Brenda-Jane and Marlene were surprised to find their mother in bed one afternoon while taking their baby dolls out to the Gruenwald cabin.

The first clue was the empty kitchen. Silence. Nothing bubbling on the stove nor rising in the oven. No cooking aroma.

The two continued down the hallway on tiptoe and peered into the master bedroom. A still form lay on top of the quilted bedspread under another quilt, hardly wrinkling the bedclothes. Brenda ventured closer. Was she breathing? The top blanket rose and fell softly.

"Mom?"

The woman stirred slightly, looking paler and more gaunt than usual.

Beside her, Marlene's eyes grew.

"Mmm," Mother moaned. "I just need to lie here for a while." She coughed. Her voice had a new octave—deep and throaty.

By suppertime, food was unheard of, and Father had exchanged the tractor for the truck to take her to the hospital in Eagle's Creek. The last time she had been there, she had given birth.

Aunt Margaret came over to sit with the girls. She, the jolliest of Father's three younger sisters— the plumpest, the blondest, and the most likely to leave the area as soon as possible.

Brenda could only vaguely remember the Eagle's Creek Hospital from a time they had visited Aunt Tina and her new baby.

There were three towns within a half-hour of each other—Hatchet Prairie, a staunch Mennonite settlement; Eagle's Creek, the oldest village that flowed along the riverbank named, you guessed it, populated largely with aboriginals; and Hazel's Crossing. Indian reservations were sprinkled around Eagle's Creek all the way to Hazel's, a truck-stop town full of debauchery motels and deep-frying restaurants. Each town had a personality as different as the population thereof, although the Crossing had aboriginals within its transient spectrum also.

Corky showed up for a visit on a bright sunny morning after Mother was admitted to the hospital for suspicion of pneumonia. With him was a gorgeous blonde woman with curly hair, red fingernails, and a lot of blue eye makeup. Her cheeks and lips were pink, and her dress, a white sundress with blue polka dots, was from page twenty-three of the spring and summer Sears catalogue. She wore pantyhose on her shaved legs and white high-heeled pumps.

Margaret told him about Mother's illness.

"What is it? Do...do...do...they know?" he stammered the way he always did. The lady dropped her eyes shyly like Princess Diana, peering up at them from the steps once in a while. The girls couldn't take their eyes off of her.

"Too bad, I really wanted to introduce her to my new wife." He had married the prettiest of a string of girlfriends.

"Where's Rusty?" He glanced around him.

"The wolves ate him," Marlene piped up.

"Th...tha...the other dog's okay?" He referred to the pup he had given them.

"He's sniffing you right now." Margaret pointed. Corky jumped at the sight of the vast dog behind him.

"*Hola!* What did you feed him?" he exclaimed. His new bride tittered into her manicured hand.

"Where's your Dad at?" He glanced around furtively again. "I need to talk to him, see if I can get my cabin back." He gestured toward the barn as if to already be talking with Father, who had to be in there.

His wife got into the middle of the truck while he darted off to the barn to deal.

The cabin got jacked up, and a trailer deck slid beneath it.

"C'mon, let's listen to records," Margaret suggested. They all piled into the forbidden living room around the record player.

Soon, Conway Twitty and Loretta Lynn were crooning "Making Believe" and the breakfast dishes forgotten.

"We'll do them later." Aunt Margaret waved them away like she was Mary Poppins. She squatted near the record pile in her tight blue denims and T-shirt, switched from the dress she had arrived in.

They picked flowers for Mother from the garden and placed them in an empty mason jar with water to take to her.

The ride to Eagle's Creek was long and the hospital grim with its drab colors and steel railings. Mother had an intravenous pole beside her and a clear plastic hose running from a bag on a hook to a bandage on her wrist. She lay very still.

The usual aura of perfume that encircled Mother had been replaced by chemicals that smelled of disinfectant.

"*Hiyah?*" (Dear one?) Father tapped Mother's arm lightly, but her eyelashes opened as soon as he spoke. Dark football player smudges lay under her eyes, making her look extremely tired and sick. She cleared her throat.

"The doctor says that I have pneumonia." She sat up slowly, weakly. One blue-veined hand grasped the bed railing for support.

The girls thrust the homegrown bouquet at her. A thin smile flickered across her face. "Are these from the garden?"

They were—pink petunias, white flocks, red sweet peas, and multi-colors of snapdragons.

"Oh, thank you."

Mother's medically issued slippers were big puffy pouches elasticized at the ankle. Her mint threadbare gown hung straight down to her knees and blueish housecoat just below.

"I should have asked you to bring my slippers. My feet are cold."

The room had four beds, but the other three were empty. Pristine, sterile, and vacant.

"You should make a list," Father suggested.

The hospital had a kitchen and dining room with a big long table like Grossmam and Grosspabeh's minus the wooden bench. There were sturdy orange plastic chairs on chrome legs instead.

"Where do you sit, Mom?" Marlene wanted to know. "Which seat is yours?" She could not fathom random seating of transitioning patients.

"They bring tray to my bed. This is for socializing," she explained. "Fuh die vot spitzeern chan (For those that can visit)."

They walked past the room and back to Mother's lonely partition. Pale yellow curtains hung from white mesh on hooks between the beds.

Brenda-Jane pressed down on the bulging vein that had the intravenous inserted in Mother's arm. It sprang back up.

"Does that hurt?"

"No, the doctor said I have the perfect veins for this."

"Who gets sick in the middle of the summer?" Grandmother wanted to know when Father dropped the girls off on their farm. Brenda didn't hear his response; she had tiptoed into the sitting room of the girl's bedroom. It had to be the prettiest room of the house—a large square of feminine knickknacks, ornaments, plants, and furniture covered in doilies. An archway was the door to their bunked sleeping quarters. The room even boasted of an electric organ; what was the world coming to?! A white ceramic swan with her neck arched held a pot of pink plastic roses on her back.

Unfortunately, her head broke off when Brenda reached past her to turn the power on to the organ. *Clink!* Quickly, she left the room, her exploration of the hope chest items on display cut short.

"Grossmam," she began at Grandma's elbow beside the giant dough pan. "I did something I shouldn't have."

She figured if she could get the "growfash" (Grandparents) on her side, they might advocate for her with her aunts.

"Oh?"

"I went into the girl's room and I broke something." Brenda-Jane felt her lip wobble and she fought hard against the demon-emotion.

"Oh!" Grandma exclaimed. "Dot vorn die maylen nicht leichen!" (That, the girls won't like!) Brenda-Jane started to cry even though she tried hard not to.

"Ass dee dot light?" (Do you regret it?) Man, there were a lot of asses in Low German!

"Um-hmm," she managed, fear of the unknown penalty swept over her, tormenting her.

"Okay. Dot mot dahn gowt zahn" (That will have to do).

The three aunts were not as forgiving, all disheveled from the garden and tired. Susanna had her usual pinched and pious expression, with more color in her cheeks. Mary looked sour in her brown gingham dress. Margaret thumped a tin pail of raspberries on the kitchen table and noisily walked away in the Whisper pantyhose she always wore under her dresses. It made her gait sound like a grasshopper.

Grossmam covered the bread dough bowl with a clean dish towel while it rose. "Girls, Brenda wants to tell you something."

No, she didn't. Brenda-Jane's stomach warmed up.

The three paused almost comically, each head and a half shoulder leaning past the other to listen.

"You are not to go in there without our permission again!" Susanna snapped. "I'll slap your hand myself!"

She flounced off in her knee-length brown dress with the pleated skirt that made her hips look wide.

Mary busied herself sorting the raspberries while Margaret set the table for supper. They worked in unison in spite of their vastly different personalities and the conflict that usually accompanied them.

Margaret was a rebel who often did things behind Grosspabeh's back. A happy rebel. Susanna was the model good Mennonite daughter with all her auburn hair so in place and wore collarless dresses. She wore sensible false leather shoes and a waist apron whenever she worked while the other two sloshed their way through farm chores heedlessly. Mary was the dark-haired baby of the bunch. She sang country love songs in her silvery thin voice wherever she went. Mary also brimmed with stories and funny jokes, yet she was serious in between.

That night, Grandpa put up an old cot in the hallway and put Brenda-Jane and Marlene at opposite ends. Margaret slept with the aunts in the double-bed wide bunk bed in their room. When the old house settled for the night, it was still a buzz with time piece activity. Clocks ticked, tocked, and chimed their medleys into the air still scented with homemade bread and lye soap. Brenda lay awake and thought of Mother and the aroma of sweet perfume she always wore.

CHAPTER 15

"Die Owning" (The Premonition)

BRENDA-JANE WOKE up to the sound of Aunt Mary's high pitched:

> "Ashes of love, cold as ice
> You made the debt, I paid the price
> Our love is gone there's no doubt
> Ashes of love, the flame burnt out."

"Pabeh champt!" (Father's coming!) Susanna's voice interrupted her. Grandpa did not approve of country love songs nor public displays of affection, and since one usually spoke of the other, both were forbidden. He had a way of embracing you with warm words but also a way of piercing your melody with his fierce blue eyes and equally fierce expression of disapproval.

The girls crowded into the bathroom off the kitchen to wash up for breakfast.

Grandpa took off his narrow-brimmed straw fedora and hung it on its hook before heading down to the cellar for an armload of cook stove kindling. The top of the hat had a dip like a cowboy hat, but that was as far old west as he got with his wardrobe. He wore army boots and khaki or brown shirts and matching pants. In spite of his horsemanship, any cowboy gear was prohibited—considered worldly.

Grandfather had been drafted to fight in World War II but had refused to engage in any sort of combat due to his staunch Mennonite beliefs. So, the government had forced him to spend the first year of his marriage in a Conscientious Objector's Camp manufacturing practical items for the war effort. Mother and Father had a running joke that it was the closest thing to birth control they had ever used.

"Sit on the wood bench until breakfast is ready," Grandma directed. "Afterward, you can help with the dishes before your father comes to get you."

"What sort of things did you have to build for the war?" Brenda asked Grandfather over a breakfast of toasted brown bread slices, poached eggs, fresh milk, and coffee.

The mess hall that was the farm kitchen fell silent, waiting for his response.

"Sawhorses." A devilish grin crept over his face. "I built sawhorses and even had to ride home to Grossmam on one."

"Obah!" (But) she protested.

"Mom," Susanna exclaimed. "The strawberries are as big as a baseball—some of them." The three had picked the berry patch that morning before the summer's heat beat them to the jam-making process.

"You can take some to your mother," Grandma offered. She hummed and half-sang "Welch Adii" (Goodbye World) as she sorted through the produce in her ice cream pail.

> "Welch adii ich been dan mude
> (World goodbye, I am now tired).
> In den himmel alle zeit, frei die ruh
> und seligkeit (In heaven all the time, free
> to rest and experience salvation)."

Brenda-Jane loved gazing up at the display case with glass sliding doors above the sink that housed Grandma's finery. It went right up to the ceiling and so did its transparent apertures. The coffee grinder sat among delicate ceramic roses on pewter stems, its wrought-iron handle saluting the big glass horse. The horse was harnessed completely, pulling a two-wheeled chariot full of silk roses. Behind it all, a mother of pearl platter leaned against the wall.

Father took the girls shopping for gifts for Mother in the only store in Eagle's Creek. The only windows in the front were barred behind metal grates one would see above a fire pit. Rusty old gas pumps still sat out front, corroding away quietly from years of neglect once the general store became less general. Plain wooden letters that spelled "gas," and "confections" had become chipped and faded. Inside, there was a wide variety of merchandise on the wooden shelves sitting on cracked tiles: overpriced dry goods, candy, liquor, knickknacks, cards, and gift wrapping.

Brenda-Jane spotted a pair of pink fuzzy slippers. She begged for them to give to Mother. Poor Mother, she worked so hard for so little. Father held a sensible plaid brown pair of men's loafers in his hands.

"Dad! Please? Those are for men. Can we please get these for Mom?" She touched the satin ribbon on the top of one slipper. "Mom never had anything this nice to wear. Please?"

At last, he relented and bought them, along with Margaret's card shaped like a basket of flowers and Marlene's silk roses.

Mother lay thin, pale, and lifeless on the shiny wheeled bed. Everyone hushed as they approached her. "Mom?" Brenda, the ever-forward one, spoke up first. "Mom, we brought you something." It appeared she still slept until they saw tears trickling down her sallow cheeks.

"Will…you…all…forgive me for all the things I did wrong?"

Marlene's face crumpled, and she began to cry too. The rest of the family froze.

"Girls," Father admonished them. They were to answer her.

"Will you?" The limp form on the bed would've wept but for lack of strength.

Dumbly, they all nodded, placed their gifts on the nightstand and, then, not knowing what else to do, edged back out into the wide hallway.

"Girls." Father lowered his voice. "It seems your mother has had some kind of "*owning." (Premonition)*

"What's an *owning*?" Margaret asked, the only family member with composure.

"It means she believes she is going to die," he explained. Then the sobbing overtook them all, and he hurried them out to wait in the car. Expressing emotions was for the English and the worldly. "I d-d-don't want my mom to die," Marlene cried.

Back at the "growfash," Uncle Dan walked in wearing a complete western outfit: a black hat with a silver band, black duster, and silver-tipped toes on his boots. He looked like a movie star straight out of a John Wayne movie or a cowboy catalogue. One couldn't help but stare at him. How handsome he looked.

"Don't you ever come to my funeral wearing those devil clothes." Grossmam wagged her finger at him.

"Huh." He snorted, stomping back outside. "Will if I want to."

Grandma kept the girls busy that afternoon, weeding and watering the garden and greenhouse. The latter was actually an old school bus stripped of its seats, bullies, and wheels. A sawhorse table sat on either side of the aisle and held plants beside the windows. All aboard.

Underneath the tables, she stored empty pots, pails, bags of potting soil, and gardening tools.

Grandma assigned the job of picking choke cherries to Brenda-Jane and herself. Of course, Brenda had to taste one and spit it out fast.

"They taste like sawdust!"

Grandma let out a thin, crystal-goblet-tinkling laugh. "They are rough, aren't they?" Made into chokecherry jam, the berries more than compensated for the tart experience.

Time went quickly, and soon, it was two weeks since Mother had been in hospital and was being discharged, as weak from the antibiotics as the illness itself.

"You will have to take it very easy," a tall thin bespectacled doctor with black hair and a crew cut admonished Mother. She smiled faintly and sat on a chair beside her empty bed, fully dressed.

"I mean it." The whitecoat shot Father a sharp look. "You people—all you do is work, work, work, and it is killing your wife. Hire a maid."

Father smiled and nodded and blushed at the doctor's direct instruction.

"Hire a maid, let the garden grow over like a jungle—there's always next year. Isn't that a farmer's mandate? Next year?"

Now he and Father both chuckled.

A very different woman moved slowly around the house, inspecting her domain for changes and, no doubt, dirt.

Mother spoke very little and easily lost her breath. She sat down wherever there was a chair or ledge to rest during her roaming, looking for all the world like a slight wind could blow her away.

Grossmam had sent ice cream pails full of potato salad, macaroni salad, canned fish, canned sausage, and pickled beans.

"The doctor said I barely made it." Mother's chin quivered.

"We'll clean the house," Margaret offered. Even though it wasn't a Saturday.

A brief look of relief fluttered over her face before Mother got up to go to bed. And it wasn't even bedtime nor Sunday afternoon.

CHAPTER 16

Along the "Shreefah" (Creek/River)

PART OF Grandpa and Grandma's driveway was actually a wooden bridge over a creek. They had named it the shreefah (Reefah meaning river, and the "sh" taken from the word shreeyen, meaning to scream). The water body was a creek, but Grossman argued that if the Indians could name the river "Eagle's Creek," surely to goodness they could name a creek a river.

In the springtime, the creek swelled up too many times its size, and the rumble of mass water movement could be heard a half-mile away. The level rose to a mere meter under the bridge down a mile. The Penners were the senior Gardeners' eldest daughter and belonged to a stricter denomination of the Mennonite religion called the Old Colony Church.

Mother, still fresh out of the hospital, went about some of her work weakly. The girls scanned the banks of the shreefah for its usual supply of wild flowering ferns, bluebells, goldenrod, chamomile, and wild daisies. Most of the foliage bloomed lavender and purple, contrasting with the yellow and white flowers. It made a brilliant arrangement when the three finished sliding the last sprig into one of the empty Cheese Whiz jars Grossman had given them to collect their natural treasures in. One now occupied, they waded into the creek to catch the tiny fish that lived in it.

Giggling with nervous anticipation, they rang the doorbell at home like some stranger, and when Mother came to answer it, Marlene thrust the crude vase upward toward her.

"Oh, you guys are going to make fine florists one day," Mother praised. Ever since her stint at the hospital, she had a new pleasantness.

"Did you enjoy your stay at Grandma's?" She smiled as the truck rumbled away back to the "folks," as Father referred to his parents. The girls nodded, Marlene stood small and bright eyed by Mother's weary shadow, still holding the bouquet.

"The doctor said I was lucky to have gotten over the pneumonia," Mother chirped. "Cuz some people don't."

The garden had been neglected during her absence, as had the lawn and laundry. So much so that by the next mid-morning, Mother was in tears.

"I almost died in the bed," she cried out. "And this is what I come back to? The doctor said, 'Take it easy,' and I can't? Because nothing is done?!"

She wept quietly as she worked, lifting clothes out of the wringer-washer barrel and feeding them through the wringer rollers.

Brenda-Jane and Margaret were instructed by Father to weed the garden. It was a relief to get out of the house; one didn't quite know how to take Mother, or which was worse—the weeping or angry harping. Secretly, Brenda-Jane preferred her mother's angry outbursts in spite of the accompanying verbal listing of all that she hated about her life.

"Hurry up!" Marg's sharp voice interrupted Brenda's thoughts. "We have a lot of work to do."

"Shut up!"

Brenda's thoughts drowned out her sibling's retort, drifting like the shreefah. The story was that the creek-named-river reached all the way to Hazel's Crossing.

The early "settlers" of Fieldarp had used the waterway as their only access to Eagle's Creek and its meager resources. People like their Gruenwald grandparents had moved to this sect of the woods in a rowboat when Grandma was pregnant with her first child. They had come in the spring, the only time the creek was wide and deep enough to float cargo on.

Brenda-Jane pulled a carrot to snack on while the sun shone noon.

"That is not working," her sister scolded, weeds flying below her rapid fingers.

"Ya, Grossmam," Brenda mocked her, dirt crunching between her teeth.

Then Father called her, and Brenda's heart sank to her knees past her warm stomach. She was in trouble for shirking on her chores, maybe, although he couldn't possibly have seen or heard the two of them from his stance across the yard.

"I'm going to go borrow Grossmam's lawnmower, do you want to come?" She accepted the respite from Margaret and her duties eagerly.

Rolling out of the yard past the garden, Brenda caught sight of Margaret's angry face and stuck out her tongue.

At the growfash, the midday hustle and bustle were momentarily lulled by a coffee break.

Aunt Margaret, in blue jeans and smelling of cow manure, brightened when she saw Brenda-Jane. She set her egg basket down and whispered, "C'mon, I'll show you something." They sidled past the kitchen table where Susanna and Mary were hovering near their parents and brother like waitresses.

In the ladies' fern-laden bedroom, bedecked with all its finery, Margaret opened the lid of the electric organ.

She turned it on, adjusted the volume down, and played "Golden Slippers" and "Poor, Poor Farmer" using one hand to play the bass buttons to create a chord and maintain a beat.

"How do you know which buttons?" Brenda was credulous. Her aunt laughed.

"I don't. You just play whatever sounds right." She was well into "Silver Sandals" when someone rapped on the outer door.

"Pabeh." She halted before the silver sandals made it up those golden stairs.

"Don't play the devil's music," Grosspabch admonished sternly. Once his footsteps retreated, Margaret turned the volume down further and proceeded again, singing along this time:

"In silver sandals, she goes walking up those golden stairs
And though we miss her so, we know she is happy to be there,
We walk with her in memory, we see her all the time,
In silver sandals walking through our mind."

Tante (Auntie) did not say goodbye before she saddled up Big Red and rode out of Fieldarp to catch a ride out of the northernmost part of Alberta.

No one noticed the horse missing or that he had been any place but his usual in the pen until he came sauntering home, saddled, rider less, and breathless.

Grosspabeh had immediately tended to the giant animal, rubbing him down while he gulped a pail of warm water. One must not ever give a horse that has just worked cold water, he had taught Brenda, or the beast would develop severe stomach cramps.

Being an old mammal that he was, it was unlikely he had been ridden far. Margaret had probably gone to meet someone with a car at the Butterhorn General Store after dark. In the nearly empty saddle bag lay a crumpled note saying she needed to see more of God's creation than the dung channels of Grandpa's barn, and that she would take a bus from Hazels Crossing to the city of Cattleline, twelve hours south. Her plan was to get a job and go to college.

Big Red was cleaned up from his impromptu adventure and followed Grosspabeh's heavy steps into the lengthy barn. He received one more rub down of his lower legs with Vick's VapoRub to prevent muscle ache.

"Dad," Brenda interrupted the milking. "What's going to happen to Aunt Margaret? Will she get an 'eatshloss?'" (A casting out or excommunication from church and family).

Shterp, shterp, shterp, the milk from the last cow squirted against the sides of the aluminum pail.

"No," he paused milking. "She was told to smarten up or leave, and she was not a baptized member of the church. So, nothing will be done until she comes back and makes it right with the folks."

"How come Grosspabeh is a deacon and not a pastor?"

"The deacon is the head of the church," he answered slowly. "He is actually the bishop of the church, then next in line is the older preacher, then the younger, then the Sunday school teacher and song leaders."

Having given the list of clergy hierarchy, he twisted a teat expertly and caught a stream of milk in his mouth.

"So is Grandpa going to lose his place in line?"

Father chuckled. "No, why?"

Brenda had overheard the adults talking once about how a leader of the congregation had to have total control of his household or else.

"Because of what Tante (Auntie) Margaret did."

"No, it would be different if she was a member, but her being young and in the bad years..." That's what the locals called the rebellious teenaged years: "the bad years." The Amish called them "Rumspringah."

Relieved, she turned to go back to the house in the dusk. Skippy and Shadow accompanied her, brushing up against her legs affectionately.

Margaret was free to live in a world of bright, shiny, pretty, and colorful things without the threat of religious repercussion.

Brenda-Jane imagined leaving the tiny hamlet on horseback one day…only she would follow the tree line along the shreefah all its way to Hazel's Crossing with all its bright lights and paved highway running through it.

CHAPTER 17

The Penners

FATHER'S OLDER sister Zedah (Sarah) had married an Old Colony Mennonite pastor who was much older than she. Uncle William Penner wore black every day of the week and had a face full of furrows. He and Tanta (Aunt) Zedah had produced as many children as his wrinkles it seemed, and they filled up the tiny space of the four-room slab house he'd built for his family.

Aunt Zedah was rotund, a younger version of Grossman really; she dressed in similar collarless dresses and bib aprons, only because the Old Colony Mennonite Church denomination had more primitive standards than any other church group, Aunt Zedah's dresses were never printed with any designs nor were her aprons. All the skirts of Old Colony females were box pleated and the cloth sewn from a solid color. Always dark.

The Penner children ranged in age from two to eighteen, the oldest Penner's being close to the age of the youngest Gardeners still at home. Subsequently, they joined a group that went socializing together on Sunday afternoons looking for other youth to befriend but ultimately to date and marry.

Ironically, after all the to-do and fuss over skirt seams and lengths, "crowd" was a conglomeration of Old Colony youth and Old Order youth. Most times that a member of one group fell in love with the spawn of another, not much fuss was made as long as the female followed the male to his denomination.

"I guess they are bored of only having family to look at." Mother shocked everyone over a pile of bread dough.

Brenda-Jane's favorite cousin was the oldest Penner boy, Heinrich. He was tall, dark, and handsome, with a headful of dark unruly hair and bushy dark eyebrows. His eyes were dark blue, concealing his thoughts and feelings from the world like a drawn curtain.

"Hein-cheh," she called him to pester him just so he'd wag his index finger at her and pretend to get angry.

"Comb your hair down!" his parents ordered frequently. So, he would oblige them, pulling a comb from his back pocket and comply, but curls and cowlicks couldn't be tamed with mere soap and water.

"I'll brush it one of these days," Aunt Zedah threatened him as he strode out the door to catch up with his siblings to go to "crowd." "Go ahead," he retorted.

Cousins Nellie, Susan, and Ernest were already in the family crew cab waiting for Heinrich to drive. They had inherited their mother's blonde hair and blue eyes.

Nellie was seventeen and old enough to pin her braids up into a bun. She'd been wearing her hair like that since she was sixteen. Ernest was stocky and sullen, hardly lifting his head when he sauntered by you. Susan wore her paper-bag-colored hair in a long wispy braid down her back.

Brenda watched them through the kitchen window, longing to be one of them except for the clothing—the girls in their starched pleated skirts that hardly moved as they walked in their dark tights and sturdy black running shoes.

Heinrich picked up a dirt clod and flung it against the house just below her. It broke with a dull thud just as her mother's sharp hiss made its impact.

"What are you doing, acting like a wallflower! Shame on you! Now go play with the other children or I'll fetch your father. Hear?"

Brenda nodded, feeling her face burning and her lower chin quivering.

"Hear? Hear me?"

"Yes." She choked out. Everyone in the house must be staring at her. When she looked up from the window, the children were all motionless and staring, the men in the sitting room chatting out of her sight. Aunt Zedah peered around the corner of the kitchen gawking at the goings on.

Uncle William had been preaching at home also. The younger children alternately used the word "zin," (sin) to manipulate each other.

Peter and David had a power struggle over a wooden truck. Both tugged at the homemade toy with four-year-old Peter growing very red faced and about to cry

"*Zin!*" (Sin!) he declared. "*Zin!*" And David let go.

"What is the sin?" Brenda was curious.

"Vote yankern vote yanna haft," (Wanting what the other has) Johan explained. "But we have to try and please God."

That was the Mennonite religion in summary: God as a distant, forbidding, white-bearded old man in the sky with a wizened face and billowing black overcoat who watched everyone disapprovingly. He didn't smile but kept a long list of rules for mankind to follow, and he kept a book of their infractions of those rules. If one managed to follow those regulations, he might maybe be pleased. Most likely not, but without trying to satisfy God, you had no chance at all. A dismal picture indeed.

The Penner cousins didn't call their parents Mom and Dad, they referred to them as "Mameh" and "Pabeh" or "Mam" and "Pap."

Brenda-Jane caught her reflection in the porch room window. She fingered her wispy blonde hair and wondered if it would ever thicken and grow into a length she could braid neatly.

"Wallflower!" a voice hissed in her ear. Her mother. Mercifully, her high-heeled shoes clicked away to the dining room table where Aunt Zedah was making faspa.

The smell of wood burning wafted through the air as the old furnace sputtered on. A woodstove crackled in the porch simultaneous with the snapping fire burning in the kitchen stove.

"Johan! Go get me more wood!" his mother called. He sighed and slid out from under the table where he had been seated on a long wooden bench, leaving his game of Yahtzee.

Brenda-Jane felt her eyelids growing heavy from the warmth of the old house, the hum of voices, and the aroma of warm bread.

The kitchen had no cupboard doors, so red gingham curtains were strung across the shelves on red baler twine, covering the cookware.

At last, the long table was laid out with the faspa feast—jams, brown and white buns, butter, garlic pickles, cold sausage, and a chocolate pancake with a whipped cream topping. Freezer jam, basically extremely sweet and frozen strawberry jam, sat thawing in a glass dessert dish. All of the food had been made from scratch. Every available chair graced the side of the great table opposite the great long bench against the back wall.

Sitting beside her sister in law, Mother looked elegant in comparison with her mint-colored store bought dress and slim waist. A large pilgrim's color edged in lace matched with white pumps and a white kerchief contrasted Tante's plain dress. Mother wore her hair swept up in a high wave off of her forehead and curled back. The preacher's wife had slicked her ash blonde hair back as if she couldn't conceal it fast enough under the large black babushka. Pleated folds on her dress skirt made her appear plumper.

As she took her turn smoothing butter on her thick slice of homemade bread, Brenda-Jane looked around the large kitchen that was more like a mess hall in a concentration camp. This the only large area the abode boasted of; all the other living spaces branched out from it. The pantry or *coma* that held the preserves and staples. The three tiny bedrooms that bunked everyone divided off from one corner. One of these served as the living room with the couch unfolding down into a bed for the Penner parents. The boys slept in a heavily bunked room, and across from their bedroom, the girls did likewise. In between the two bedrooms, a closet-sized opening held a claw-foot bathtub, U-Haul toilet, and sink that drained into a five-gallon bucket under it.

"I do believe the Shepnards are at it again," Mother trailed her hand loosely over some imaginary crumbs. She referred to the archenemies of the Gardeners. The Shepnards were wealthy business owners of a trucking company and farmed grain only where the Gardeners did mixed farming and were dirt poor.

"Nah!" Aunt Zedah snapped at Johan for reaching across the table for the freezer jam. "Nah," "Bah," and "Obah" were the sounds of a German speaking Mennonite protesting and sounding disproval at their offspring. He retreated, and the story continued.

"Grosspabeh purchased a new combine, and the Shepnards had found out about it. It hadn't been hidden—the new red Massey Ferguson sat in Grandfather's yard briefly before it was put it to use in the field. From across the creek where the youngest Shepnard son lived, the forestation was thinned like the hair on most male Gardeners, and they could easily see into Grandpa's yard a way. The next thing anyone knew, there were two new red and white International Combines parked beside the Gardeners. "How they were parked was a sad sight to behold," Mother continued, stroking the tabletop, brushing imaginary crumbs to the wooden floor. "Like they were kissing, with the headers almost touching."

"Margaret came home from the bus with the story that the Shepnards had called her a 'messy farting son' because of her grandfather's farm machinery," Mother rambled on. William and Zedah gasped at the language."

"Ni yo," Zedah soothed, meaning "okay then."

Besides, the one-word declaration, *zin*, that cancelled any unwanted activity of the Penner children, there was the term *mot* (have to).

"Why do you all wear suspenders?" Brenda-Jane asked Johan sitting beside her. The children had moved into the entrance of the house to play out of sight of the adults.

"Dot mot zo" (It has to be), he replied.

"*Mot*," little Peter echoed.

The Shepnards had also tried to lay claim to the bridge that joined William's land to Grandfather's. The creek was on Penner property, yet a sign magically sprouted up one day bearing the slogan "Shepnards Creek." The older Penner cousins touched it up with spray paint and electrical tape to read "Sheepnerds." After all, removing it would be a sin for sure. The post, along with its offensive lettering, soon disappeared.

"I don't think the shortcoming is money," Uncle William spoke slowly of their wayward neighbors. "But all the other things…" he left the sentence hanging. It was true. The Shepnards owned a logging company and had a lot of money.

Grownup conversation turned to gardening, fieldwork, and weather. The three teenagers returned home and took a spot at the table the younger children left when they resumed playing with the wooden blocks on the floor.

"I am going to need help with canning," Mother announced. "I don't have the help that you do."

"Why not?" The Penner children all had assigned chores according to their age and ability, and their household ran like a button factory.

"I only have one big enough to help, and she is always outside with the barn chores."

'Nah," replied Tante Zedah. "Nah" was the cousin of "niyo," and it meant placation of the protest.

Evidently, Mother won the argument as she invariably did, and Susan came home with them to stay and help with the canning for a week.

Brenda-Jane fought the sleepiness that swept over her on the way home like warm honey on sliced tomatoes. Her head sagged onto her mother's arm and was promptly elbowed off in one bony thrust. Marlene lay curled up in her mother's arms. The next thing Brenda knew, her father had picked her up and was carrying her into the cold dark farmhouse where the fire in the stove had gone out.

Susan was a quiet, reserved girl who kept her secrets as tight as her hairstyle. It was parted in the middle, pulled back on each side, and held by a metal hairclip before it was pulled back into a braid. Her braid kept falling forward as she worked, and occasionally, she impatiently shrugged it back over her shoulder.

Whenever Susan was in between tasks, she stood back with her feet spread, toes pointing out with her arms at her side, waiting for the next directive from Mother.

"Land sakes!" Mother exclaimed, snapping the tea towel, folding it in half, and whipped it over her shoulder.

Susan had gone out into the garden for another basket of beans.

"That girl will drive me bananas yet with all her hanging back when there's work to be done."

Margaret came in with the milk pails, singing loud and off key, "A poor, poor farmer praying it won't snow!" She poured the milk into the cream separator that stood stately in the entryway corner in the beautiful new mud room that had just been erected over the new cistern.

The black metal base that curved up and inward with its gold lettering looked sharp in the white and gold room.

"Where's that girl?" Mother fumed and fussed over the bowl she was chopping beets into for cooking and canning. "Pay her enough for a new dress," she singsong mimicked Susan's mother. Brenda-Jane watched the point of her kerchief jerk with each vivid motion of her cutting up vegetables.

"Why get a new dress if one is made the same as all the others?"

A mound of sliced beets grew by Mother's elbow. Then a new idea caused her to drop her knife and dry her hands on her flowered apron. Heels clicked across the kitchen and down the hallway to the linen cupboard.

Reaching high, she took a package from the top shelf wrapped in meat packing paper. A large bolt of navy-blue cloth had lain dormant on the shelf since the fabric sale at the general store last year.

Little pink, blue, and red flowers flooded the dark cloth on tiny green vines and dainty leaves.

"Are those—?" Marlene breathed when Mother laid it out on the table.

"I was going to make an apron for everyone last Christmas." Mother stroked the fabric. "Then your Aunt Valerie came up with her foolish ruffled teapot covers, and there I went, helping HER!" Swiftly, she rolled the bundle back up.

Susan slept on the black patent leather couch that folded down. She had packed her belongings in a homemade bag fashioned from a former flour sack. When the week was over and the green beans were snapped, beets cooked and canned, yellow beans pickled and canned in half-pint jars, Susan would go home in the same outfit she arrived in.

When mother presented her with the vast bolt of fabric, her eyes lit up, but her face remained expressionless.

"Oh," she muttered, touching the tiny design and feeling the material between her thumb and forefinger.

Mother had also unearthed the spools of thread, piping for trim and colorful buttons she'd purchased for her project. It was brighter than anything Zedah had ever used in her preacher wife's wardrobe, but she'd hate to waste good supply.

"Here," Mother also thrust a twenty-dollar bill into Susan's dry, chapped hand. "It's not much. Still, it's a thank you."

Father drove his niece home to his sister in the blue Ford truck he used for work, and Mother busied herself with the bed linens to be washed.

"Sure, will be glad to get the lye smell out of these," she remarked, piling them into the wringer washer.

Aunt Margaret had sent a letter complete with a new photo of herself.

"Bah!" Grosspabeh scoffed, looking at the made-up face, lipstick smiling in the midst of layered blonde curls, a ruffled blouse, and missing glasses.

He laid it face down on the homemade expanse of the kitchen table where Father, Aunt Zedah, Grossmam, and the two remaining aunts were having midday coffee.

"That won't go unpunished forever," he growled.

Mary and Susanna pounced on the picture. "Can we see?" They fought with it and both lost hold, dropped it, and the room fan blew it through the air and straight to Brenda's feet.

"Bring it here," Grossman demanded sternly. Slowly, she picked it up and carried it, studying the pretty face that smiled and resembled the new Aunt Margaret. Susanna and Mary peered over her shoulder at it before it was jerked from Brenda's grip and flung into the woodstove. It seemed whatever did not get resolved behind the barn got handled in a lit cook stove.

CHAPTER 18

School

THE MENNONITES of Hatchet Prairie were leery of the public-school system and reluctant to enroll their offspring in its authority. Mothers kept their children at home until they were at least six years old, some seven years of age by the time they embarked on the first grade.

Butterhorn Public School had a trial first day of school for would-be first-graders, and Brenda Jane had not been more excited. She picked a dress to wear; a blue denim ensemble with a ruffle at hem and bottom of the sleeves made of red cotton. The garment wasn't new; the material faded to a light blue, but Mother had added white eyelet lace trim in between the red and blue. It saluted the upcoming big day smartly. Brenda-Jane packed her orange plastic lunch box with her mother's egg salad sandwich on brown bread and an apple. She placed the matching orange thermos full of juice in the lid, snapped the clasp, and set it in the fridge.

Margaret was unhappy with the added chore of taking her sibling to the bus that morning.

"You'll sit with me for the day," she instructed. "Once you go to school, you'll sit up front with the grade ones."

Brenda-Jane felt grown up and sophisticated, wearing her new sneakers for school to school and leaving the farm with her older sister.

"Watch over the younger," Mother instructed. "Don't let anyone bother her." "Yes, I know!"

"Don't take that tone with me!"

Across Grosspabeh's ripening field, the orange school bus was retreating from the one Shepnard home and heading for the gravel road to another.

The families that kept their children out of school as long as possible were sometimes questioned by board members and even the family doctor, "Is little Jacob going to school yet?"

"No, we want to keep him home a bit longer" came the terse, carefully rehearsed phrase.

The cumbersome orange rig rumbled to a noisy halt in front of the sisters with all the grace of a farm cow.

Mr. Heinrichs opened the bi-fold door and grinned down at them. Brenda-Jane struggled up the stairs behind Margaret and followed her to her seat.

"You go to school too?" He closed the door and glanced at the mirror above him that allowed him to see the students. He feigned shock as he closed the door and revved the engine.

"Are you a grownup then?" He roared with laughter at Brenda's second nod. She decided right then she liked him.

The bus population was scattered with Heinrichs children of all ages, rivaled only by the Penners in number. They lived in Fieldarp also and attended Uncle William's

Old Colony Church, which was why the Gardeners and the Heinrichs didn't socialize a lot. Once you chose a spouse and decided on a denomination within the Mennonite realm, you stuck with your peers.

From the first-grade classroom, sounds of weeping and sobbing emitted from the children who had not previously been separated from their mothers other than Sunday school. One little boy stood in corduroy trousers and a growing yellow puddle on the floor and stood helpless and forlorn while a pretty young lady with curly dark hair and shiny blue eyes scurried to assist him.

"There now." She took his hand and led him to a cupboard with a bright orange door. "I've got just the thing for that." She reached in and withdrew a bath towel and a pair of blue jeans. The towel was spread over the puddle and the boy led to the boy's bathroom to change clothes.

Ms. Whittingham was as kind and charming as she was attractive and energetic. She wore a purple dress with a skirt that swung out every time she turned, and she pivoted and swirled a lot. The skirt had other shades of lavender stripes running across it, and when she spun on her heel, it flared like the stripes on Brenda-Jane's tin spinning top when you pressed the plunger rapidly and then let go.

"There now." Ms. Whittingham pressed Kleenex into his hand when he returned from his clothing exchange.

"Now." She closed the big orange door with the glass and mesh window. "Let's make some nametags." Every desk was already laid out with crayons, stickers, and construction paper.

Once everyone was engrossed in their artwork, she swished over to a record player and turned it on. Brenda recognized a familiar sound when Ms. Whittingham walked by, the same as the wispy noise her Gardener aunt made when she walked wearing Whisper pantyhose.

"My Bonnie lies over the ocean," Children's voices sang as the record circulated. "My Bonnie lies over the sea, my Bonnie lies over the ocean, so bring back my Bonnie to me..."

Many of the class knew only scant phrases of the English mottled with German words.

"Teacher, ah, *mot ich* (I have to)—can I go to the bathroom?"

"It's 'may I', and you certainly may." Ms. Whittingham winked at a young man nervously "*fragging*" (asking).

She paused over Brenda-Jane's craftwork, bringing a cloud of scent—nay, a thunderstorm mingled with sweet pea flowers and strawberries flooded with sugared cream.

"What a pretty dress," she remarked, while Brenda glued a red border over her yellow nametag. A happy warm feeling spread over Brenda and grew warmer as she looked up into the smiling face with the porcelain doll skin and sparkling cornflower eyes.

By lunchtime, Brenda-Jane's thermos of Kool-Aid had leaked all over her egg salad sandwich, and she was daydreaming that Ms. Whittingham was her mother.

She imagined the two of them going shopping for store-bought clothes together, smelling of that perfume, and unconcerned about money. At night, they would curl up and read books together until it was bedtime and the glass lamp with the light glancing off its crystal body had to be shut off. In the morning, a white Uncle Ben alarm clock would buzz from beneath its gold trim and gold numerals instead of a rooster crowing, tin pail rattling, and off-key singing.

"Here." A jovial voice startled her. It was a white bread cheese sandwich sliced in half, plastic encased and thrust into her hand.

"Don't eat soggy bread," Ms. Whittingham chided gently. The new sandwich tasted heavenly, fluffy white and almost sweet. Brenda-Jane closed her eyes. In an instant, she heard laughter that sounded like china dishes rattling, fine and pealing.

"It's only a sandwich." The curly haired teacher shook her curls and tinkled her silvery laugh as she turned to help with a lid on someone's canned lunch item.

Even Ms. Whittingham's bangs were curly; they came down her forehead and curled out and up again. Brenda-Jane had never seen anyone prettier than her first-grade teacher, she decided.

Just then, her admiration was interrupted by another yellow flood at the feet of another young man distraught over the separation from his mother. Little Davy Harms gulped and sniffled, trying not to call attention to himself with noise. He wiped his nose on his brown gingham shirt and dropped his head dejectedly in his crooked arm with his tin lunch box unopened.

"Davy! What's the matter?" Ms. Whittingham swooped down to his level, putting her arm around him. He flinched like she was about to strike him.

"There, there, old tears," she soothed.

"Miss, miss!" Another boy pointed to the floor where her baby doll patent shoes were close to touching the creeping sea of yellow.

"Oh! Here! I'll get some more towels to clean that up!" She whirled around and grasped an entire package of brown paper towel, undid the brown paper wrapping, and scattered the pieces on the floor like an autumn wind with leaves.

"He couldn't get his lunch kit open," a helpful neighbor of Davy's explained as he was led away for a change of clothes.

At recess, Brenda-Jane went in search of Margaret at the end of the long hallway. She wove in betwixt children she had not seen before, some she recognized from the school bus and a few from Sunday school. A fist struck her arm, and the smirking face that it belonged to was Johan Penner.

"I'm gonna fail my grade so I can be in your class next year." He smiled eagerly. Brenda-Jane felt uneasy and ducked around him.

"Our new horse is prettier than yours." His older brother, Ernest, was sneering from the door of Margaret's classroom.

"Is not!" indignation flared up from inside her. He was a big, blue-eyed, blonde boy enlarged from hard labor and farm work, and he blocked the entrance effortlessly.

"Move!" Brenda-Jane glared up at him. He laughed soundlessly to himself, casually scraping his nails with a pocketknife.

"Ernest!" a shrill voice turned his head. A plump, gray-haired woman walked toward him, shaking her bespectacled head. "How many times do I have to tell you—" Brenda-Jane caught sight of Margaret and pushed past him.

The sixth-grade girls were credulous that the two Gardener girls were siblings; Brenda-Jane was small for her age, pale in complexion, with straight wispy blonde hair and blue eyes. Margaret shared the blue eyes but was a plump freckled girl with curly brown hair.

"Hah yine!" exclaimed one.

"Obah!" (But!)

"Zitz mole!" (Look once!) came from a sarcastic Ernest, sullen now from his encounter with an authority figure.

"Mean pe-at zit fail shmokah" (My horse is much prettier), he taunted, reaching out to tug Benda's hair as he sauntered by.

"Not with you standing beside her." Margaret kicked him in the shin.

"Ow!" he bellowed. The girls all giggled, which seemed to infuriate him more. A crimson color spread from his plaid collar to his white blonde hair.

"Well? You are mixing up girls with horses means you get kicked."

"Take him to a vet," someone called out, and the group all dissolved into mirth again before the recess bell rang to summon the end of the lunch segment of the noon break.

Outside, the vast lawn was sprinkled with brightly painted teeter-totters and swing sets, "monkey bars," and a tetherball pole. The primary colors were the common theme throughout—red, yellow, blue alternating with green on all sets.

Benda Jane got on the teeter-totter with a shy girl named Mary on her nametag. They got going in a bobbing sync when a gust of summer blew up as Ernest and Johan walked by. It caught Brenda Jane's skirt and she frantically pulled the ruffle down, but they had already peeped at the show.

"Such fat thighs," Ernest mocked.

"Ya, fat thighs," Johan echoed and then added, "You will be my wife one day." They laughed as they continued together.

Brenda-Jane felt more stripped bare just then than when the wind had defamed her. She dismounted the painted two-by-eight board and retreated to the swings. Behind her on the monkey bars, a group of children played fox and goose, calling out happily and laughing. Below them, holding the brightly painted metal bars in place, lay a cold cement slab.

The bars were really metal frames stacked one on top of the other and welded in place. A plush shaped trail ran through their clover-leaf position, which allowed for a circular motion around the outside by the "geese" trying to sneak by the fox in the middle.

Brenda-Jane could not shake the shadow off her mind. Most of the day had been bright and cheery, and sun still shone June light like before.

The recess bell signaling them to the white brick school building went unnoticed to the occupant of the red slab on two chains. She swayed slightly only with the breeze now until a laughing voice and flowery scent came up behind her.

"There you are girl. Come along now, we're late for class." Ms. Whittingham took her hand and led her to the school. Once she returned to the classroom, she dismissed the other teacher of her watch duties and gathered the children onto a large throw rug for a story. Everyone knelt or squatted "Indian style" on their behind with their legs crisscrossed in front of them. She read with such exuberance and enthusiasm one could practically smell tar when the rabbit punched the tar baby for not speaking to him. The children giggled when Ms. Whittingham punched the page lightly.

"I SAID HOW DO YOU DO?"

The class giggled.

"Home time!" came too soon. Ms. Whittingham handed everyone a multi-colored lollipop with the colors swirling toward its center. Margaret came to the door to walk Brenda-Jane to the bus. In one swoop of purple and sweet scent, Ms. Whittingham was gone from sight until school started again in the fall. Brenda's first day of school was over, and the summer yawned ahead.

The bus was crowded and noisy, appearing fuller than the morning for an increase in activity.

Margaret sat across from the Penner cousins, Ernest and Nettie, so that placed Brenda-Jane in the same seat next to the aisle.

"Branna! Hey Branna!" Ernest mocked. "I still think my horse is prettier than yours."

Brenda-Jane thought about the dozen Morgans Uncle William kept around as literal horsepower to get his farm work done where most used machines.

"You don't have one. Your dad owns them," she retorted.

"That's what you think. Pap gave me one. He's pretty. His name is Scaredy Cat." Beside him, Nettie drew her lip into a straight line and kept reading her library book, *Little Women*.

"Scaredy Cat is better than better than Little Red or Star," he gloated.

"Is not!" Brenda-Jane felt panic and anger rising simultaneously. Little Red was Big Red's daughter—quick, nimble, and as hot-tempered as her father was slow and gentle. Star was a Shetland pony with a white patch on his forehead.

"Is too." His beady blues mocked her, daring her to counter him more.

A shrill voice that could have cut the chrome off a Chrysler interrupted.

"Nee haveh dot yeah heat vayen dot pee-at! (Now we have heard about that horse!) Say another word and see what happens!" Margaret challenged him, blue heat sending chills from her eyes.

Ernest swallowed, looked out the window and clenched his fists. Nettie, next to the window, turned the page, oblivious and pinch-faced.

The bus ride was an hour long, and when at last it rolled up to the end of their driveway, Brenda Jane was relieved to see home again. The sprawling white farmhouse with its new porch jutting out like a nose, with a square window flanking each side, greeted her like a smiling face. The brick basement wall that rose from the ground ran its crimson rectangles all around the base of the main floor.

Screams filtered out of the house through the kitchen window screen.

"Hah! I didn't say that! I have to work and work all day like a wretched mule while you do only what pleases you!" The statement ended in a sob. Inside the house, the scent of cinnamon and brown sugar melting wafted throughout the front yard.

Father sat at the head of the table in sullen silence, chewing and staring down at his slice of apple pie, a cup of coffee streaming by his enormous hand. He picked it up and took a slurping gulp.

"It's been that way since day one! You work as you want, when you want, IF you want. And most likely, for someone else! Our chickens need a henhouse, so you fix your mother's?!" Dishes clattered.

Margaret changed into her chore clothes—an old pair of jeans and a worn T-shirt—and went outside quickly, Marlene in tow.

"Mom, can I have a slice of pie?" Brenda-Jane ventured.

With curt motions, Mother wordlessly crossed the kitchen floor in her high heels, cut a slice, picked it up with the knife, and flicked the pie onto a saucer from a stack on the table.

"There." She shoved it to the opposite end of the table.

Father finished his coffee and pushed his chair back.

"Well, the folks said they'd give us a few more laying hens—"

"What does that even mean? We need roosts for the bloody chickens we've got!" Her shout followed his retreating back while the dishes clattered their own complaints.

"School was fun today, Mum—" Brenda-Jane was interrupted by a loud crash followed by a string of German curse words.

"Fublingedeh devilce upvoshtich!" (The devil's dirty dishes!)

Brenda-Jane escaped to the garden to smell the flowers like the scent of Ms. Whittingham's perfume.

"Skip to the loo my darling…" filtered across the farmyard where Margaret and Marlene were feeding the horses oats.

The screams of frustration continued to emulate from the orange muslin-clad kitchen windows. The house, emptied of all family members, did nothing to dissipate Mother's frustrations.

Brenda-Jane inhaled the sweet pea blooms. They were the most like her teacher's fragrance. Her mother wore perfume and a lot of it, but it was mixed with the aroma of Mr. Clean, Lysol, and other cleaning products.

"I'll tell you a story," a voice startled her. It was her father, grinning broadly. He held an old flat iron in his hand.

"Do you know what this is?" Brenda shook her head.

"This is what caught the house on fire and nearly killed your mother when she was carrying you."

Before the farmhouse was built, Mother had set the iron on the wood stove to heat up in between strokes on the laundry she was ironing. A can of speed starch stood on the ironing board and heated up when she set the iron beside it to go to another task. It exploded upon her return and covered her upper body and the linen in flames.

"It was God who turned my head to the house," he explained. I was on the tractor, and Margaret was shouting something. I would have never heard Mother's screams for help, but HE made me look." Brenda thought of the scars around Mother's neck.

'She had first, second, and third-degree burns. They flew her to Cattlelina and put her in the burn unit."

"What does first, second and third degree burn mean?"

"Well, we all have three layers of skin. She had burns through them all in some places."

Brenda-Jane thought of the sizzling, whistling sound that hot dogs make over a snapping campfire and shivered.

"Brenda! Here! Come here!" a shrill voice traveled across the lawn in the June warmth.

Her mother stood in the back porch where the clothesline was strung from one of its posts and led to a powerline post in the backyard.

"Come!"

On wooden legs, she moved slowly toward Mother, knowing what was next.

"Come pick up the clothespins I dropped. Do I need to haul you by your ears?"

So, Brenda-Jane picked up the wooden pins that had already fallen on the ground and traced the trail beneath the line for more. These she passed to Mother to be reused to hang more wet clothing and linen, some weathered and gray, some new, still golden.

The line above creaked as it rotated dry around the pulleys that enabled Mother to load and unload the wash from the back door.

The sheets and billowing dress skirts danced on the line to the tune of the June breeze, weightless and carefree.

CHAPTER 19

The Little Brown Hens

SOME OF Cornielius Timber's brown chickens wandered onto the Gardener farm again, and their dark interruptions in Mother's white flock reminded her to remind Father to build a proper fence.

Next, a spindly cow tottered over and began grazing in the pasture, followed in delayed fashion by the unfashionable Corny a few days later.

His face was blackened by a scowl and the road dust that was his yard, and he was clad in his usual pinstriped denim bib overalls and sweat-stained plaid western shirt rolled up at the sleeves.

"Is it possible to get my animals back?" he growled in German to Mother from his pickup in front of the porch where she was washing beets.

"Soon as I figure out a bill for what it cost me to feed them," she snapped.

His countenance crimsoned, and he chewed for a couple of moments.

"And don't worry about the cow," she continued. "I have called the vet and made an animal mistreatment report. He'll be around shortly. There isn't enough meat on her for our dogs to steal off you once you butcher her. And lastly"—she raised her vegetable brush— "GET OFF MY PROPERTY."

Get, he did, making a racket and churning up a dust storm by gearing down and revving his engine down the driveway.

"Brock louse-it hingah ayne!" (Useless rear end!) she swore after him, shielding her eyes from the sun with her arm.

The purple gas tank now touted a padlock, and the gas lasted longer. So did Father's tools now that he locked the garage.

"Wish I had told him I was keeping the animals to make up for the gas he stole," she grumbled.

She turned to Brenda-Jane and Marlene.

"You don't just stand there. Make yourself useful and go pull enough carrots for supper."

Despite the animosity between Smelly and the rest of Fieldarp, when someone gave them an old house on skids to upgrade from their cabin, the Gardeners went over and helped them move. Their generosity was made easier by Corny's absence. Mother brought a casserole, and the girls had a good old time running back and forth between the two abodes, carrying household items and entertaining the two Timber toddlers. Margaret and Father carried the bigger furniture pieces into the four-room house with an attic and a dormer.

"A palace." Mrs. Timber breathed, pausing to gaze at the square auction-block purchase with fading paint and storm windows. A narrow staircase led up to a single room in the attic with red carpeting, of all things.

Mrs. Corny Timber had been pretty once, now her tired sunken eyes had dark rings around them. Her eyes were blue and tadpole-shaped, roaming everywhere, exploring the corners of her new digs. Her long brown straight hair was pulled into a long glossy ponytail and hung out from under her kerchief down her back. She could have been the twin of actress Sissy Spacek before the Corny effect. Now barefoot and most likely pregnant AGAIN, her red dress was as dirty as her cabin.

"A sewing room," she marveled, gazing at the square room upstairs in the stifling heat of an attic. Mother set a box down on the chrome legged kitchen table.

"I have some things for you if you can use them," she announced. "It's not much..." came another one of her carefully rehearsed phrases. "A few things my sister gave me. I can't wear them; I am such a Giraffe."

Mrs. Timber gasped.

"There's a few jars of canned sausage, pickled cucumbers, beets, carrots, and a loaf of bread." She concluded the inventory.

Mrs. Timber looked stricken. "Oh my." She sighed. She sank down into a ripped vinyl chair. "Oh, this is all just too much."

Her tots, a boy and then a girl, undoubtedly nine months and five minutes apart in age, squatted by her feet, their noses running, playing with an empty pork and beans can.

Once the furniture was reasonably placed, the Gardeners excused themselves and walked home.

"What an ugly house," Margaret remarked.

"Shh," Mother admonished, glancing furtively over shoulder. "We're not that far off yet."

Next door, another family was moving into the former Bart Timber home. The older Timber brother had abruptly sold off and moved out—no auction, no goodbyes.

The new family was a noisy bunch, hollering and laughing while they unloaded a grain truck of their household artifacts.

The "Benjamens" were a family of eight children and their parents. Both parents hailed from Mennonite backgrounds but spoke mostly English. The only visible aspect of their lives that was traditionally Mennonite was the number of children they had.

"Englishers," Mother called them. Rumor continued that they had a television in their house, and no one had to do chores during *Gilligan's Island* or *Dallas*. The entire clan dropped whatever they were doing and watched the show before continuing their duties.

"Devil's box" was what the Mennonites called the television set. Unless, of course, they were the liberated kind like Aunt Valerie and had a set themselves.

The Gardeners had record players and radios, but only Christian music was played on records when company was present. Mother turned the radio on for "Tradio," at two o'clock on Saturday afternoons while she worked, of course.

It fascinated the children to listen to the voices coming out of the slated plastic box as if their sources were right there with you. Callers would phone the radio station and verbally advertise their goods for sale, trade, or asking for something they wanted to purchase. Lost or found items were also listed by the radio hosts.

A male voice that sounded very familiar phoned in to report a lost couple of laying hens and a brown cow. Corny.

"How many chickens?" the radio announcer pried. "How many chickens?" "About four or five." "Hah!" Mother said.

"In the field—I mean, Hatchet Prairie area," Smelly stammered. Fieldarp was only a German to English translation meaning "field village" that was an unofficial name for the settlement around Grosspabeh's field.

"And the phone number?"

That was the last straw in the roost. Mother dropped the mound of butter into a big aluminum bowl and covered it with a clean T-towel. She wiped her hands on her red flowered apron and strode briskly outside. Soon, loud squawking filled the farmyard. The girls gathered at the laundry room window to watch the slaughtering of the brown hens. The newly headless fowl hopped around for a while before succumbing to reality and laying still on the weedy ground in various brown mounds of feathers and blood.

Mother's axe quit swinging. She called across the yard to Father. "He-ey? Will you get a hold of your folks and ask if we can borrow the plucker?"

The plucking machine made the removal of feathers from chicken corpses more effective. The motorized tumbler on a wooden stand had protruding rubber knobs scattered facing outward from a cylinder that turned once the gizmo connected with electricity. The fingers struck the feathers off the chicken held up to its proximity after the dead bird had been dunked in a metal pail of hot water propped up on rocks with a blowtorch trained to it. The canopy behind the cylinder caught the gobs of wet feathers and kept them from splaying in all directions. Next, the hand plucking began. The blowtorch was used again to singe off and lingering hair and fine feathers. After that, the chicken was ready for butchering.

The cow had promptly overeaten and died. The vet either had not been called or could not find the farm. Father had found her stiffened body on her back, legs protruding out like a wooden sawhorse. He stripped the carcass of the hide and meat, saving the bones for dog food.

At butchering time, the girls were assigned to hand plucking and watched the necks get circumcised, in a manner of speaking, before being cut open just below the breastbone.

Father was sullen and nearly silent, displeased at his wife's actions.

"I would have given them back," he voiced.

"Of course! Always sucking up and making me the bad guy! Enough is enough! He steals from you, and you hire him and give him access to more. How much stuff have you donated to his charity now? Gas and what have you!"

Mother reached into the slit she had just made out of the casualty in front of her and pulled the innards out in a heap on the makeshift plywood table in the barn.

"It is no wonder he gets away with what he does."

Now that the "English Mennonites" had purchased the former Timber estate, it meant Smelly Cornelly lived on their property.

"If I know Helen like I did when we went to school together, she won't stand for any shenanigans," Mother remarked.

"I don't know Zeke Benjamen, but I remember Helen."

Brenda-Jane knew that, soon, another care package would be gathered, and a visit paid to the new neighbors. Although the overall purpose would be to welcome the Benjamens to Fieldarp, Smelly would come up in the conversation. Mother would make it happen.

CHAPTER 20

Sunday School

SATURDAYS WERE sinfully busy with cleaning the house for company on Sunday and going into town to purchase groceries for the following week. So, Brenda decided to simplify things a little. Mother forever said, "If it isn't moved, it hasn't been cleaned." Brenda took a rag and dipped it in the wash bowl like her sisters, wrung it out, and walked around the living room with it, tweaking the furniture and garbage can, the ornaments—anything she could move slightly.

"Aren't you fast today?" Mother praised. And Brenda felt guilty. Not enough to go dusting and washing for real, but guilty, nonetheless.

Some of the staples bought were for feeding guests and those few items the Gardener household always kept on hand. For entertainment purposes, there had to be sunflower seeds in the house that the adults would eat while gossiping, and Mother and Father both encouraged them to spit the shells directly on the floor.

"Don't worry, we've got three girls that can sweep that up," they'd soothe.

Another item that always landed on the faspa table was smooth peanut butter that stuck to the roof of your mouth like a denture. Dill pickles, homegrown and pickled, were sliced, and their slippery surfaces slathered with gobs of peanut butter.

Brenda-Jane loved Mother's "paypa-nate," a sweet bun made with white bread dough and cinnamon, black pepper, and sugar. They were topped with white icing and coconut and served on a Blue Onion Corelle supper plate.

Everyone helped with Saturday keeping, meaning the house cleaning and having a bath to be presentable for church the next morning.

Mother wore her kerchiefs and square high-heeled shoes to match her dresses, unlike a lot of her peers who wore black running shoes and black babushka's every day. On Sundays, the women wore black, navy blue, or dark brown dresses, and flat-heeled pumps.

Mother had been raised by a colorblind alcoholic in a modern Mennonite home where there was a Christmas trees, gift wrap, and other glimmering or colorful objects. So, she splayed color wherever she could. It was uncanny how she found matching spectrums from so many unrelated thrift stores. Silk scarves from new stores were sewn into squares to be worn as a kerchief with print that complimented a home sewn dress. Today, it was a bright blue handkerchief with white polka dots as a head covering and a white and blue dress printed like her weekday dish set. A pair of white patent leather pumps completed her look.

"Dot ass nicht mowed," (That is not the custom), Father disproved her ensemble.

"Hah! Says who? On MY side of the family, it most certainly is!" she retorted. "I don't know why everything has to be about YOUR upbringing."

He drove to town in sullen silence, so she turned her attention to the girls.

"Have you decided what you are going to buy?" She tried to be cheery, but her "buy" wobbled a little.

"We don't have money," they reminded her. At which, she opened her large leather purse and pulled out her wallet. Clearly, Mother had not overcome the diaper bag phase of her life, because that bag held everything except the neighbor's cat and a sledgehammer.

Mother pulled out two scarlet two-dollar bills and a blue five for Margaret.

"Here." She handed them the paper pesos. "It's from my egg money."

Mother sold chicken eggs at a dollar a dozen and kept the brown eggs for her family.

"Your Aunt Valerie thought she was too good for brown eggs." Mother grimaced. "City slicker." After grocery shopping, the family went to a restaurant for the usual—fish and chips with a glass of fountain pop. Sometimes, they switched for chicken fingers and fries, and the fingers were a whole lot different than the fowl legs mother cooked at home. There were only two eateries to pick from, and Mother didn't like the cafe where Aunt Valerie waited tables, so they paid homage to "The Steakhouse."

Improperly named after a high-end meal, The Steakhouse was about three sea cans jimmied together. A hand-painted plywood sign hung weathering against the building above a windowless metal door. A few square single-pane windows punctured the front of the restaurant which was the length of the containers. Inside, dark paneling matched the dark wood tables placed on an orange indoor-outdoor carpet.

CHAPTER 21

The Englishers

SURE ENOUGH, within a week of the Benjamens moving into town a sturdy cardboard box was wrapped in an orange and white striped bath towel like a gift. Mother stitched the ends together after combining an impossible amount of food into the festive package: a pound of butter, two loaves of brown bread, canned sausage, canned fish, a jar of pickled cucumbers, a half-gallon jar of summer borscht, and three dozen chocolate chip cookies.

"Now we wait until Dad gets done with his chores, and then we can drive over." Mother tucked a piece of light orange muslin over the box like a netting.

"Oh! Margaret, would you go get me the pail of milk from the porch? Never mind. Just cover it with this." Mother tossed a white linen T-towel over to her.

After a supper of noodles in cream gravy and hamburgers, they loaded up the Ford by carefully, setting the boxed goodies on Margaret's lap. The rest of the family lined up in the lone seat in the usual sequence: Father, Brenda-Jane, and Marlene on Mother's lap.

A makeshift baseball game was in progress when the Gardeners pulled into the yard. The entire Benjamen family was involved, some stationed at overturned tomato sauce cans and a tree stump first base.

The Benjamens were a long-haired, dirty, and happy clan. The father had a crew cut while the rest sported curly long tangles.

Helen's tresses were streaked with gray, and she wore thick glasses low on her thin hooked nose. Her gray-blue eyes flashed when she laughed or emphasized a point.

"Boys continue against the girls," she called as she and her husband left the game to greet the visitors.

"We didn't mean to interrupt," Mother assured.

"Nonsense! We're too old for this shit anyway!" Mrs. Benjamen giggled as she was presented with the care package.

"We've been living on spam and toast." She embraced the box, still chuckling happily.

Father handed the aluminum pail of milk to Mother for the Englishers and then hung back to visit with Ezekiel Benjamen, his name twin. The two women carried their domestic burdens into the house, chatting.

Shyly, Brenda Jane and Marlene followed their mothers' rigid back while behind them, Margaret was handed a baseball glove and drawn into the shade tree tournament.

Once inside the house and after her eyes adjusted to the darker lighting, Brenda Jane was astonished at the changes to the former Timber house. In one short week, the contrast between the dugout basement and the elegant upstairs had lessened. Dirt lay on the orange linoleum floors that had been exposed when the creamy carpet had been torn up. All that remained was a rich green indoor/outdoor carpet in the living room where the gold carpet had also been taken up also. The Lino contrasted loudly with the pink rose wallpaper.

An odor of a U-Haul toilet and the chemical used in great futility to mask it hung heavily in the air. It stood in the exact spot where the white porcelain toilet had been. An old aluminum bathtub squatted low and plain in place of the former white claw foot bathtub. The carpet had been removed by the décor Nazis and now gold and brown flecked vinyl flooring lay bare in its memory.

"—Wanted to warn you about your neighbor," Brenda-Jane overheard her mother discussing with Helen Benjamen in the kitchen.

Marlene clung to mother's side during the visit while Brenda hung back waiting for an invitation to sit in the dining room with the ladies.

The brown beer glass insets in the walls beside the archway between the kitchen and dining room had been covered with shelving.

"He's constantly stealing and sneaking around," mother stroked crumbs off the table. She kept stroking. "Mind you, we started locking up a few things now."

"He's living on our property now," Mrs. Benjamen pondered, taking a sip of her watery coffee. "We'll have to have an 'eat-shloss,'" (disfellowshipping) She cracked up at her own joke.

An out casting, or "eetschlossen," was only conducted by church officials. Those meetings were called "Darnehdach," meaning Thursday because there were held on that particular day of the week in the evening whenever necessary. If the sin was severe enough, like a sexual sin such as premarital sex, the sinner had to go to "No-choyk," or "after church."

The Benjamen offspring in all their shaggy headed glory were named; Basil, Hillary, Jillian, Tilly, Barclay, Emmet, and Mitchell. The three girls were dubbed "Hill, Jill, and Till," in all humor.

Brenda Jane and Marlene wandered into the living room where the television was on. Two long silver poles jutted from the back of it and made a giant "V" shape above the false wood box and its glass contoured face. It was fascinating to watch people moving and talking in it like they had been shrunk to fit the screen. A man's face loomed life sized up to the glass and Brenda Jane jabbed him with her finger just as he adjusted his glasses. Marlene gasped in unison. After that, they tapped the screen several more times but to no avail.

Marlene gripped the knob and twisted it and suddenly, he was shouting to them, his voice blaring in the room. Mrs. Benjamen came running with their mother in pursuit looking shocked.

"There now," the lady of the house snapped the television off with her ragged fingernails. "The boys must have forgotten to shut it off."

Mother shot Brenda a fierce look that said this was not over yet, grabbed Marlene's hand and heel clicked it into the kitchen. She wore white high heeled pumps with a stacked heel and a running shoe tops with a tongue and laces. Her dress was a mint fortrel, a-line cut that didn't move.

"Go get your dad," she snapped over her shoulder.

Meekly, Brenda, let herself out through the screen door and found her father in the main barn, talking with Mr. Benjamen about mixed farming.

"I'm told it's not good soil here," the new neighbor stroked his chin and stared thoughtfully through round wire glasses. "I wonder if that's why Timber sold out."

"No, he retired," father corrected him. "Before that I never heard of any trouble." In spite of this reassurance, the other Zeke looked leery.

"Shame on you!" mother scolded Brenda Jane on the way home. "Turning the devil's box on like that!"

Brenda's ears burned and her bottom lip trembled.

"I'm always ashamed of you!"

"THAT KID—" she explained to her husband's quizzical expression, "went into the living room and turned their devil's box on full volume!"

A ditch separated Corny Timber's plot from the Benjamen's yard. A ditch that trickled water into a big pond at the end of the garden where the girls used to play with Colleen Timber.

To plumb his house Smelly had simply ran a tin pipe from under his bathroom to the ditch and his family's excrement was carried into the neighbor's watering hole.

Only a thin fringe of trees ran between Corny's place and the Gardener farm. A wispy lot that disappeared into a clearing before continuing again. The opening was a view right through his backyard to the Benjamens.

It wasn't long before a loud altercation filled the clearing one summer afternoon.

Everyone at the Gardener's lunch table ran to the living room window and peered out at the ruckus. Mother snatched father's binoculars off the desk and dashed out to the back deck. The girls followed.

Helen Benjamen was yelling at Smelly; in fact, he had grabbed a hold of his arm and stood hollering up at his six-and-a-half-foot frame.

"Ooh." Mother breathed. "I wouldn't want those fingernails in my arm." "Let me see! Let me see!" The girls' clamored for the binoculars.

"Shaw!" She shooed them away like chickens.

"—expect me to water my garden with your SHIT?" Mrs. Benjamen screamed. Mostly, only snatches of her indignation could be heard. "Lying dirty hobo" carried across the pasture. He seemed to be pulling away, but she did not let go, a hundred pounds of blue jeaned fury bent on making her point.

"—drinking water" and "Lazy good-for-nothing" came next.

Abruptly, she released his arm so fast he stumbled backward.

"You get off my property!" the little woman shrieked, backing away and yelling.

Soon, Corny drove noisily into the Gardener yard, looking pink-faced and sheepish. He went straight to the garage where Zeke tinkered on small projects, a gate latch for the fence, a new feeder for the pigs.

Zeke walked over to his handmade deck trailer and motioned with his hand for Smelly to back up to it.

"The heck—" Mother stopped her sentence and lowered the binoculars. "What's he doing?"

The men hooked the trailer up to Smelly's pickup, and then Father climbed in with him, and they drove over to the Timbers.

"Ooh." Mother sighed. "He'll never see it again."

Brenda-Jane got on her yellow bicycle, a castoff of Margaret's, and rattled over to Corny's.

Her father and Smelly were jacking up the cabin while the truck idled, the trailer backed up and waiting. It was a long process; once the men had placed wood blocks under the front end, they moved to the back and proceeded to raise it and repeat process. The Timbers were moving, that was evident.

Brenda-Jane grew tired of observing and cycled home.

In the late evening, Father returned home on foot, looking weary and limping.

"Did you give him the trailer?" Mother was credulous and funny. "Cuz it ain't Christmas nor his birthday, you know."

"Well, a man needs to help out where he can." He lowered himself into his chair heavily. Mother bustled around warming supper.

At first, the vacant spot the hut left was obvious and barren, with only the empty house and a few rickety outbuildings left for dead weeds to blow against. Then a few rains later, grass grew tall where no one drove anymore, and the Benjamens burned the brief Timber home down. Fireweeds appeared rapidly, and wild raspberries pushed over onto the driveway from the fence line.

The Englishers were known as the people living in the old Timber place and always would be. If a decade passed, the Benjamen home would still be labeled the Old Timber place. Fieldarps present was defined by the past, and its future was expected to remain the same.

Then Mother threw a fork into it and deemed the English Mennonites "the Timbenjamens." That was Mother.

CHAPTER 22

That Kid

THERE WERE days when everything set Mother off. Usually, it involved Brenda-Jane, and today was a humdinger for that.

At breakfast, Brenda discovered a lump in her porridge and carefully spooned it aside. As if a motion detector had erupted, her mother pivoted from the stove, caught sight of the offending mass on the table, and exploded. She stomped across the floor, snatched up the bowl, and flung it into the sink of dirty dishwater. Suds flew up and hit the curtain above it, clinging to the ruffled orange curtains.

"There! Now see what you made me do! Rotten evil kid. I will punish you yet!" Danger flashed in her glittering brown eyes. Brenda-Jane cowered in her chair, unsure of what to do. Breakfast was over, but if she left too soon, she would be ordered back or even hauled by her ears to remain seated.

"Sit there like a dumbkopf!" Mother's thin mouth twisted into a sneer. Passing by a basket of laundry, she picked up a pair of brown boys' summer shorts and held them up gingerly just as Margaret entered.

"Heh?" She dangled them in front of Margaret's nose. "Valerie gave me all Karla and Kenneth's old clothes. I was going to give some to the neighbors, but I think Brenda wants these." Margaret's eyes twinkled, and a smirk crossed her ruddy freckles.

"Yeah, make her put them on," she agreed quickly. Her compliance didn't appease her mother for long.

"Go! Do something about that rat's nest on your head!"

Brenda-Jane fled to the sandbox; visions of herself going through the day naked except for the boy's shorts ran through her mind.

Marlene wandered outside, spotted Brenda-Jane, and they built a sand farm by pushing the dry sediment aside and pressing the wet sand underneath it up into fence forms.

The sun was directly overhead when Brenda spotted the picnic drink cooler on the front porch step. She retrieved it to pour sand through, but of course, it didn't. Sand clogged the spout, and the button could no longer be pushed.

"BRENDA-JANE GARDENER!" As if on cue again, her mother's shrill voice sliced the sunshine from across the yard.

"WHAT HAVE YOU DONE TO MY COOLER!" She tore through the pigweed that covered the yard where grass or the odd footpath did not, snatched the plastic container out of the sandbox, sand billowing everywhere. Mother groped wildly for the lid and missed, swearing and snarling in German; after all, cursing in Deutsch was not nearly the sin of cussing in English.

"I'll tell your father about this." She swatted at Brenda-Jane's bare leg. Hard. Quickly, like a windup toy, Marlene jumped up to follow Mother, chattering nervously.

Pink welts rose on Brenda-Jane's thigh, and she cried quietly to herself. On days like this and times like these, it appeared like Mother could not pour out her hatred thick enough.

Brenda-Jane knew there must be something horribly wrong with her for Mother to be so angry and treat her as she did.

Margaret, with slicked hair in metal clips and wearing an old dress of Mother's, came outside with a mouth as fresh as her hairstyle and the laundry on the line.

"You're going to get it when Dad comes home," she taunted, shielding her eyes from the sun with a plump arm.

"Shut up, your fat cowl"

"You're not my sister!" Margaret shrieked, stopping in her gum boots. "You're adopted! My real sister was killed when Mom got in the house fire. The doctors gave her an Indian baby to make her feel better!"

Brenda-Jane was shocked. Relieved. Stunned. This butcher's block wasn't her family? Her real family lived someplace without her. Were they kind and quiet people like Grosspabeh? Or loud, boisterous, and happy like the Benjamens?

Grandpa. Oh no! She wanted to be related to him. To keep him. At the very least, she decided, he would both know and tell her the truth. The next time she saw him, she would ask.

When Father came home from the field wearing the usual sweat yoke around his T-shirt collar, he was yelled at and denied any affection from his wife. He stepped in the house and started for her, but her grimly pinched lips offered nothing.

He started to ask but for a torrent of words tumbling at him. "All day I've had to stop what I was doing and deal with THAT KID!" "Branna?" He knew.

"Who else? She threw her porridge on the table. Filled the drink cooler with sand. Anything to torture me, she did. Do something about that kid!"

"Bren—" He opened his mouth to yell, but she had reached the screen door in a futile attempt to escape. A beefy hand jerked it open while grabbing her upper arm flesh, pulling her across the room. He took off his belt, buckle and all, and twisted her arm above her head while he struck her back, her buttocks, and thighs with the belt and buckle.

Hot burning pain seared over her body so fiercely it took away her breath.

"Um-mmm." Brenda mustered a tiny amount of oxygen. "Uh-uh" when a little more air flowed.

Then great sobs. A scream. His yelling.

"YOU SHUT YOUR MOUTH! HEAR?" he jerked her arm tighter.

"YOU SHUT YOUR MOUTH OR I'LL GIVE YOU MORE!"

Pain like there was nothing else to her seared and burned over her body. Brenda Jane shivered a long sob sigh, shuddering. He so abruptly released her she was forced to grab his leg for support, loathing herself for it.

"My father used to spank me a lot when I was young," he said absently toward the ajar screen door, as if talking to himself or expecting someone.

Lunch was a hostile event. No one spoke except mother, who had raided her private closetful of alternate personalities and plucked out a new outfit, so to speak. One that crooned sweetness and oozed sugar.

"Want me to cut that up for you?" she hovered near Brenda Jane's chair. Lunch was moose-meat cooked to all tenderness with tomatoes and onions in the same roaster, served with mashed potatoes, gravy and peas.

Brenda ignored her, who jumped up and announced brightly; "I know what the girl wants!" She retrieved a margarine container full of cookies and elaborately tore off the lid. Reaching in, she grasped a molasses cookie and dropped it near Brenda's full plate. Dessert came after the meal, never before or during.

"There. Now what do you say?"

A long awkward silence followed. Brenda had to keep shifting in her seat to be able to sit. Her bottom burned with an unquenchable fire.

"Well?" the sweet voice continued.

Still, she said nothing. Desert was not allowed first. That was against the rules, and she was taking neither bait nor bribe.

Finally, Father spoke.

"If you're not going to eat, leave the table."

Cautiously, she slid off of her chair and went to the bathroom. Carefully, she set one dirty bare foot on the edge of the bathtub and pushed herself up by grasping the wall between the tub and shelves behind it.

The bathroom medicine cabinet covered by a mirrored door was directly across from her now. She kept her back to it and lifted the back of her dress, peering over her shoulder. Already, angry red welts were forming, purplish stripes crisscrossed her back, bottom, and legs.

Brenda dropped her dress and stepped down. If she went outside, she'd have to pass through the kitchen again.

She decided to retreat to the bedroom she shared with Marlene.

Lying on her quilted bedspread, she daydreamed about the family she would meet one day. The ones she'd been stripped from as an infant. There could not be sisters.

This was her daydream, and they were abolished. Perhaps a few brothers, or maybe she would be an only child. Gracious mercy and providence did her body ever need an ice pack.

CHAPTER 23

The Gospel of Murphy's Law

BRENDA-JANE WAS clumsier than a five-horned Billy goat and had the bruises to show for it. The Smurfs had nothing on her, nothing at all.

Stepping back in the house from gathering eggs, her toe caught the baler twin rug, and she started falling, groping wildly for a hold. The eggs were scrambled by the time she grabbed the spout of the cream separator to catch herself. It tipped over on her, baptizing her in milk while stainless steel parts pelted her heavily.

She could not breathe. Above her, Mother screamed epithets.

Brenda-Jane tried drawing air. She pushed herself to her knees from the floor, but the room spun and her ribs nearly drowned Mother out.

Struggling for air seemed to seal it off more. A rough hand seizing her left arm and jerking her to her feet caught a rush of oxygen for her.

"Go!" her mother yelled, viciously swabbing at the mess with both hands.

Brenda's dress dripped milk as she walked.

"WAIT!" followed by a string of descriptive complaints about messes, horrible kids, and too much work.

Her mother unzipped her dress and yanked it up over her head, slip and all, leaving her standing there in tights and shoes.

"Take your shoes off! And those tights! Don't just stand there like a dumb-dumb!" Brenda complied, leaving the chaos with just her panties on.

"Go!" Mother yelled again, cleaning and clanging as she scrubbed the machine.

Redressed in her bedroom, Benda picked up the songbook Grandpa had given her and held it to her face, inhaling deeply.

In the vestibule, the tirade continued—how lousy a kid she was to have created more work for someone who only ever worked.

"Rotten kid!" Mother bellowed, still raising a racket.

Brenda traced the outline of a carnation flower on her quilt etched with liquid embroidery. The fringed scarlet-haired face winked up at her impishly. An azure morning glory hung her head and gazed down at the ground.

High heels clicked across the kitchen floor and down the hallway briskly.

"There!" Mother's long bony finger shook with rage at her. "Lying around while I do all the work! Shame on you! Great big girl!" The statement ended in a growl. Mother's eyes were blazing.

Brenda-Jane cowered on her bed atop the smiling, winking floral creatures.

"Make your bed!" Her mother picked up a patchwork bedspread and flung it toward her. Out of habit, Brenda winced, but it fell short of the bed and on the floor. She froze, knowing that one wrong gesture could trigger a storm of blows on her sore body. Yet not doing as she was told could accomplish the same.

For a long tense moment, Mother stood in the hall like a cat ready to pounce feet apart, eyes afire, fists at her sides.

Brenda-Jane did not look up. She dared not. The moment was about survival, nothing else.

Mercifully the heels began clicking again, down the hall, back to the kitchen. Supper was soon in full crescendo, pots crashing, plates slammed on the polished kitchen table.

Slowly, Brenda made the bed by pulling the pieced cover over the quilt. Fiery bolts of pain darted over various parts of her body. If she could just lie down.

After a meal of hostile silence and tinkling of weekday dishes, Brenda ignored Marlene's baleful stares and Margaret's overextended elbow and slid from the bench.

"Dishes." Her father's command interrupted her escape.

Margaret usually washed the blue-patterned Corelle and Amway pot ware, and Brenda-Jane dried. Sometimes, Marlene joined by rinsing until the gravy boat bobbing on top of the clear water grew too distracting or got excused for being too young to join in the after-meal cleanup.

With a smirk, Margaret splashed and tossed suds and dishes everywhere. Customarily, Brenda Jane would give her a good return for her shenanigans, but not today. Her spirit already crushed, she dried the dishes and put them away with the numbness and agility of a wooden doll.

As soon as the last piece of_moss green Tupperware was dry and placed in the cupboard, she pushed her tea towel over the green oven door handle and fled to her room on glazed footsteps.

The evening sun was still bright overhead when Brenda lay down on top of her bed clothing and fell asleep.

Loud voices stirred her awake.

"Ice cream," her mother announced. "Sure, is good ice cream."

Other voices mingled in, but the words "ice cream" echoed repetitively.

Brenda-Jane sat up, groggy and fully dressed. Dusk had replaced the June sunlight in the window above her head.

"We're having ice cream," Mother lamented again.

Brenda rubbed the sleep from her eyes and got up. As soon as she walked down the hallway, mother and her two siblings sitting at the table exploded with laughter.

"Ha-ha-ha!" Mother mocked. "We fooled you! That'll teach you to sleep the day away. How could we have ice cream with no milk?!" Her mirth gave way to an angry shriek. "HAH?"

Brenda-Jane had reached the hall closet before the tears brimmed over. Quickly, she turned away so mother wouldn't see. She had contained herself all day and couldn't compress her feelings anymore; she squeezed her eyes shut to keep from giving way to audible sobs.

As Brenda-Jane made her way back to her bedroom, footsteps suddenly descended upon her.

Mother.

"YOU DON'T TURN YOUR BACK ON ME WHEN I AM STILL TALKING TO YOU!"

Slaps reigned and rained all over Brenda-Jane, complete with the accompanying laundry list of what an awful kid she was. Mother slapped her head over and over until satisfied, finally.

Long after the house had grown quiet and Marlene had kicked Brenda's bed customarily on the way to hers, Brenda heard yelling.

It alternated between a man's voice like her father's and a woman's like her mother's, only deeper. Across the hall, her parents lay sleeping—Father even snored as usual, so there was no explanation for what was happening to her.

Barooong barooong! The voices chased each other back and forth—his, hers, together. Louder and louder they grew, until Brenda-Jane sat upright, holding her head in both hands quietly. The volume threatened to detonate from within.

Gradually, they disappeared, and Brenda drifted back to slumber. They returned louder than before, shouting that strange language louder and louder again.

Barooong *BAROOONG!*

She pulled the covers over her head, but the voices were already there. When the air grew too stifling, she uncovered her face to breathe.

She imagined Roman soldiers from her Bible storybook coming to catch the man and woman for behaving so rudely and making so much noise. They thundered into the house on horseback, riding up to her bed in their armor and steel headdresses. Horses nickered and neighed, hooves rumbled.

When the night was finally serene, it was morning. Dishes rattled and coffee percolated. Sunlight streamed in between the white cotton curtains sprinkled with green ivy vines.

Brenda-Jane closed her eyes and daydreamed…she was Ms. Whittingham's daughter, an only child living in the three room "teacherage" with her mother. There were no spankings, no siblings, just love, hugs, and ice cream for real.

The phone rang four short rings, and her mother answered it. A chair scraped the linoleum in the kitchen, and heavy footsteps boomed across the domicile and faded down the edge of the deck.

Her father…who would he be? Ms. Whittingham wasn't married. Picturing him was difficult until Brenda thought of thin, tall Mr. Shales, the principal of Butterhorn Junction. He wasn't handsome, but he seemed kind—too kind to be a disciplinarian. He wore a large moustache on his long face and kept his thick gray hair military short.

Brenda-Jane decided he would do but resolved, in her daydreams, to send him out on a frequent truancy ventures and parent/teacher meetings. *Crash!* The phone rudely hung back on its claw drew her out of her wool gathering again.

CHAPTER 24

Raising My Mother

BRENDA-JANE LEFT Marlene sleeping in the usual telltale yellow crescent on her bed and ventured into the kitchen. She could see Mother was angry by the short abrupt motions she made kneading the butter she was making. Butter was worked to squeeze the excess moisture and air out of it so that the finished pound didn't resemble Swiss cheese.

Squish. Squish. The holes in the golden mass gave up their secrets.

A box of cornflakes, Rice Krispies, and a bag of frost-colored puffed wheat were lined up neatly on the table.

"Use the brown sugar for the puffed wheat—it's better for you anyway! So, your Aunt Valerie phoned. Wants to host a family gathering at our house. HAH!" She brandished her one-pound wooden butter mold. "Dirty up my home and take the credit for the party? No dice!"

Once the butter mold was full of butter, she poised it over a sheet of rectangular wax paper and pushed down the plunger. A perfect gold brick landed in the middle of the printed wax paper.

"Trust your father to leave before I have a chance to talk to him about this." Two worn hands expertly drew the paper taut along the long sides of the pound, and then one layer on top of the other.

The sides were folded like the ends of a boxed Christmas gift, three of them triangulated.

When the pound was wrapped, the blue stamp read "Pure Home Grown," on both sides.

"Why did Aunt Valerie want to have a gathering?" Brenda-Jane inquired.

"Nah! Fuh dee growtellern!" (Well! For the grandparents!)

"Grandma and Grandpa Gruenwald? But they live in Saskatchewan now," Brenda-Jane suggested hopefully.

"Bah!" her mother exploded. "Don't ask me all these questions when I am already so upset. Don't be like your father." The last syllables ending in a snarl, she pivoted and clipped over to the fridge on her heels.

Margaret entered the porch with the morning's milk.

"TAKE YOUR SHITTY BOOTS OFF BEFORE YOU COME IN!" her mother bellowed.

"I know!"

"Want me to come box your ears?"

Brenda-Jane often wondered why parents asked children those questions. Do you want a spanking? Do you want me to box your ears? It was an inevitable penalty—a dark predecessor to corporal punishment. Do you want your ears boxed translated meant they were about to be!

Only a sniffle came from the addition amidst the clanging of pails as the cream separator was loaded with fresh milk.

"HAH?" Mother shouted. "ACK FRUCH DE VOT!" (I asked you a question!)

"Nay-ay!" Margaret wailed. Quickly, her mother's footsteps beat an angry rhythm across the floor and vibrated the lids on the cook stove in the front entryway.

Slap! Slap! Followed by a whimper and a sob. Heels clickety-clacked across the floor as rapidly as they had departed.

"THE THINGS I PUT UP WITH AROUND HERE!" Mother detonated.

Brenda-Jane finished her cereal as a brick wall of butter was formed on the marble-look counter. Her sister sniffed as she brought the empty milk pails to the sink to be washed.

"I'm sure going through a lot with your aunt," Mother remarked to Margaret, as if there had not just been an explosion.

Margaret brushed her arm across her face, wiping her nose on her bare wrist.

"Oh?" Like a programmed rat, she jumped for the opportunity to redeem herself before her mother's caustic regime.

"Well, first she called to ask if we could have a gathering here for when Grandma and Grandpa come up. They are staying at her house, the little teacher's pet. I said no to that. We both hung up and then it was settled."

Margaret sat down beside Brenda-Jane to pour herself her post-chore breakfast.

"Uh-huh?"

"That was last week Saturday. Today, she calls and asks again, only with a list of reasons why it can't be at her house—her home is too small, too old and too crowded. Well, tough!" she spat.

"All my life, I have never been good enough, and now, when they want to use me, only NOW I'm important? No dice! No dice!"

Mother turned into an adamant Yahtzee auctioneer whenever she got this upset.

Marlene appeared and mounted her wooden stool steed. "Is your bed wet again?" Mother asked. Marlene's eyes expanded and her chin wobbled. She nodded.

"Hah?"

"She nodded," Brenda piped up.

"ZEE SHTALL ZEE!" (Shut up you!) Mother roared. "You haven't said a dad-ridded thing all morning that was useful, so just zip it!"

Brenda felt her own lip quiver and tears forming.

"No crying either! You may as well go play for all the good you are!"

Brenda crept quietly from the bench, tiptoed across the floor toward the outdoors, fearing the sound of vicious heel tapping at any moment. They didn't follow her, so once the screen door was closed, she bolted across the yard for her yellow bicycle.

She had taught herself to ride the castoff by getting on a standing position and pushing down on one rusty pedal hard and then the other before it tipped over. She had zigzagged wildly until she learned to shift her weight slightly back and forth to keep the balance.

The fenders were loose and rattled on the gravel road past the "old Timber place." A twinge of nostalgia flitted over her as she cycled by the pond and the clearing behind it. The front steps to the Benjamen house already had a broken board, and the grass grew tall on the lawn that Bartholemew Timber had kept immaculate. Brenda-Jane missed the fair-haired Colleen Timber, who lived in Hatchet Prairie now.

A sudden tug on her skirt almost jerked her off her bike. The hem of her dress and the end of one tie thereof had become tangled in the chain. Brenda-Jane's mother's angry face flashed by her.

The sound of giggling emerged with its source from the driveway immersed in lilac trees.

The three Benjamen girls, dressed in blue jeans and T-shirts, walked out of the thicket bearing ice cream pails.

"Hey, neighbor," Tilly called out gaily, and her sisters halted briefly before changing direction and heading for her.

"I'm stuck," she announced, her right leg hurting from her own weight resting on the bar between the seat and handles.

Giggling, the three dropped their berry pails and surrounded Brenda. Fear gripped her momentarily as the three got as close as a punitive parent.

With a Benjamen at each end of her bicycle steadying her, she had only to maintain her balance while the third yanked her dress free of the chain. An ugly dark smear of dirty grease appeared on the red-flowered blue gingham. For the second time, her mother's countenance descended upon her thoughts like the grease stain on her skirt.

"Thank you. How do I tell you apart?" Brenda-Jane blurted out.

"It's easy—I'm the oldest and the biggest." Hillary giggled, shaking her brunette curls and rolling her cornflower blue eyes upward.

"She also has the biggest butt!" Jillian swatted her sister's behind.

"I do not!" Hilly Anne retorted and then dissolved in titters again.

Jillian had darker straighter hair and wore a wool hair ribbon to keep some of it back. She was shorter and quieter than her siblings.

"I'm the middle and Tilly's Margaret's age," she retrieved her berry pail. "Just remember the order like this: 'til Jill got up the hill."

When the laughter subsided, Tilly asked where they could find a good berry patch.

Across the gravel road from the little runoff pond, a thinning of the forest on Grosspabeh's field lay a half-circle he didn't use, said it was too hard to maneuver equipment in around the trees. Strawberries grew wild, large, and succulent there, tucked in between the trees and wheat crop.

After pointing them to the berry patch knowing Grandpa would not mind, Brenda turned around for home, walking her bike and worrying about Mother's reaction to her soiled dress.

CHAPTER 25

Anticipation

IN THE middle of Grandpa's field lay a dry smooth patch of dirt where nothing grew, not even fireweeds. The sun merely cracked many lines across the soil and packed it dry, creating a paved bicycle circle. Grosspabeh always said if he sprouted a bald patch, then it couldn't hurt his field any to have one also.

Brenda loved circling "the acid patch" on her bike. The ground was fairly smooth in spite of the dry mini-furrows, and she rode uninterrupted from the sparse local traffic from the gravel road.

Today, she had to postpone her adventures in pursuit of justice at her mother's mercy concerning her soiled frock.

With an exuberant jolt of carelessness, she pumped the pedals of the rattling old yellow bike and careened home. Dropping her two wheeler beside the flowerbed with the rear still spinning, Brenda clambered for either grace or a quick penalty.

"Mom! I was riding my bike and my dress got caught in the chain—"

"You know how to ride a bike?" Mother's credulousness surprised Brenda.

"I didn't know you could ride a bicycle."

"Uh-huh! I taught myself. Do you want to see?" The stain forgotten; Brenda-Jane scrambled back outside to raise the fallen and gain credibility by demonstrating her skills.

"Margaret! Come quick! Brenda-Jane is riding your old bike!"

Brenda saw their faces in the porch window briefly before fleeing away. Happy excitement welled up inside her. Mother cared about her and was interested in her bicycle riding.

"Wait until Dad sees this" had a positive note this time.

When Brenda finally did present her dress skirt to Mother, it was merely dismissed.

"Just leave it beside the dirty clothes bin."

Mother's lighter mood didn't last long, and the lamenting over her sordid upbringing in the shadow of her older sister returned. Valerie had been favored over the rest of the children in the Klaus Gruenwald clan, let off from any grueling chores and allowed to take up smoking without repercussion.

"I know!" She brightened in mid-rant. "We'll all write letters to Grandma. We won't mail them we'll bring them to Tante (Aunt) Valerie's house when we visit. They'll be so pleased."

As she spoke, Mother gathered paper pads and red pens from a drawer in the cupboards, ceremoniously distributing them in three places at the table.

"Use red pen—Grandma likes that. She does all her writing in red ink."

Brenda-Jane and Marlene sat flabbergasted for a moment.

"You could draw something," Mother suggested perkily.

Brenda sketched a row of daisies at the edge of a flower garden, but the red on ice white paper looked odd. Like a candy cane in July.

"Mom, can we color with your pencil crayons?" she dared. They were so much neater than stubby wax box crayons. She shivered as she remembered the beating, she got from her father once for coloring outside the lines of a coloring book.

"Do you promise to be careful?" Mother hesitated. Three choruses from the kitchen table choir assured her, and she wiped doughy hands on her apron. Cautiously, she lifted an old wooden container from the stationary drawer that had housed her pencils in school many years prior.

Sunday after church, the family turned right at the white corral fence that bordered the church parking lot instead of left to make the journey into town for Aunt Valerie and Uncle Bill's house of beige carpeting and rosebud soap.

The house in town between other houses was white and pretty, with lace-treated windows and three wooden butterflies clinging to the siding. The garage was attached to the house beside the black and purple butterflies. Blooming white lilacs trees added another edge of lace to the grassy yard. Cement crept out from under the wide wooden garage door and ran up to the big burgundy Suburban Father had purchased recently.

Mother clutched a handful of enveloped notes and picture letters in one hand—a small spider plant in a dainty robin's egg blue pot sat cupped in the other.

As soon as the door flung open, loud greetings erupted like so many angry seagulls over a bread crust. Grandma was behind curly haired Valerie with her own head of frosted curls, an austere Grandpa behind her.

No one embraced but, rather, shook hands enthusiastically. Grandma wore a black dress printed with pink roses and wore white polka dotted pumps with dainty bows on the toes. Her ankles rose thick and puffy above them. Grandpa's bifocal glasses, as usual, were dark and foreboding. He stepped down the staircase to enjoin the circle of handshakes and birdcall salutations, remaining gruff and somber.

CHAPTER 26

The Party

THERE WAS that awkward moment where everyone has saluted everyone else at a get-together but have not yet graduated onto the next phase of the party.

"Oh, here." Mother handed the envelopes to Grandpa, who promptly frowned and backed away. "More bills?" he said credulously. Uproarious laughter flared up like a flock of startled geese in Grosspabeh's field.

"N-no," Mother explained quickly. "The children missed you, so they wrote to you." She thrust the little spider plant in Grandma's direction as she spoke.

"A corsage?" Grandma cradled the delicate gift. "You shouldn't have, you naughty girl."

The group turned to mount the short staircase that led to the house of baubles.

At the dining room table, tucked into an alcove built for it and the mahogany bench that framed it sat Karla with a toy typewriter.

"I'm typing Grandma MY letter." She beamed. Brenda-Jane sidled over to her Sear's-catalogue clad cousin, ruffled and curled, to behold the majestic plastic machine.

"I have a toy of everything Mom has for real," Karla bragged. "I'll show you."

She rustled when she walked, wearing a dress that looked like a skirt and blouse sewn together. A white muslin top with a keyhole in the neckline and puffed sleeves that ended in a lace ruffle. A black satin ribbon around her waist into a bow at the back hung above the blue three-tiered ruffles that made up the skirt.

Karla flicked a heavy peach curtain aside to enter the narrow room she shared with her twin brother, Kenneth. Kneeling and reaching under the bunkbed, she pulled out a collection of toy kitchen appliances, hair dryer, and doll's head on a stand with curlers in its hair.

Brenda was transfixed. A doll without a body, a face like Aunt Valerie's—blue-lined eyes and big pink lips and cheeks, only the head was blonde where Tante (Aunt) was a brunette.

Back down the entry steps and around the corner, a long narrow cement staircase led to the basements. A mountainous heap of high-heeled shoes spilled in one corner were the decor for the main room. Behind "Stiletto Hill" was a row doorway to bedrooms of Aunt Valerie's offspring.

"Mom wants to sort them." Karla waved airily in the direction of the pile Brenda-Jane couldn't stop gawking at. Shoes, Pumps, and sandals of every color lay there. Marlene, Brenda, and Karla played dress up for a while, wobbling around on pastel pumps or lacing up ribbons on sandals.

In the living room, cigarette smoke amid raucous laughter floated heavily around crystal hanging lamps, and most of the adults held an alcoholic beverage. Everyone except Mother and Father, Brenda noticed on her path back downstairs from the white porcelain and pink ceramic bathroom.

Uncle Bill, Valerie's heavily mustached husband and avid trucker, was home on this rare occasion. He reminded her of Tom Selleck in the movie, *Night of The Grizzly*, the community had watched on reels in the gymnasium of the Butterhorn School.

Uncle Corky suddenly got up, set his drink down, and lunged for Aunt Valerie, who screamed and spilled her drink. The recliner reclined her on her backward descent, sending her polka-dotted dress billowing around her.

"Don't be a WALLFLOWER." Mother's voice snagged Brenda's attention and dragged its rusty claws through her spirit. "GO."

CHAPTER 27

A Mennonite Mystery

CORNY TIMBER had made it to his next home in the Blueberry Hills past Butterhorn Junction on his last tank of fuel with his tiny house loaded on Father's deck trailer. Soon after, the farmers of Fieldarp breathed a full quota sigh of relief at the local hoodlum and thief being gone. Now, once again, garage and barn doors could be left unlocked and purple gas reservoirs unchained.

Father's flat deck ever returning to its rightful position somewhere in the yard was a Sasquatch theory: everyone talked and pondered about it, but no one believed it would happen.

Then the chickens mysteriously began laying less eggs even though their coop remained lit at night, and the walls were whitewashed to encourage the most production of white eggs.

"Huh," Mother mused one morning while inspecting the contents of the aluminum pail Margaret presented to her. "That's the third day I only counted half a dozen."

A gap in the bale stack by the horse barn yawned loudly. Several alfalfa bales also lay where they had fallen from a splintered avalanche.

"Say, uh—" Father paused over dinner." "Have you girls been playing by the gas tank?" He pinched his face together and peered over the wire rims of his glasses. "I noticed there is a little bit of a fort under the stand," he singsong. "Did anyone maybe play with the nozzle and forget to shut it off?"

Marlene and Brenda both shook their heads.

"Are you sure?"

"Dad! It stinks under there!" they chorused.

"Well, the tank is empty, and it usually lasts me a month, not two weeks. And I haven't—"

"Hold on a minute!" Mother interrupted. "The eggs seem to be disappearing—"

"The bales have been knocked down."

"Is Smelly making round trips?" Mother ventured. "ACK DOCHT VEE VEERN DEM LOWSE!" (I thought we were rid of him!)

"Nah!" Father protested. He still favored the underdog slightly, even a thieving conniver at that.

Nothing more was discussed over dinner. The aroma of dill and vinegar in Mother's summer borscht filled the wordless air and was soon gone.

An expression of pure defeat landed on her mother's face, Brenda-Jane could tell. Mother relied heavily on the sale of farm eggs to neighbors at a dollar a dozen. That and the unconcerned dismissal of her husband once again over her concerns now clouded her face and tightened her lips.

All day, the thought of burglars lay heavy on the minds of the Gardener persuasion. It plagued them as they weeded the garden, searching for unfamiliar boot prints, missing vegetation, and glanced over their shoulders infrequently.

The dogs lay in the shade of the lilac trees and panted in the summer heat, tongues hanging.

"How could anyone get by Skippy?" Margaret wondered, turning the garden hose on the German shepherd and then the black lab. Skipper and Shadow lunged for the stream of water that lashed and coiled unpredictably between them.

"They must come when we aren't home," her mother straightened, wiping a dusty hand across her sweaty brow and leaving a streak of mud.

"Look!" She pointed to the disruption in the third row of carrots. A foot and a half had been ripped up.

"Uhh." She sighed, slumping. The four continued to work in silence, pulling weeds from the rows of corn, peas, and poppy flowers.

Brenda-Jane loved when the poppy flower morphed into a hard acorn-shaped hull that held a mouthful of poppy seeds.

"Don't eat too much of that." Her father would chuckle. But he'd never answer her question why.

Brenda and Marlene liked to play in the big metal tank used to haul water for the garden. They had to wait for it to be nearly empty and then they'd climb into its murky depths through a jagged square hole on the top.

Inside, it was rusty and humid, but they could poke their heads up for air by climbing the sides with legs outspread, one against each side. It was water from the Shreefah that contained tiny fish and often a frog or two. Usually, by the time the water level dropped low enough to wade in, any unfortunate frog was floating on its back, but the fish were heartier. It was a hilarious good time trying to catch them with their hands and screaming when they briefly felt the flicker of life between their palms before it escaped.

Brenda-Jane also enjoyed the way the tank altered their voices, so she sang the ditty Ms. Whittingham taught them on the trial day of school: "Froggie went a courtin' and he did ride, uh-huh. Mr. Froggie went a courtin' and he did ride, uh huh. Mr. Froggie went a courtin' and he did ride, a bag of parcels by his side. Froggie-oh baby-mine." Both girls were giggling by the time the song finished.

After the peas were picked and shelled, it was suppertime. Mother hadn't had the time to cook while tending to the garden, so she reheated "pigs'n blankets," pork sausage wrapped in a dough and baked together. She also sliced watermelon and thawed rollkuchen (roll cookies, a sugarless, deep fried biscuit) in the oven.

"One day I'd like to have a white fridge and stove," Mother mused out loud. The General Electric stove, refrigerator, and her sewing machine were all moss green. A second fridge in the porch was a yellow Moffat, perched across from the wood stove to hold the eggs, milk, and butter that were for sale. The wringer washer and the dryer were white.

"Hey!" Mother yelled out the frilled kitchen window. "Supper's ready!"

The rest of the kitchen was orange and brown, the cupboards stained medium oak, and the curtains and floor orange. The walls had been wallpapered between the cupboards and were otherwise white mock paneled wood.

Brenda-Jane would sometimes squint really hard at the recipes printed on the wall pasting among dancing salt and pepper shakers, willing herself to be able to read them.

The cupboard above the fridge was enmeshed with Mothers burgeoning ivy plant that crept all over the unfinished ceiling boards, catching on the rustic splinters. Sunday "yast" (guests) commented on the expansive plant.

There were no moldings or trim against the base of the wall or bottom of the cupboard where the linoleum ended, so it curled up at the edges.

"Your father never finishes anything but a plate of food," Mother often remarked dryly.

Marlene sat up on her church-painted highchair and poked at her food.

Brenda-Jane helped Mother clear the dishes while the sinking sun slanted the shadows across the yard and added another hue of orange to the kitchen.

CHAPTER 28

Whitewashing the Henhouse

FOUR DAYS of heavy rainfall shut the farm down to the basic activity and enabled the unearthing of forgotten hobbies and crafts. Father puttered in the garage with his welder, welding pieces of rebar together to form the skeleton of a scare-a-crow.

The canner bubbled on the stove, full of jars of stewed tomatoes. Mother got out her sewing machine and sewed octagon-shaped fabric patches together for a quilt she was making.

The three girls dug into the liquid embroidery kit, an assortment of ink in pliable tubes with a ballpoint applicator. Mother had laid out the kit and a stack of drawings on white fabric ready to be colored in.

Brenda-Jane chose a smiling flower with a baby face below its blooming hair.

"Do a good job or I won't be giving you another," her mother admonished.

It was a cozy kitchen full of warmth, food cooking, and the scent of meatloaf wafting out of the oven.

During rainy days, Mother usually told stories of her childhood once the females of the family had settled in around the table with various projects.

"I sure wish your father would do something about the slat barn now that the goats are sold. Chop it up for firewood or something."

"Otherwise Smelly will move back here?" Marlene piped up innocently. "No dice!" Mother cried out. "The nerve of that hobo—"

"What's a hobo?" Brenda interrupted.

"Hach dee yoma!" (What a pity!) Mother leapt from her chair and swan dove for the stove. The potato pot was boiling over.

Giggling, the girls asked, "What's a hobo?"

Mother tried to appear stern and failed, succumbing to the humor of her linoleum Olympics and topic of conversation.

"It means the stove's getting dirty." she choked on her own mirth.

"No. Mom! What's a hobo?"

"Every once in a while, a vagrant or two would come through Grandfather Gruenwald's farm, looking for work for the summer. They're homeless young men that wander the countryside—unmarried, dirty, and unkempt. I remember one tried to get my oldest sister, Susan." The sewing machine hummed for a few moments, a high pitched "heeheeheehee" that reminded 3602 Brenda of Aunt Valerie's laughter.

"Grandma was very strict and would only allow the men to eat on the front steps. They slept in the grain buildings at night. Well, after a month, one of the two

Dad had hired for the season asked for Susan's hand in marriage, and that was IT."

"What happened? What happened?" the girls chorused eagerly.

"We were all at the table when the men got up to go back to work. One of them turned back and asked, 'May I have your daughter's hand in marriage?' Grandma bolted out of her chair and grabbed the straw broom to strike at him. She told them both to leave and never come back unless they wanted an old-fashioned ass-whooping from a woman."

Loud footsteps thundered up the stairs. The door was thrust open so hard the knob hit the wall and the tin pot on the woodstove rattled.

"The chicken coop is flooding! Come help me!" Father slammed the door shut and galloped 3614 noisily toward the barn.

Rain had done more than merely turning the soil everywhere to a mire that clung heavier to each boot step. It had flooded the dung troughs behind the cows, and now the chickens were either crowding on the roosts or trying valiantly to navigate their abundant new water supply.

"They'll drown!" Father had a spade in one hand, readily digging a trough in the dirt to lead the flow away from the barn. He moved with the fervent agility of a farmer trying to save part of his livelihood.

Margaret and her mother grabbed five-gallon pails, tipped them in the dark fluid, and filled them gingerly, then both grabbed the handle and struggled out to the yard away from the barn to dispose of it.

The yard already had a slight ditch that ran in a half-circle that extended past the barn to the garage fifty yards away. A wooden plank lay over the trench on the trail that led from the house to Margaret's responsibilities. Now, Father furiously dug another little gulley that would lead into the new breach.

"What about your sump pump?" Mother yelled over the clatter of rain on the tin roof.

"It's at the folks!"

Brenda-Jane and Marlene scooped water into five gallons with an old metal dustpan and a broken handled shovel. While the pails were being emptied outside, they caught distressed chickens and helped them to the crowded roost until they gained a foothold.

When the water level was reduced to a dull sludge of chicken poop soup on the floor, Brenda-Jane and Margaret swept it with a push broom and an old straw broom while Marlene held a shovel level to use as a dustpan to catch the bog.

Outside, Father and Mother were throwing straw bales down in a row alongside the channel to block the water from creeping over to the barn again should the drain flood.

In the chicken coop, the girls swept and scraped the dung until the cement floor was clear of flood, fowl, and foul. Margaret plunged into the rain and got a bale of straw from the stack that was not yet drenched and lugged it into the barn. She was as strong as an ox and about as ornery.

"C'mon! Help me spread this around!"

The fresh gold straw on the damp floor smelled sweet and looked so inviting. A few birds dared land from their safe perch and venture back to the feeder.

Margaret grabbed the baler twine that it hung from and gave it a vigorous shake to loosen the chopped wheat in the barrel and send it downward into the open ledge for them to eat from. She bustled away and returned with another bale.

"Dad says I give the animals too much bedding, but I don't care," she declared stoutly.

It seemed a long time before everyone was seated around the kitchen table, warm and dry again, eating meatloaf, potatoes, and peas.

Mother and Father discussed moving the former goat barn closer to the farmyard and having the chickens migrate to it and then using that section of the cow barn for a mother pig and her brood.

"It still had better not flood like that again," Mother admonished nature.

"How high's the water, Mama? I said it's two feet high and rising—"

"Dad!" Mother protested. "We'll have to whitewash the new henhouse of course. Well, I can't do it. My back is so sore from work already, and I'll be stiff for days now from today's workout."

Father's face brightened. "Well, what do you think you have those three girls for?" He beamed at them all in turn.

After deciding on the goat barn as the new coop, Father undid the fence so he could cross the line with the 1070 case tractor, hook onto the structure still on skids since manufacture, and pull it through the pasture. He parked it next to the big barn, and he and Margaret set to work shoveling years of straw bedding and manure out of it. Mother collected the dung in her wheelbarrow and trotted off with it to dump in the garden for fertilizer. Nothing ever got wasted.

Father and Margaret had abandoned the little shed to go touch cows below the waist, so Brenda poked her head into the project. A shelf with wide spaces in between the boards remained in the way of potential whitewashers, so Brenda picked up the sledgehammer to desecrate it and make the path smooth for the task ahead of them. How pleased they would be once the evening's chores were done and the cabin was ready to be whitewashed, she mused happily, splinters flying.

After she had disassembled the spindly rack, Brenda carefully dragged all the boards out and laid them neatly beside the stoop.

Next, she carried the hammer and Roger's Golden Syrup bucket of nails out and set it beside her neat pile of kindling.

Pleased as a laying hen with her industriousness, Brenda resurrected her rickety bicycle and rode off to the acid patch on Grandfather's field. It was her oasis away from the clamor of the Gardener farm and what little traffic the neighborhood afforded.

Yelling interrupted her figure eight, so Brenda turned her front wheel homeward. Whatever it had surely excluded her, but curiosity propelled her forward.

Father, Mother, and Margaret stood in a noisy huddle in front of the new chicken coop. Margaret brandished broken bits of wood and yelled in unison with her mother. Father turned and spotted Brenda-Jane in the driveway. He waved for her to approach.

Dread spread arthritic fingers across her stomach and clenched a fist. Slowly, Brenda-Jane pedaled toward them, yet it seemed a fault line beneath her quickly swept her before the hangmen.

"I tried to help." Brenda knew now she had made a mistake.

"You undid all our work!" Margaret spazzed.

"Do something about THAT KID," Mother hissed.

Father picked up a stick and grasped her forearm. Brenda wondered why she instinctively tried to cover herself with her free arm when it always proved to be of no avail.

Phwat! Phwat! The wood hissed before it stuck her lower back and behind. Hot and fiery pain seared every nerve and gulped the last breath of air she needed for itself. Someone, maybe the devil, screamed a hoarse high-pitched scream. Oh, the pain. Such pain. One could not move for the pain but had to move to try and ease the pain of a thousand knives.

"Uh-huh-uh." she drew a stuttering breath and wailed.

The voice shrieking had been hers.

Tears streamed down her face and sobs devoured her equilibrium.

"SHUT UP!" he yelled in her ear. "YOU SHUT UP, HEAR ME?" His beefy grip tightened on her arm as his breath rasped her ear.

"Go." The cold dismissal and lingering disapproval hurt deeper than the path the board had carved in her backside, but there was no resolution. Brenda stumbled forward to run to the house.

The little henhouse remained the homework assignment of the three girls the next day for whitewashing. Margaret was being drippy-sweet, and Brenda ignored her. She picked up a sawed-off broom handle and dipped it into the thick white paint and mud mixture. Though your sins be as scarlet, *they shall be white as wool*, Brenda remembered a scripture verse she had been made to memorize. "It's like playing with icing," Marlene chirped.

"Mom says to do the bottom half of the walls and she and Dad will do the rest," Margaret instructed.

Brenda-Jane shoved her broom brush into the gooey mixture and extracted it, heavily laden. She couldn't help but think how good the concoction would look on her sibling.

"You'll be there forever the way you're going," Margaret suggested to Brenda-Jane who, in turn, wished her sibling would go away and do something else.

Margaret thrust an empty ice cream pail into the larger container and withdrew it nearly full and oozing down the side.

"Ice cream," she remarked, drawing a finger through the gel and dropping her jaw as if to lick it. She waited for a favorable reaction from Brenda-Jane, whose spirit still lagged from the previous days' penalty.

A lump of wash fell from Brenda's brush onto the floor.

Quickly, Margaret scurried over and stepped on it with her rubber boot, smoothing it over.

"Just don't let it dry in globs on the floor," she ordered.

Brenda resented her friendliness. It insulted her after yesterday's incident, a Band-Aid on a gushing wound.

Marlene chattered while she painted—how the chickens would be thankful for their new house and show their gratitude by laying extra eggs. Margaret laughed and bantered back while Brenda-Jane's fury grew.

"Look, I'm Santa Claus." Marlene smeared a glob of white around the bottom half of her face and left it dripping from her chin.

Margaret exploded into a ball of laughter. Brenda merely exploded. Deftly, she plunged her brush into the white mud and pulled it out of the pail with such force a wave of wash was released upward in her offending sibling's direction with a resounding *thwap*.

The wad of gook struck Margaret's forehead and fell down her face, leaving a trail of white that half-masked her freckled face. Her shocked expression added to the effect. The fight was on. Mud globs flew like melted snowballs, transforming them into August snowmen.

A shadow in the doorway became Mother. Rage darkened her face.

"YOU! ROTTEN KIDS. BRATS! BIZZEH CHINGA! (Evil children!) What do you think we are around here?! A rich man?!" she shrilled, stalking up to Margaret and striking her across her left ear with a right hook.

"YOU! BIG GIRL, big help you are. A more useless child never lived! Now clean this up and finish the job or I will go get the belt!" She ground her heel into the floor to pivot and stomped out.

"Here!" Mother beckoned to Brenda-Jane and Marlene.

"Here. Come here," she snarled. Meekly, they filed in behind her.

With her back straight, kerchief point jerking with every stocky-heeled footstep, Mother led the way to the rain barrel. Picking a shoe brush, she baptized it in the water and began furiously scrubbing at Brenda-Jane's hands, arms, and head.

"Bizzeh chingah!" she burst out intermittently.

Whitewash oozed from the cuff of Brenda-Jane's jacket.

"Ach!" the brush was flung to the ground. "Take your coat off!"

For a long time, Mother scrubbed Brenda with the stiff dirty bristles of the shoe brush like skin was optional.

"There. Now get inside and wash your face." Mother laid down her weapon and picked up a rag. She ordered Marlene to strip out of her dirty clothing and then gently washed her face, hands, and limbs.

"I was Santa Claus," Marlene interjected happily.

Mother's head dropped to her chin, and a gust of air escaped her through a smile. Mennonite laughter worked like that.

Marlene crept closer to Mother, and Brenda wondered what it would feel like. Mother finally finished with her darling and erected, tall and angry. "Get in the house," she growled, saliva escaping through her splintered gray and yellow teeth.

CHAPTER 29

Making Good

ALTHOUGH TRACES of whitewash still lingered in their hair, Mother drew the old plastic foot wash bowl from its place under the bathroom sink and filled it with tepid water. Brenda watched her expression, but it revealed no clues to the next event.

The once orange plastic dish had faded to peach. Mother sat it on the bathroom floor and picked up a moss green basin, filling it to the same level awkwardly under the sink tap since the oblong pans did not fit well under the stream.

Reaching under the vanity again, Mother extracted a bottle of Pine-Sol and a flask of something labelled Dettol and poured a generous amount of each into each bowl.

"Now take off your tights and underwear and dunk your bottoms in the water until I say to stop," she instructed.

"Why?" Marlene quizzed, gingerly lifting her dress and lowering herself into the shallow solution. "Because I don't want you to get itchy." The sentence ended in a breathy laugh.

Brenda-Jane sat in the chemical sitz bath and waited with Marlene while Margaret came in from her punitive chore. She heard Margaret and her mother talking rapidly back and forth.

"Are your bums tickled yet?" their mother shouted over the bathroom fan.

"Does it tickle?" Margaret mimicked, eager to redeem herself before Mother.

The household products burned, so Brenda-Jane and Marlene raised and lowered their bodies above the water to allow relief to their private areas.

"SIT, or I am going to bring bleach," Mother threatened. The hooting and hollering continued while the water cooled off. At last, Mother stuck her gleeful face in the bathroom and allowed them to get up.

Father came pounding in the house just then and asked Mother where the girls were.

Brenda pulled her fresh pair of panties on quickly in the bedroom and tried to decipher what they were saying. She couldn't make out every word, but it sounded like Mother was telling Father about the whitewash fight. Her conclusions were right when he bellowed out their names.

"Margaret! Branna! Marlene!"

Meekly, they all gathered in the kitchen. Father was smiling that certain smile of his that said trouble. Dread warmed Brenda's stomach.

"Macht yunt gowt odeh kree yee schach" (Make yourselves good or you will be spanked), he admonished.

"Making good" was forced affection between two siblings. One had to somehow embrace a feuding sister in spite of the anger that still simmered like Mother's summer borscht on the stove.

Awkwardly, Margaret stepped toward Brenda-Jane, now wearing the same queasy smile. Inwardly, she cringed when Margaret's skin brushed past hers and their arms crossed each other.

"Not good enough," Father declared. "Do it again." So, they draped their arms loosely around each other and endured the close proximity for a small eternity. Brenda-Jane cringed when Margaret's breasts touched the side of her face and she caught Father's expression of pure delight.

Margaret scooped tiny Marlene up in her arms and squeezed her hard until they both squealed and giggled. Brenda-Jane felt stripped bare of something beyond clothing. She was standing there naked of all personal choice, human rights, and decent boundaries. Warily, Brenda wrapped her arms around Marlene, recoiling inside and watching her father out of the corner of her eye. As long as he wore that pink look and sickly smirk, all was well, and they were off the meat hook. Abruptly, she released Marlene and fled into her bedroom. Mercifully, he didn't call her back.

CHAPTER 30

Making Father

SUNDAY MORNING was the usual on the Richter scale. The house rattled and shook with Father's loud footsteps and bellows.

"C'mon, everybody! Get up! We're going to church!"

"Ack vanch du hadst mole eineh off-shitz" (I wish you had an off switch), Mother complained bitterly.

Bah bang! Bah bong! Bah bang! The stove elements and wood stove lids clattered along with the doors and the floor.

"Hee ah!" He jerked the bedroom door to Margaret's bedroom open and let it strike the wall. *Crash!* Her full-length mirror fell off of the wall and splintered.

"Oh shit, oh shit, oh shit!" She wailed.

"Do you want a spanking?" he growled.

Bah dong! The bedroom door to Brenda-Jane and Marlene's room flung open ceremoniously. It stuck the wall and vibrated while he stepped on their clothes to approach their beds. The covers were jerked off of Brenda-Jane first. She lay exposed, wearing nothing but a pair of panties and a T-shirt. A big rough hand swooped down on her, grabbed her panties in the back and twisted them, hauling her upward. She dangled there in his grasp, her buttocks fully exposed and herself fully helpless. He started laughing his snickering, wheezing laugh.

Seeeer seeer. Air whistled from his leering mirth. She didn't have to look at him to know he was laughing at her.

It seemed like he hung her there forever, sneering and enjoying himself. When Marlene stirred under her covers, he dropped Brenda-Jane from his grasp and went over to her bed to tickle her through the blanket.

"Hey. Hey. It's time to get up. We're all going to church," he announced before leaving.

The church yard was filling with dark-colored vehicles and people dressed the same in navy, dark green, brown, or black clothing. If anyone spoke at all, it was in hushed tones.

It was Father's turn to teach Sunday school. He wore a dark green suit with a square-shaped blazer. The boys jostled and teased each other on their bench, trying not to laugh out loud as they inched along to one side until one got shoved right off the bench. Father cleared his throat.

"Do you all want to sit down?" he began. He pinched the pages of his book so hard between his thumb and forefinger it made a sound everyone could hear.

"Today, we'll talk about Elijah," he said slowly. "Have any of you ever eaten what a bird brought you in his beak?"

The question brought giggles from a few pupils.

"Your dad always tells such good stories," a blonde girl whispered to Brenda-Jane. She was from town, and her yellow dress was store bought and trimmed in white lace.

"Shnowbowl." the boys repeated the German term for beak and chuckled behind them.

"In the time of Elijah, there was a bad king in power named King Ahab. He told people to pray to idols and ugly statues that he had made instead of having them pray to God. But Elijah—he wasn't like that. He went to the king and told him there would be no more rain until the people prayed to God. And then he quickly left the king's house and hid beside a small creek."

Brenda-Jane pictured all this happening beside the Shreefah that ran through Grandfather's property.

"Elijah had to stay there for a long time," father continued in German, "and he had no food, but he could scoop water from the creek and drink as much as he wanted to. The ravens brought him bread in their beaks every morning and night for him to eat."

As hard as she tried, Brenda couldn't picture drinking from the Shreefah. It was always muddy from its movement and the activity of bovine creatures.

"Then the water dried up and the birds flew away to a greener land, but there was still no rain because of all the evil in the land. Elijah had to go looking for food. In a nearby town, he found a "vatefruh" (widow) with a son gathering sticks to make a fire. He asked her for food. She said she only had enough for one more bread meal for herself and her son. After that, they must wait for death."

The image of her mother's Festive Faspa table wafted by Brenda-Jane, the Blue Onion Corelle looked sharp against the dark wood around all Mother's crystal jam dishes. White and brown buns filled a red plastic basket in the center.

"And after the vate-fruh gave Elijah some of her bread, her flour bin and oil crock never ran out again," Father continued.

Grossmam had a handle on her flour bin that looked like a handle on a cupboard turned sideways, and instead of the door swinging open, it tipped out of the cupboard forward, revealing its full, triangular bin.

The next segment of the Bible story was the burning of the altar. She had watched her father light brush on the homestead as more land was cleared, sometimes sprinkling gasoline from a jerry can on the pile of branches to boost the process.

"And then Elijah heard another word from God to go to the place where the King's preachers were screaming and dancing around heaps of stones. They wanted their god to light the wood and the things they had piled up on top. Nothing happened after they prayed. Then Elijah set up his altar. He prayed for fire to the only God. Fire came and even burned up the water. "Alles vahrt fuhbrandt" (everything burned up), Father concluded.

Brenda-Jane pictured the homestead, nestled at the base of the Blueberry Hills. She could smell freshly cut birch trees and rich earth newly turned over. Bluebells hung their lavender-tinted heads like submissive women. After a fresh rain, the air was full of scents all clamoring for attention like a houseful of children once a kind father came home.

The shuffling around her brought Brenda-Jane back to reality. It was recital time. She scrambled inside for her High German verse: "Gelobet sei derr Herr tatelich." She had forgotten what it meant. Something about God being loving today. High German was a lot harder to understand than Low German. The first seemed to require a lot more spit, and a great deal of noises from the back of the throat.

A sharp jab in the ribs from Margaret told her to stand up and recite. Soon, they would be separated by a makeshift sliding wall painted the same color of death as the rest of the interior of the Sunday school, death house, and church. Margaret would go into catechism class for those aged twelve to sixteen or until they were married, whatever came first.

Mother was crying as she descended the gray church steps in her white polka-dotted black pumps and black brocade wedding dress. Marlene walked beside her, hand in hand.

Somberly, the older sisters filed to their red and cream-colored Suburban behind their father.

Quiet tension filled the air in the vehicle after Father started the motor and waited for his turn in the Sunday morning traffic. Tension and sniffling.

For a long time, no one spoke. Ripening fields flashed by. Harvest season hung low over northernmost Alberta; leaves gilded and turned crimson. School would be starting soon, forever altering life like a hand-me-down garment in mother's grip.

She thought of her plastic orange lunch kit; a big rectangle with a matching handle that she had opened and closed so many times the plastic had weakened. The inside still held the scent of new, cradled in its white strap holder was her orange and white thermos. Brenda-Jane secretly wished it wasn't as large but had said nothing for fear of reprisal.

"What seems to be the problem?" Father finally asked uneasily while Mother wept on.

When she finally spoke in a wail, one craved the silence.

"He hammered at the women," she sobbed a great rush of air.

She heaved great breathy sobs while Father said nothing. He turned from the gravel road to a straight dirt way before he spoke again.

"Zus vote?" (Like what?)

"Nah!" she exclaimed and then hiccupped. "All the things we are to do perfectly. The home has to be clean and orderly, the children in order, wear long dark dresses and a matching kerchief." "That is the church beliefs," he mumbled.

"Then after all that—and believe you me, there was more—he says we can only hope to go to heaven!" Mother dissolved into a fresh gale of weeping.

"I worked myself half to death at home on the farm, but it was never good enough. Ack racka me yedah dach! (I strain myself every day)." Now Mother was crying like a child, audibly weeping.

The suburban turned into the driveway of the farm. A foreign vehicle sat in the yard exactly where Father usually parked, a navy-blue van.

"Eltestah Vielah" (Elder Wheeler), Father breathed.

A second man in black left the vehicle to approach Father. Their suits were long-tailed and black, their smiles toothy and mirthless.

Father stopped adjacent to the men. "Gundag!" (Good day) he greeted them.

Mother blew her nose hard and then pulled her handkerchief away from her face and examined it.

"Send your children in," Elder Wheeler ordered, frowning as he said it.

The girls timidly slid out of their seats to the ground and ran into the house, immediately stationing themselves at the laundry room window.

CHAPTER 31

When the Saints Come Marching In

ELDER WHEELER was as large literally as he was a looming figure in the office he held in the church. He had a big portly nose, a thick head of silver hair brushed backward, and a pair of thick eyebrows forming a breaker should it slide down over his forehead.

"Yuna elern combmen uk" (Your parents are coming too), Mr. Wheeler barked. The other man smiled a perfect denture grin and talked small talk with Mother and Father while they waited. Mostly with Father. He had a brush cut around his head with slightly longer hair on top slicked to one side.

"What are they going to do to Mom and Dad?" Marlene whispered, credulous.

"Shh." Margaret stooped down and set Marlene up on the stool beside her.

A low, wide chrome less black sedan rolled lazily into the yard on the two-wheel tracks not covered by pig or chick weed on the driveway. Grandfather and

Grandmother parked behind Father's Suburban and left it sandwiched between the two visitors.

Stealthily, Margaret slid the window open, keeping the vinyl-lined curtain cracked.

"We have seen your wife's clothes getting brighter and brighter, and now your truck is red and white," the smaller church leader spoke up in Low German.

"Eltesta Volfe." (Elder Wolfe) Margaret identified him under her breath.

Grandmother nodded and smiled that same overstretched smile.

"We cancelled the eldership meeting and decided to just make quick work of it here." She nodded, beaming.

Mother shriveled visibly, sagging against the side of the offensive vehicle.

"The church started with a belief that wearing black to attend services and driving black cars was right," Elder Wheeler began. "And since that is not always possible, we have allowed brown and dark blue."

Grandfather said something very quietly. Whenever he spoke a little too quietly, it was a sign he was angry. Very angry, like the stillness of a volcano overdue to explode. Complying meant forbidding the explosion and its impending wreckage, according to father.

"And that does not mean that when church is over and Sunday done with for the week that all the devil's colors are to be let loose," Mr. Wheeler snapped. "The kerchief and shoes shall stay black!" Grandma nodded and kept smiling her elegant thin-lipped smile.

"Vee zahn dee elern ava dee choyk, and dee choyk ass unzeh chingah!" (We are the parents of the church and the church is our children!) Grossman chirped happily.

Ass. It showed up all the time when even the holiest grownup spoke German. Brenda giggled into the sheer curtain and reaped a shove from Margaret to place her out of earshot.

The ultimatums were given; paint over the truck and its chrome, trade it in for a darker model, or face an eat-shloss or excommunication.

Mother held her emotions in check until the clergy were driving away, and then a geyser came that lasted for a very certain eternity. Father became her caregiver, walking her like a grieving member of a funeral procession.

"Why did you let them do this to us?" she cried in a voice that was deep and hollow.

The crying spell lasted for days, and no trench was large enough to catch the floodwaters. Dishes piled up, and meals went uncooked while Mother stayed in bed and cried and slept.

The girls ate in the garden throughout the day, and Father spent a lot of time at "the folks."

In the middle of the third day, Father came home from the growfash and called the girls into the kitchen.

Uneasy, they all slid behind the table together on the bench. Apprehension filled the disheveled room.

"Have you been keeping up with the milking?"

"Of course!" Margaret answered stoutly.

He nodded. "I want you girls to clean up the house, do the dishes, and then I'll take you to Grandma's for a few days."

Worry clouded Brenda-Jane's bright sunny hopes for the first day of school. Would Grandma make their lunch and send them to school on the bus from her bridged driveway? She had imagined Mother in her blue and white Corelle dress waving from the porch as they walked to the road to meet the bus.

During the past few days of crying and staying in bed, Mother had quit speaking to anyone.

"Are you taking her to the doctor?" Grandma whispered to Father as the girls settled around the world's biggest dining room table with coloring book and crayons. It was a collection of pages other cousins had also colored in and written their names in.

Brenda-Jane strained to hear the whispers from the porch but couldn't decipher the conversation above the rustle around her.

"Look at Petey's work." Margaret pointed out. "He made the grass blue, but he does well with crayons." Petey was the youngest Penner, a tiny toddler with white blonde hair and giant blue eyes like a breathing Precious Moments figurine.

Later that afternoon, the Penners rumbled into the yard in their big old bumper less van. An army of children dressed in navy blue spilled from its paint-scabbed sliding door.

Brenda-Jane and Marlene joined Johan and David in the double-benched swing on the front lawn.

"Your mother gave us this cloth," Johan bragged to Brenda. "And there was enough for all of us! Elder John Giesbrecht said it was okay with tiny print!"

"But not for Papa," David argued. "He's a preacher, and he only wears black. Just black."

The boys sat across from the girls, the four of them holding their legs out to avoid the pinching of lower leg flesh whenever the floor rose on their side and the bench dipped forward.

"Branna," Johan called her. "Hey, Branna. Someday I will marry you, and David will marry Marlene."

Gooseflesh grew instantly where her skin had been. Brenda-Jane felt the way she did whenever father forced them to embrace each other.

"No," she said. "I don't want to."

"It's not up to you. When a boy wants a girl, he takes her and marries her." With that statement, he leapt off the swing and tumbled in the grass to exaggerate his fall.

"I do that when I get bucked off my horse!"

"I'll tell Father you were showing off," David warned, shaking a chunk of long blonde hair off of his forehead. The boys all sported brush cuts with a long strip of hair down the top of their head they were expected to comb over.

The Penners could not stay long; they had a family to visit that was one of Uncle William's parishioners. When it was time to reassemble, Uncle reached into his van through the driver's window and honked the horn twice.

Like they had previously all spilled out of the vast vehicle before, all the Penners ran for it now, all but their dignified parents. Uncle William and Aunt Zedah always moved with deliberate slowness, as if not to startle or offend a tyrannical God.

Pastor William Penner looked twenty years his wife's senior, and rumor had it that he was. He wore a homemade black baseball cap with a wide flat top, a broad band encircling his head, and short blunt brim. He also wore a black suit with no tails, beveled edges, or curves. It was a straitjacket and a straight pant leg made by Aunt Zedah.

Brenda-Jane often wondered why God liked black so much and hated people, why he could not be appeased, and why anyone bothered trying to please him. Why not just let 'er rip?!

The days at Grandma's were hectic and noisy; there was weeding to be done in the garden and eggs to be gathered. Margaret and Mary washed out the milk house while Brenda-Jane and Marlene tagged along with Susanna to pick raspberries.

"Don't eat them all," Susanna scolded beforehand. Brenda-Jane wished she could work alongside Mary instead, who was always giggling and telling stories.

Shrieks of laughter came from the milk house as the two milkmaids of sorts splashed sudsy water everywhere the evening sun shone.

"I hope the milk house is as clean as you are soaked?" Grandmother smirked over cooked chicken and mashed potatoes.

"Yo, Mameh" (Yes, Mother), Mary managed. "The cats do not like us!" Margaret giggled with her. "Girls!" Grosspabeh chided them for unruly conduct.

"We caught raspberries!" Marlene chirped. That was Marlene. She didn't speak. She made announcements. "Vee die-den die ala yreepen!" (We caught them all!)

The choice of terms erupted the entire Gardener clan. Tears formed as cooked vegetables were passed. "After supper, you can catch some dirty dishes," Grandpa managed.

CHAPTER 32

A Close Call

BEDTIME CAME fast for the busy household, Margaret bunked with Susanna and Mary while Brenda-Jane and Marlene slept just outside Grandma and Grandpa's bedroom on the army cot. The backseat out of a car that usually sat up on blocks for the grandchildren to sit on had been pulled aside to make room for their squeaking, makeshift bed.

Everything in the big farmhouse was brown, black, or a shade of navy blue. The mottled brown indoor/outdoor carpet in the hallway argued silently with the royal blue car bench. Furniture was homemade, wooden, square, and stained dark walnut. Every piece was of necessity and sat uniform to the piece beside it.

Brenda explored each item of the living room like it was the first time when they slept over at the Growfash. The only pretty thing in "the great room" was a clock with the face of a china platter, gilt-edged with a floral pattern around the outer edge. Long gold chains hung from it, weighted by gilded cylinders.

After a few days at Grandmother and Grandfather's house of religion and work, Father came to get the girls and take them home again.

"You'll stay for supper," Grandma admonished Ezekiel junior. "I made perogies, your favorite." "How's is Elizabeth?" she quizzed him.

"Oh." He paused heavily. "She sits in a chair now instead of staying in bed."

Mother was doing better indeed. She smiled when the family walked into the living room. Marlene snuggled into her lap, making her chuckle deep in her throat.

"How was Grandma's?" she asked warmly.

For the next few days, Mother was kind and loving. She made *cringles*; leftover pie dough rolled up after brown sugar and cinnamon was sprinkled on the raw dough.

Mother said nothing when Marlene and Brenda-Jane bickered over the last piece nor when Margaret snatched it.

The three began to test the new limitless limits, searching for a boundary and the mother they were accustomed to. They fought with each other valiantly, teased, and tattled and received no response, achieved no reaction.

There was no fixing the troubles of life like getting on a bicycle and riding down the gravel road, away from the busy farm and the turmoil of the household. Brenda-Jane often rode away, listening to the familiar rattle of the loose fenders and crunch of gravel beneath her tires.

A fire and the two oldest Heinrich boys tending to it interrupted the usual view of the empty overgrown lot that used to be home to Smelly Cornelly Timber. When they saw Brenda, they hollered something in German and tittered, passing a cigarette back and forth.

Brenda-Jane pedaled past the Benjamen farm, strangely quiet. A soft glow from the living room window before the trees shrouded her view hinted of a family evening around the "devil's box." (Television set.)

She pushed on, past a windbreaker of trees on Grandpa's field that lined the sweetest wild strawberry patch in all of Fieldarp.

In thought, wondering what was wrong with her mother, Brenda-Jane got to an intersection and realized she'd gone farther than she could go.

Grandpa's field had ended, and a road ran in between his and "Bus Driver" Heinrich's Field.

Brenda turned around and started for home as dusk drew heavy drapes around her.

School started tomorrow, and an uneasy knot had tightened around her stomach in spite of her anticipation of it.

Laughter and high-pitched chatter drifted up with the smoke from the campfire as she neared it, intermittently joined by a loud *clank, clank* noise.

Brenda-Jane found her wheel-trail in the ditch and veered off the main road, through the ditch, and into a clearing in the trees. It was a shortcut onto the Gardener farm that could only be navigated on a bicycle or a tractor.

Wild strawberries grew across two old wheel marks along with chamomile, fireweed, and goldenrod.

"Woo hoo hoo!" Wicked laughter rollicked behind her. Out of the corner of her eye, Brenda-Jane saw her hair swishing in the slight breeze right before a loud *clank* and a wisp of hair was cut by something whizzing beside her head. Startled, she jumped and regained her composure quickly by bearing down hard on her pedal, one and then the other.

At the house, she dropped her bike, wheels spinning, and bolted into the living room where her mother and father were sitting.

"Mom! Dad! I was riding my bike, and I heard the Heinrichs boys laughing and then a loud noise and a piece of my hair flew off because they—"

"I thought I heard gunshots." Her father was on his feet and storming out of the house before she could finish.

The blue Ford pickup started and was revved loudly as he tore out of the yard in a dust cloud.

"The nerve! Sending your father off like that! He's finally going to spend time with me, and now you're making him leave!"

"Where's Dad?" Marlene wandered in from the hallway where she'd been playing jacks with Margaret, who got up and trailed her, wild eyed and curious.

"You look like a ghost!" she exclaimed to Brenda-Jane. "What's wrong?"

"Nah! Dot streck!" (Well! The brat!) Mother snapped. "Comes blasting in here with crazy stories and now Father's out searching!"

Margaret stopped, glanced back and forth between Mother and Brenda-Jane, regained her composure, and said, "C'mon, Marlene. Let's play pickup sticks."

Mother's face was pale, gaunt, and angry. Brenda-Jane turned on her heel and walked out of the room to get ready for school tomorrow. She tensed, waiting to be ordered back sternly for more contempt and condemnation, but none came.

Father drove back in the yard quieter than the demeanor with which he left. He walked in and threw his hat on the porch floor with flourish.

"Well," he announced. "I couldn't find the boys next door, so I drove to the Heinrichs farm and cornered the old man himself." He took off his boots and sank heavily into his chair at the table while the girls clustered around him and Mother sat crying in the living room.

"Then what? Then what?!" they all chorused, oblivious to the plight of their mother in the dark recesses a handful of steps away.

"I told him in no way was he to allow his boys to have rifles unsupervised and let them trespass on other people's land. I also said this was his first and last warning. From now on, I only talk to the police."

In her bedroom, Brenda-Jane re-examined her pile of clothing and articles for school the next day. She had laid out her green corduroy jumper and matching book bag that her mother had sewn. A cloth "A," "B," and capital "C," had been cut out of other cotton fabrics and zigzag stitched onto the outer pocket.

Putting herself to bed, Brenda-Jane relaxed under her quilt. Mother was back to her old snarly self, and Father had resolved the problem with the Heinrich hyenas. She fell asleep thinking of Ms. Whittingham and her colorful dresses.

CHAPTER 33

School

WHEN THE door of the school bus opened the next morning, Mr. Heinrichs greeted Margaret and Brenda like old friends.

"You gonna make it?" He chuckled as Brenda struggled up the seemingly insurmountable steps.

A few families into the route, and the bus already halfway full, thanks to the Penners and Heinrichs families. Scattered among them were the Shepnards, each one snootier than the last.

The next stop was the Benjamens. They were all lined up in bright new satin baseball jackets, girls and boys alike. Silence and the scent of old vinyl mingling with new plastic filled the air.

"Morning!" Mr. Heinrichs' greeting drew a few giggles from the girls as they boarded, looking chipper in the primary colors they wore.

"I thought they were on welfare," Jacob Shepnard whispered loudly to his seat buddy, Cousin Ernest Penner.

"*Ni yo*" (uh-huh), Ernest answered politely.

Ms. Whittingham's classroom was a blaze of fiery fall colors, big construction paper leaves with student names emboldened upon them were Scotch-taped to the desks. She wore a dark brown dress with an orange and yellow leaves pattern across its full skirt and patent brown leather shoes.

"Teacher, your dress needs a rake," one of the boys commented and sent her off in a gale of giggles.

There was less pant piddling this time than the first day of school, balanced by some tears and several students speaking German to the schoolmarm.

By lunch time, when all the homemade egg salad sandwiches emitted their flatulent odor amid the chalk dust, Ms. Whittingham had the class paired up with bilingual and Low German-speaking kids.

The school day went by as fast as the one-hour bus ride, it seemed. However, the bus ride home was noisy chaos compared to the sleepy morning journey. Sweat replaced the new plastic scent; an apple core was tossed by the boys while the girls cringed and squealed.

"Did you eat all your lunch?" Mother asked when they got home. Brenda-Jane couldn't wait to pull her "Surprise, surprise!" reader out to show her mother.

"We're going to have to cover the pumpkins, squash, and peas tonight. There's a frost warning." Mother looked worried.

"What about the flowers?" Brenda-Jane worried.

"No, but you can pick a bunch for Ms. Whittingham tomorrow." Mother scurried away. After the supper dishes were cleared, washed, and put away, Mother raided the open linen closet of all the blankets and bedspreads.

“Here. Here.” She dumped a stack of gray flannel into Marlene’s outstretched arms. All the red and gray bedclothes had a thick black patriotic stripe down near the ends. Brenda-Jane was laden with the red pile plus a fortrel bedspread.

“C’mon.” They panted to keep up with her rapid pace out into the garden. Dusk was falling heavily and unfurling linen along with it. They took turns once Mother had all the blankets on the ground, smoothing out the folds and overlapping the ends.

“I’m running out of blankets. Bring me your bedspreads,” Mother ordered.

Once the last of the vegetation was tucked in, Mother hobbled toward the house gingerly, the girls following.

“Why are you walking funny?” Marlene queried just as Margaret burst out of the barn singing

“I’m So Lonesome I Could Cry” loud and off key.

“My back,” came the terse reply.

“—hear that lonesome whip-poor-will—” “Margi, sing something good!” Mother yelled.

“Ahh-mayzing Graaa-ay-ay-sss.” Margaret couldn’t carry a tune in a wheelbarrow with a knot around it nor a board nailed across it. But God bless her for trying, and the cows didn’t protest.

School became an oasis for Brenda-Jane. She dreaded Friday and looked forward to Monday. Ms. Whittingham was a lively adult friend a child could talk to where, at home, it was the opposite. Mother did all the talking unless she needed reassurance. Then God help the child who didn't pick the rightly phrased response.

Brenda kept the first-grade teacher's desktop decorated with handpicked floral bouquets from Mother's garden, complete with the odd spider's web and straw flower.

CHAPTER 34

In the Red Zone

TO HER great delight, Father announced one Saturday morning that he needed help finishing with the combining, and he wanted Brenda-Jane to go with him.

"Dad!" Mother protested. "She's only six years old!"

His eyes sparkled behind his studious wire-rimmed glasses.

"Well, I don't have any boys." Her face fell and she was silent. The only sound was of spoons clinking against porridge bowls.

"What about town?" she tried.

"We'll go to the junction," he reassured. She tightened her lips in a grim line and rose to clear away the dishes.

Out on the back quarter, Brenda-Jane started her new career by steering. It was exhilarating to be that high off the ground over the golden swaths she kept centered in the spiked conveyor belt.

When Father got out to check the hopper bin, Brenda-Jane had to take over the foot pedals. She found the Massey Ferguson walked itself along without pressing on the foot feet, but when Father hollered, "Heah up!" she had to stand on the brake to stop the machine.

Around and around the field she went, sometimes stopping to let Father go check the moisture level of the wheat by rubbing his hands together with a few stalks between them or to empty the hopper into the parked grain truck.

By late afternoon, Brenda-Jane was bursting with pride like the wheat stalks bulging with ripe kernels. Father took over driving home, and she sat in her usual spot in the cab—on the hard-red metal ledge beside the driver's seat. The combining was finished for the year at the Gardener farm. As the combine hobbled over the furrows, her father sang "Poor, Poor Farmer," and Brenda Jane always joined the chorus:

> "Oh, I'm a poor, farmer always on the go
> A poor, poor farmer filled with rabbit stew
> A poor, poor farmer always on the go
> A poor, poor farmer praying it don't snow!"

They always shouted the last part and then laughed.

Mother met them in the yard by the grainery buildings.

"He-ey? They close at six o'clock." Meaning the local general store.

"I guess I'll bring the grain truck back later," he mused. His face lit up, and he glanced at Brenda Jane.

"You can drive the three-wheeler back."

They all piled into the chrome less blue suburban and drove to Butterhorn Junction, past the fields of everyone they knew. Fieldarp was a patchwork of farms and families, all interconnected by lot, block, plan, and usually blood.

The Benjamen field stood aging and sparse, unswathed.

"Are they waiting for rain?" Mother snapped sarcastically, wearing her third best. It was a straight cut beige dress that flared at the bottom and stopped at her knee, the print was pink roses and tiny Blue Baby's Breath surrounding every cluster of flowers.

"Mom, your dress looks like wallpaper," Brenda admired.

Mother stiffened in her seat. "Did you hear? That kid calls me a wallflower?!" She turned to Father. "Well? Do something about that kid!" On cue, like a programmed rat, Marlene swiveled her head from the middle of the front seat and glared at Brenda. Margaret glowered at her from the bench seat she shared with Brenda-Jane.

Brenda-Jane thought fast. "N-no, Mom. I meant I wish I had wallpaper just like that!"

"Oh." A brief smile flitted across Mother's face like a cabbage moth. "Sorry."

At Buttermilk General, one could fuel up, receive mail, and buy all household goods imaginable, it seemed to Brenda-Jane. The musty old structure had two stories covering a wooden sidewalk along the store front.

Wooden block letters painted red stated their purpose against the peeling white paint: "Buttermilk General Store."

A stack of "Christmas wish books" sat on the bench under the post office window. One of the spinsters that worked as a cashier scurried from the cash register to the scarred wooden door of the little room that served as the post office. Mother and Father had a post office box here as well as in Hatchet Prairie.

The store was run by the oldest Humboldt brother; a thin, freckled, bespectacled man who was raising his orphaned siblings and never married. He had hired two unmarried sisters of school bus driver Mr. Heinrichs to work in the store during the day while he and his brothers fixed cars across the road at their garage.

Susan and Sarah were older than Isbrandt Humboldt and as round and cherubic as he was gaunt and skinny.

"What a machine," Mother mumbled as Susan's Whisper pantyhose clad legs called the wild in passing.

"You girls want a wish book?" she sang out of her post hole window.

Eagerly, the Gardener girls nodded. Beaming from his place on the counter, Father reached beneath him and picked up a shiny new catalogue and plunked it in the child's seat of the shopping cart.

On the dusty way home, the girls were tense with anticipation over the Christmas catalogue.

"I want to see it first!" Marlene chimed out.

"No one sees anything if you're gonna fight!" Mother snapped and glared back at Brenda. "And for goodness sake, don't mark it up. Make a list on paper. Not that we have money for Christmas presents."

Every year, their mother said there was no money for Christmas, and Brenda-Jane's hopes sank readily, buoyed intermittently by hope drawn from the brightly embossed pages of the Sears Wish Book. Each Christmas brought gifts to the kitchen table beside their bowls.

"The farm is in debt—" Mother was interrupted by Father.

"I'm going to work in the bush for the Shepnards this winter," he announced. "Maybe I can get the combine paid off—"

"And buy presents?" Brenda-Jane piped up. Mother shot her a withering look. "You don't even behave well enough for gifts!"

Father's solution, of course, was to break into singing:

> "We'll get ahead someday!
> We'll get ahead someday.
> If the sun comes up and we both
> cut down, we'll get ahead someday!"

Once they arrived home, there were still groceries to unpack and a grain truck to bring home from the field. Margaret and Marlene scrambled to help Mother while Father ordered Brenda to return to the field with him.

"We'll take the trike." He strode to the garage so fast she ran to keep up with him. "You'll take it back."

The red international grain truck sat in the freshly threshed field awaiting its next purpose. Father shut off the three-wheeler and dismounted.

"Dad, are we poor?" Brenda-Jane wanted to know.

He chuckled. "What makes you think that?"

"Cuz you said the combines not paid for, and Mom said no money for presents."

"Well, we're in debt. Everything colored red on the farm is not paid for yet. Here, put the choke there, turn the key, and as soon as it starts, push it all the way over."

Brenda-Jane felt a shiver of excitement go through her. This was her first trike ride alone, and she was helping out to boot.

"I need a boy." Her father's lament swallowed her thrill. "A farm is not a one-man operation." He swung up onto the running board of the truck, got in, and the grain truck growled in response.

White knuckled, Brenda-Jane drove the trike over to the rugged terrain, fearing it would tip over. The truck rumbled past her in a veil of dust, making the dusk seem darker. She gripped tighter a move that dug her thumb against the throttle and shot the three-wheeler forward. She zipped through the dust cloud and past Father's shocked expression. It was hurtle and lurch all the way from the uneven terrain to the back quarter which was beside the farmyard.

Back at the weather-streaked garage, she released the throttle and grasped each brake handles hard against the handlebars to stop the machine.

Father parked the truck beside the grainery and threw a tarpaulin over the bin.

"Give me a hand, will you?" Brenda-Jane was suddenly boosted up to grasp the tarp corner, standing on the narrow ridge along the truck bin with tiptoes and holding the sideboard with one hand.

"Is the case paid for?" she hollered while the tarp billowed over the truck.

The engine was a burnt orange color, making it hard to tell. The paint had faded before the title was inked.

"*Ass dot rote?*" (Is that red?)

"*Yo!*" (Yes!) Father shouted. "Now pass me the strap!"

"Even the barn?" Brenda-Jane was credulous. Her loathing of the color orange was expanded to its deeper hue now.

"What's red is in the red. The strap." Father held out his hand.

"Dad!" Brenda lost her patience. "Marg and Marlene will already be into the wish book!" "Go." He laughed, dismissing her with a wave of his beefy hand.

In the living room in the pathway that led to the back deck and end of the clothesline, Margaret and Marlene lay stretched out with the book in front of them. They hadn't gotten far when Brenda-Jane dove to a spot between them on her belly.

"Nothing with batteries, and no Barbie dolls!" Mother snipped from the kitchen. "And no fighting, or I'll throw the book into the fire!" Mother meant what she threatened. Many an object of her frustration landed in the flaming recesses of the cook stove in the porch, one casualty had been a doll named Helen that Marlene and Brenda had fought over.

The peering three were soon lost in a land of embossed pages, smiling faces above beaded angora wool sweaters and dolls that walked, peed, and cried.

CHAPTER 35

Teacher's Pest

BEFORE BEDTIME on Sunday nights, Brenda-Jane took her customary detour out to the garden to pick flowers for Ms. Whittingham.

The vibrant first grade instructor's blue eyes twinkled like the March birthstone in the catalogue's jewelry section.

"Oh, for me? They are so beautiful! If they weren't for me, I was going to steal them!" Brenda felt herself blush.

"Wow, thank you!" Ms. Whittingham buried her face in the homegrown bouquet.

"Ms. Whittingham, may I ask you a question?"

"Only if you tell me what these are."

Brenda-Jane obliged her by pointing out the Black Eyed Susan or pansy, a black centered flower, the Dwarf Petunia, with its red and white stripes, and the tiny flocks.

"Hmmm." The pretty young teacher inhaled.

"How come you call yourself a 'Ms.' Instead of a miss or a missus?"

Ms. Whittingham paused her admiration of the florals and thought for a moment while students began filing into her classroom.

"Because I'm piggy in the middle. I'll go get some water for these." And at that, she scurried away.

Ms. Whittingham had a bulletin board of chores for her pupils that rotated every week. Someone was selected to change the Velcro name tags for the chores, cleaning the chalkboards and erasers, desk checks for cleanliness, and choosing the story at day's end. Brenda-Jane loved running the felt erasers over a little machine in the janitor's closet that vacuumed the dust out of them.

Another first grade delicacy was reading class. Brenda-Jane gathered up the English language like she picked strawberries from her secret berry patch between the Benjamen/Gardener property line. And like she devoured the sweet succulent fruit; she ingested any book she could borrow.

After Ms. Whittingham read her lively rendition of *The Three Billy Goats Gruff*, Brenda-Jane floated home, barely aware of her cousin Johan smearing his peanut butter sandwich on her sleeve.

"Trip, trap, trip, trap!" she chanted happily, walking down the driveway from the bus.

Marlene waited by the power pole with the yard light for them. Soon, Brenda-Jane had her engaged in the story of three goats tramping across the bridge to their encounter with an unsightly beast.

"Trip, trap, trip, trap!" They marched breathlessly around the table.

"Don't leave your schoolbags on the floor!" Mother bellowed, coming with in armful of laundry.

In their bedroom, Brenda-Jane and Marlene pulled the mattress off the wooden framed bed and pushed the boards that supported the mattress together. They donned on a pair of mother's old shoes and discovered they could trip-trap and traipse well on the makeshift bridge. Taking turns, they played the role of goat versus the troll and catapulting off the bridge in triumph after the goat charged and pushed the troll to her demise.

The troll was living the lives of a cat and maintaining her tenacious bridge patrol when Mother, putting sheets away in the hall closet, spotted the room.

"What are you doing? I have so much work to do! Put that bed back or I WILL spank you!"

"Brenda-Jane," she continued, "you have been such a hyper rectum since you started school, and when I get finished with you, your rectum will quit."

That night, the angry male and female voices careened around in Brenda-Jane's mind when she tried to sleep. They shouted but spoke no words, only sounds.

Barrongl Barrong! Barrongadongah! They grew louder and louder until she cringed and winced, covering her ears to no avail. They were on the inside. She thought about calling for Mother or Father but knew it would be another futile effort. Her parents were not loving, affectionate, or understanding people. "I love you" was a term unknown, and for good cause. Anger and impatience ran the Gardener home.

Around and around, the man's baritone chased the shrill female voice until it seemed they were saying something.

"HYPER RECTUM" reverberated in her head. "HYPER RECTUM, HYPER RECTUM!" On and on it went.

The next day was surreal. Brenda-Jane woke up in a fog, struggled through her Wheaties, and nodded off on the bus.

At school, Ms. Whittingham handed out a black and white picture she instructed the class to write a story about. The mother bear scrubbing the floor on her hands and knees made it no contest for Brenda-Jane.

"Mother had no time to play with a floor to wash. Soap and a brush were all she needed."

The educator flounced around the classroom, jovially picking up the papers before sitting down and thumbing through them. She seemed enthralled with one story in particular.

"I found a winner!" she exclaimed.

Of course, with the rambunctious first grade schoolmarm, life in itself was reason for exclamation marks. Reaching into her desk drawer enthusiastically, she produced a little red leather-bound book and handed it to Brenda. It was the tiniest storybook ever built, to be sure. Inside the two-by-two-inch pages was the story of *The Little Red Hen* in small print.

Carefully, Brenda carried her minute treasure home in her coat pocket as to not get hand sweat all over the sturdy little book.

An aroma of fresh baked gingersnaps and cow's milk greeted them as soon as they entered the porch.

"Hi," Mother greeted them sweetly. The cookies were still warm and chewy, not long removed from the orifice of the green stove. Mother sank heavily into a chair despite her slight build and sighed. "What, Mom? What?" the girls chorused.

"Ahh." She sighed.

"Mom?"

"Oh, it's nothing."

"Tell us, Mom! Tell us!"

Mother sighed and lowered her head, lips in a pout. Listlessly, she stroked imaginary crumbs off the table in front of her.

"Well… Dad's been spending a lot of time at Grandma's again. He knows I don't like it. I would think by now she would catch on to cut the apron strings. But I dunno… Winter is coming, and he is going to be off to the bush skidding for the enemy—the Shepnards."

The kitchen, stuffy from the days baking and cooking, made Brenda sleepy. The room swam around her. Quickly she shook her head.

Margaret rose and mumbled under her breath about the time and her evening chores.

"That's right don't care about me," Mother simpered.

"Grandma's a sow no one can ship," Margaret quipped on her way to her bedroom to change her clothes.

At that, Mother's features relaxed, and she smiled that rush-of-air smile that meant laughter.

Marlene stretched her large eyes wide and said, "Why doesn't Dad just stay home, Mum?"

"Brenda-Jane! You look sick. Go lie down for a while, hear? I'll wake you in time for supper."

When she woke up, Mother was strangely attentive. She hummed over setting up for supper and beamed at Brenda.

"See, our big girl who goes to school is still small. She has to take a nap." The family all glanced her way for a moment, and Brenda-Jane's face burned with the sudden unusual attention.

Mother's kindness hinted of a sinister nature more so than her angry outbursts. Rage was a familiar devil, and at least her anger and abuse was real and predictable.

Father ate quickly and noisily.

"Aren't you going to chew?" Mother teased him.

After supper, Brenda dried the dishes and listened to Mother's tale of woe and concern. How she had married Father to get out of her alcoholic home and ended up no better off. Grandmother controlled all her sons except the ones who moved away and joined other churches. Dad got to see his parents every day, and she could not see hers. The Gardeners followed Gardener traditions, never Gruenwald family traditions…

"That's not fair!" Brenda-Jane offered. Then wishing to share a part of herself with Mother, she started, "Today in school, we—"

"I mean, just because the Gardeners are big church leaders doesn't mean they are better than my parents! Sure, my father drank—DRINKS—but he is still a Christian…"

Brenda-Jane wondered if Mother would read to them again once the fall canning had been done. Last winter, she had infrequently read from *Uncle Arthur's Bedtime Stories* on winter nights. Other times, she read a chapter out of a James Herriot book.

"Mom, will you read *Papa's Daughter* to us this winter?" Brenda ventured.

"Ahh!" Her mother waved her away with the dish rag still in her hand. "You're not listening anyway!"

Mercifully, the voices stayed quiet that night.

CHAPTER 36

Sure Shades of Brown Sugar

FALL CAME and, with it, daily frost and the need for winter clothing. Mother constructed whatever she could from behind the sewing machine, complete with many descriptions of a garment that did not turn out right and even more German swears.

Brenda-Jane and Marlene looked forward to shopping in Hazel's Crossing over an hour away from Fieldarp on paved road. It was a busy, blue collar town full of truck stops in comparison to the sleepy junction general store and the bare necessities of Hatchet Prairie.

Mother had engaged in hurrying Father about visiting the Gruenwald Grandparents or, her folks, this upcoming Christmas.

"Annsch (name of Penner cousin) told me we shouldn't go to Saskatchewan, it's too far into the world," Margaret began from the back of the Suburban.

Mother's head shot up, spun back, and danger flashed in her eyes. "Is Annsch YOUR mother?

"Huh? Your grandmother?" Her voice was cracked and gravelly with rage.

"You tell that old grandmother that travelling the world is not the same as worldliness! Hear?"

The three children shrank back in the back seat. Brenda-Jane saw Margaret's chin wobble, but she steeled herself and did not cry.

"Growtmurkeh," (Grandmother, pronounced in a derogatory way) Mother growl snarled. "Ack val meaneh cownt uk noch mole ziin!" (I want to see my side once too!)

Lights glowed everywhere once they arrived in Hazel's Crossing. Streetlights, billboards, and store lights were lit everywhere.

"Take me to Robinson's," Mother instructed.

Once in the store, Brenda-Jane's hopes of choosing her new winter attire ensemble faded like her old attire when Mother and Father plucked boots off the discount rack and ordered her to try them on. They looked nothing like the slightly heeled boots of Cousin Karla's she had outgrown and was still wearing. The coats were also streamlined; a brown overcoat like the married women in church wore over the entire length of their dresses.

Brenda secretly hated dressing like a miniature adult.

She eyed the puffy red satin baseball jacket styles with elasticized waists and wrists.

"They ride up when you're playing." Mother shot down her idea. "You'll just get snow down your back."

On the way out of town, Margaret read every billboard and sign out loud, "Vacancy, Monday night rib special, 5.99, Red Rooster Convenience Store," and "Stardust Hotel."

"Are you happy with your new clothes?" Mother asked warmly. Expectantly. Brenda-Jane hung her head and wished she didn't have to answer.

"Huh?" Mother sounded irritated.

"I have to get used to it," Margaret blurted out. That seemed to satisfy Mother, but when Brenda-Jane looked up, Mother's piercing brown eyes were still boring a hole through her.

"Well?"

Brenda shook her head slowly.

"YOU DON'T LIKE IT?" Brenda looked down at her brown false sued coat with dark yellow fluff trim around the hood, cuffs, the zipper, and bottom. It was a shapeless cloak, and the fluff near the hem made the backs of her knees itchy.

"I liked my old one better," she ventured. "I could wear that and save this one."

That infused Mother, and she exploded. "There! See? That's what I must put up with from THAT KID! That's the thanks I get! Hear? Do you hear that? I spent my hard-earned child tax money—" She was drawing Father in. "May as well turn around and take it back. Hear? Well, aren't you going to do something?"

"Branna," Father snarled. "You will wear the new coat for school and church, or I will stop the truck right here and spank you, hear?"

She felt tears coming and bit her bottom lip to steady it. Brenda could get in as much trouble or more for crying, and she knew it, but the tears and quiet sobs came anyway. She lowered her head right into her chest and stroked the faux fur down her front to appear to be admiring it and hide her emotions.

Marlene's coat was royal blue with white false fur that enhanced her cherubic eyes until they looked like two jewels in Aladdin's cave.

Margaret's *yowp* (garment) was identical to Brenda's except bigger and with a big buckled belt at the waist like something Peter Pan or Robin Hood would wear. It made her look like a packing box on two feet, and worst yet, Brenda would inherit the coat once Margaret outgrew it. Brown suede was here to stay.

She slipped away in her thoughts...she daydreamt she was Ms. Whittingham's daughter and her father were away working. They lived in the teacherage and walked to school hand in hand every day, went skating on the big rink whenever they wanted to, and ate wieners and beans for supper sometimes. Teacher's iridescent eyes sparkled and glistened with mirth rather than glittered and flashed with hatred and unbridled anger. Father never spanked her, and no one slapped her around.

Suppertimes were candlelit roasts and bedtime signified a cuddle and a long story, sometimes from a book and other times, they took turns making one up until Brenda fell asleep. Bedtime stories were year-round, not just in the winter months.

"Dream sack," mother shook her gently. "Dream sack." They were home

"Tell me what you dreamt about," Mother sing sang. Alarm warmed Brenda-Jane's stomach. How could she have known? What could she tell her? Mother would be upset if only she— "Come along then." Mother bustled out of the car briskly. "Just come on."

Snow came, and Father left for work in the bush for the Shepnards. A coziness settled over the Gardener farm like the growing white blanket outside.

Mother had clung to Father, already in his overcoat like a needy child before his boot steps thundered through the porch and out into the night.

After school, Margaret changed into old blue jeans from her button front school dress and beelined for the barn to get the chores done ahead of the dusk that came earlier in the evening now. Mother joined her, drowning in her borrowed coveralls to drag straw and alfalfa bales down from the hayloft to bed and feed the livestock.

Brenda-Jane and Marlene stayed inside with the Sears Christmas Wish Book, writing lists while the soup pot bubbled merrily on the stove with biscuits warmed in the oven.

Mother came in with her glasses fogged over, panting with exertion alongside a disheveled Margaret.

"Winter is here!" exclaimed Mother, shucking her barn clothes. "Did you two get along?" she demanded of the two who brandished lists on the step between the porch and kitchen.

They nodded eagerly while the fire in the stove snapped. As she set the table for supper, Mother sang:

> "The Lord's our Rock in him we hide
> A shelter in the time of storm.
> Secure whatever ill betide
> A shelter in the time of storm.

O Jesus is a rock in a weary land
A weary land, a weary land—"

"Margaret! Did you bring in wood like I asked you to!" "I've already changed!" Margaret wailed. Mother sighed.

"Well, do it tomorrow then! Don't forget again!"

"How come the younger don't have to do anything!"

A peculiar look crossed Mother's face. She gathered all the soup bowls and sandwich plates off the supper table and redistributed them all over the kitchen. A bowl ended up on top of the fridge, a plate along the unfinished windowsill, another in the toaster oven, and so forth.

"There! Now you girls can set the table," she admonished playfully, her dark eyes laughing.

After the supper dishes were washed, dried, and put away, Mother brought out the liquid embroidery and her sewing machine, and the button box with all its stories...

"Go ahead, pick one," she urged each one. "I'll bet I can connect it with a story from the clothing it came from. Try." Brenda steered clear of the brown and picked out a small metal rose. On principle.

CHAPTER 37

Saskatchewan Never Comes

ONE EVENING, on a Saturday night, after the pigs were slopped and the cow udders dropped, Father announced the family would start singing hymns one night a week. He got out his guitar, a stack of beaten hymnals, and began strumming while he waited for everyone to conglomerate in the corner of the living room.

Mother finished the dishes and hung the tea towel on the green oven door handle before submissively walking across the orange linoleum on her stacked heels.

"C'mon, kids! You heard your father! I won't be the bad guy if you resist and then get spanked!

So, come! Let's sing!"

Margaret sulked into the living room. Marlene and Brenda-Jane groaned simultaneously from their bedroom where they were playing school.

"*Malice!*" (Girls!) Father bellowed. "You come now, or I will come get you in here by your ears!" Meekly, they crept into the front room.

"Grab a chair! Take a book!" The orders came swift and stern.

"I don't want to sing—" Brenda ventured.

"Then you WILL get a spanking!" Mother snarled, glaring.

"Number 586," Father commanded.

Liltingly, Mother's beautiful soprano voice blended with and then rose above Father's baritone.

> "Is my name written there? On the pages bright and fair? Is my name written in the book of life?"

Brenda remembered her parents often telling them how their bad deeds were being recorded by God so he would have had to write their names down first. Other times, adults would say, "Yo, vee chan mole bloss hopen fuh den shinen himmel (Yes, we can only hope for the bright heaven)." It was confusing to wonder about a name in a book when it was clear to Brenda-Jane, from seeing Ms. Whittingham's mark book, that names were recorded beside marks—good, bad or mediocre. And rewards were doled out accordingly, so if mundane things of earth were a certainty, how could one's destiny remain a question mark?

Brenda-Jane mused silently that, perhaps, earth and heaven were separated by grades like school, and if one studied hard and got a lot of one hundred percent marks, one would surely be passed into the next class

"Dream sack!" Mother's voice sounded kinder now. "I can tell you are not with us."

After a few hymns, it got easier to sing and feel the conviction in the age-old words of "The Old Rugged Cross," "Amazing Grace," and "Sweet By and By."

Father stopped playing his guitar, propped it up against his desk, and retrieved his 120 bass button accordions from its case in the coat closet.

"I'm going to play this, and you are going to sing as loud as you can!" He beamed.

"Dad!" Mother protested. "You know I hate that thing!"

"Brightly beams our Father's mercy—" Only he had none. They sang until their throats were raw and the yard light came on.

"That's enough for today." The accordion was contracted and tenderly laid in its velvet-lined box. Father was about to close the lid when Brenda-Jane and Marlene scrambled to run and stroke the smooth red velvet lining before he closed the lid. He chuckled.

"Dad," Brenda-Jane wanted to know, "why does the hymn ask if our names are written down in God's book if he's writing our behavior down? Doesn't he have to write our names down first and then our doings?"

"Oh, that's a different book. He writes all our deeds down and then decides if we're good enough to go into heaven. If we are, then he writes our names in THAT book."

"But we can only hope to ever do enough good."

Crestfallen, Brenda-Jane went to bed under the liquid embroidery flowers on her duvet and wondered why children couldn't just get a free pass for being "awshullich" or innocent. There was also an old wife's theory along with even the most horrid sinner repenting in their death throes and squeaking into heaven on an honorable mention.

Brenda's pastime when company came on Sunday without children was to eavesdrop on adult conversation. "Upshnakken", it was called in German. On Sunday, a childless couple visited after church, which meant the girls were to quietly entertain themselves and not disturb the adults.

The men and women were dressed in collarless attire much like the Penners in plain, dark navy blue with sensible black shoes. His was a square cut suit; her dress was starched, the upper half covered by a black sweater.

Brenda-Jane and Marlene got out a card game and played "Go Fish," in the hallway just outside the living room. Marlene was unaware of Brenda's ulterior motive.

The grownups did not disappoint her ear. Soon, a lively discussion of who was pregnant and wearing store bought or Sears clothing started between the women. The men exchanged crop talk and who owned how much, met quotas, and so forth and so on.

Sooner than later, Brenda knew religion would cross the topic of conversation, with possible drama at its ugly flat heels.

"We can only hope to make it to heaven one day," the man drawled in German. Father agreed heartily. Repetitively.

The couple was known as "The Friesens with no children" in the community. Mother always said that's how that woman stays young. Brenda wondered if that meant Mother disliked Mrs. Friesen because she referred to her as "that woman," and goodness knew what THAT meant.

"Obah, die manna neaten han ein gooden ohnfangk" (But the Mennonites have a good start), he added piously, still pondering the ever-elusive admission to the ever-elusive heaven.

The talk drifted to death, funerals, and burial procedures of the culture as the card game progressed to Memory. Mennonites didn't hire professional undertakers; there were people self-appointed who built the plywood casket. There were others who washed and dressed the deceased in a large shapeless white men's dress shirt before laying them on a white cotton sheet stapled taught across the perimeter of the coffin. The body was also supported by a layer of sawdust and wood shavings underneath the linen. Then another white sheet was draped across the bottom half of the torso and rest of the corpse and attached to the wood frame. The material sagged toward the foot end increasingly to allow for foot room so that the sheet stretched across the lower torso and legs had no bulges. The hands were folded in silent prayer, with a black ribbon trimming the cuffs and running the entire outline of the casket to cover the staples. The collared white shirt also sported a ribbon that ran under the collar and emerged in the front in a thin, meagre little bow. The bow was only five millimeters wide since, apparently, God took issue with those also.

The grownups discussed how white was not worn until death to show purity, and only in death did one cease to sin.

"I often wonder why the black ribbon then," Mother simpered.

"It's for mourning—that is for the grieving family," the man instructed.

The married women also had a black fringed kerchief tied around their chin in death, the pink and red floral stamp at the back hidden from view. The visiting woman wore one just like Grandma Gardener.

Mother's quick footsteps delivered their sharp jabs to the brown and gold linoleum, and she was above them in an instant.

"Obah! Varum shpiel yee krickt heah?! Go! Fuhtz in yuneh shtove nan!" (Exclamation/protest. Why do you play right here?! Go! Right away into your bedroom!)

Meekly, they gathered up their cards and scrambled to obey quickly enough as to not raise Mother's ire further.

"If in this life only we have hope in Christ, we are of men most miserable." 1 Corinthians 15:19.

Brenda ran her index fingernail along the word "hope" in the index of the little New Testament Grosspabeh had given her as a secret prize, he had put it. Like all the religious books from his library for sale, it was mock black leather bound, with gold calligraphy lettering.

Brenda hid it from her parents and sisters. She had her German Bible she couldn't decipher but pretended to read with the testament tucked into its guilt—ahem, gilt-edged pages.

A possible pending trip to Saskatchewan was added to the list of items to threaten with as soon as Mother caught a whiff of enthusiasm in the children.

"We won't be going if the ground doesn't freeze on time," she would say. "Dad cannot work in the logging camp as long as the trucks can't drive into it. And if he can't make the money, then we just don't go."

If the girls quibbled over whose turn it was to wash or dry the dishes, Mother would snap, "Okay then, we're not going to Saskatchewan."

CHAPTER 38

With Father Gone

MOTHER RUMMAGED through the button tin and laid several purple pearlescent buttons on the table beside it. She held a nearly completed navy blue dress with faint squiggly designs that the puce orbs would bring out once they adorned the front bodice.

"These came off of a gaudy satin blouse of Aunt Valerie's," she mused. "She wore it when she started smoking Grandpa's butts. And all he did was laugh and give her real cigarettes—at fourteen years of age. It's no wonder her sheers are gray and the air in her house is blue and she turned out the way she did." Mother bit off the thread she was unwinding.

"I am not looking forward to that part of going to Saskatchewan." She tied a knot in the thread at the end of her needle.

"Does that mean we are going?" the girls chorused.

"If we have the money. If you guys behave."

"Anyway, Grandma and the rest of us were pretty mad at Valerie for taking up smoking, so she hid it. One day, Grandpa went drinking with the friends he drank with and won a bet where the fellow paid him in sausages. He brought them home and went to hang them in the smoke house—only, he went to the outhouse accidentally, where Valerie had been smoking all day. He hung the pork up in between the seats from the ceiling boards. They got flavored all right. We had to feed them to the dog!" Everyone laughed. Mother made the story so real.

"Well." She held up the dress with its row of buttons and full skirt. "I wonder if the elders will be satisfied with this new Sunday dress."

"Why would they? It wouldn't fit any of them," Marlene remarked innocently. They all roared with laughter at the thought of male leadership in church in a skirt.

One night, Mother put on her blue jeans and a pink flowered blouse and directed exercises on the living room floor until they were all breathless and laughing. It was a sight to behold, Mother in her blue handkerchief, pink blouse, denims, and nylons on all fours, kicking back like a farm cow at a milk stool.

"Kick high—high as you can. Now with the other one!" she instructed.

Another night, they played hopscotch on the kitchen floor where the square designs in the orange linoleum fell into something of a pattern. They used potholders to mark their place, and that meant girls had to avoid the marked squares where the others had left off as they jumped their turn.

The Christmas season was exceptionally busy for the Gardener children; there was a church Christmas program as well as reciting the same verse for the Gardener grandparents at the family gathering. They had a part in the school productions and choir like most children in their community; children who didn't have to recite at their grandparents or, if they were Old Colony members, didn't have Sunday school. The Gardener girls had to perform, perform, perform.

Mother began cutting out pattern pieces for new dresses for her three daughters. This year— 1986—they would be royal blue velour.

Her own dress was a second-hand store find that resembled Christmas itself; long, black, covered in quarter-sized red roses and bright green leaves. A white knitted elasticized waistband joined the skirt and top together like a snow on a scenic card and then resurfaced between ruffled tiers. The collarless neckline was elasticized within the fabric and didn't come high enough to cover Mother's breastbone and throat. Not only would it be considered immodest and cause a church meeting, but it revealed the burn scars from years earlier.

"I guess I'll tie one kerchief around my head upside down and backside front," she vowed, letting the heavy knit material drop from her hands. "And I'll have to shorten the hem to please your Father." "No, Mom! Don't!" the girls protested. The dress was too beautiful to alter in any way. Mother smiled her pleasure and then went to change back into a work dress.

Brenda rummaged through the scrap box and pulled out a crocheted white scarf that had been attached to a lavender angora wool sweater.

"Mom! You could wear this over your dress. See? It matches!"

In the meantime, she flicked Margaret's ear triumphantly, who in turn, punched her like an ox kick and nearly knocked her off her chair. Marlene rushed into the fray, hands flying, pulling hair, yelling.

"Hey!" Mother barreled out of her bedroom without her head gear on, busily pushing bobby pins into her hair.

"I'll tell Dad, and you'll get a spanking when he gets home!"

And that's how winter went, Father off to the bush every Sunday night and back every Friday evening. After a late meal, he would push his plate away and, for dessert practically, ask Mother, "Well, how were the kids?" And one by one, their heads would drop. Mother would smile and list the demeanors of the week if there were any, by deed and child.

Father would snicker and then call them one by one to his side, starting with the oldest. From his sitting position, he undid his belt and drew it from his pants.

"Turn around," he'd order. Instinctively, the victim obliged but covered their posterior with their hands—an act of pure futility, because with one hand, he jerked a self-protecting arm up and struck with his free limb.

The sounds that emitted from the beaten were indescribable as pain threatened to obliterate one's entire existence. All the while, Father shouted for the disciplined one to just shut up.

Once he released Margaret, Brenda-Jane's turn was next. Very slowly, she approached Father in the same stance as her sister had. Fists balled up behind her. One was jerked up and away from her body while the belt lashed away at her backside and pain burned until her spirit went numb.

Crying, she ran to her bed while Marlene received a much lighter spanking.

Saturday evenings were spent singing hymns to a God Brenda-Jane was learning to detest for giving parents the power to beat their children.

"When I was a little boy, Grandpa used to beat us really hard," Father said at bedtime from the doorway of Marlene and Brenda-Jane's bedroom. As soon as he was gone, Brenda turned on a flashlight she had pilfered from his toolbox and read her testament.

"When my father and my mother forsake me, then the Lord will take me up." Psalms 27:10. The words shocked her. This God who endorsed the whipping of children cared for them instead? She reread the verse over and over until sleep and Sunday morning's clatter came.

This particular Sunday morning brought an unusual presentation at the breakfast table. Wrapped around the back of three chairs were the straps of bright red overnight bags with the slogan "Shepnard Logging" in white lettering across the side.

"Do you know what this means?" Mother stood nervously rubbing her hands together. Father sat, beaming at his end of the table, opposite to the end that housed the sewing machine.

"We're going to Saskatchewan!" the girls sang out. "We're going!"

"That's right. And you get to miss the church program and the Gardener gathering because we'll be on the road!" Mother sang out gleefully.

That meant they only had one performance that year—singing soprano in the school choir. The Gardener girls were shy, withdrawn children that were not chosen for main parts in school plays; usually, they operated the string on the school curtain or made backdrops. Its suited Brenda-Jane just fine; attention was usually negative at home, so not being noticed felt safe.

CHAPTER 39

Still Christmas

THE SUNDAY school teachers gathered at the Gardener household and carefully measured cups full of peanuts and hard candy into brown paper bags the size of a lunch sack. Each bag received an orange before getting folded over three times and stapled once.

When the night of the school play came, Father was still deep in the woods, and Mother called on Mrs. Benjamen for a ride to the Christmas program. She wore her pretty black three-tiered dresses with its white lace trim and bright red roses with green leaves.

Helen Benjamen wore gray dress slacks and a black satin jacket. She drove the largest van they'd ever seen, and the Gardeners were easily seated among the Benjamens on the benches behind Mr. and Missus at the front.

"It was this or a school bus for us," Ezekiel Benjamen joked about their newly acquired used wheels and family size.

The Christmas program had all the charm that tinsel wound around coat hanger halos could muster. Ms. Whittingham had cut holes in the center of twenty-five white sheets, and the choir wore them with a gold braid tied at the middle.

"Angels we have heard on high, sweetly singing ore the plain, and the mountains in disguise, echoing their joyous strain..."

Brenda-Jane looked for her mother in the darkness of the auditorium, but only the front rows were visible.

"Glo-oh-oh-oh, oh-oh-oh-ria." The chorus was breathtaking.

Afterward, the principal handed every child a brown lunch bag like the ones the church gave out, and Brenda-Jane finally found her mother in the crowd. Mother clung to Marlene, who clung to her bag, her long burgundy dress coat covering most of the festive dress. Behind her was Helen Benjamen in her black satin jacket open to reveal a white satin blouse. Her peppered hair waved up off her forehead and curled back down around her bespectacled face. She looked stylish, almost pretty. "You look nice," Margaret ventured shyly.

"Oh, thank you!"

All the way home, the Benjamen family bantered about who snored when they slept and who sucked their thumb while Mother sat in stony silence.

When the van pulled up to the darkened farmhouse and deposited the Gardeners, Mother spoke only to thank the neighbors tersely for the ride.

They stumbled up the dark steps, the yard light's rays blocked by the porch. Even in the dusk, Mother's face was grim. "Had to wear my dress just so my neighbor could get a compliment," she gripped.

Margaret looked like she'd been slapped.

"Get me some wood."

Margaret almost tripped on the braided baler twine rug to hasten to Mother's bidding.

"You look pretty, Mom," Marlene chimed. "You always do."

Mother allowed herself a grim smile. "Oh? I thought Mrs. Benny looked pretty."

"No, Mom. She looked nice for a change. A lot nicer than usual. You look pretty all the time," Brenda-Jane hurriedly interjected.

"Oh." She seemed pleased with that.

Margaret returned with an armful of wood and stood waiting for Mother to relieve her of her burden.

Mother snatched the pieces one by one and dropped them into the stove before closing the round opening at the top. She finished unloading Margaret by dumping the rest of the kindling beside the stove on the floor.

Meekly, they all prepared for bed and shivered their rhyming High German prayers from under the cold covers before falling asleep. "*Ich gehe un she-roo, mine mude augen zu, mine heliand vache du, Ahmen.*" It meant I am going off to rest, closing my tired eyes, may the Lord watch over me. Amen.

Saturday morning, Mother announced that Christmas would be celebrated early—later that day, in fact, because they were spending the holiday with the Gruenwald grandparents. And with that comment, Mother singlehandedly lengthened the day and shortened the attention span of the three girls.

"Work still has to be done," Mother warned. "I need help washing the cream separator, dusting, and Saturday cleaning before I give any presents."

Somehow, Saturday proceeded at a much slower pace than the anticipation and excited thoughts of young children. The house was swept, and floor polished, gleaming stainless-steel machine parts propped up to dry, and shallow baths poured.

"Don't use too much water" came the ever-weary reminder. They were not allowed to have a full bathtub, and Brenda-Jane and Marlene had to share their meager supply by bathing together.

Mother poured in some L.O.C. as the water ran into the tub. "For bubbles," she said tensely, but Brenda flashed back to the Pine-Sol and Dettol baths and felt dirty to the core again.

A pair of aluminum milk cans stood waiting for the trek into town, along with a box of homemade butter to sell at the grocery store in Hatchet Prairie.

"Maybe Isbrandt Humboldt will trade me straight across for groceries so I don't have to wait for money," Mother mused while she stirred the soup on the stove.

Brenda-Jane secretly longed for gift wrap on her presents at Christmas—shiny paper and a pretty bow. She had seen them in the store window in town and admired their sparkle at each visit.

"Mom," she blurted out while she set the table. "Could we have our presents wrapped this year?

Even just one?"

"I'll ask Dad."

A dinner of vegetable soup and sourdough biscuit were eaten and cleared; the green rimmed dinnerware baptized in sudsy water for their sin of uncleanliness, dried, and put away.

It was an oddity in a world of order and routine to interrupt so much tradition for a trip to Saskatchewan in mid-winter. The Gardener family gathering would be skipped, and Christmas Eve celebrations brought several days forward.

After the trip into a town of few stores where local gossip and red and green lights circled the windows, the fire at home had gone out again and left the house cold. Father cursed and coaxed the fire to life in the furnace downstairs, clattering and banging the furnace door while mother started a new flame in the cook's stove that warmed the porch. The three girls huddled together at the opposite end of the stove.

"I thought you added wood," Mother remarked crossly as she closed the wrought iron lid and Father rose heavily from the basement.

"I thought so too." He rubbed his dry calloused hands together.

Only suppertime lay between the children and their Christmas gifts now. Margaret set the table while Brenda-Jane went shivering to the cold storage for a jar of marinated carrots.

Sometimes, Marlene and Brenda played "store" in the storeroom of shelves brimming with neatly labeled jars of canned vegetables, fish, sausage, and soup. Carrots embedded in sawdust in their wooden crate stayed crisp all year.

Flicking light switches on at each opportunity, Brenda-Jane silently hoped her mother would let her have the green Tupperware bowl this year. After all, she was a year older and bigger than last year.

Tradition was to set bowls on the table by your designated seat on Christmas Eve before calling the children out of their bedroom. The Gardeners didn't wait for the next morning to present the filled bowls and gifts on display. Everything happened on Christmas Eve in true German tradition.

Mother's voice calling her brought Brenda-Jane's attention to her mission and the sight of all the festive colors shelved before her.

"Carrots. 1981." She found her assignment and cast a glance at the potato bin which doubled as the counter that housed the imaginary cash register.

"Dream sack," Mother chanted when she delivered the jar full. "You were down there a long time. You were daydreaming, weren't you?"

Christmas and Father finally arrived on the kitchen table where everyone filed to their places, each beset with a stainless-steel bowl full of mixed nuts and hard candy.

"Silver bowls," Mother sang in her high-pitched soprano. "Silver bowls. Its Christmas time in the country." She smiled sweetly.

Brenda-Jane found an Etch - A - Sketch, a Spirograph kit, and a set of mini pots and pans at her place. There was also a game called "Perfection" that consisted of a platform of various shapes that one had to fit in their groves before the dial ran out of time and forced the platform up, popping the shapes out of place.

Usually small gifts were buried in the bowls, so Brenda-Jane dug for a new pencil, a small harmonica, an eraser, and a Christmas orange. Something metal touched her wandering fingertips, and she pulled out a metal Donald Duck in a matchbox-sized car.

"You can each choose a gift to bring to Saskatchewan." Mother beamed and stood with her fingers laced together.

Marlene and Brenda-Jane's gifts were usually similar, and they both chose the Spirograph kits. Margaret held up her paint-by-number set.

Mother and Father had filled each other's bowls and exchanged practical gifts—a package of work socks for him and a new casserole dish for her. They normally retreated to the living room to piously read the Christmas story, but they were leaving in the morning. After the gifts had been examined, Mother ushered everyone to bed to get sleep before tomorrow's early start on the journey.

CHAPTER 40

The Wagging Train

CHURCH MORNING crank-started the day of travel. Father stomped around, merrily shouting: "ALL ABOARD!"

The range vibrated and the floor shook as Mother packed blankets, toiletries, water, and snacks for the trip.

Father had borrowed Grosspabeh's blue Chevy Impala for the trip at his insistence. It had a white roof when it was purchased and had been painted over by the three single aunts at his direction. Now it had a navy top and royal blue body, immaculately kept with the ashtrays superglued shut.

Once the vast trunk had been laden to capacity, everyone piled in in their usual order; Brenda behind father, Marlene in the front middle or the back middle, depending on her choice.

Brenda-Jane secretly envied Marlene, who seemed so loved and adored by their parents while she and Margaret were on the outside looking in yet pitted against each other in the competition of acceptance.

"We should pray." Father took of his brown corduroy baseball cap and lowered his chin to his chest.

"Grossen Gott" (Great God), he began. "Vee yayven uns layven gownz avah tow dee" (We give our lives completely over to you).

Little shivers ran up and down Brenda-Jane's spine. At that moment, God seemed so real, so large and powerful and not the miserable old coot in the sky who made parents beat their children and women dress unattractively.

Father finished his petition and put his hat back on.

"Dad," Brenda wondered out loud. "Why did you call God 'dee' just now? You make us call you 'yee' for respect."

"Yeah, Dad, listen to your children," Mother ragged.

"Well, I guess I made a mistake then," Father drawled.

"We've never been past Hazel's Crossing before," Margaret mused.

"We're going to Rosedale, Saskatchewan," Mother perked up. "Grandma always wanted out of here."

"How come?" Father queried.

"She wanted out before one of those dad-ridded kerchiefs was cemented to HER head!" Mother's crisp head piece was folded and ironed into a perfect traffic triangle in the back of her head, with the point centered precisely to the middle of her neck. Although they were all color coordinated to her outfits, Mother would just as soon not wear a "duke," as kerchiefs were dubbed in Deutsch, but she claimed Father made her wear them.

"They are among the English," Father said slowly.

"Oh! We always lived English when I was growing up," Mother exclaimed.

"English" was a term coined to describe the rest of the world in dress and lifestyle.

For the first few hours of the trek, anticipation and excitement kept the children intrigued. With Hazel's Crossing behind them, all sights and scenery were new and previously unchartered territory for the Gardeners.

The Penners had reluctantly agreed to look after the animals while they traveled to Saskatchewan, disapproving the trip.

"You'll only mislead your children, taking them out into the world like that," Tanta Zedah had told Father.

Apparently, worldliness wasn't only sinful behavior and immodest attire, it was a geographical plague.

"Isn't Hatchet Prairie part of the world?" Mother scoffed, shoving a Kleenex into her gigantic purse.

For the one who had the mis-notion that the trip to Rosedale would be the essence of a Mennonite baptism in time consumption had another misnomer coming. Rather than a few sprinkles on the noggin and a spiritual flogging, the road stretched on and on in between towns.

Margaret read as many road signs and billboards as she could in passing. Brenda-Jane admired the pastel Christmas lights that glowed hazily in the falling snow.

"Season's special, 29.99," Margaret chanted. "Vacancy. Clean and Dutch, you won't pay too much."

They drank water and snacked on jam-jam cookies; a shortbread cousin made with syrup stuck together like Oreos, but jam was the adhesive.

Marlene slept on her mother's arm while Father drove on. When Brenda-Jane woke up, Mother and Father were arguing bitterly over directions. Mother had the map covering her side of the front seat, and Margaret lay tipped over on the couch-like back seat, sleeping.

They pulled into a drive-through restaurant, and Father rolled his window down to order when the waitress came up to the car.

"You got any suggestions?" he charmed, chuckling. He had never eaten at a drive-through A&W before and wasn't sure of himself, so he covered up with charisma.

It was eating epiphany for the girls to discover that chicken fingers were not actually cooked chicken feet like mother served at home. Brenda-Jane had never tasted anything like it before, and to have the meal clipped to the driver's side window to boot. It settled the matter for her; A&W chicken fingers trumped cooked poultry limbs at home as well as fish and chips at Mary's Diner in Hatchet Prairie.

The motel was a dark, flat-roofed building with painted orange doors. Father disappeared into the door that had a "VACANCY" sign flashing on and off while Mother waited with the girls in the car.

"Where are we?" Marlene whispered.

"Hydelan," Mother spoke. "We're almost halfway there."

It seemed like they had been driving for a down payment on eternity or at least become permanent residents of the ship called Chevy.

Father reappeared with a bright orange object in his hand.

"Hydelan Haven," Margaret read sleepily.

The motel room had carpet and a television set with a convex screen and several television knobs that clicked when you turned them. A smaller button turned the set on when pulled, and a rustle of static grew into voices talking and a picture of people to go along with the noise. It was fascinating to observe humans as short as Barbie dolls walking around and talking to each other.

There was the desk the television sat on and two matching double beds made up with factory made brown bedspreads. The wall-mounted nightstands were dark wood like the desk and chair. Everything, though stale and musty smelling, was matched in pairs or colors or both. A pot-bellied clay lamp sat bolted to each floating nightstand with a beige-fringed shade and mock-burnished brass base.

The best part was filling up the bathtub with water right to the overflow without worrying about the supply.

Mother sprinkled something mysterious in the water just before Brenda-Jane and Marlene got in to bath, and it seemed to make the water as slippery as butter. They couldn't stand up nor get a foothold in the slimy tub; they slid and fell whenever they tried. It was great fun to splash in so much water, and they didn't get out until Mother returned and ordered them out.

Since there were only two beds, Margaret was to sleep on an army cot with a fuzzy red blanket with the Hudson's Bay black stripe across the ends.

CHAPTER 41

Culture Shock

THE NEXT morning in Dixie's Restaurant, with red carpet, red tablecloths and painted waitresses, all they could do was stare.

"Stop staring like a bunch of wallflowers," Mother hissed, glaring at Brenda-Jane.

The pretty dark-haired young waitress wore her hair in a long Farah Fawcett shag with feathered layers and blue liner around her eyes. She brought everyone glasses of water with laminated menus, singing out cheerily when she spoke.

"Are you folks from town?" She wore pink blush and pink lipstick. Brenda-Jane decided right then that, one day, she would look like that. As soon as she could break away from home, from Mennonite ways, and the confines of Hatchet Prairie. One day, she would be snazzy instead of submissive.

"I said quit it!" Mother hissed from under her transparent scarf. Her anger always seemed directed at Brenda-Jane; whose stomach knotted around itself. She was only halfway through her pancakes with whipped cream scallops and sliced strawberries when she pushed her plate away.

"Clean your plate," Mother snapped. Brenda-Jane shook her head.

"Dad, do something about THAT KID." Father reached over and drew the plate toward himself and began eating it.

"Oh, that's teaching a kid."

Mother called her "kid" and "that kid" a lot when she was angry.

The endless journey began again, with less interest in new landscape and more desire to arrive at their destination on the children's part.

Hank Williams droned of Fairweather Friends on the eight-track player and Mother's scarf kerchief slid lower with every mile.

Cattlelina was their first experience in a big city where the pavement widened, lanes multiplied, and buildings of concrete, metal, and glass rose to the heavens. The land lines had disappeared.

"Himmelshtendah" (heaven stander). Margaret breathed, leaning to crane her neck upward to follow the heights of the skyscrapers.

"I told you the streets and avenues run North and South!" The navigational argument resumed from the front seat.

It seemed Father was going in circles while simultaneously getting deeper into the heart of the city where it was busier and thicker with traffic. Brenda-Jane had a nagging feeling there was something about the city she should remember, so she peered out of her window and tried to decipher what it could be.

Outside, Christmas lights glowed in steady pastels or fire engine red intermingled with what was crayon green. Some flickered on and off amid streetlights and lit novelty theme shops. People spilled all over the sidewalks like milk from a kicked-over bucket to shop Boxing Day sales. They dressed like models from the Sears Wish book, with store-bought clothes and bobbed haircuts curled under the ladies' knitted tams. Men strode briskly with wrapped packages in their hands or a woman's arm linked through theirs.

AUNT MARGARET. Brenda-Jane remembered her long-forgotten, muchly shunned Aunt.

"Aunt Marg lives here! Aunt Margaret!" She burst out. "Can we go see her?"

"Brenda-Jane Gardener!" Mother whipped around. "Do you see we are trying really hard to get out of here? At this rate, I will never see my parents again!"

"Brenda," Father spoke up sternly. "Margaret has made a choice to go the way of the world, and we have to leave her to it."

Father finally turned Grandpa's car into a gas station and asked for directions from the gas attendant after he paid for a fuel up through the window.

"Thank you and Merry Christmas," Father said pertly.

Sleep came intermittently and broke up the miles between the big blue army-tank-sized car and Grandpa and Grandma Gruenwald. Mother slept with her neck stiff and upright, her chin sagging down every so often and then jerking back upright. Brenda giggled at the sight, and Margaret glared her to silence.

Then Brenda woke up with her mouth so dry she couldn't speak. She tried to ask for water but could not utter a sound from her parched throat, so she slid forward and tapped Mother on the shoulder.

"Yine ack zay! Vote reyeat dee?" (Exclamation I say! What is wrong with you?) Mother hissed icily.

The water thermos was at Mother's feet along with the cookies in the Styrofoam cooler. She turned away.

Brenda-Jane strained to speak as hard as she could while tapping Mother's shoulder again. She pointed to her mouth, only able to make an eerie hoarse croaking sound.

"Stop touching me, you homo! Here!" Mother flung the thermos over the back seat, where it landed on the floor after narrowly missing Marlene's head.

When Brenda lifted the drink to her face, she noticed Margaret snickering out of the corner of her eye.

Darkness fell heavily, and just when it seemed they were to live out their days in the beltless seats of the Chev Impala, lights twinkled and gleamed across the upcoming path.

"Is that Rosedale?" Margaret whimpered.

"Should be," Father mused.

"Well, what's your mileage? The guy back there said fifty miles north from the café." Mother sprayed words like a machine gun.

"Rosedale, five miles," Margaret interrupted. In 1982, cars had no seatbelts nor kilometers on the speedometer.

Anticipation raised everyone's heads again as Father drove through Rosedale and Mother read the directions like a preacher.

At long last, they pulled up to a house with white siding and a whiteboard fence encircling the yard. Snow covered the roof, yard, and everything else not painted white, giving a winter wonderland illusion.

CHAPTER 42

The English Grandparents

THE BRASS doorbell was rung, and the door sprung open for an exuberant exchange of greetings, Gruenwald style. Grandma was bedecked with strings of necklaces and pearls fit to compete with a Christmas tree, wearing a red satin dress and matching satin pumps. Grandfather's bifocals were dark, and he seemed to scowl even when his mouth was saying friendly words.

Although it was a late hour, the adults gathered around the kitchen table and visited while Grandfather smoked, and Grandma passed nuts and Chinese oranges around. The girls yawned and fought off sleep. Marlene rested her head on Mother's arm.

Then finally, through a smoky haze, Grandmother led them to their beds in the living room while the adults sat up and visited more. Margaret laid down on a couch printed with pictures of covered wagons and teams of prancing, energetic horses all over it. "Colonial Style," Mother called it. Brenda-Jane and Marlene were to sleep together on the hide a bed of the other chesterfield.

A ceiling-high Christmas tree stood at the end of their bed, adorned with large pastel light bulbs glowing. It was slathered in silver tinsel icicles, delicate foil orbs, and oblong-shaped baubles. A few gifts wrapped in red, green, and white striped paper lay scattered at its base, but Brenda knew better than to inspect them for her curiosity. She would be harshly reprimanded, and besides, she was exhausted.

Sounds of a radio announcer woke her up from dreams of Etch A Sketches, Spirograph doodles, and hard candy. Grandpa's glasses glowered at her and then glanced back at the television set from his armchair beside the unlit Tannenbaum.

Brenda-Jane sat up and looked for her sisters, but they were not in the room, having left rumpled bedding and a wet circle beside her. She scrambled out of bed, scraping her legs on the metal frame of the hide-a-bed upon her hasty descent. Grandpa made her uncomfortable somehow, and she wasn't hanging around to figure out why.

She found everyone else in the kitchen eating breakfast and talking animatedly or listening wide eyed to a storyteller. Mother's two younger brothers still lived at home, and Corky was back after a failed marriage to the page thirty-four model.

"Mother," Brenda-Jane whispered, standing beside her chair and waited. "Mom." Mother held up a fork of food and then dove for it like a hungry baby bird.

Corky spotted her, "Hey, blondie, what do you need? Maybe I can help?"

Mother turned to her, and for a brief moment, Brenda looked into her cold, hard eyes. They lit up to a glittering glare.

"Scat," Mother snarled.

"There's a wet spot on the bed," Brenda pushed on, growing hot as the noisy conversations died down.

"Hah?" Mother swallowed hard.

"Mom, will you come with me?" She felt hot all over and was sure she looked as red as a Christmas bulb.

"What do you want?!" Mother exploded in a spurt of crumbs.

"Mom, there's a wet spot on the bed—"

"Someone peed the bed!" Corky sang out. "I thought big girls didn't pee the bed." Could her face burn any hotter, Brenda wondered?

"It wasn't—I didn't—" she began, but a hustle and flutter started up around the table. Mother and Grandma rose to accompany her to the makeshift sleeping quarters.

Once Mother saw the damage, she never stopped chattering and scurrying; apologizing for the mess, asking to borrow the washing machine and explaining about poor little Marlene. Once the machine was agitating the pee out of the bedding, the two women attacked the mattress with boiled soapy bleach water and rags.

When Mother was finished with the story of her poor, underdeveloped baby cakes, Grandma wanted to go out and buy her presents.

After a breakfast of cold toast and a table littered with used dishes, Brenda joined everyone in the rearranged living room.

Casey and Finnegan were playing hide and seek with Mr. Dress up in the screen of the floor model set.

Gramma wore a dark dress with a flared skirt and pink flowers chasing each other around like wind-blown leaves. On the wall behind her, a mural of a lake surrounded by autumn trees had been pasted over an entire wall.

Grandpa tapped ashes into an overflowing ash tray on a brass stand beside his chair. The uncles sat on the couch, smoking and urging the girls to open the gifts under the glistening tree.

"C'mon! Mom, can they open their presents now?" Corky coaxed excitedly.

"You beat me to it." Grandma fumbled with a 110-millimeter camera, a slim black machine the size of a pencil box.

With everyone watching, Brenda-Jane crept up to the tree feeling naked, vulnerable, and unaccepted. Mother sat, glaring and skinny in her long dark dress with red flowers, green leaves, and white lace trim.

"C'mon!" she urged, almost snapping.

Slowly, they knelt beside each other. Grandfather leaned over his armrest, jostling the tree as he shoved the gifts toward them. The three wide, blue-eyed uncles sat on the couch in their tight jeans and stared.

"There. Open them," he said gruffly.

Brenda and Marlene's parcels were the same shape, and they both pulled a fifty-piece jigsaw puzzle out of the wrapping. Brenda's was a picture of a basket full of German shepherd puppies, and the other was of one little pup.

"Skippy!" she cried out, and everyone chuckled.

Margaret's gift was the Parker Brothers Game "Sorry!" where people were pricks to each other and sent each other's pegs back to the starting point of their journey around the board.

"Well, whaddya say? Huh? Whaddya say?" Mother chanted.

They chorused a thank-you as Grandma reached under the branches and pulled out one more gift and handed it to Marlene. "You have this too."

Brenda-Jane's face burned with hurt. She picked up her puzzle and hugged it to herself, hoping her feelings wouldn't show for fear of reprisal.

Marlene beamed and held up her prize; a velvet-coated rabbit that looked real except for his brown plastic eyes and a slot on his back for coins.

The young men exited to ride their skidoos in the backyard and alley, which left the girls and Father sitting with Grandpa in the smoke-fogged living room in an awkward silence.

Margaret disappeared to help the kitchen clean up, and Brenda-Jane tackled the overflowing ash trays. She carefully lifted the heavy brown glass out of the brass holder and stand and dumped them into a moss green plastic garbage can in the kitchen the size of a diaper pail. Then she gathered the gold-glass ashtrays from the coffee table and emptied their ashes and cigarettes out.

"There's more in the house. Go look in every room," Grandpa barked. She studied his austere countenance for a moment, forever a shade of scarlet, it seemed. Beneath his bushy moustache lay a thick-lipped sneer penetrated only by a cigarette or the few terse words he exchanged with Father in stilted conversation.

Brenda-Jane busied herself gathering ash trays. When she had collected all of them in a precarious stack between her elbow and her chin, she wobbled into the kitchen with them.

"Goodness." Grandma laughed. "A helper."

When Brenda-Jane returned to the living room with her assortment of depression-era glassware, she found Grandpa tapping his ash into the brass stand without the tray. He almost smiled at her.

CHAPTER 43

The Long Way Home

DAYS IN Rosedale, Saskatchewan, passed with a lot of television, flushing the toilet after each use, filling the bathtub at bedtime, cleaning Grandpa's ashtrays, and avoiding Mother's tickling, teasing brothers.

Marlene and Brenda-Jane liked watching Casey and Finnegan and suspected Margaret did too— on the console "devil's box" in the living room. They also enjoyed *All My Children* and switching the channels back and forth with the remote. They were balancing precariously above the bathroom sink while dangling the teardrop baubles from the light fixture off their ears when they overheard Grandpa grousing about them.

"These kids are using up all my batteries and water." Brenda heard Father say something and get interrupted.

"I HAVEN'T GOT MY BILL YET! But I am sure it will be a humdinger."

Mother's hamster-quick footsteps materialized at the bathroom door, Margaret behind her.

"Grandpa says you're flushing in the bathroom all the time—remember, if it is yellow, let it mellow, if it is brown, flush it down!" she spat. "And quit using the remote! He says it is costing him batteries!"

Brenda-Jane kept up her ashtray mission around the house. It was an endless project since the three uncles smoked like their father. In their bedroom, she found a magazine half-covered by Corky's blanket. She pulled it out, heart hammering in her chest over her misdeed.

Naked girls lay eagle sprawled and open mouthed, with naked hairy men standing near them, kneeling over them.

"Branna," Father admonished from the door. Swiftly, she shoved the magazine back under the covers.

Her father was laughing silently, looking down at her with a berserk expression. It followed her around all day whenever he looked at her.

Mother accompanied Grandma to the second-hand store with the girls and bought high-heeled shoes, a pair of tight blue jeans, and translucent scarves.

Margaret purchased high-heeled sandals and Penny Pincher Romance novels.

Grandma found adorable frilly little dresses for Marlene. Brenda admired the jewelry and noticed her mother's bare head for the first time.

Mother joined her brothers' dressing style with her blue jeans but wore a blouse over her denims instead of a Waylon Jennings T-shirt. Her brown hair was curly like her three brothers, only longer, and she had brown eyes, but they were all tall and thin.

It felt strange hearing Mother called by her first name, "Elizabeth," by her family. Of course, none of her siblings went by their birth handles; the three snowmobilers were simply referred to as Corky, Pug, and Slim.

Slim was the youngest, tallest, and loudest. He had hair so curly it looked like an African afro and his father's thick sneer, although he joked around a lot and seemed a happy-go-lucky kind of guy. Pug was the runt of the family—a short dark fellow with a five o'clock shadow at any hour of the day.

"GO SHAVE!" Grandpa would bellow at him. "You look like a Mexican bank robber!"

"I shave everyday just like you, Dad." Pug stood up to the old man. Corky and Slim stepped in behind him literally during one such exchange, and the old troll backed down.

In her jeans and without her kerchief, Mother reminded Brenda-Jane of the back cover of the Chatelaine Magazine where the Marlboro cigarette advertisement quipped, "You've come a long way, baby." The scene was in black and white, with a woman of the 1950s sneaking a cigarette in the pantry room off of the kitchen where no one could see. A colored part of the picture was a modern-day woman smiling with an unlit smoke in her elegant fingers.

"Doesn't look like my wife," Father muttered, walking past Mother.

The next time Brenda-Jane saw Mother, she was weeping in Grandma's pink, rosy bathroom.

"Mom, what's—" *Click.* The hollow wooden door swung shut.

Soon, the rest of the family was uneasy and asking questions.

"What's wrong with Mom?" Corky stared at Brenda-Jane and puffed a cigar.

"I don't know," she half-fibbed, suspecting Father's comment.

Christmas in Saskatchewan was officially over, such as it had been. The Gardeners packed up and concluded their vacation tensely. Mother cried all the way to the hotel.

CHAPTER 44

The Family That Eats Itself

IT WAS a stark contrast between city-living and farm life. Although the memories of Christmas lights, trees, and fake snow in store window displays glowed in the mind for a while, real snow fell, and Mother's baler string of Christmas cards came down. It was over for another year.

The Sears Wish book was put away, Mother's two decades of catalogues saved, and the gardening brochures brought out.

Ms. Whittingham had the class transcribe their experiences of the holidays.

Brenda-Jane was the first student to complete the assignment and brandished her scribbler eagerly in her raised hand. Beaming, Ms. Whittingham collected it and began reading it as soon as she sat down behind her heavy wood-top and turquoise metal desk.

Watching her hero with a smile that rapidly turned into a frown, Brenda-Jane felt an uncomfortable warming of her stomach.

> For Christmas, we borrowed my Grandfather's car and drove to see my English Grandma and Grandpa in Rosedale, Saskatchewan. We drove and drove. It snowed a lot. My Dad was lost. Mom got mad at him. Grandpa drinks a lot of whiskey. Then Dad said something that made Mom cry. We had to leave then. And now my toys feel old.

Brenda-Jane thought she was in trouble when the bubbly elementary school teacher returned her transcript.

"How about," Ms. Whittingham suggested, "you make a list of what you got for Christmas?" And Brenda obliged, not sure of her misdemeanor, and as always, afraid to ask for fear of setting off a grownup to burn with anger toward her.

"That's better." Ms. Whittingham pinned the list to the "special stars" bulletin, decorated with an enormous amount of little gold, silver, red, green, and blue foil stickers.

Brenda-Jane had not yet learned, and it would take a harsh lesson later in life to understand that no one rewards you when you tell the truth about coming from a generation that put the "f" in family.

After Christmas, winter stretched on with deep snow, split kindling and bright daylight glancing off of the peaks of snowdrifts in a cascade of colors.

The vast farmhouse seemed hollow and empty, bare walled and bald floored, without soft carpeting and glass chandeliers and glass-beaded light fixtures.

On a rare Sunday afternoon, Hilary, Jillian, and Tilly Benjamen wandered over to the Gardener farm to visit Margaret. For a while, they were content to hole up in Margaret's room, giggling and tittering as usual.

Brenda-Jane and Marlene had been cutting paper dolls out of an old Mary Maxim catalogue and snipping ladies rings out of another old catalogue, slitting them in the middle and creating "crowns" for the be-sweatered model. It reminded her of a hymn they sang under compulsion on Friday nights, "Will There Be Any Stars in My Crown?"

Father had acquired a few sets of cross-country skis, and they were leaning up in a corner by the basement entrance. Brenda-Jane sprung an idea, and when she knocked on Margaret's bedroom door next to the playroom door next to the playroom, the usual "Vot vas du anna vay?!" (What do you want anyway?) Didn't deter her.

While mother and father "napped" the afternoon hours away, the group of girl's scissor-legged and slid along the pasture as best they could, laughing as their feet became disengaged from their bodies and sided with the skis.

The Benjamen females were inspired to poke the middle of a frozen cow pie with their ski poles and try to keep it attached as long as they could. Hysterics won over hilarious, and then Hilary ran her ski through a fresh brown mound. It finalized anyone's chance for mobility, as they rolled helplessly in the snow, ass over tea kettle, and then Father bellowed for them to come in for faspa.

The trek back to the house was sobering, and tears were wiped from mirth and cold-pinked cheeks by the time they got to the door.

"Rosy cheeks!" Mother crowed, putting on her best face.

Then the large dollop of peanut butter was passed around, and Tilly snorted, setting them all off into gales of laughter again until even Father snickered ruefully.

"What's the joke?" he managed.

"There's a brown icicle on the—" Margaret dissolved again.

"On the ski pole!" Brenda added.

"Did you ski through a cow pie?" Mother wanted to know. Now, all decorum and propriety at the table was doomed by snorts and guffaws.

Father made a raspberry sound with his mouth, and Mother choked out, "Hey! They've skied through enough for one day!"

The town of Hatchet Prairie hosted a table sale in the hall, and as usual, Mother and Father were short of money and seized the opportunity. It cost five dollars a table, and vendors could sell anything from baked goods to farm eggs, Amway/Watkins/Rawleigh/Avon products, household items, and furnishings provided they fit in, on, or around the table somehow.

The girls could gather up a few toys they no longer wanted to sell for walking money. They conglomerated their tin spinning tops, a plastic cube full of holes and cut shapes that had to be matched, and a few plastic doll prams.

Mother assembled eggs, Amway soaps, and a couple of her Afghans and patchwork bedspreads.

"Bring up a box of gingersnaps, pin wheels, and one of jam jams," she instructed Margaret. "We'll sell those. I've got lunch packed already."

"What about my horse carvings?" Father queried, rummaging through his desk. "Think they'd sell?"

"Nooo!" the girls chorused. "Keep them! We like them!" Father could carve a horse from a chunk of birch two-by-four that looked lifelike without any paint.

"I don't think we'll ever have a boy," he remarked, cradling the biggest horse in his hands.

"But, Dad! We like them!

"What about the skis?" He brightened.

Mother looked disgusted. "Now you're just plain being foolish."

The town hall had been old for a long time; a dirty beige abode squatting beside the parking lot it shared with the fire hall. The brown trim, roof, and brown doors over the small vestibule that served as an entrance flaked paint and sagged.

Inside, the dim lighting and dark green indoor/outdoor carpeting in the hallway led to a large room with an uneven floor covered in dark carpeting. At the end and middle of the big room, directly across the hallway, was a concession window filled with the odor of warm deep fry and the sound of giggling Benjamens.

"Oh, heat da mole" (Oh listen once), Mother snorted.

Not only had the neighbor lady scored the bid to run the concession; she had rented a table for her Amway products, liquid embroidery tubes, and pre-stamped white pillowcases and tablecloths.

Mother fumed as she set out a stack of white doilies beside the Amway cookware set and used toys. Brenda-Jane had added a wooden block puzzle and a Dick and Jane hardcover book.

Once the toys sold, Mother handed the girls their profits. Brenda had made a whopping 12.50 and spent half at the concession stand on a hotdog, cherry blossom, and cream soda.

Margaret coveted the Chantilly Doll across the room on a neighboring table. They were in style; a doll with a large head and eyes and an enormous curved hat trimmed in lace. It matched her puffy dress, tight and low cut at the bosom and bodice but flared and full in the skirt. This doll held a parasol in one hand and supported her elbow with the other. Some of the dolls had a lightbulb growing from their disproportioned noggin and a lamp shade balanced above them.

Brenda-Jane watched as Margaret stroked the silky glued-down hair that ended in ringlets attached to each side of the doll's breasts. Mother and Father smiled at each other.

At the end of the afternoon in the dingy community hall, Margaret toted her new ornament out into the dazzling sunlight.

Mother and Father stopped at the Super J grocery store on the way home and left the girls sitting in the Suburban.

"Now I can bake a cake for your birthday." Mother smiled as she got in her seat. "I can grow most anything

I need on the farm but not baking soda, pastry flour, or sugar."

Brenda-Jane's seventh birthday was coming, with an angel food cake topped with cooled strawberries and homemade whipped cream. The celebrated blew out white power outage candles, received an unwrapped gift and a card before life on the farm resumed, caring for barn animals, cleaning the house, and waiting for springtime.

Carefully, Mother would wipe the candles clean and store them back in their cardboard box until the next power outage or occasion.

CHAPTER 45

Browbeating

ON BRENDA-JANE'S birthday, Ms. Whittingham made an orange crown out of construction paper and drew jewels on the peaks with colored markers. The she had the class sing "Happy Birthday" to her. Brenda felt both pleased and embarrassed, and a full body blush poured over her head like warm paint until she was drenched. The energetic first grade teacher handed her a bright yellow pencil with purple bows scattered across its newness.

Best of all, the class started on its third reader in language, *Pets and Puppets*, and sent Brenda off to dreamland.

Sock puppets with button eyes and red flannel tongues lolling spoke when real life limbs animated them from the draped table beneath them.

Springtime transformed the dull gray world of winter into a dripping place of rivulets and frozen puddles to slip on. A large ice patch beside the ice rink barrier had formed, and the preacher's daughter and her friends had claimed it. Every recess, they formed a line, grabbing hold of the weathered ledge that housed the ice rink, and spun out with their feet as fast as they could go. Had they known how ridiculous they looked—like one large foot-producing machine from a Dr. Seuss novel—they might have ceased their activity. But there they were, the song leaders' daughters and the preacher's offspring in a heap of billowing skirts and tights-clad legs, pedaling their boots.

Brenda-Jane dared venture into the Old Order Mennonite gang only to be rudely shoved back with a hand on her chest. When she tipped backward and landed on her bottom, skirt flying, a laughing crowd sent her scrambling to her feet and away from everyone until the urge to cry subsided.

Ice puddles formed and froze alternately in true menopause fashion. At home, they broke out the rubber boots and clomped around the farmyard in the slush.

Ice puddles sent your feet up and your arse, down into the icy water, soaking dress, leotards, slip, underwear, and all.

Mother came over to Marlene and Brenda-Jane in her gum boots, trotting as brisk as a horse to the grain trough.

"There!" She slapped Brenda-Jane's soggy rear several times, hard.

"That's what you get for bringing your sister out here and making me work!" The spanking stung right through the wet clothes, magnifying her slaps like an electric current. "Now get in the house, hear me?" Mother grasped both their hands and jerked them forward so hard they had to run to keep up with her.

At school, a boy's snowball posse had formed against the old Order Clergymen's children, and they took cover behind the weathered planks of the skating rink perimeter whenever a teacher passed by.

Brenda picked up a crusty mound of half-frozen snow and ice, aimed, and fired right for the bare forehead of the preacher's daughter. David slew Goliath and she fell, blood gushing from her forehead.

Everyone screamed and ran away, leaving only the stern old fifth grade teacher to descend upon them. Brenda-Jane ran to Matilda Jacobson, sitting up bleeding from her frontal lobe.

"I'm so sorry! I only meant to throw a snowball! Are you okay?" She panicked. Every vein in the bloated red face of Mrs. Bechtold was bulging, her long overcoat billowing as she came in for landing.

"YOU'RE GOING TO THE PRINCIPAL'S OFFICE!" she snarled.

Matilda spluttered. "No-no-no, it was an accident. She s-said she was sorry."

The Lord's Prayer and the strap were present in public schools those days, and Brenda-Jane knew which she was destined for unless they could convince the geriatric educator otherwise.

She took Matilda's arm awkwardly and helped her stand to her feet.

Mrs. Bechtold took out a handkerchief and dabbed at Matilda's head. The small, Y-chromosome shaped wound was not as big as it was letting off blood. Her expression had softened.

"Well, come along then, we'll get a Band-Aid. Brenda-Jane, you'll stay with me for the rest of the recess."

The cantankerous fifth grade teacher was an enormous angry woman who always sounded like she was choking on a hot potato when she spoke. The older students called her "Hitler." "You're sorry, right?" Matilda shivered in a sudden cold breeze and piety.

"Um-hmm." Brenda-Jane trembled under the ferociousness of Mrs. Bechtold's glare and fear of Matilda's father, Pastor Jacob Jacobson, holding a meeting with the men of the church about her. A warm knot formed in her stomach. What had she done?

As the day wore on in the scratch of lead pencils and occasional sampling of Elmer's School Glue, visions of a willow rod beating at home intruded on Brenda-Jane.

Nervously, she chewed her pencil.

At last recess, the wiry, bespectacled principal walked right by her in the hallway in silence. Brenda began to relax. Maybe she had been forgiven by all concerned. At school anyway.

The hour-long bus ride home seemed longer, cut up only by Markus Heinrichs remarking on how the Gardener family always brought a cow-pie smell to the bus.

"Aw, du riks bloss dee zelse!" (Awe, you are only smelling yourself!) Margaret sang out. Laughter circled around the bus.

The Gardeners were the last ones unloaded off the bus. When the cumbersome machine rumbled down the last stretch of gravel road, Brenda slipped to her knees and whispered a quick prayer, "God, you know it's hard with Mom and Dad. Please don't let them be mad at me for this too." She didn't have time to elaborate. The orange mud-streaked beast squealed slightly as it stopped. God knew everything anyway, she reasoned with herself with each mud and snow-splattered step.

The aroma of apple cinnamon pie baking mingled with Mr. Clean once they opened the porch door.

"Get back with those muddy boots," Mother screeched. She had moved the crocheted baler twine rug and placed cardboard and newspaper in its place, making the stepping zone smaller. "I don't want my rug all gummed up with Fieldarp clay!" "Shaddy-ya blot" (Shabby mud), she added with vehemence.

Marlene sat on her church-pew-colored highchair and proudly smeared icing onto sour-cream sugar cookies, beaming as they entered the kitchen.

A roll of kringle sat cooling in a tin plate with its red poppy design chipped and faded. Kringle was leftover pie dough rolled flat and brushed with milk and then sprinkled with brown sugar and cinnamon before it was rolled up and baked. Mother sliced up the banana-shaped treat and offered it to Margaret and Brenda-Jane, who devoured the flaky delicacy eagerly.

"How was school?" Mother asked carefully in English, meaning she was trying out a new role or uncomfortable or both.

Something retightened the knot in Brenda's gut just as Father banged the porch door shut. "I accidentally threw ice at—"

"Hey! Your boots!" Mother yelled.

"Yo hilya ack vite," (Yes honey I know) came the resigned response.

"I had a snowball fight with Matilda Jacobson, you know, Preacher Jacobson's daughter?" "Isn't she a grade ahead of you?" Mother interrupted again.

"Uh-huh. We were playing, and they wouldn't let us on the ice, the grade two-ers, and the piece I threw had ice and it hit her and—"

"Bah!" Mother waved her hand, dismissing her. "Kids' stuff. Kids' stuff."

Brenda-Jane needed not have worry; her parents were eternally preoccupied with the farm chores, Marlene, self-imposed duties, and their personal pain.

CHAPTER 46

"Blot" (Mud)

SPRING BLEW in with the usual force, turning Fieldarp into a giant melting clay pot and flooding the fields and roadways. Mud in this small fragment of the universe wasn't ordinary mud. The thick tar-like substance stuck to the bottom of rubber boots and gathered more with each beleaguered step until the trotter became heavy footed.

Visitors on Sunday afternoons parked on the dry areas of the dirt road and walked tentatively toward the house, advancing through the mire slowly. At the door, Mother greeted cheerily, "Wear your boots in, that's clean mud!"

Once inside, the sunflower seeds were brought out, and the guests encouraged to drop their seeds on the floor. "We have girls for that you know."

Brenda-Jane always felt the dark clouds of low self-worth when the comment was made.

Mother always rose from a cantankerous tyrant that screeched complaints and cursed in German about how tired she was from her heavy workload to a gracious hostess.

If the guests had children, they were divided up among the Gardener children according to age and sent off to play. Woe betide the Gardener offspring who resisted or even hesitated to entertain the company.

"Don't be a wallflower!" Mother would snap." Or if there was no audience, she'd hiss, "Do I have to get your dad over here with his belt? HUH? You answer me!"

Springtime continued to make everything weep. Eaves troughs flowed with melting snow water, and trees dripped as it dissolved from their branches.

Brenda-Jane and Marlene played "baptism" under the garage eaves, catching just enough droplets to constitute a Mennonite sprinkling on the top of the head.

Meanwhile, Margaret blared her usual off-key singing during her chores.

> "I'se the byse that builds the boat,
> I'se the byse that sails her,
> I'se the byse that catches the fish,
> and takes them home to Liizer!"

Only Margaret didn't have a water vessel, she pushed a wheelbarrow through a muddy barnyard.

"Oh? It makes me feel like traveling on—" Now she'd gone from sailing to bleating about heaven.

Mother's sewing machine was beset with cut out patterns and lavender velour fabric pieces as she designed Easter outfits. Twice a year, they received new clothes unless an aunt or a cousin cast some off in their direction, Christmastime and Easter were the sole occasion otherwise.

This year, Mother had cleverly cut out three dress patterns that would appear to be three-piece skirt suits with a velour skirt, a white cotton bodice, and vest that matched the skirt.

Brenda-Jane's turn came to stand facing Mother while her work-softened hands pinned the incomplete pieces together around her. Mother's fingertips were gentle as she maneuvered Brenda in a slow circle, tickling her torso as she prodded and pinned. Brenda couldn't help but giggle as Mother's hands grazed her ribcage.

Mother's stern, concentrating facial expression relaxed, and she smiled.

"What?" She removed the last pin from her mouth.

"That tickles!" Brenda-Jane giggled again. It was also the only time Mother touched her.

Mother laughed and gyrated her fingers into Brenda's belly for real. "That'll teach you."

When the three outfits were complete with a row of faux white pearl buttons down the front of the blouse and topped by a purple ribbon at the throat below the white collar, the girls looked sharp.

Like a trio of Easter penguins.

Mother lined them up by the stairway door and took a picture with her 126 camera.

Easter wasn't as high maintenance as Christmas time, although there was a light and frothy concert put on at school during the day, and there was a family gathering at the grandparents.

At home, Mother allowed the girls to carefully chip a hole at the opposite ends of an egg and then place a bowl underneath to catch the yolk as they blew it. One the egg was drained, they carefully colored on it with pencil or wax crayons.

Father came from a family of twelve, and when all the married siblings and their spouses came home for a gathering with their children, Grandma's house was teeming with bodies, minus Aunt Margaret.

In Sunday school, Father told the Easter story wearing his green and beige plaid bellbottoms and green corduroy blazer. In church, Pastor Jacobson wept as he told the story of how Jesus was murdered and how the congregation was to blame if they didn't turn from their sins and repent. He wiped his eyes, blew his nose, and listed all the sins he could muster—stealing, lying, murder, wearing worldly clothes and styles, technology, women cutting their hair, men growing theirs long, and people driving brightly colored shiny cars. Weeping and chin wobbling still as he spoke, Pastor Jacobson announced that Catechism classes would start the following Friday for those wanting to repent, be baptized, and/or get married that summer. The process of joining the church was an all-inclusive package.

Grandfather sat up on the deacon's platform, enclosed by a red-stained wood pony wall. When Brenda-Jane's eyes met his, a twinkle popped into his otherwise stoic expression.

On Easter Sunday, pastel baskets with plastic straw appeared at each daughter's plate filled with various Easter Candy and a foil-wrapped chocolate bunny.

"What did the Easter Rabbit bring you?" Aunt Zedah asked the girls at the table full of cousins eating Easter dinner.

"Himself!" Marlene declared as the household cracked up.

There were "holy days" that followed each holiday; two more days after a Sunday that were treated like a Sabbath Day. The first was the original Sunday, the second "holy day" was the Monday, and the third was the Tuesday. Grandmother always deemed the "ershten halyeahdach" (The first holy day), the day for the gathering at her home.

Grossmam and Grosspabeh's house didn't yield much in the way of entertainment in the off season. The male teenagers were sequestered off downstairs to Uncle Daniel's old room while the pre-adolescents hung out near the chalkboard on the wall of the wood block storage room to play hangman. The young woman gathered in the "great room" attached to the bedroom that housed Susanna and Mary to exchange stories and gossip.

The toys consisted of a Roger's Golden Syrup pail full of broken crayons, a few well used coloring books, an assortment of wooden blocks, and a necklace made of dark colored buttons Aunt Susanna had made.

"I'm going to marry you when I grow up," Cousin Johan declared to Brenda-Jane, eyeing her up and down playfully. A warning spread over her, like someone had poured black tar on her.

Quickly, she turned and fled up the cement stairs, catching her stocking on the cracked linoleum as she did.

"New tights and what have you done already!" Mother hissed. "I'm telling your dad."

When spring finally dried her tears and warmed up the earth with her warm, sunny smile, the work on the homestead began.

Nestled at the base of the Blueberry Hills, the air was filled with the scent of freshly turned soil and moss.

Father had built a Quonset there on the hill, and one day, a new home for the Gardeners would flank it.

"A log house," Father dreamed aloud, shading his face from the sun. They were breaking for supper on sawed off log stumps in a circle around the campfire. Mother's camera captured the wiener roast, blue-jean-clad children, and the purple bluebells hanging their bashful heads everywhere.

There was brush to be piled and rocks to be picked endlessly on the homestead. Father had acquired a skidder and a bright red shiny new rock picker, but some of the finer work still had to be done by hand.

Then he had the inspiration to put twelve-year-old Margaret on the skidder to brush-pile while he ran the tractor hitched to the rock picker.

Father shouted instructions and gestured above the loud machine. He stood on the ground and watched Margaret climb up and seat herself. The yellow giant lurched forward and zigged and zagged violently across the field until it rose up on a hill and vanished down the other side. Then all was silent. For a moment, everyone froze and then began running. Mother, Father, Marlene, and Brenda-Jane rushed toward the neighboring field in horror—not knowing if Margaret was hurt.

Down the knoll, the monstrous machine was parked at an awkward angle, and beside its near tire, dwarfed in comparison, sat Margaret with her head in her knees, weeping.

"Yahoo?" Father whooped in relief. Margaret began sobbing audibly.

"What seems to be the problem?" He sing sang in English.

Margaret lost all composure then.

"YOU COULD HAVE HAD ME KILLED! IS THAT WHAT YOU WANT? IF YOU DON'T LIKE ME, WHY DON'T YOU JUST GIVE ME AWAY TO SOMEONE WHO WILL?"

"Well—" But she cut him off.

"You work us to death! Mother and I! You treat us like horses. I'm sick of it! You are horrible, Father!"

Brenda-Jane felt her mother's hand grab her shoulder and pull her behind the big rock the skidder had nearly struck. Marlene cowered beside them.

"Is Dad gonna spank Margaret?" Brenda-Jane whispered.

"Shh!" came the terse reply. The gesture of hiding from sight while remaining within earshot seemed a lesson in futility. Oddly, there was no repercussion for the outburst.

CHAPTER 47

Stipulations

"PINKSTEN" CAME fifty days after the anniversary of the resurrection of Christ (Pentecost) or Easter Monday, and every holiday came with a message from Mother and Father. At Easter and in the days leading up to Pinksten, if a child misbehaved in the Gardener household, it was confronted with "Jesus died for all your sins, and you just helped nail Jesus to the cross."

Grandmother had complained about the white bodice of their Easter outfits, so Mother threw a package of red and one of blue powdered dye into the wringer washing machine, weeping as she did. The white turned a rich shade of purple as mother's eyes and nose grew red.

"I wonder what I ever did to deserve THAT woman in my life," she moaned to Brenda-Jane. "I should never have married your father."

"It's okay, Mom, honest. I always slobber mustard—it wouldn't have stayed white anyway," Brenda-Jane soothed her. Mother's face brightened, and she pulled a swatch of pink fabric from the linen closet. It had white lattice work designs crisscrossing behind purple flowers.

"This is exactly what my flower garden looks like in the summer." Mother stroked the cotton fabric gently. "Now, tell me, does God really have a problem with these colors?" The three daughters stroked the fabric and admired it.

"One of these days, that old woman isn't going to meddle with me anymore," Mother said threateningly, having recovered from her earlier sadness.

On Sunday, the Gardeners visited the Heinrichs family after church. They only lived a few fields over in Fieldarp, so they were neighbors, yet it was strange to see Mr. Heinrichs out of the driver's seat of the bus and in his black Sunday-go-meetin' clothes.

The Heinrichs family consisted of nine boys and five girls, although the older boys and their sisters Susan and Sarah had gone off to "crowd." That left three girls, the Gardeners, and the five younger Heinrichs boys, so they formed teams and played "Anty Anty over" by the woodshed.

The brothers gathered on one side of the low building to play against the girls, even though the sides would soon be mixed according to capture.

"Anty anty over!" Margaret called and then tossed the volleyball over the wooden shingles, cocking her head to listen and detect whether it was caught. Footsteps descended on the female team. "Corny" had the dingy white ball, and they were fair game to be captured for the foes. Shrieking, the girls fled to the opposite side of the shanty—a safe zone. If you made it to the opposing side of your own volition, you were safe. Tagged and dragged to the other force signified defeat. Once all the members of a group were hostages, the game was over.

Time passed in a flurry of homemade skirts billowing and suspenders sagging. When faspa time came around, mud-stained children trooped into the large front room that encompassed an enormous table.

John-Jacob Heinrichs—bus driver, farmer, and father of the male children seated with the adults—beamed at the guest children and said, "You need a couple of boys."

Father smiled and replied, "These are my boys. I tried to teach Margaret how to run the skidder." He laughed his carefully measured public chuckle.

"Oh?" heads turned to Margaret in brief admiration, but she hung her head in embarrassment of the story to follow.

"It almost cost me an expensive machine," Father continued jovially.

Mother perked up, grabbed her plate like a steering wheel, and pantomimed jerking it violently to the right and then left. "She went like this all the way until she hit the neighbor's brush pile and nearly struck a great big rock."

The hosts chuckled slightly. "See? You need a few boys," he repeated.

Brenda-Jane's face burned as she spread freezer jam on her white bun over top of the homemade butter. The message was constantly and consistently; boys were better, girls were inferior, and it infuriated her.

On the way home in the navy-blue suburban, Margaret exploded. "Mom! Dad! You don't have to tell that story to shame me! I hate it!"

"What?!" Mother turned from her seat in the front, looking shocked. "Listen to the lip." She tapped Father's plump arm lightly as he drove.

"Margaret, shut your mouth!"

"Yeah, you guys always try to embarrass us in front of company!" Brenda-Jane surprised herself. "Then you wonder why we are shy and don't want to be around! And then you call us wallflowers!"

Mother's bottom lip trembled, and she gave Father a sideways glance. He reddened and said nothing. Brenda fully expected to be hauled out of the truck by her ears at home and dragged behind the wood pile for a beating, but an eerie peace came over the family.

Mother didn't drive except a bicycle occasionally. Lately, she had been studying the learner's book of driving so that she could get her license and bring Father's lunch out to him at the homestead.

It seemed in the Gardener family that things were expected of children that adults were incapable of.

At chore time, Brenda-Jane thought she heard peculiar noises coming from the barn. Like a sheep bleating but ending in a low moan, and the Gardener farm had neither goat not sheep housed in a slat board shelter by the garage.

Brenda-Jane followed the sound toward the cow barn where it intensified. They were deep, guttural groans of someone or something in pain. Fear froze inside her, and she forced each subsequentially step forward.

The massive door creaked as she pushed it open and stepped into the dark recesses of the building. Yellow fuzzy marshmallows danced in front of her vision as her eyes adjusted to the dim lighting. An orange electrical cord hung from the beam above the cement aisle in the empty milk stalls. She followed it down to a curly head of hair—Margaret! It was Margaret, sobbing, choking, and kneeling, trying to hang herself just before milking time.

The trouble was the cord kept stretching, and Margaret had hung it too low to successfully commit suicide.

Brenda-Jane grabbed the old pruning shears and clamped them around the cord. It wouldn't cut all the way through, so she stood beside Margaret and wriggled them until the wires snapped and fell.

Her older sibling had the most depraved look on her crimson, tear-streaked face. Her eyes glared unblinking while Brenda tugged at the noose around her neck.

"Margaret—" the words stifled. A large silhouette darkened the doorway. Father. A gasp beside her told Brenda volumes.

"What are you girls up to? It's milking time."

Brenda-Jane still held the broken extension in her hand.

"Look, Dad. We tried to make a swing!" she chirped brightly, Marlene-style.

Margaret rose to her feet slowly.

"Well, you wrecked my good extension cord." He stepped forward and gingerly touched the mangled end still dangling from the ceiling.

"It was an accident, Dad! Promise!" Brenda-Jane insisted.

Deftly, he reached up, untied it, and took the two broken pieces with him as he turned on his heel and marched off.

"Bring the cows IN!" he bellowed.

"See, I can't do anything right!" Margaret whispered. "Next time, I'll—" She made a gun with her right hand and made like she shot herself in the chest.

"But that's a sin!" Brenda was shocked.

"If I can't ever get it right, I don't want to be here." Margaret opened the back-barn door to let the cows in. "Besides. Everything is a sin." She sniffed and wiped her nose on the sleeve of her chore coat.

Crestfallen and dazed, Brenda-Jane retreated to the barn loft that housed a nest of baby kittens. She cuddled a baby cat that had just opened its eyes and lungs and thought how dreary life could be indeed.

CHAPTER 48

Covert Incest

PIG BUTCHERING season came when the ground was still a mixture of mud and a few lone snow drifts clinging to the hills.

Usually, three of four families got together to alternate households to help each other get them butchering done for the year. For the children, it meant getting dropped off at a different location on the school bus to free up those preoccupied with meat processing. The Gardener girls usually went to Grossmam and Grosspabeh's.

This year, Mother and Father decided to combine childcare and the butcher site and simply joined the growfash (grandparents) at the senior Gardener farm.

The entire car garage—a distance from the house and a different direction—was cleaned out for the occasion. Sawhorses were set up to hold a sheet of plywood and serve as a table with the hand cranked meat grinder bolted to the makeshift workstation. Once the pig was shot, it was hoisted up by its hind legs and suspended from the front loader of the farm tractor. Its throat was cut, and blood drained from it before the men skinned it from its position.

A hose was hooked up to the end of the intestines, and they were flushed to be reused as sausage casing.

Brenda-Jane knew the procedures well because whenever a child got to be too rambunctious for Aunt Susanna and Aunt Mary, they were sent out to "help the grownups."

This year butchering was strictly a family affair; the rotation starting at the Deacon Gardeners. Once the first family's pigs were butchered, the other three went home with packages of sausages, spareribs or "rap shpah" (spareribs) the laborers had cooked in a boiling pot of water while working.

It meant spareribs for school lunch with mustard or de-ribbed meat placed in a homemade brown bun. Sausages in a dough wrappings— "pigs'n blankets"—were left on the table to grow cold and serve as a snack.

This spring, the Penners gathered with Isaiah Gardener and his flock of children along with the Ezekiel Senior and Junior families, which put a lot of nieces and nephews in the small farmhouse with Susanna and Mary.

Aunt Susanna was engaged to be married that summer in name and date only. The Old Colony and Old Order Mennonites did not believe in wearing jewelry.

"Susan is very good with children," Grossmam always said. "She will make a fine mother one day."

Besides cooking for those working in the garage, the two young women tried to keep a houseload of youngsters entertained. Susanna got out a large ice cream pail of buttons and divided them up between the fifteen children above the age of eating them.

"This is money," she declared. "I am paying you to be good. If you misbehave, it will cost you, and if you spend all your buttons, come see me and you can earn more."

"B-but I'd rather have money!" Johan Penner spluttered.

"We're playing. Now," she said, her blue eyes twinkling," who wants to buy a cookie? I charge two large buttons or three small for each jam-jam."

After a cookie and a glass of raw milk, Susanna offered to show everyone her wedding dress.

They crowded into the sitting room of the girls heavily decorated bedroom to view the black brocade dress made like the plain dress she wore, only with black buttons down the front of the bodice instead of an obscured zipper in the back. It was knee length, with accordion pleats in the skirt and sleeves down to the wrist, ending in a buttoned cuff.

"That's thick material," Johan lamented. Then he looked up and pointed to Brenda-Jane. "I'm gonna marry Branna when I grow up."

Susanna laughed as Brenda-Jane cringed.

"You can't marry your cousin. Not first anyway."

"Why not? Earnest and I, we can make her if she—"

"You are too closely related." She folded her dress up firmly.

"*Nee mean* ovence klite (Now my evening dress)." She shook out a cotton burgundy dress, identical in style. The custom was to change out of pitch-black wedding attire and slip into a lighter colored dress and matching shirt made from thinner material by mid-wedding day. The bride to be sewed the shirt for the groom out of the same material as her dress. Often, that was the sign of the engagement, going around half-dressed half-alike in the weeks before the wedding day.

Brenda-Jane loathed the darkness of her aunt's clothing.

"How come God doesn't want women to be pretty?" she blurted out. Aunt Susanna frowned and shooed all the children out of her plastic flower bedecked room.

The next thing Brenda knew, she was sent to the slaughterhouse to help scrape the membrane out of the pig guts turned inside out. First, they were rinsed with a water hose and then the mucus membrane scraped carefully from the slippery intestinal wall to prepare them for their purpose as sausage containment.

Each family butchered two pigs; one was divided up to pay the laborers so that every family had fresh meat no matter whose pigs they slaughtered.

"Are you going to take some "varscht" (sausage) to your teacher?" Mother asked Brenda-Jane sweetly.

"How are my children doing?" Aunt Tina asked. Uncle Isaiah and his missus had five children in as many years of marriage.

Brenda-Jane pondered. She hadn't paid attention to the sleeping babies nor the menagerie of toddlers in the farmhouse, so she lifted her shoulders and let them sag in an I don't know gesture. "Speak when you are spoken to!" Mother snapped. "You haven't fallen on your mouth yet!"

"Um, they were sleeping and playing," Brenda-Jane stuttered.

Fieldarp slowly dried up enough for Brenda-Jane and Marlene to ride their bicycles to the end of the driveway and back up to Mother's big lilac tree in front of the house. The sun shone longer and brighter, warming the icy spring winds that once pierced the down-filled coat.

Brenda-Jane took to hiking out to the back pasture, past the goat-barn, down a small treed valley, and over a hand-hewn footbridge, up the other forested side and into the sunshine beyond to the horse pasture where Little Red, Star, and Blizzard were kept.

Busily daydreaming of swirling dresses with rainbow colored skirts and eating the last of her Easter candy, Brenda jumped when a voice spoke.

"I think the horses are in heat," Earnest and Johan approached on horseback, passing through the Gardener field.

"Yah. Look how they are lifting their tails and sticking out their ass. One day, I'll make you do that," Johan pitched from his bareback stance.

"I will tell your Dad what you said," Brenda retorted. Their faces blanched.

"Let's go." With a clicking noise in the back of their mouths, the boys urged their mounts forward.

CHAPTER 49

Stampede

THE HORSES were restless. A fourth unfamiliar beast had joined the three—a male. Star was a gelding, and there was nothing he could do but keep moving in nervous circles away from the two jostling females.

The strange horse raised his gray head high and nickered loudly, deliberately, at length. They moved faster now, and suddenly, Brenda-Jane recognized him as "King," a Heinz 57 from the Benjamen farm. He was rumored to have a vicious nature and to be untamed. King reared up and pawed the air with his front hooves, neighing magnificently. He wasn't about to service anyone without putting on a show.

Brenda-Jane grew ill at ease and turned to run back to the yard. She hadn't gone far when she heard hoof beats beating the ground behind her. Over her shoulder, she saw the four drifting in a line that headed toward her.

Panic turned her steps to a bolt. The hooves beat faster also.

A sputtering engine roared from the encompassment of the forest that housed the hoof-bridge. Father drove up on the Yamaha trike.

Brenda-Jane veered right and dashed for her father's protection. In her wake, the horses ran left, away from the struggling yellow machine.

She looked up for reassurance and a ride on the seat behind him out of the hormonal equine madness, but Father was furious, every vein in his spectacled face bulging.

"I have been looking all over this blasted world for you, and you were nowhere to be found! How are we to help you if anything happens?" he sprayed, epiglottis vibrating.

Brenda-Jane motioned toward the three-wheeler, but he gunned the engine and blew off in a cloud of blue-gray smoke. The horses had wound a tight circle and were circumnavigating back to her. Running until her ribs ached, she half-expected to be stomped to the soil and to her demise at any moment. The trees blurred, came to focus, and blurred again as hoof beats thundered and the ground shook.

She dove for the trees and tripped and fell on a weathered ladder half-hidden in the woods. Jerking it upright, she propped it up on the birch beside her and to climb up to the platform left behind by the Henry kids.

Her arms strained to pull her weight up the last two feet the ladder didn't span up to as the horses veered another circle in her direction. Brenda mustered one last bout of adrenalin, hoisted herself up, and collapsed on the flimsy slats, gasping for air.

Anger welled up in her throat over her father's behavior. He didn't know where she was now either, or she rebelled at the notion to hurry back to ease anyone's curiosity as to her whereabouts. Screw them, she thought, trying not to cry and failing. He had abandoned her to a field full of restless, unpredictable horses to whatever may come.

Brenda-Jane didn't know how many hours passed after her adrenalin slowed, and she drifted to sleep.

The sun was casting extended shadows by the time she awoke and scrambled down the ladder hurriedly.

According to the light, she was late for "ovenkust" (supper).

The rest of the family was seated when Brenda-Jane entered the kitchen of silence and tension. The atmosphere was thicker than the" keel chee" (thick noodles in buttermilk) they were all quietly spooning in.

Although Brenda-Jane's place was set as usual, it was clear she was being shunned for what Father had told the family. As a result, and not for the first nor last time, she felt as though she was on the outside looking in.

To escape the terse environment, she crawled deep inside her thoughts and concocted a story she would write at school for Ms. Whittingham's pleasure. It was an anecdote of a young girl who ran away from home to live in the woods just a few miles away, so she still had access to her mother's garden and cold storage for food.

She lived in a willow sapling teepee and crept in and out of the farmhouse on Saturday afternoons to steal food and clothing out of the rag box.

The idea so gripped Brenda-Jane she decided to make a runaway package and stash it away in her red Saskatchewan duffel bag in case she ever eloped for real.

She would find an old Cheese Whiz jar for holding water, baler twine for tying her willow sticks together, books to keep her company in the solitude, Margaret's old rain poncho, an old sheet, and a long dress from the rag box. When she finished her incomplete survival kit, Brenda shoved it under her bed and pulled her bedspread down lower to cover the legs of her box mattress away from Mother's prying hands and snooping eyes.

CHAPTER 50

Second Cousins

SPRINGTIME WAS over when the baby chicks Mother and Father had housed in the basement were ready to move outside into their own coop. The plastic wading pool was washed out and carefully dried and filled with straw and baby chicks at Easter. The makeshift pen was kept warm by a red heating bulb that hung from the beams down to the center of the pool.

Even though the little balls of fluff with small black eyes and tiny clawed feet faintly peeped and seemed so delicate, they had a meanness for an injured gosling among them. If a chick got hurt and hobbled around, he instantly drew attention to himself and got pecked on.

Mother had to remove the injured bird and keep it in quarantine in Father's tin lunch kit until it was well enough to rejoin the flock, or if it declined, it had its neck wrung.

When the shipment of baby chickens arrived by bus in Eagle Creek, Father picked them up and brought the peeping perforated flats home in time for Easter.

"Eagle Sheet" (Eagle's shit), as the Mennonites called the hamlet nestled along the North River, named after a large rock, that had once housed an Eagle's nest. Or so the story went according to the local natives.

Eagles Creek was a drab little place that included a liquor store with grates covering its minute windows: a grocery store that also held a post office and sold gasoline, and a stucco-sided hotel that leaned toward the river. And of course, there was the old hospital right on the main, not to mention a bank with slat-bar windows that leaned into the hill behind it as if for protection.

Brenda-Jane and Marlene spent hours huddled over the wading pool, scooping up one peeping fuzzy baby to another and cuddling them. It was fun to stroke their yellow fluff until their eyes slid shut and flimsy legs gave way underneath them.

"I had to get them away from the Indians before they turned brown," Father joked with their mother.

"Oh! I don't know why there ever had to be Indians!" Mother explained. "People like that will never be saved."

"Um-hmm! Um-hmm!" Father agreed.

Unbeknownst to them, mother's cousin Eva Gruenwald, a single mom of a daughter who worked at the local cafe with her, also had a son from an aboriginal. It was rumored in whispers that she was hiding her son as much from the public eye as she could, as far as Hatchet Prairie went. He was shipped to school in Eagle Creek with his relatives, and his father was rarely seen in the upright position.

The knowledge came as a shock when Eva called to ask for a visit one Sunday after church. When they arrived, a boy between the ages of Brenda-Jane and Margaret stood shyly between his mother and thirteen-year-old sister.

Cousin Eva introduced Jacob Benjamen Gruenwald to them all for the first time, a very Indian looking boy indeed. He had thick black hair cut short into a brush cut, glasses, big lips, and big square white teeth.

Sometimes, Father and Margaret sang a song called "The Indian's Place" while they milked the cows. All Brenda-Jane could remember, looking at her unlikely relative was part of the chorus that went:

> "Son don't go near the Indian's place
> stay away.
> Son don't go near the Indian's place.
> Do what I say."

Margaret sometimes screeched a jauntier tune.

> "One little two little three little Indians,
> Four little five little Indians…"

All the way to a triumphant shout. "TEN LITTLE INDIAN BOYS!" Apparently, someone had not heeded their parental warning.

Both Eva and her daughter Maria had pale-colored complexions, cornflower blue eyes, and almost white blonde hair.

"Well, c'mon, take your guests to the hayloft and show them the baby kittens," Mother coaxed.

"Don't be wallflowers." There was a hard edge in her voice that she meant business.

"Cowce du mat forn?" (Can you ride along?) were the first words out of Maria's mouth to Margaret.

"Mat forn" was the female in dating among Mennonites. "Girlin' forn" was the male role. As soon as boys turned fourteen, they got their learners, and at sixteen, their driver's license. The family vehicle was borrowed on Sundays until the son could afford his own and he drove to the homes of eligible females and asked to take her for a ride. Usually, several boys travelled together and gathered a girl per stop until everyone was matched.

Alcohol was often a factor in the drive by dating game, and many Mennonite girls were pregnant on their altarless wedding day.

"I can go next year, when I'm fourteen," Marie argued. "Mom says."

Margaret was twelve and wanted a boyfriend badly. She often pretended to be wrestling and giggling with one in her bed after dusk. Brenda-Jane overheard her once at bedtime and asked her about it but got told to mind her own beeswax.

Jacob didn't speak much German, so the visit was kept English speaking while he was within earshot.

"What are their names?" He sank to the straw-covered floor in amazement. Upon learning they had none, he proceeded to name them all after Disney characters. "That one is Donald Duck, that one is Daisy." He pointed.

The girls giggled. "You have to check and make sure if they are boy or girl." Brenda-Jane grasped a kitten and turned it upside down to show him. "See the two bumps? That's a boy."

Jacob's credulousness with farm life grew as did theirs with their proximity to a real-life Indian. His skin was a rich dark brown and his glassed eyes nearly black in the dimly lit hayloft. He reached and pulled a tiny tail.

"Don't do that, Jake the headache!" Maria berated him.

"Hey! Mom said—"

"Well then, don't do that."

"You're not the boss of me!" he retorted but lifted the baby kitten by its belly instead and brought it to himself, me-yowling all the way.

The girls took their company to the goat barn next, showing off a little.

"C'mon, let's go visit the treehouse the hoodlums made," Brenda suggested. Jacob looked fascinated and scrambled to his feet in anticipation.

Margaret shot her a withering look of pure jealousy. "Off-vesah" (Show off), she snarled under her breath. With that, she led the way down the packed dirt trail toward the slat barn.

"So, when can you?" Maria prodded Margaret.

"Vanneyeah coss du mat forn?" (When can you ride along?)

"Ah!" Jacob covered his ears and bolted ahead of them, chanting. "Mat forn! Mat forn! Blech!" (Ride along, ride along! Yuck!)

He lacked the Mennonite German so greatly they all giggled at his phlegm-less pronunciation.

"Ack vite nicht" (I don't know), Margaret answered wistfully.

Maria's mother did not attend church nor wear a babushka, and many locals frowned on it. The kerchief was worn by the women to show marital status, submissiveness to their husband and church, or just plain sexual activity.

"I don't care if I get pregnant," Maria chirped on, pausing to push her blouse into her skirt. "I'll just wear a dueck, (kerchief) on my wedding day!"

Another purpose of the unforgiving headgear—to reveal sexual activity to the church during the process of joining the membership by getting baptized. After the customary eight weeks in the pastor's study with the High German catechism, the navy, brown, and black-clad young men and women began marching behind the pastors to sit in the front row. Catechism study was done during the church service in question and answer format. The young women who had succumbed to her boyfriend's sexual overtures wore a kerchief while he was hidden in the lineup on the men's side, not even placed adjacent to her to reveal who he was.

"Why are the men allowed to wear all color suits and nothing for their part in the deed?" Mother often fumed. "My brother Corky said they should have to wear a ribbon on their fly."

Brenda could just picture poor Corky with a stream of ribbons flowing from his middle fit to join a powwow.

A Mennonite youngster caught an early that romantic affection was the only kind allotted so to get that need met, you got involved in a relationship as soon as able. The only other physical contact was violence from a punitive parent.

CHAPTER 51

Negative Prophesy

THE DISTINCT "Hoy!" from Father notified them of faspa time.

Cousin Aunt Eva wore store-bought clothes and dressed her children the same. Her blonde hair was permed and hugged her round face gently.

"Who has goat dung on their shoes?" Mother announced loudly, peering at Brenda-Jane.

"Something smells wunderbar!" (wonderful, sarcasm).

Mother notoriously did her best to humiliate her children in front of the guests, especially Margaret and Brenda-Jane.

Jacob giggled. "What's vunder-bar?"

"Did you wear boots? Did you change your boots at the door?" Mother persisted.

Brenda-Jane sensed Margaret's head hang from her position on the bench beside her while her own face burned. She wished the creaking floor would break into a total abyss beneath her, but of course, the linoleum-clad stage made no gesture to rescue the ashamed.

Satisfied with her disgrace fix, Mother turned to her cousin. "Have you heard about Uncle John's cancer?"

Father sat at the head of the table, staring at Cousin Eva's ample chest, smiling pinkly to himself. "How do you like our farm?" Father refocused on Jacob, who had a mouthful of cold, canned sausage.

"Do you know we make most of our own food here?" Father continued.

"Woo." Jacob breathed.

"Would you, maybe, like to come and stay with us for dis somer?" Father's German accent colored his English.

The boy's eyes widened, and he looked at his beaming mother. He swallowed.

"What would I call you?" he addressed Father, who chuckled out loud.

"I gas you could call me Uncle Zeke."

Eva's large round blue eyes sparkled. "You're lucky to have a family."

"Well, you could have been widowed," Mother offered generously.

"Jakey" was eight years old and growing to be a regular handful for his single mother. The purpose of her visit to the farm in her old brown Chrysler New Yorker had been to find a father figure for her son.

"Sure, could use a hand around here," Father boomed jovially.

"It's another mouth to feed," Mother snapped after the gargantuan vehicle had rolled away quietly.

"I wouldn't have had an Indian kid. I would've made sure it didn't stay." Her voice trailed off as she glanced at her children.

Father was immovably for Jacob coming to stay at the farm for the summer.

Feeling dejected by all the commotion over a boy from another family, Brenda-Jane crept closer to her mother, hoping for a morsel of affection.

Mother noticed and jerked away. “Get away from me, you homosexual! Hey! Do something about that kid, will you?”

Father turned and glared so fiercely at Brenda-Jane she wished she was never born.

“Honestly! I don’t know what I will do with such an evil girl some days!” Mother spat. Brenda-Jane found her rattling yellow bicycle and went for a bike ride. The road had dried enough for two packed wheel marks to form and make for a smooth journey past the Timber place. From the dirt road, through a clearing above the pond, she could see the Benjamens sitting around a bonfire.

Although she couldn’t hear what they were saying, the sounds that filtered through the tree branches were happy. Whoops and laughter chased each other in the cool springtime dusk.

Soon, strawberries would bloom their tiny white flowers with fuzzy yellow centers. Purple fireweed would grow, and goldenrod and white-flowered chamomile would grow right along with it in the ditches lining the fields.

A bright red object lay on the road, starkly contrasting with the mottled, dull colors of the dirt and gravel road. Brenda-Jane picked it up an empty DuMaurier cigarette case with a blonde lady’s head on the cover, wearing a blue hat that matched her eyes. Brenda tucked the pretty paper in her pocket and headed home.

"WHAT DO YOU HAVE THERE?" Mother demanded when Brenda-Jane entered the kitchen, hands in her pockets. "Show me!" she demanded.

Brenda-Jane reluctantly pulled her find out of her pocket and laid it on the kitchen table where Father and Mother sat drinking tea.

"Foy! Shmeet dot vaych!" (Gross! Throw that out!)

Brenda did as she was ordered, stepping on the brown pedal of the green metal garbage can to open the lid.

"Those who smoke should just give that money to me," Mother remarked tersely.

It was bedtime. They washed their feet in the foot bowl one at a time, and then Margaret lifted the oval yellow plastic vessel and carefully dumped it in the toilet.

The girls went to bed without brushing their teeth or exchanging affection with their parents.

Ms. Whittingham had given everyone a toothbrush, tube of toothpaste, and a Styrofoam cup with their name inscribed on it. After lunch, she insisted on everyone trekking to their gender respective bathrooms and performing this rite of personal hygiene.

Just before suppertime, Father would line everybody up behind him at the washroom door by the light switch. The light and fan control being outside the washroom made for great pranks for the child in the hallway. For the unfortunate on the pot—not so much.

In spite of the cistern having been added to the indoor plumbing, water was still a controlled substance. The bathtub could only be filled a quarter of the way, one could not flush the toilet without Mother bellowing from the kitchen to stop wasting the water, and a basin of water was reused in the sink.

As spring faded into a dusty prairie summer, the water Father left in the moss green plastic wash bowl grew muddier. Margaret washed next, then Marlene, and then Brenda-Jane.

Once summer afternoon, exasperated with the arrangement, Brenda-Jane burst out with, "Dad, you should go last—you're the dirtiest!"

His beady blue eyes turned steel cold, and he turned to her with an icy voice. "If you don't learn to obey, you're never gonna amount to anything. You are going to be nothing but a criminal and a divorcee."

The words poured through her like dirty wash water until she was soaked to the spirit. Despondent, Brenda slunk away and walked to the supper table and took her place.

Mother's fist-sized perogies filled with cottage cheese were delicious and mealy. There was a choice of choice toppings, either cream gravy or cooked strawberries in their own sauce. "Soon you'll bring me wild strawberries, won't you?" Mother purred to Brenda-Jane.

CHAPTER 52

Home On the Strange

ON SUNDAY mornings, sweet-faced Aunt Susanna took her black shod place at the front of the church to join the membership. The baptismal candidates on the female side of the congregation were usually engaged to their male counterparts across the aisle but seated in no particular order. Rarely did one sign on for the process without the intention to marry. That simply was the system.

"Why do people only get baptized to get married?" Brenda-Jane scoffed out loud one day.

"Brenda-Jane Gardener! That is evil! Evil child!" Mother exclaimed. "Is that a Godly child?!"

Father pondered for a moment. "At baptism, you decide to change your life and live better for Jesus. What better time than is there to get married when you are changing your lifestyle anyway? They both change your life."

"Really?" Mother sneered at him. "You changed your lifestyle when we got married? Seems to me you do whatever you feel like!"

"I'm the head of this family!" he bellowed.

That week, Father loaded the grain truck with firewood and took Mother with him into town. He was off to an auction, and she was writing a learner's test to get her license so she could drive the old sea green-blue Ford pickup to the homestead and back.

"Wish me luck?" she chirped happily as she stepped up to the running board of the red international.

The girls all said yes and waved them off.

"Now," Margaret announced cheerily. "Let's clean house. Mom will be surprised when she gets back." And as ever, Margaret couldn't function without singing, as it were.

"The more we get together, together, together, the more we get together, the happier we'll be!"

"You sound like a Billy Goat," Brenda-Jane dared. And the fight was on. White faced and enraged, Margaret turned, bulging eyes to Brenda.

"You! You are not a Christian! You are the reason for the problems this family has! You're the worst kind of all—"

"Fine. Clean the house by yourself then." Brenda-Jane tossed her rag to Margaret, and it flattened across her freckled face in a wet spatter.

Brenda-Jane took a Tupperware container and escaped to the pasture to look for wild strawberries. Truth be told, she was afraid of Margaret's vicious temper and ox like strength. Hence her method was to tease the bull, tuck in her red cape, and hightail it away.

Ms. Whittingham added dancing to the music class that she taught. Everyone made a circle by placing their hands on the shoulders of the person ahead of them. Instantly, Brenda-Jane was uncomfortably with the proximity of her cousin Johan and the barn odor that hung in the air. The record started.

"Did you ever see a lassie, a lassie, a lassie? Did you ever see a lassie go this way and that?" Instead of doing the bunny-hop, Ms. Whittingham showed them how to step right and then left, making the circle expand and contract.

She taught the class "Home on the Range." It was a pretty lullaby, and when the words "Where seldom is heard a discouraging word" came, Brenda-Jane remembered her father's curse.

After class, she sidled up to Ms. Whittingham's desk. "What's a criminal?" she asked timidly. "Spell what?" Ms. Whittingham leaned closer. She smelled of fresh lavender soap and Head and Shoulders shampoo.

"N-no. I need to find out—what's a criminal?" She could feel her face start to burn. Like the entire class must be scrutinizing her and wondering what sort of clown she was.

"Oh! A criminal is someone who breaks the law—the rules," she explained.

"And a divorcee?" Brenda-Jane pushed on.

A rare frown crossed Ms. Whittingham's porcelain doll complexion.

"It's someone who decides not to be married anymore," she answered thoughtfully. "Are you reading library books from the wrong section?"

Brenda-Jane hung her head, shaking it no. "Mmm." Ms. Whittingham studied her.

Emmet Benjamen barreled up to the desk, tripped on his shoelaces, and landed, kneeling with his face parallel to the garbage can.

"What says this?" He still managed to hold up his reader.

The class dissolved in laughter at his dedication to the Dick and Jane story, and Brenda managed to slip back to her seat, relieved.

CHAPTER 53

Scapegoats

MS. WHITTINGHAM got called to the principal's office later the week after the class danced the circular bunny hop and returned, crying.

The class was busy reading a chapter in *Pets and Puppets* when she sank into her desk wearing her pastel striped dress and full skirt. Brenda-Jane sensed the flood near the rainbow-clad elementary school teacher.

She watched Ms. Whittingham barely moving, drawing tissues out of the bright orange plastic box and wiping her eyes.

One by one, like silent dominoes connecting and falling, the class raised their heads, some riddled with dandruff and head stink from lack of washing and noticed their teacher. It was awestriking to see the vibrant beautiful porcelain doll in motion so still and so sad.

Alarm spread long hairy fingers across Brenda-Jane's middle and squeezed. Uncomfortable warmth expanded from her belly to the rest of her innards, surging to her skin. Ms. Whittingham oversaw happiness, sunshine, and bright colors, so what had happened to the flagrant first grade instructor?

Chill replaced the prickly warmth and raised the hairs on the back of her neck. Mother had crying spells, not Ms. Whittingham!

Ms. Whittingham glanced up, ran her red-rimmed jewel-like blue eyes around the room, and startled a little.

"Would you guys like to listen to a record?" she asked in a falsetto voice.

"Yes!" they all chorused. Sniffling, she got up to oblige them, and soon, the familiar crackle of a needle on an imperfect vinyl track led to "A Farmer in the Dell" and "O Susanna."

Rumor was a parent of one of the Old Colony children had complained about the dancing in music class resulting in the meeting between Mr. Shale and the first-grade teacher. Another whispered version hinted of the termination of the vivacious Vivian Whittingham.

"Our teacher cried today," Brenda-Jane told Mother and Father over supper. No one spoke, only chewed their hamburgers, and stared down at their plates full of burgers, mashed potatoes, peas, and browned cream gravy.

She tried again. "Ms. Whittingham cried today during school."

"You'd cry too if you had a rotten girl like you!" Mother snapped, glaring ferociously over the table. Brenda shrank into herself and wished she were invisible, not merely treated that way.

Jake joined the Gardener family for a week as a trial visit with his new mentor, Father.

"What should I call you?" he quizzed Father in the garden as they all worked, pressing beans into zigzag pattern in the ground.

"Does God have a wife? Uncle Zeke?"

Father had built a wooden plow with three stakes at the end to dig three garden rows at a time.

He hitched himself and Mother to it, and they pulled so hard Mother's wallpaper-flowered dress stretched tight against her back.

Brenda-Jane and Marlene planted peas and beans after Mother taught them how place the seeds two-and-a-half inches apart in a diamond pattern.

"Whoa! They look like peas, only shriveled up!" Jacob breathed.

Skipper and Shadow sniffed him curiously. The pup had grown to be a big strapping German shepherd who still held his head slightly tilted from Smelly Cornelly running over him with his pickup truck. Shadow was getting old and grouchy, showing his yellow teeth a lot.

"Why do you zigzag them?" Jake wanted to know. "Do plants know how they are planted?" Everyone chuckled at that.

Margaret burst into raucous song:

> "I've been working on the railroad, all the livelong day! I've been working on the raaaaaaaaaayelroad, just to pass the time away!
> Can't you hear the whistle blowing?
> Rise up so early in the morn!
> Can't you hear the captain shouting!

Dinah! Blow your horn!"

Corn was sown three seeds to a shallow hole dug by one smooth motion of Mother's hoe.

"One for pleasure, one for waste, and one for good measure," mother chuckled.

They planted sweet pea, flowers, petunias, dwarf petunias, striped petunias, flocks, and poppies in the discarded tractor tires painted white near the driveway in front of the house.

"How come we never plant black-eyed susans?" Brenda-Jane wanted to know.

"Because your grandmother only plants those!" Mother snarled.

They carried the seedling tomato plants from the house in reused tin cans filled with dirt out to the garden.

When each row was done, Mother took a broken slab from a picket fence and shoved it straight through the empty seed packet and into the end of the row it represented.

Father ran a hose to a tall sprinkler on a rebar pole stuck in the ground in the middle of the vast garden. Water was drawn from the tank on the wagon parked beside the upturned soil, and the sprinkler head was rigged to reach the far corners thereof.

The warm sunshine and Jacob's excited chatter urged them on to finish the planting of the potato patch using sprouted spuds from the previous year. Some of the larger were cut in half and placed in the hole, raw side down.

Late spring cast fervent rays through the single-paned church windows, stifling the baptismal candidates in their swarthy attire. Most carried a handkerchief in case the sermon of that particular morning drew tears of repentance, but now, they patted their perspiring faces.

"If you are good enough to be accepted into God's kingdom, those ends of hair you once cut off on earth will one day be much needed in heaven," Pastor Jacobson droned at the women.

Jacob sat beside Father on the men's side, silent, wide eyed, and credulous all the way home.

"Man alive! What was he saying to make all the ladies cry?" Jake exclaimed.

"Picking on them," Mother remarked dryly.

"I couldn't understand a thing he was saying! Uncle Zeke, was that German again?"

"High German." Father chuckled at his shirttail nephew. "We speak Low German all week and High German in church."

"The singing was awful," Jacob continued.

A rueful smile tugged at the corners of Mother's mouth, and she quickly hid it with the back of her hand. Father flushed pink with discomfort and smiled his slippery smile that he wore whenever he forced the girls to embrace or was about to beat them.

"What's the difference between High German and Low German?" Jake pestered on.

"High German," Brenda-Jane squeaked in a falsetto. "Low German." She ended in a gruff voice.

"Brenda!" But everyone laughed. Even Mother, once she had glanced Father's way and saw that he was.

"You're bluffing!" Jacob challenged.

Dinner was cooked chicken and mashed potatoes with the chicken-water as gravy. Their guest puckered up with disgust when Mother grabbed the foot, claws and all, and plopped it on Brenda's plate.

"You love the feet, don't you?" Mother poured in her syrup-smooth tone usually reserved for company. Brenda nodded to keep her happy.

"Here. Have both."

Jacob's amazement over farm life and religion dissolved into disgust. "I can't eat that!"

A hard expression crossed Mother's face. Father opened his mouth. "Well, if you don't—"

"What? We're gonna treat children differently under the same roof now? Listen, just try it. You must try the food before you know if you'll like it, okay?" Mother had an edge to her cheery suggestion.

The young boy's dark expression blanched, and he slid back on the bench. Meekly, he received the cooked peas, juicy breast meat, and chicken fat gravy all over his potatoes.

Watching him try to use the salt and pepper shakers was a nearly painful experience. He picked them up carefully, examined them like a geologist does a fossil, and then tried to hold one like a cigarette between his thumb and index finger. He tapped it with his pointer and managed to speckle his potatoes sparsely in turn.

CHAPTER 54

Sunday Again

THE WILD strawberry crops came in full in the ditches between the driveway and garden, in the main pasture, and along the dirt and gravel road around Fieldarp.

Brenda picked everyone she found with the anticipation of the naturally sweet jam mother would make of them. When they showed up on the school playground, the berries provided nourishment for the raiding school children at recess.

After dinner, father took Jacob and Marlene outside to play catch with a baseball while mother, Margaret and Brenda-Jane cleaned up.

"I don't know what Eva was thinking, sending her son over here and then asking how I stay so thin. Hah! As if more work will fatten me up like her?" Mother scoffed. Her tirade continued with how she suspected Eva had the hots for Father even though he was ugly and fat. How food was her enemy and she couldn't eat like everyone else did. Why couldn't people understand that?

"You always look nice, Mom," Margaret soothed.

"They're just jealous, Mom. That's all," Brenda-Jane declared, drying a pink glass serving bowl that had held red Jell-O for dessert. Margaret drew her arm back as she lifted a pot and bumped BrendaJane, knocking the pink bowl to an explosion on the floor. Glass flew everywhere across the kitchen's perimeter.

"Brenda Jane Gardener!" Mother yelled, slapping her about the head viciously. "You are the reason this family does so poorly, and then you go and do a thing like that! We have nothing as it is! That bowl was a wedding gift from my folks! Now go get me the broom and dustpan!"

Crying, Brenda-Jane crunched over the broken glass in her Sunday shoes to the unfinished broom closet without a door. Quivering, she picked up the moss green metal dustpan and broom.

"Hurry up! Before we all cut our feet open!" Mother stood in true Mennonite stance, high-heeled patent leather white pumps slightly apart with her toes pointed outward.

Margaret stood ashen, blue eyes gawking at Brenda-Jane, her face twisting in disgust.

Brenda-Jane started sweeping the drinking fragments of glass together. Mother shot forward and grabbed the handle. Instinctively, Brenda flinched back.

"Go!" Mother shouted hoarsely.

Brenda needed no second bidding to escape the tension in the kitchen, and fled to the treehouse between the pastures, past the now empty spot that once housed the goat barn. Father had sold "the seven dwarfs" and their mother "Snow White," whose former barn was now the chicken coop.

Dress and all, Brenda-Jane hauled herself up to the platform. She remembered Psalm 27:10 from her leather-bound little testament. "When my father and my mother forsake me, then the Lord will take me up.'

Sniffling and wiping her tears with the back of her hand, Brenda tried to sing, but her voice cracked and wobbled. Above her, a robin chirped, "Dur-reet! Dur-reet! Dur-reet! Wheedle wheedle."

Sadness never lingered long when Brenda was off by herself in the midst of animals or nature. Time slipped away, quickly swallowed by the melody of birds freely warbling to an unbridled tune. She decided to lapse into a fantasy world, calling the domain surrounding her the "magical forest."

Fairies in long, flowing translucent gowns and gossamer wings floated in and out of sight, weaving in between the trees.

No! No. She must not play magic nor fairy lest she slip and tell Marlene as they played and then end. up getting into trouble.

A squirrel chirped and chattered on a branch near her. Catching her breath, Brenda Jane rose to her feet slowly. If only she could touch him—what a pet to have! She could see his rapid heartbeat as she leaned over, stretching out her hand to grasp him. He was so close she could see his small round black eyes like the buttons on mother's black church sweater.

Yeek keek keek keek! He scolded and dashed past her down the tree with his tiny feet so fast he was a blur.

A familiar bellow from the distance signaled Brenda to get herself home or else. She scrambled the ladder, ripped her pantyhose, and landed clumsily on her patent shod feet.

After a rain, the robin would change his song to Deet! Deet! Deedelah deedelah deedelah! Brenda-Jane reminisced as she passed the spring calves frolicking near the barn, carefully stepping in between the cow pies.

"Eww, you smell funny." Mother shied away from her as soon as Brenda stepped into the kitchen where Cousin Eva sat in her Sears catalogue dress. She had arrived to pick up her offspring after a Sunday visit and looked for all the world like an argument between a sailor and a pilgrim with her blue pin stripped ensemble and huge white collar. Mother was slicing pickles in preparation for faspa and jawing about something as usual.

Brenda noticed Eva didn't have hairy legs like all the women of the Mennonite culture did. Bodily hair was allowed to grow freely, and rumor had it, doctors shaved those child-birthing candidates just before delivery.

Mother had dark hairs showing through her support hose, standing against the counter with her high heels together and toes apart.

"Did you step in cow dung?" Mother asked sweetly. She wasn't about to drop the opportunity to embarrass Brenda-Jane in front of company; it was as tradition as peanut butter for faspa.

"No." She tried not to snap at Mother for fear of future reprical but wasn't going to cooperate with the game either. "I always know when my shoes are dirty, and when they are, I shuck them by the door, MOM."

"Set the table then!" Mother ordered. Brenda obliged, getting out the Blue Onion Corelle dishes and the matching mugs for the adults.

"My Marlene is going far if she keeps up." Mother began one of her "Marlene, my favorite child, is meant for greater things" spiels.

"Oh?" Eva politely asked.

"Well, she's so kind and loving, intelligent, and generous. Not like—" Mother shot Brenda-Jane a glance silently. "Aren't you done yet?" she snipped.

"Almost." Brenda hadn't done the cutlery yet, and she hurried to finish the chore to escape the "Marlene is the next Princess Diana" speech.

In the living room, Jake, Margaret, Marlene, and Father were engaged in a game of Battleship. Brenda retreated to her room to read *Johnny* Wondernose before it was due back to the school library.

Jacob's older sister was on a date, her mother answered the question on her absence proudly over her chocolate cake and white icing.

After the guests had left, disgust ran rampantly in hand with judgement.

"Hasn't she had enough trouble without turning her daughter into the same thing she is?!" Mother spat as she washed the faspa dishes and Father dried them. That was a rare feat.

Margaret was already outside, bleating, "Jesus Loves the Little Children," and swinging her empty tin milk pail.

"Red and yellow, black and white, all are precious in his sight. Jesus loves the little children of the world!"

"Ni yo," Father solemnly agreed with Mother in all piety.

The day's socializing wasn't over yet. A familiar royal blue Chevy Impala turned into the orange muslin-clad window; Mother groaned out loud.

"Zan di verklich heah?" (Are they really here?)

Two dark shapes emerged from the heavy metal, chromeless beast.

The girls ran to greet them. "Grossmam! Grosspabeh!" and stopped a step length back from Grandmother. No one touched so much as a hand because any public display of affection was strictly forbidden as a sin.

Company in the evening meant another round of faspa at bedtime, just before they left.

Grandpa paused on the top step of the deck and glanced at his three granddaughters. A grin crossed his chiseled face and lightened his blue eyes.

"Hello, boys," he teased as always.

Once seated stiffly on the black vinyl chesterfield, the church leaders wasted no time.

"I hear you have taken on an Indian boy," Grandfather spoke.

The girls knew better than to visibly hang around near adult conversation, so they scattered coloring books across the table within earshot.

"A boy needs a father, and a farm needs a boy," Father answered evenly.

"I thought we were deciding," Mother interjected.

"Help for you means work for me. I mean—you've already got Margaret outside." "Ass dot ein britt?" (Is that an Indian?) Grandmother asked pointedly.

Crayon encircled the ears of Mickey Mouse while the girls listened. The red crayon was labeled "Indian Red," but Mother had told them there was a fuss being raised about the designation.

"Big deal." She had sneered about the issue. But Brenda-Jane was sure if the black crayon was dubbed "Sunday go-meeting-black," there would have arisen a similar issue.

The conversation rotated around the sex life of Eva Gruenwald; had she worn a kerchief when she visited the Gardener farm? For indeed, she had when she was baptized but no longer attended church. Was there a man in her life now? But of course, no one had known about the other two. Perhaps Eva was looking to get married and pawning off her son would make it easier to attract another mate; after all, the daughter would soon be out of the house and married off.

Gossip wafted down the hallway long after night lunch had been cleared away, but Brenda's curiosity could not even keep her awake.

CHAPTER 55

The Greenhorn

AFTER DELIBERATION, Grandmother and Grandfather must have blessed Jacob Gruenwald's presence onboard the Zeke junior farm, because he started showing up every weekend.

Rainy days slowed the activity of the farm down to a union speed. Everyone dropped the hectic pace to pick up a hobby or their handiwork. Father puttered in the garage with Margaret and Jacob tagging along with him.

Mother got out her liquid embroidery and sat down with Marlene and Brenda-Jane and taught them to "shade" by pushing a blending tool across a still wet, freshly marked surface past the original stain.

"The rain will sure help start the garden," Mother praised, hiding her relief at a reprieve from daily labor.

Marlene pricked her finger with a marking tool and started crying. Swiftly, Mother rose to her feet to the medicine cupboard above the fridge. Down came a tin of Band-Aids and a bottle of Maltlevol liquid vitamins.

"Here." Mother pulled the two tabs apart equally and smoothed the bandage around the wounded finger.

"Now take some of this." She poured some of the dark brown liquid into a transparent cup and offered it to Marlene.

"Brenda, you may as well take some too."

"Why?"

"To strengthen your nerves." That was the Gardener family way. Tears, like affection, were forbidden. One considered worldly, the other a sign of weakness requiring more vitamins.

Maltlevol warmed a path clear down into Brenda's stomach like fear and apprehension did. So, while the sky cried steadily on the shoulder of the Gardener estate, the heat from her gut reminded her she wasn't allowed.

Mother turned on the radio to Tradio as she did every Saturday afternoon on her flat cassette recorder player.

"Soon, you'll hear me on the radio." She beamed at her embroidery pupils. "Dad said I could put the old lawnmower for sale."

To make it more interesting, Mother high-heeled into the living room to Father's desk to use the white rotary phone instead of the wall-mounted black one in the kitchen. It was a running joke that the cord of the cook room telephone stretched longer with every use.

"Hello, you have reached Tradio," the male announcer answered in his baritone. The girls waited with bated breath.

"Yes, I'd like to place a lawnmower for sale?" she put on her best English voice.

"All right, what is the make and the price you are looking for?"

"It's a general electric brand, and we'd like fifty dollars, firm." Mother kept up her businesslike prattle.

"Okay, and the number to reach you at?" he prompted.

Mother's voice passed through the talking rectangular box on the counter one last time as she recited the Gardener home phone number.

"How did I sound?" she smiled broadly when she returned to the kitchen table. "Did I sound like the English?"

Vividly, the girls all nodded, causing Mother to smile even more.

After the Artex pens had been replaced in their upright tray and stashed in Mother and Father's bedroom closet, the girls played dress-up.

The cardboard trunk of miscellaneous clothing was kept on the floor of the doorless linen closet. Mostly it contained long dresses that Mother's sisters had given her that hadn't been shortened enough for anyone to wear yet.

Marlene pulled out a peach knit dress with an outlandish white collar and a lot of gathering around the bosom, giving the impression she had one. Brenda-Jane donned on a long beige cotton gown with brown piping around the collar, bell sleeves, and the hem. They rummaged to the bottom of the box for high-heeled shoes. Marlene found a block-heeled pair of pumps with a large gold buckle on the arch. Brenda chose the red pumps with spiked heels and a matching red clutch purse.

They hobbled gamely down the hall, holding up their drooping skirts and stepping in foreign footwear.

Mother chuckled at her sewing machine. "You pirate."

They traipsed through the house for a while, then revisited the cardboard container again. Marlene turned a large white purse with a gaudy gold buckle on it over her head and wore it as an Arabic turban. Brenda abandoned the dowdy beige ensemble for a red dress with tiny four-leaf clovers all over it and tied the belt around her head like a headband.

Mother got her 126 camera and struck a flash cube on top of it.

"Smile!" she took their picture standing against the pale paneling wall that held the kitchen phone with the curly cord dangling between them.

"Now quick! Go change before Dad and Jacob come in and see you," Mother urged, peering outside. "We mustn't encourage menfolk to stare at us," she warned.

Margaret, Father, and Jake came in for lunch, smelling of rain and speaking English.

Summer Borscht bubbled merrily on the stove as it boiled above the light and flaky shnetya (biscuits) Mother had warming in the oven.

"Just a few drops of water sprinkled among them, and they'll turn out like they were freshly made," she told no one in particular.

Eating Mother's soup was a treasure hunt in Grossmam's beige stoneware. Every vegetable known to be grown in the garden appeared as expected; the game was to recognize it in its cooked format.

Jacob pulled an assembly of herbal products out of his overnight bag and set them around his plate until it was wreathed in bottles.

He glanced up at the stares of the Gardener family.

"My mom wants me to take those," he said matter of fact.

Margaret picked them up one by one and read mock titles on the bottles. "Smart pills."

"Hey!"

"Muscle grower."

"It does not say that!"

"Don't wet the bed pills—" Jacob searched the snickering faces around him and relaxed. Quickly, he snatched up a bottle.

"Dumb girl pills—these must be yours," and he passed a bottle to Margaret labeled "Odorless Garlic."

"Ogre's Garlic—must be yours," she shot back.

Jacob was a complete city slicker and had to be taught every detail of the farm, including slopping the pigs.

Mother kept a "pig's pail," in the kitchen for potato peels, watermelon rinds, and assorted leftovers of each day. After supper, the pail went outside with Margaret and was dumped into the pig's trough along with water and shrout (shredded grain).

The rain stopped, and a rainbow had silently unfurled above Grandfather's wheat field. Marlene and Brenda-Jane donned on their rubber boots and trotted out with Father, Margaret, and Jacob across the drenched pig-weed-shrouded yard. The four pigs were lined up at the trough and grunting in anticipation.

Pigs were dirty creatures true to their reputation—for lack of alternatives. They stood in mud, lay in mud to cool off on a hot day, and never bathed like humans did. Highly unnoticed went their organization, however. They used a corner of their pen to eliminate, one as a napping area, ate at their trough in the third corner, and rooted in the fourth. The middle of the back fence was interrupted by their low-rise shelter, a building equal to the fence in height and weathered the same dark gray color.

"Are they dangerous?" Jacob queried, peering down at the four porkers.

An idea popped into Brenda's mind. She clamored up over the fence and dropped into the mire below.

"Of course not! You can ride them!"

"Ride them!" Everyone exclaimed simultaneously. All but Mother, who had stayed behind at her place of permanent residency as she so often put it—in front of the sink.

CHAPTER 56

Rodeo

BRENDA-JANE KNEW she could not back out now, not without demonstrating her harebrained idea once. She sidled up to Socks, the only black pig with white ankles, and scratched his back to relax him. When she thought he was least expectant of her ruse, she draped herself alongside his back and quickly wrapped her arms around him just behind his front legs. Socks made short history of his rider, depositing her into a mud puddle in the rooting corner.

"Let me try!" Let me try!" Margaret, Jacob, and Marlene pitched into the mire beneath them. Sally, Sue, and Sissy were the pink pigs that were once hard to distinguish from each other but now defined riders on their backs.

Pigs don't run in a straight line; they zigzag and circle. Sally ricocheted Jacob neatly into the slop trough with a sharp turn. Sissy ran with Margaret on her back to the door of the little barn and neatly scraped her off like a cheese slicer, but Margaret scrambled to her feet.

Marlene fared better, being lighter weight, but Sue dropped to her knees and slid her burden over her snout.

"All right, you guys." Father was laughing and wheezing so hard he could barely speak. "Leave them for another day. They've just eaten."

Brenda-Jane and Marlene returned to the house, happy, muddy, and reeking of pig while Father, Margaret, and Jacob ambled to the barn.

"Hold it!" Mother barked as they stepped on the baler twine rug in the porch. "I didn't clean all day just to have you kids muck up the house! Now back outside!"

Meekly, they obeyed. From their uncertain vantage point on the front porch deck, they shivered. Thunder grumbled from deep inside the trees, enshrouding Brenda-Jane's platform oasis.

"Here!" Mother emerged from the house of cooking soup and Lysol scent. She carried the faded orange foot bowl full of steaming, frosty colored water. Brenda-Jane knew the odor all too well. Dettol and Pine-Sol.

"Take those filthy clothes off!" No one moved. Brenda-Jane remembered her earlier instruction not to encourage males to gawk at them, glanced over at the barn and cringed.

Mother must have caught the thought, because she abruptly changed venues.

"Go around back," she ordered, retrieved her steaming shallow caldron.

On the paint-chipped deck off the living room where Mother maneuvered her clothesline on pulleys from, they stripped to their underwear and flinched while Mother roughly sanitized them. She used a piece of sackcloth that could have exfoliated a moose.

At the end of the bath, Mother had them wait, shivering like a pair of wet pups on the back stoop while she bought a second steaming bowl.

"Here." She laid two sets of clothing on the loose board of the deck, including panties. "Take your underwear off, sit in these for a while, dry yourselves on the towel, and then hurry up, get dressed, and come in."

Mother didn't stay and mock them as she customarily did with the chemical baths but, instead, withdrew into the house.

As soon as the fiery orange door shut behind her, the two made short work of the sitz bath. They pulled their panties down, squatted briefly, dashed the dreaded rag over themselves, and dried off to get dressed. That way, they could honestly say they had obeyed orders.

Thunder growled again, raising the hair on Skippy's neck. He and the two older dogs had joined the duo at the back deck but stayed at the foot of the stairs. Lightning flashed like the flash cube on Mother's 126 camera.

"God is taking our picture,' Brenda told Marlene, who promptly ran into the peach farmhouse.

The house had been decorated with remnants Mother and Father had picked up at auctions or been given by other farmers. Hence the pale peach siding, the burgundy trim around the windows, doors, and the heavy back door itself. The deck had been painted a red- brown once, but Brenda-Jane couldn't remember a time when the paint wasn't chipping and peeling.

"BRENDA-JANE!" The door behind her burst open, and Mother exploded from it.

"Telling Marlene that God took your picture?! That's blasphemy! A sin! A big, BIG sin! Don't ever let me hear you say such things again! Hear!?"

Swiftly, Mother dumped out the water from the wash bowls and collected the clothing before jerking the door shut behind her.

At night lunchtime, everyone watched Jacob stab his pig- in-a-blanket cautiously with his fork as if afraid.

"What does your mother feed you?!" Mother detonated again.

Jacob paled. His eyes looked like large brown marbles behind his strapped-on glasses. He ogled his plate, Mother, and his plate again.

"The Daniel diet," he struggled to say. "A-at home, we eat like Daniel—nuts, seeds, and berries. And a lot of oatmeal porridge."

Lightning cracked, knocking loose another downpour. The naked bulb above the table flickered and died. The power was out. Dusk settled over the house.

Next to rainy days, power outages were Brenda-Jane's favorite times.

A chair scraped. Mother got up and retrieved her stash of plain white candles from the drawer that held her wooden slide-top pencil box. A match scraped sandpaper; a flame rose and fell.

Expertly, Mother tipped the candle sideways to drip wax onto a saucer to hold the candle in place. Three candles later, they were eating by candlelight.

Brenda-Jane watched the flame and shadows compete for dominance across Mother's angular face, illuminating her cheekbones and darkening her cheeks. In this lighting, she looked ghoulish, sunken eyed and sallow faced. The horn-rimmed glasses added to the sinister appearance.

"Will you call it in, or shall I?" Mother said in English to Father.

Power outage meant several hours of cozy darkness, candlelight, and flashlights. Another break from the monotonous drudgery of farm work for the adults, thus more time spent with the children.

Brenda-Jane and Marlene wriggled under Marlene's bed with a flashlight and a Dick and Jane reader.

Mother couldn't wash the dishes or run the cream separator without power, so the house fell unusually silent as the parents retreated to a dusk lit window in the living room. Margaret and Jacob could be heard playing Battleship by candlelight on the freshly cleared kitchen table.

Outside, rain massaged the roof gently and patted the window of their bedroom while thunder rumbled from further away and lightning crackled with less fury. Electricity or none, the day was winding down to a snug resolution.

CHAPTER 57

Baptism

SUNDAY MORNING was an oddly somber, silent event instead of its usual auctioning off by Father.

Brenda-Jane and Marlene woke up, still curled up under the bed by the furnace vent.

"Girls," Father stomped into their bedroom, stepping on the clothes, books, toys.

"Today is baptism at the church. We won't have any Sunday school. All the children will join their parents in church or stay home with the oldest.

It was Aunt Susanna and her fiancée's baptismal day, however, and everyone knew better than to offer to stay home.

Mother wore her black wedding dress and bow-toed pumps for the occasion, with a black babushka made of veil material. Today, Susanna would wear her morning wedding dress for the first time and again on her wedding day for the second time.

The church was swaddled in inky clothing on the women's side. The men's side afforded more browns, royal blues, and Saturn grays.

Preacher Jacobson had no sooner marched in with his band of ebony-clad clergymen and declared, "Die freide des Hern zie mitt uns allah, ahm (The joy of the Lord be with us all, amen)." Then he launched into a fire and brimstone spiel.

Preacher Jacobson, like Uncle William Penner, was twenty years his wife's senior, but today, he resembled Old Moses himself. White hair bristling where he still had any. He could always be counted on to cry during a sermon, but today, he also shouted, gripped the beveled edge of the pulpit, and glowered.

"We cannot watch all of you!" he thundered gloriously. "But God sees everything you do!"

"Today, we rejoice in new recruits joining us to do God's will! And instead of us preachers, deacons, and bishops running after you to see that you obey our great God, you all observe these newly baptized!"

The women all around them wept. Brenda-Jane looked up at mother and saw her chin trembling and tears flowing down her cheekbones.

"These young men and women want what God wants!" He bellowed on. "They have confessed their sins, given up things they know are wrong, and now we will baptize them into the Father, Son, Holy Ghost, and church membership."

At last, the be-robed and the berating stepped down from his half-hexagonal shaped pulpit and approached the first male constituent holding his water pitcher.

Pastor Jacobson asked the young men in turn if he promised to uphold the church ways and customs, lead a godly household, a godly personal life and, if called on, to step up and help run the church. The candidates said, "Ya," and knelt to receive the two and a half ounces of water on the top of his head.

The congregation continued to sniffle quietly while the preacher's voice chanted and wobbled, "Valcom, bruder, in deeze yeahmindeh!" (Welcome brother, into this denomination.) With that affirmation and in a rare moment of physical affection, he seized the brother by his elbow and hauled him back to his feet.

The ladies also had to agree to adhere to their husband's leadership, raise orderly children, and be damsel in black with her hair pinned up. They "Ya'd" their way to a ruined hairstyle, as the last Ya meant a douse of water from the pitcher would run down their heads.

At the close of the baptismal service, Preacher Jacob fired several more warning shots.

"Now, you watch over your new brothers and sisters, be ready to steady them if one should falter. And make sure they can look to you for a good example, not a misleading one."

Jacob Gruenwald sat in rapt attention beside Father throughout the entire process. "Woo!" he breathed once seated in the Suburban. "How much coffee did that guy drink?!" Mother blew her nose loudly into her handkerchief and said nothing.

"Your mother was baptized once," Father admonished him.

Jacob rolled his eyes. "I know." He sighed in mock exasperation. "She was supposed to marry my sister's dad, but he chickened out and left town. Then she had me six years later with my dad who's a drunk Indian, so they kicked her out, and he won't marry her either, but it's okay, because she's a Seventh Day Adventist now and they don't care!" he finished triumphantly.

Mother's Cousin Eva had been excommunicated and shunned for sinning a second time sexually, apologized to the church but refused to wear the kerchief and thus remained kicked out of the congregation.

"If that blasted piece of material did so much, why did Jesus have to come?" Mother asked no one in her hollow sob voice.

CHAPTER 58

A Walk in the Woods

"GET DOWN from there, they'll never hold your weight," Mother remarked crossly to Brenda Jane on her ketchup can stilts. They were nail-holes punched twice each while overturned and then threaded with baler twine for handles. The user pulled up on the twine with their hand while stepping.

"You're not petite and cute like Marlene. She's built like me." The criticism carried on.

Brenda-Jane clomped through the kitchen on her stilts, expertly stepping down into the porch.

"Hey! That's new linoleum you're cutting up!" Mother screeched. "You're the reason I can never have anything nice!"

Ms. Whittingham had inspired Brenda-Jane to build a pair of props with a story she told, and she had been eager to manifest the idea.

"Get them out of my house!"

Skippy and Shadow joined her trek to the garage to put her heightened heels in storage at their origin. The younger canine playfully cut in front of the older, playfully biting his ear. Instantly, Shadow's neck fur raised, and a dangerously low growl followed in his throat. He flashed his teeth and dove for junior's gizzard, not playing.

Skippy yelped, and Brenda-Jane yelled for help. Tins flying, she ran for the barn just as an ashen faced Margaret appeared and Father close behind her.

"Shadow's killing him!"

A full dog fight was on. Father ran toward the battle, yelling for the old Lab to stop. The German shepherd was bigger but younger, inexperienced, and taken by surprise.

Brenda-Jane picked up one of her cans and threw it at Shadow. It struck him on the head, and he released Skippy and lunged for her, growling and barking, showing full teeth.

"Dad!"

Father ran into his shop and came out with a gun, shouting something. The dog rose, half-dove for Brenda, and then flattened his front legs on the ground to lunge. All the while, he snarled ferociously and curled his lip back to reveal all his pointed yellow teeth.

"Hunt!" (dog) Father shot into the air once and then swooped down and grabbed his collar with his free hand. Turning away, he jerked the dog with him, and the Black Lab half hung, half walked alongside him into the woods.

Skippy cowered behind Brenda now. He had always cringed around Father's guns, no one knew why. He had come to the Gardener farm as a puppy with no unusual history that anyone knew of. Other than being a gift from Corky.

Shadow had simply grown old and tired, which in turn, had made him less tolerant of the young dog's antics and human interaction.

Brenda-Jane found Skip's collar buried in his long fur and held on to keep him with her. He whimpered. Margaret tried to sing from beside her.

"My bonnie lies over the ocean. Let's go inside," she suddenly urged.

They took refuge in the porch on the rug—all three of them, Margaret, Brenda, and Skippy. Mother clip-clopped to the door to inspect the admission into her precious Cleanville, but Margaret beat her to it before she could shriek.

"Mom, Dad has taken Shadow into the bush, and young Skip's afraid of guns. Can we stay here until Dad comes back?"

"No more questions!" Mother burst out. She reached in behind the freezer door and pulled out a plastic ice cream pail of frozen soup.

"I think animals go to heaven after they die," Brenda-Jane declared stoutly. "And I don't think they need a soul to get there. They just do somehow."

Marlene's eyes brightened. In the distance, the sound of a rifle cracked the air. Everyone flinched, then a long segment of deafening silence that seemed fitting to honor the faithful dog's service, followed.

From his porch refuge, Skippy barked as Grosspabeh's religiously correct dark brown pickup rolled into the yard.

Aunt Mary clambered out of the truck while Grosspabeh retrieved his rifle from the gun rack behind him.

Grandmother stayed in the middle of the bench seat.

"There's a bear loose," was the understatement. Bears generally were in Northernmost Alberta.

Father reloaded his 30-03 from the corner of the deck and walked into the pasture, over the electric fence with Grandpa and Aunt Mary.

"Where are your dresses?" Grossmam peered over her round glasses from her perch.

"In the closet!" Marlene replied pertly. "Do you want to see?" Mother turned her face away to hide a smile.

Farm life often required blue jeans—in fact, Mother was raised where a dress was a reprieve from pants and their accompanying work.

Grandmother declined the invitation to come in for tea, so she and Mother made tense small talk before Mother excused herself to recoil behind the kitchen sink.

Mary returned to the yard, downcast. Evidently, she had been ordered to leave the men to scout the farm and remain with her mother.

"Do you really think there's a bear here, Mom?" Brenda-Jane approached Mother cautiously.

"Ahh!" Mother wiped her brow with the back of her arm. "It's an excuse to check up on us."

The menfolk had quickly scanned the perimeter of the farm for bear tracks, dung, or defining noise, and found none.

Grandfather frowned upon hearing of the Labrador's execution at his master's hand. He started the excrement-colored vehicle, sapphire eyes flashing passionately as he said, "Next time, get one of the boys to do it. A man shouldn't have to take his own dog down." He meant one of Father's siblings.

CHAPTER 59

Perverts in Training

SUMMERTIME WAS a mixed blessing in the wardrobe aspect. Tights that never properly reached the height of those forced to wear them were shucked. However, this meant susceptibility to the prying eyes of perverted boys that crawled around the floor in class and in gym, hoping for a peek under a skirt.

"I can see two holes," Johan announced to his band of creeps kneeling a yard away from Brenda Jane's desk. She froze for a horrified moment and then jumped out of her seat to tell Ms. Whittingham. One could hardly expect better than that from the backwoods Penner boys; raised with only a mind game to play with and that was if the gears worked.

The class carried on as, one by one, the boys were called out to the hallway for a meeting with the teacher. Her normally jovial face was drawn into a grim line.

"Okay, everyone! Let's get ready to brush our teeth!" Ms. Whittingham had the voice of forced cheer she had used after the principal had scolded her.

Since the beginning of the year, Ms. Whittingham had ensured that everyone brushed their teeth after lunch recess. Brenda-Jane's parents didn't endorse oral hygiene and, apparently, neither did anyone else's. She like the clean smooth feel of her teeth afterward and kept running her tongue over them.

In journal period, Brenda-Jane wrote about Father shooting Shadow and telling the family animals don't go to heaven because they have no soul. She added her differing opinion in the safety of her kind audience—strictly Ms. Whittingham—that she thought animals had souls and went to heaven. It came back marked with a big yellow happy face sticker.

Saturday, the Gardener family went blueberry picking; Jacob included. Mother donned on her blue jeans and pink flowered blouse; her look, with a transparent pink scarf around her hair folded double, appearing almost English. The glaring detail that dampened her perky look was her rotten, splintered yellow-gray teeth where there were any at all.

Jacob stared at Mother, shocked at her alteration.

Once all the short ropes for hanging tin pails around necks and a lunch was packed, everyone boarded the two-tone burgundy Suburban. The farm now boasted of two such wagons—a navy and royal blue beast that had just been added minus its chrome grill, bumper, and trim. Father had the auctioneer announcing, "number one the buyer!" more than once.

"This is our weekday car," Father explained to Jacob. "And the blue one is for Sunday."

"You think God knows the difference?!" Jacob's mouth hung open. "I thought Jesus rode a camel."

Mother went on a real bender about Marlene this time around. Sometimes she carried on about her stilted relationship with Grossmam, her problems with father, or food.

"People think I diet," she'd say. "I don't. I like my food. Food just doesn't like me."

Today, it was Marlene; how small and cute she was, how intelligent, generous, good, and well mannered.

Not like Brenda-Jane or Margaret, who were big, clumsy, stupid girls as dumb as cows.

Marlene was headed for a bright, shiny future with all her good graces, talents, and great beauty.

Brenda-Jane felt a hatred curdling inside her for her mother and sister both.

"They're bragging," Jacob whispered to her in the back seat. "People shouldn't brag."

Margaret stared out her window, tight lipped and silent. Jacob sat in the middle of the red velour seat the size of a small chesterfield. Brenda-Jane zoned out in her spot, daydreaming of belonging to a mother that loved her.

She nearly longed for Margaret to sing something to break up the monotonous oppression of mother's endless rendition of "Marlene is so wonderful the rest of you suck."

They passed Eagle's Creek, passing a Catholic graveyard littered with crosses and peaked roof like covers over graves.

Finally, Father turned down a gnarly dirt road with ruts that jerked the Suburban in all directions and tossed the passengers like a ship in the Galilean sea. At last, they arrived at the blueberry patch.

Mother switched to Mr. Benjamen, Father's namesake twin. He had come over to borrow a hedge clipper when Father wasn't home. In fact, lately, all his visits were when Father was on the homestead, and she thought he was coming on to her.

"One of these days, I am gonna give him a piece of my mind," she proclaimed. Which begged the question, could she afford to live on the difference?

Mercifully, Margaret burst into a high-pitched plea of "Ashes of Love," and that swallowed the next few minutes.

Father carried his rifle on a leather sling across his back in case a bear turned up.

"Marlene's already got the bottom of her pail covered," Mother declared. "She's a hard worker. Might even be the first one married off if she keeps up." Marlene's bright future suddenly took shape. She was five years old and headed straight for a man. Hip-hip-hooray for Marlene.

Brenda-Jane pretended to drift away from the group, picking further away until she was out of earshot. An idea hit her like a pulled branch snapping back on the second hiker.

She would hide near the edge of the berry thicket until someone noticed her missing. They would panic—fearing a bear had dragged her off into the woods to kill her for his digestion. They would realize their erroneous ways for mistreating her and favoring Marlene.

It seemed a long time of solitude though. Brenda listened to the sounds of summertime around her—birds chirping, singing, and calling to the purple fireweed, goldenrod, and white flowering chamomile growing in the ditches.

Grasshopper's hind legs buzzed. Sometimes, Father had the girls catch them to use as live fish bait.

"BRENDA-JANE!" Father stood glowering above her. "I've been calling you and looking all over for you! Now get back to the family! You are NEVER in with the rest of us!" She obeyed meekly, defeated. Her ruse hadn't worked.

CHAPTER 60

The Visit

"HOLD FAST to the right, hold fast to the right, wherever your footsteps may roam…and forsake not the way of salvation, my boy, that you learned from your mother at home," Father sang with his guitar in the living room after his bath Saturday night.

Mother was attempting to comb out Marlene's long tousled hair in the kitchen after her shared shallow bath with Brenda-Jane.

"Look at the long beautiful hair," Mother praised.

Marlene bit her lower lip and looked like she was trying hard not to cry as the teeth jerked through her brunette tangles.

"Silky tresses." Margaret walked by, lifting one straight wet lock.

Brenda-Jane stuck out her tongue at Margaret.

"I wish you three all had hair like this," Mother continued, picking through the web of snares.

Brenda's hair was short, thin, and wispy, like it was afraid to grow. Margaret's was absolutely frizzy like Mother and Uncle Corky's.

Jacob finished his turn in the bathroom, leaving a thick ring of dirt around the washbowl and tub alike. He unloaded his stock of herbal supplements and began washing them down with milk.

From the living room wafted the strains of "Grandfather's Clock" on father's twelve string.

> "My grandfather's clock was too large for the shelf
> So, it stood ninety years on the floor
> It was taller by half than the old man himself
> Though it weighed not a pennyweight more..."

When Father got to the chorus, a sadness fell on Brenda-Jane like a shadow.

> "Ninety years without slumbering (Here, Father always picked a clock ticking sound.)
> His life seconds numbering
> It stopped short, never to go again
> When the old man died."

Grosspabeh had a clock like the one in the song, but the thought of his passing placed a rock in her chest. Brenda-Jane could picture his eyes twinkling light blue at her even now. He always paid handsomely for each cupful of wild strawberries—better than Mother's rates, in fact. No, Grandfather must not die.

"Do I HAVE to go to church tomorrow?" Jacob piped up. "That guy scares me, and I don't understand a word he says!"

"Ask Uncle Zeke." Mother smirked. She and Margaret were engaged in a lively game of "name that herb" to tease Jacob.

"Take your smart pill first," Margaret interjected. "And your 'talkalots,'" Mother bantered.

Jacob approached Father, and the rest of the house fell silent to eavesdrop on the conversation. Getting up too late for church warranted a beating in the Gardener home, everyone anxiously anticipated Father's response to the proposed church truancy.

"Can I stay home from church tomorrow? I can't understand anything!"

Father cleared his throat and sounded uneasy. "Well, you don't have to understand High German to go to church—as long as God understands. Besides, don't you want to learn German?" "Not the church kind! Just what you speak!" Father chuckled and everyone exhaled.

"Margaret!" he bellowed. "You'll stay home with Jacob tomorrow, hear?"

Sunday dawned with bright sunshine, twittering birds, and Brenda-Jane's first pair of spice colored pantyhose.

Nylons were the first cousin of tights, whose crotch never met with your true inseam. Where tights were too short and the crotch stayed halfway up one's thigh, pantyhose wrinkled around your ankles even after they were pulled up to your armpits.

Brenda-Jane had a pair of wooden sandals with a one-inch heel and leather straps like Cousin Karla's. Once she saw them, she had begged Mother for a pair until she relented.

Ready ahead of time for church, Brenda-Jane decided to go for a bike ride on her rustic bicycle.

At the end of the dirt driveway between the birch trees, she turned onto the freshly graveled road to go halfway to the Benjamen residence. The morning was alive with blooming ditches of purple, white, and yellow flowering weeds and herbs alike, now joined by the pink Alberta Rose.

The loose gravel grabbed her hind wheel, and the bike slid to the earth, bringing Brenda-Jane to a stockinged knee. It ripped her nylons and her flesh. Blood oozed from the new opening in her knee cap. In fact, a large round flap hung like the door on a compartment in a Ford pickup.

Crying, Brenda-Jane limped back up the driveway. Blood from her knee smeared against the skirt of her "Pinksten" dress, mingling with the dirt.

"What have you done!" Mother was horrified. "A new outfit! Look at your pantyhose! Stop crying! Now! Ach! Dad!" she called. "We haven't got time for this." She reached above the fridge for the Band-Aid box. "Look what that kid did," she scolded, running a paper towel under the cold-water tap. "Take your hose off!"

Father's steps were bah-bah-booming down the wide hall. Quickly, Brenda-Jane shucked her ravaged stockings.

Mother dabbed at the big hole on Brenda's knee to clean off the dirt, small rock collection, and blood before smearing a glob of Ozenol on another folded paper towel.

She attached it to the injured knee with Band-Aids until it was covered like the ground in a fresh snow.

"Look what she did—I haven't got time to wash her dress. She may as well stay home too."

Whenever Marlene fell or hurt herself in some way, Mother and Father made a big show checking for a hole in the floor to distract her from crying. They did whatever they could to make her laugh and smile again.

"Heah op mit dot yeah bimmah!" (Stop that crying!) Father commanded Brenda. "You'll stay home with Margaret."

Margaret and Jacob played Scrabble, Battleship, and a card game called "Dutch Blitz" all morning on the dark walnut wood kitchen table. Brenda-Jane knew better than to ask or offer to join, so she changed her dress, pulled on knee-high socks, and went for another bike ride.

Both dogs trotted beside her for a while but were soon distracted by a rustling in the ditch.

She stopped at the former Corny Timber yard to eat wild raspberries and avoid an oncoming vehicle. She recognized one of the Shepnard families rushing to church late, given their speed.

After a lunch of fluffy white buns with butter and summer soup, the phone rang, and Father spoke English gravely when he answered.

"We're getting company," he announced. "Ms. Whittingham and Miss Valen are coming over." Miss Valen was a roommate of the perky grade one teacher who taught grade three.

Mother and Father swung into action. Father swept the kitchen floor while Mother urged the girls to hurry up with the dishes. She descended into the basement in a clatter of high heels on hollow steps to gather the best baked goods and pickled delights from the deep freeze and cold room.

Next, she raided the china shelf for a woven ceramic basket, red with tiny white bulbs around the edge, to use for buns. Mother also took her crystal desert bowls out of the middle section of the entertainment center in the living room.

Father put a record on and turned the volume down. Organ music lapped at the white paneled corners of the parlor where the linoleum curled up.

The ladies drove up in a large green Ford Crown Victoria—of course, all cars were cumbersome then. Both wore frilly dresses from the Sears Catalogue and baby doll patent leather shoes.

"Keep your shoes on this is a farmhouse," Mother demurred.

Ms. Whittingham's face lit up when she saw Brenda-Jane. She reached out and tickled her as she walked by in an aura of rose perfume, carrying her burgundy clutch purse.

Mother poured coffee into her best tea set—an elegant china set with white scalloped edges and patterned with a floral bouquet on the sides of the teapot and curve handled cups. She daintily set the steaming cups on her silver-plated tray and carried the jaunty arrangement to the living room.

"So, have either of you been to this part of the woods before?" Father made exaggerated circle motions with his big beefy hand.

Instead of the usual sunflower seed spitting and gossip over who was pregnant, getting married, or driving with chrome showing, Mother and Father talked about gardening, the farm, and the homestead.

They brought out the photo albums and told endearing stories. Mother trip-trap-tripped gaily in and out of the kitchen and living room, keeping the coffee, cream, and sugar cubes flowing.

Father got a small blackboard out to demonstrate the difference between German lettering and the English alphabet.

Brenda-Jane remembered how the High German "s" and "f" were backward, so "sassy" would appear as "faffy."

"Can you ride a bicycle yet?" Miss Valen spied Brenda-Jane peeping around the corner of the living room. She was a Marilyn Monroe type where her comrade was dark haired and freckled.

"Oh yes, she took a spill off it this morning," Father answered for her.

"More coffee anyone?" Mother leapt to her feet and bustled by Brenda-Jane, pulling her around the bend.

"Listen you spook," she hissed, showing her ghastly gashes of splintered teeth. "Don't be a peeping Tom or a wallflower. Go play with the other kids until faspa, HEAR?" Brenda-Jane withered as her mother's fingernails dug into her flesh.

"Hear? Or should I get Dad." Mother sprayed saliva.

Brenda nodded. She walked to her room to find Marlene but remembered Margaret had taken Marlene and Jacob downstairs to the playroom to play hangman.

Walking past the wide-angled doorway of the sitting room, Mother caught her again.

"Brenda-Jane—come here. Come on," she urged sweetly.

Reluctantly, Brenda sidled closer to her mother's stiff upright seat.

"Let me check your knee," Mother said tersely. She lifted Brenda's hem slightly and peeled back the makeshift bandage.

Brenda cringed as Mother pulled back the paper towel that had dried to her wound.

"Hold it," she peered behind the dressing. "Seems okay."

Mother reattached the Band-Aids. "You can go." The brittle edge in Mother's voice also suggested she had better skedaddle.

There was a personality to be put on for the benefit of outsiders, Brenda was learning.

CHAPTER 61

Third Party Goodbye

BRENDA-JANE FOUND Jacob and her sisters' downstairs in the playroom in front of the gigantic chalkboard Father had bought at a school division auction.

Jacob wore his white starched shirt and black jeans, looking like one of the music stars on a record.

Margaret looked like she enjoyed her chalkboard tricks, making him guess phrases in Low German he didn't know.

"Stop with the 'du bist ein shween!'" (You are a pig!) he exclaimed. "My mom didn't teach me any German!"

The playroom had once been the kitchen, dining, and living area when the family lived downstairs. The only remaining relic of those days was the deep freeze and the white muslin curtains on baler twine above both windows. Now it was Jacob's bedroom by weekend and a museum of odd furniture on weekdays.

An old gray flannel blanket hung across the door edge to Margaret's "new" room and the stairwell, creating a barrier between Jacob's room and hers.

The children played hangman until Mother called them for faspa. The table glittered with Mother's best crystal and china. Napkins were triangulated under the cutlery. Lacey doilies sat under each cup and mug.

All finery aside, the whole eatery event was mercilessly tense and uncomfortable. While the two teachers seemed oblivious to all the put-ons, the children were silent and nervous. To speak was to risk saying the wrong thing and getting lashed out against later. To remain silent meant to be accused of being a wallflower or stuck-up.

Jacob fell silent for his own reasons; he was in the presence of those he was usually at odds with.

Father told charming stories of growing up without luxuries like plumbing, electricity, and a telephone. The two schoolmarms exclaimed over the enormity of the garden in view of the kitchen window.

There was no dining room segregating from the kitchen upstairs either; the table was situated in the middle of the large room lined by cupboards and counters.

Brenda-Jane saw Ms. Whittingham study the diamond-shaped gouges in the golden walnut-shell colored cabinet doors. They'd been blackened as they had burned the wood and matched the dark handles sharply.

"Did you build the cabinets yourself?" Ms. Whittingham asked Father.

"No, I designed those and had them built for me." He laughed. "I built the house, but I had to quit while I was ahead."

The two educators chuckled. Brenda-Jane waited for her mother's customary mutter of how the house was still not finished. It didn't materialize.

"I got the idea—" Father wiped his beaming face on his white napkin, "—from the Diamond Willow tree. In fact, I still have an unfinished table out in the garage that will have Diamond Willow legs."

Again, Mother's lips went in a grim, unhappy line instead of denoting Father's unfinished string of projects.

"What is your favorite farm chore?" Ms. Whittingham asked Brenda-Jane. Everyone turned to Brenda, whose face burned with discomfort.

"None," she replied, to which Father roared with laughter and the teachers giggled.

After they left and the sudsy dishwater subsided, Mother and Father broke wind and news alike; Ms. Whittingham was leaving Butterhorn School at the end of the year.

Brenda-Jane felt sadness curtain her relief. The tense visit was over, but she hadn't thought of not seeing the bubbly schoolteacher in some capacity next year. "Why?" she ventured.

Mother glanced at Father furtively. Father licked his lips nervously.

"Ahem, she got into some trouble with the principal—no one knows exactly what or why."

Jacob's mother's big brown Chrysler New Yorker rolled into the yard lazily, with Skippy braying at its wheels.

Cousin Eva brought her albino daughter and a stack of books in.

"Has Jacob been taking his allergy medication and vitamins?" were her first words. Mother bristled visibly.

"What? I thought those were for the pigs!" she feigned confusion.

Eva looked genuinely shocked and horrified until she noticed Mother fighting back a smile. Then she launched into her book spiel on Adventist literature for children without regard for the day being Sunday.

Father got out his check book and purchased two sets, five Uncle Arthur's Bedtime stories, and five Bible stories. They were richly pigmented, hardcover books. Eva included a hardcover book called "*The Desire of Ages*" as a gift for looking after Jacob.

Eva declined an offer to stay for night lunch, collected her children, and drove away.

Mother fumed as she put on another pot of coffee. "The idea! Selling us books when we feed her kid and babysit for free!"

Father started to drawl a protest, but she ran over the top of him like a runaway horse.

"Asking me if I have stuffed him full of herbal medicine and allergy pills! Hah! What do I look like? Like I need the inconvenience? No dice!"

From outside in the dusk came the nearing sounds that the chores were completed, and the milk was coming in.

"Sandwiches are beautiful! Sandwiches are fine! I want sandwiches! I eat'em all deh time!"

CHAPTER 62

Almost Doesn't Tie Up the Cow

THE LAST few weeks of school were whipping by. Many classes were held outside on the grass amid the yellow dandelions and a slight breeze.

Dandelion bouquets were often picked and brought into the classroom to grace Ms. Whittinghams' desk in a Styrofoam cup only to whither instantly.

Chirpy decorations inspired by Dr. Seuss were removed from the bulletin boards, artwork taken down and sent home with the children. Ms. Whittingham divided up her leftover school supplies among the children, and they lapped them up greedily.

Mennonites in those days were either poor or acted as though they were, seizing every opportunity to gain something for free.

Brenda-Jane was between looking forward to summer and sadness over saying goodbye to Ms. Whittingham.

Mercifully, the last day of school was like all the others, only shorter. The bulletin and blackboards were stripped down to mere borders. Ms. Whittingham handed everyone a giant Mr. Freeze as they left the classroom and said goodbye like tomorrow would come.

The Gardener kids arrived home to a flurry of the usual shouting and German cursing by Mother who was overwhelmed with work but never too tired or busy to say so. Father had taken Jacob to work on the homestead, and there were chickens to be butchered. On and on.

Brenda-Jane retreated to her platform in the trees to read *Little House on the Prairie* and breathe the fresh birch scent mingled with wildflowers.

"Ashes of love, cold as ice? You made the debt; I paid the price?" Sounds of the evening chores pierced the growing shadows when Father turned in the yard in the dark Suburban to end his day. Not that he owned any.

Skipper scampered off to the barn, Skippy at his heels. A burst of noise and a shot of laughter indicated they had successfully interrupted Margaret's broken country song.

"Are you nearly done picking rocks?" Mother sighed, sinking into a chair still wearing her apron.

Father slurped his coffee, sweat staining his worn dark T-shirt.

"*Mace*" (Almost). He studied the dark liquid in his cup.

"Mace bingt chineh kuh an!" (Almost doesn't tie up no cow!) Mother sighed, sinking into a chair still wearing her apron.

"—and the moose said 'Ooyah! Ooyah!'" 'Jacob brayed through his nostrils.

Mother glared at Father. "Moose? You didn't go hunting, did you?!"

Father pursed his bottom lip. "Nope. But we saw one."

The family ate their meal of keel-cheh (cold homemade noodles in buttermilk) with raw cucumber slices in silence.

Afterward, Father pushed back his chair and beamed at them all. "Well, who wants to go swimming?" The household dissolved in all directions. Father and Jacob went out to the garage to inflate a few inner tire tubes. Margaret poured milk into the shmontah (cream separator), and Brenda-Jane and Marlene helped Mother clean up supper.

Only the menfolk packed swimming trunks. The females wore old torn dresses from the scrap bag. Father had crammed their previous bathtub—a big aluminum bowl—into the middle of a big tractor tube and made a raft. Jacob dove into the dugout on Grandfather's field like an alarmed beaver. Brenda-Jane and Marlene got into the raft and drifted like the early settlers into the unknown. Once they got too close to the middle, Father hollered at them to paddle around the perimeter instead.

"Where you are is deeper than I am tall!"

Margaret discovered a leech on her thigh and screamed.

Father ran to the Suburban and retrieved a lighter. He held the flame to the brown stain until it writhed and rolled off her. How could anyone has known the futility of the exercise since she would end up marrying one in just a few years.

Someone had built a dock but laid a board across it too heavy and too long for the base. Brenda-Jane abandoned ship, leaving Marlene to paddle on her own as she tried swimming for the plank platform. Once she reached the edge, Margaret stepped on it, and it came down like the occupied end of the teeter-totter. The board struck Brenda's head and pushed her underwater simultaneously. She caught a glimpse of Father's face just before the water closed over her. He was terrified.

A meaty hand caught hold of Brenda-Jane's arm and jerked her upright. There was yelling. A lot of shouting.

Blood ran into her mouth from her nose. The board slid down on her again as Margaret stepped off of it. Water swallowed her whole, but father pulled up by her arm. Jacob's white face flashed before her.

Margaret got a tongue-lashing from Father, then that cancelled the carousing.

Back home, Mother was folding up freshly laundered sheets on the kitchen table. Margaret was sobbing by the time she walked into the house.

"Margy, it's okay—" Brenda-Jane tapped her arm, but she jerked away.

The children all washed their feet in the oblong foot bowl in turn and changed into their pajamas and flowered cotton night gowns made form an old sheet.

"What's Uncle Zeke so mad about?" Jacob whispered. He had missed the translation of the German lecture on the way home but caught the undertone.

"Cuz I could have drowned, you nitwit!" Brenda-Jane slugged him.

A hiccupping Margaret sulked off to bed while the rest of the family had cold sausages for night lunch. Mother sat, glaring over the table at Brenda-Jane.

"Dad favors you." She wiped a pie plate furiously. Which wasn't entirely true; in a dispute between Brenda-Jane and Marlene, the latter was favored. A rift or odds amidst Margaret and Brenda-Jane usually ended with the younger party mollycoddled.

A border collie puppy came home in the back of the "work-burban" with Father to replace Shadow. He was agile and foxlike, and he and Skippy immediately touched noses like boxers do gloves and then circled, sniffing each other's rear.

"Where did you get him? What's his name?" The four children clamored around the newcomer. He was black with an interruption around his neck of white and brown-gold wobbly rings.

"Snoopy," said Father tentatively.

Jacob shook his head. "Snoopy is a Beagle."

"Aww, shucks," Father snickered. "I wanted to name him after the cartoon."

"Charlie Brown!" Jacob exclaimed. The women folk fell back and observed men and beasts.

Margaret had taught Skipper to rear up on his hind legs and place his paws on her shoulders in an embrace.

The two dogs parted long enough for Charlie Brown to flatten his front legs and bow to Skipper. Then they laid their heads across each other's necks and seemed to embrace.

"Look, a hug," Marlene commented. Skipper separated, bee-lined for Margaret, and stood up to her, literally, only with his penis out this time!

"Margaret has a boyfriend!" Brenda-Jane sang out. Jacob laughed so hard he had to grasp his dragon T-shirt-clad abdomen with one brown hand.

Charlie hadn't been around long when the Gardener farm was turned into absolute carnage.

Everyone had slept through the night and typically did unless the dogs alerted Father that wolves or coyotes were near. They woke up to Margaret's screams and panicked footsteps up the burgundy steps to the porch.

A trail of blood and feathers led to the barn, along with chicken organs and mangled fowl. The new dog had gone on a killing binge and enticed the other to join in. He had a baby kitten in his mouth when Father arrived at the barn where the trail ended and had begun.

Brenda-Jane hollered for Father to stop the dog. There was a lot of yelling. For a moment, Father stooped to pick up the tiny kitten dropped on the barn floor, and a tender moment ensued. The little feline clung to the large calloused hand it was dwarfed by, and Father cradled it as he returned it to the rest.

A murderous expression crossed Father's face, and he grabbed a chain hanging from the nails on the barn wall. He strode back to the front porch, pausing only to grab the leg of a dead bird. He tied the chicken up with the rope and then roughly grabbed Charlie Brown's collar.

The dog yelped as he tied the chain and fowl to his collar and attached it to the cemented base of the homemade boot scraper at the basement steps.

"As for you!" Father lunged for Skippy's ears and yanked the big dog up and down by his grip.

The dog howled and wailed as Father beat his head into the ground, up and down.

"YOU KNOW BETTER!" He shouted as he reached for the German shepherd.

All day, family members had to pass the chained prisoner, who looked up hopefully and tentatively wagged his tail. No one could pet nor comfort him.

Brenda-Jane felt bad for the canines despite the half-dozen or so chickens they had slaughtered.

One could always tell what member of the dog family had killed or otherwise made chickens disappear. Wolves and dogs played with their prey before the kill, creating a telltale trail behind them. Coyotes and foxes stealthily crept in, mouthed up their victim, and ran off with them, leaving no trace.

CHAPTER 63

The Repenting

SOME SUMMER evenings were spent riding the pigs, with Mother and Father watching from the weathered board fence.

The girls wore old blue jeans of Aunt Valerie's under their dresses and rubber boots. The trick was to sneak up to the pig and start scratching him along his back until his contented grunts slowed down to a sleepy rate. Then the would-be rider flung herself onto the back of the unsuspecting pork, and off they went in circles until the pig pitched them off.

Mother wore her black wedge shoes on one such pork-drop occasion and stepped into a grassy pothole. Her scream halted everyone, and Father scrambled to help her to her feet.

White faced; Mother crumpled as soon as she tried to stand.

"Margaret, you're in charge. I trust you kids all to behave," Father called over his shoulder as he loaded Mother into the Sunday mobile.

Dusk closed on the farm as the children took turns at the foot wash bowl. No one wanted to go to bed, so they sat in the forbidden living room in pert near unbroken silence until the yard light came on, drawing an instant cloud of insects to it.

"Will Mom die?" Marlene's bottom lip quivered. "She always says she wants to. If Mom dies, I want to die too."

"Shh." Margaret hauled Marlene onto her lap. Jacob and Brenda-Jane exchanged glances of disgust.

Brenda-Jane went to bed and then got out her flashlight and read a chapter in *Little House on the Prairie* before falling asleep.

The next morning, Mother set her knee on Father's office chair and hopped around the kitchen on her good leg. The badly sprained ankle had been swaddled in an elasticized bandage and had to be kept elevated. A pair of crutches leaned up beside the metal moss green garbage can with its cluster of fruit design stamped in the center.

"You look funny," Brenda-Jane ventured, to which Mother bristled.

"That proves how much you care about your mother," she snarled.

"Branna," Father admonished sternly. "You make sure you help Mother out extra today. She's going to need all the help she can get."

Jacob stared as mother wheeled around the kitchen on one foot like some kind of dancer.

"What's everyone staring at!" she snapped! "I'm going to need extra help for the next month!"

Father's latest trip to an auction had produced bottle-fed baby goats who were growing in size and attachment to the farm kids.

"The Bible even teaches to have goats," Mother had emphasized dramatically over faspa company, much to an awkward silence. Only preachers professed to know what the Bible said.

Outside, they frisked along with whatever the girls did like two little white shadows. Having lost their mother, the goats took them on as a substitute like some animals do.

From his rotting carcass-clad position in the shade, Charlie Brown watched them all and wagged his tail hopefully.

Marlene and Brenda named the plump boy goat Snowball and the smaller female goat Snowflake because of the slight skiff of darker white hairs on her forehead that looked like a pattern.

Jacob stayed home for a couple of days with his mother and didn't witness the tension between Mother and Margaret mounting. In fact, when he was around, the family gears shifted to Sunday company mode on low.

Mother was impaired by her impaled ankle and tightly wound. Margaret was increasingly frustrated with the extra demands to run up and downstairs to fetch canned goods and told it was the wrong product.

"I said the wurst from 1980, not last years! Can't you ever do anything right?" "No, I can't!" Margaret wailed truthfully, almost in tears. "You make sure of that!" *Slap!* Sobbing, Margaret's footsteps resounded down the stairs.

"Useless, useless girl!" Mother shouted to the kitchen condiment patterned red and beige wallpaper.

Brenda-Jane lay on her bed in a belly flop over one of the new books Father had purchased from Cousin Eva, reading to her sibling.

Mother continued her harping, and when Father came in for dinner, she hooted and hollered about how awful Margaret was and how he had better do something.

Brenda-Jane's eyes met Marlene's. Wordlessly, their expressions made the same statement. Something negative was brewing. Unless Margaret kept quiet…

Beatings at the farm were so regular the children couldn't protect themselves nor prevent them, so at times, they simply acted up or lipped off to get it over with.

Father began berating her, "Mom says you don't obey, and you talk back—"

Brenda and Marlene clung to each other as Mother and Father's voices got louder and louder, intermingled with Margaret's. She was breaking down, her volume decreasing and her voice wobbling and shaking. Shrinking.

Lectures rose and grew, turning Margaret into a chew toy for the adults, declaring her evil in God's sight, dishonoring her parents.

The whipping started, and they covered their ears as Margaret unsuccessfully tried to cover her behind.

Deep, spirit-broken sobs gushed from Margaret by the time some invisible force propelled her siblings down the hall toward her in a lopsided huddle.

"Now, ask you mother's forgiveness!" Father roared, towering above Mother. At Mother's feet with her head down knelt a crumpled Margaret. Her shoulders heaved;

her head rested on Mother's lap without any comfort nor any other contact.

"Do it! Nicht bless mace!" (Not just almost.) Father demanded. After all, this family didn't function on nearly doing things. They thrived on overkill.

CHAPTER 64

Mockingbird Hill

JACOB RETUNED to the Gardener farm brandishing a new BB gun his mother had allowed him to buy.

"Dad!" Mother hissed, grabbing Father's beefy arm. "Dad, do something!"

"Ah, maybe wait to use it until we get to the homestead," Father murmured. Mother's face fell.

The summer blazed by in a flurry of berry-picking, weeding, watering, noise, confusion and work.

Mother's ankle injury didn't affect her tongue any, and it wagged like the tail of the new serial killer on the farm, Charlie Brown. Saliva sprayed from her splintered yellow and gray teeth as she ferociously spat out her troubles on the children listening, usually Marlene and Brenda-Jane.

Whenever she paused her tirade of how Grandma Gardener didn't like her and favored Aunt Mary, the two girls were expected to catapult comforting words at her to fix her feelings.

Ms. Whittingham had taught the grade one class all about feelings last year, displaying them on colored construction paper according to happiness and hue.

"Yah! Grossmam is not nice like Grandma," Marlene suggested agreeably.

Mother stared pointedly at Brenda-Jane, waiting. The kitchen fell silent, and the silence screamed.

"Mom, you're t-too nice. T-too good for her anyway," Brenda stuttered. A lot of the family on Mother's side stammered; most of her brothers did.

"Ach!" Mother dismissed them with a wave of her hand.

Marlene and Brenda-Jane took their "Baby Brenda" dolls and some oversized dresses from the linen closet and went to play in the hayloft.

In the sweet smell of the alfalfa bales with the sunlight streaming into the two square windows at the mid-peak of the hip rook barn; they played house. Brenda-Jane was strong enough to push and pull bales into an outline of a room. Then another. Soon, she had maneuvered bales until the entire hayloft was a prickly bungalow.

Mid-grown kittens darted in and out of the walls like rambunctious children at play while their calico mama mooned over them from her hollowed place in the straw.

Mother got her learners license one hot summer weekday in Hatchet Prairie and drove home at about twenty miles an hour. It felt eerie, Mother in the driver's seat and Father on the passenger side.

"I did it so I can run meals out to the homestead," she spoke as if measuring herself. "So, I can bring Dad his lunches."

Jacob and Margaret had stayed home to "demuckify" the chicken coop and unmire the cow dung channel.

When the Suburban rolled up to its place near Charlie's penalty zone, he was loosed and went into a frenzy of barking and carrying on. No one thought much about it, just that he must have been happy to get out of his confinement.

The two baby goats were nowhere in sight. Jacob looked pale under his nationality, and Margaret belted out "Mockingbird Hill" a little louder than usual.

> "Tra la, tweedle dee deedle it gives me a thrill
> To wake up in the morning to the mockin' birds trill
> Tra la tweedle dee deedle
> There's peace and good will
> You're welcome as the flowers on Mockingbird Hill."

Charlie Brown kept up his racket all evening.

"I'm gonna wring his neck!" Mother declared, painting an instant mental picture of her unsteady hands on the wheel deftly squeezing the dog to death.

Brenda-Jane and Marlene had abandoned playing house and had drifted to the picnic table where Mother was slaying beets.

"I don't want this mess in the house!"

Marlene suddenly froze in mid-coloring. "THE LITTLE GOATS! Snowball! Snowflake! They always come around to greet us. Where are they?"

That started a commotion. Father thundered out of the house in his boots, pausing only to reach for his rifle from the inside the pickup rear window. Mother left the beet bathing, limped behind Father, and wrung her hands into the apron she wore. Brenda and Marlene followed the procession.

"Margaret and Jacob!" Father bellowed, lumbering past the barn to the gate that would allow him to search the pasture.

Two pale faces peered around the big red door. They shook their heads wordlessly; no, they hadn't seen the kids.

Skippy and Charlie Brown trotted lazily along, aimlessly sniffing the odd cow pie.

The front pasture yielded nothing. Father took big strides down to the dirt trail through the windbreaker led to the rapeseed crop behind it.

Two white mounds lay a short distance from each other on the dirt in a sparse area. A small hole in Snowballs belly had begun to loosen innards but beside soil, there was no mark other than dirt on Snowflake.

A sob rose from Marlene. A warm tightness wrapped around Brenda-Jane's throat like she would soon be unable to swallow.

"Get me a shovel and spade," Father ordered without looking up. He bent to grab Skipper's collar and tightened the chain by twisting it.

The two girls ran back to the barn. Horrible sounds of a man's rage and a dog's agony mingled with Marlene's sobs. The band across Brenda-Jane's chest tightened and tears welled up anyway. Their frisky little friends were gone.

"STUPID DOGS!" Marlene managed. She grasped Brenda's hand, and they rushed to the cow stalls together, crying.

As great as the distance was from the field to the barn, it was insufficient to drown out the sounds behind the yard.

They found the tools hanging from the wall where Margaret was threatening to dump the contents of the wheelbarrow on a protesting Jacob. He was laughing as she shoved the one-wheeled vessel, wobbling toward him on her way to deposit the load on the clompen (pile of manure) outside.

The image of the quarter-sized gap in Snowballs stomach haunted Brenda-Jane. A dog couldn't have made such a neat and tidy mark on the little goat.

Mother returned with Father, shielding her eyes from the late afternoon sun, and scowling.

"I don't think the dogs did this," Brenda dared as she handed Father the spade. "That looked like a bullet hole."

"That's what I said!" Mother exclaimed.

Father detonated. "The dogs ran those baby goats to death! Now get in the house!" he bellowed, flinging a load of dirt at Brenda's feet angrily.

Meekly, Mother led the way back to the house. From the pasture side, the tar-papered side of the unfinished structure showed. The weathered plywood entrance squatted under the attic door.

"Look at that Indian cabin," Mother scoffed. "Your father never finishes anything unless he's beating a dog."

"Or us," Brenda offered.

"Shaw!" Mother made her chicken shooing sound like she did when the free-range hens clustered around the porch step. Only now, she meant "shut up!"

Margaret and Jacob were anointing the bathroom and each other in a water fight when they entered the house.

"HEY!" Mother yelled. "You two clean that up right now! And Jacob—" she snarled, sticking her face into his— "Let me catch you just once using that BB gun around here, and it's gone, you hear?"

The boy's eyes widened behind his wire-framed glasses, and he shrank backward from Mother, nodding rapidly.

Supper of hotdogs, buns, canned beans, and cottage cheese was eaten in taut silence by all but Marlene, who didn't eat at all. Big tears streamed out of her large blue eyes as she sat perched on her church gray/blue painted pedestal.

"Why don't you get yourself a jam," Mother suggested, which usually worked. But this time, poor Marlene couldn't be comforted.

Mother wished aloud the dogs had killed the rest of the older chicken flock and saved her the work of butchering them.

CHAPTER 65

A "Yeah" Woman

UNCLE ISBRANDT and Aunt Betty Gardener were invited to join the chicken butchering in exchange for half of the flock for help with the slaughter.

They came and brought their ten homeschooled children and Grandfather's plucking machine with them in their mammoth van.

Uncle Isbrandt was loud and obnoxious when he finally surfaced from his sequestered life behind the poplar tree curtain on the Shepnard property. He was only nine months, three days, five and a half hours and a bit younger than Father. Most people mistook them for twins at least once.

"All right! KINDER!" (Children.) He bellowed for the fourteen youngsters to gather around him.

"Everyone ten years old and over, stick around and help. Nine years and younger—make yourselves scarce or you will be put to work, hear?"

Aunt Betty was a sister of Uncle Isaiah's wife, Tina. Both were Mother's second cousins— slender, tall, and dark haired, with snapping dark eyes.

"Yo, ack vol mole nicht neh vohtayteh fruh" (Yes, I didn't want a watery wife). Uncle Isbrand launched into one of his stories. This one on how he once asked his younger brother if his girlfriend had an older sister.

Watery was his term for the near albino coloring many of the blonde blue-eyed Mennonite women had.

Twenty-four chickens were beheaded at the chopping block and left to flail and squirt blood as they finished perishing. Brenda-Jane and her cousins played tag with the flopping fowl which seemed, at times, to be headed straight for them.

"We should wait for the men to do the plucking." Aunt Betty was no fool. "They want to be the head of the house; they can be the head of the barn too and do the heavier work!" Mother chuckled at the sawhorse table.

When the men returned, they plunked the chicken carcasses in the boiling water while holding them by the feet and then dangled them above the plucker. Feathers flew as the rubber knobs on the new machine knocked them off and spit them out of its hopper.

A canopy like a baby carriage kept the sodden plumage from flying everywhere and channeled them into a funneled aluminum pipe.

"How did you manage to borrow the new model?" Mother asked Uncle Isbrandt cynically. "Oof!" He snorted. "I just told Mother if I ceased borrowing, I ceased being me! Say, whose boy have you go there?" He motioned toward Jacob.

Brenda-Jane wanted to eavesdrop on the adults but got drawn into a game of dodgeball followed by capture the flag. Cousin Hendrix, the oldest who was her age, made a crossing line in mid-yard with branches, and they were on.

The adults, Margaret, and their cousin George helped hand pluck the finer feathers off the scalped birds. The fathers held the fowl by their legs over a blow torch to singe off any fine hairs remaining. Next, the chicken would be neck-circumcised before an incision was made under the breastbone and its legs wrenched wide open. The butcherer then forced her hand in, hooked her index finger around the ribbed esophagus, and dragged it out with all the guts following.

"What's for dinner, chicken?" Uncle Isbrand joked.

"For you, we'll keep it raw," Mother teased as if giving him a hint.

"Don't always start something," Aunt Betty chided him.

Their offspring lined up like a checkerboard, George was dark. Edith was fair. Hendrix again had his mother's dunklet (dark color), and Martin was a blue-eyed blonde. Jeremiah had his father's cut-up personality and a dark complexion. Helen was a tiny angelic creature with gold curls, and a few dunkleh (dark) *kinder* later, at the bottom of the family tree was a bald cerulean-eyed toddler.

Most of the males in Father's ancestry were as bald as chicken eggs.

Mother watched as the two dogs gobbled up the chicken heads.

"My parents tried to make me eat chicken brains," she remarked. "I refused them for breakfast, and so out they came for lunch."

"Raw or cooked?" Aunt Betty was credulous. "Raw," Mother said grimly.

"*Heat-a-mole!*" (Hear it once!)

"At lunchtime, I sat there until supper. Finally, she left the room and I flung them into the *cheat amah.*" (Scrap pail used for collecting leftovers to feed the pigs).

As the story went, Grandma had rewarded Mother with a cookie for allegedly eating the innards, and it had gone uneaten also.

Talk cycled into Aunt Susanna's upcoming nuptials and her finance, a Steinburger uncle of the orphans that lived behind the junction store. The cabin they were moving into was on the edge of a relative's property, two rooms up on stilts without a bathroom.

"I built them an outhouse as my wedding gift," Uncle Isbrandt boasted. He and Father were gifted alike in the ability to create unique artifacts and items out of almost any ordinary materials.

Mother and Father had purchased a Big Ben alarm clock they never used; a beautiful white metal time piece with a gold band encircling it. The numbers were gold, so were the hands and knobs on the back. It was still in pristine condition, so they were wrapping it in gilded paper and giving it as a wedding gift. Bridal presents were always wrapped unless they were too large.

Talk turned to topics like "debt" and "farm credit," and worry crept into the voices of the grownups.

Aunt Betty's chin wobbled. "We could lose our three-room shack as it is. At least Susanna and Isaac will own theirs.

Uncle Isbrandt burst into belligerent song just then.

"Oh, give me a home
Where the buffalo roam
And the deer and the antelope play
Where seldom is heard
A discouraging word
And the skies are not cloudy all day!"

"Enough!" His wife hushed him, and the women excused themselves to make lunch.

"Why do you have two names?" Uncle groused at Brenda. "Couldn't you sell one and buy your folks something nice?"

At dusk, the chickens were butchered, soaking in the bins of water and the relative's portion loaded in the abyss that was the rear entry of the vast van.

Uncle Isbrandt played guitar sometimes, but not in the style Father did. He strummed like he hated stringed instruments and blared like a bull with his testicles caught on barbed wire.

Aunt Susanna and the new Uncle Isaac's wedding was a solemn affair, with the couple entering at the front of the church through the men's door side by side without touching. Pastor Jacobson's officiated, preaching on how Jesus knocked on the door on our hearts and marriages, asking to be let in to make it sweeter. He went on to say how men were in control and women were to suck it up, toe the line, and be there for the men.

Brenda-Jane watched Susanna's pious pale face encircled with braids she pinned up like Ellen White wearing her black wedding dress.

Their wedding invitations had been wine-colored parchment paper printed with black calligraphy lettering to hint of the colors to come in the evening and her only wedding finery.

"Give each other your right hand," Preacher Jacobson ordered as they said their vows, agreeing, not repeating, with a simple "ya."

Once the congregation finished singing, "Zoe Fleegen Unzer Tageh Hin" (How Quickly Our Days Fly By) acapella style, as usual, the groom and bride fled the church with the groom at the head, the bride following her new leader to symbolize how marriage should be.

After a few photos were snapped with Polaroids and 126 cameras by the congregation, the feasting began. A table of glittering gifts strewn with several plainly wrapped "yeah-shenken" (presents) sat waiting outside along the Sunday school building.

Everyone ate potato salad, white buns with homemade butter, roast beef cold cuts, and pickled vegetables. There was desert of every kind, from jelly rolls to Rice Krispies squares and pan-baked cakes with frosting but no designated wedding cake.

Nine months later, the bride would be pregnant and every nine months or so consecutively thereafter because birth control was a sin.

There were no confetti flung adieu nor any display of public affection — also a worldly sin.

The tall, big-boned bride and short, lithe little groom left in a brown pickup truck undecorated, with the bride sitting beside her new husband behind the wheel, so close.

CHAPTER 66

Discipline

SUMMER BLEW by in a flurry of chicken feathers, trips to the dugout, and work on the homestead. As soon as the July page of the calendar turned, August roared to life, and devoured everything warm, scented and blooming.

School supplies appeared on the store shelves while the evenings grew cooler. The children picked bluebells on the homestead and chewed on stripped fireweed stems around the campfire. A feeling of nostalgia and melancholy crept over them.

Mother still shouted about Father's shortcomings and how Jacob got away with all his shenanigans on the farm and that she hated Grossmam.

After Sunday school, the class joined the tail end of the church service and Lord love a duck! It was stuffy. Usually they ended at the same time true to order and "ordung" (organization) unless the visiting Preacher had extra spit.

Anyone getting married later that afternoon sat segregated in the two front rows of the men's and women's side, sweltering in their fortrell clothing. At the end of his spiel, Pastor Jacobson dismissed the couple with a nod first, who promptly scuttled down the middle aisle and existed from the men's entrance. These were the few times a couple would enter and leave a church together.

"Die flee-en zick emma in deh zocken" (They always flee in their socks), Mother greased on the way home.

"Nush tah bah zihn" (Nothing to see), Father quipped.

"I wish you would treat that boy like one of your own." Mother changed the subject to Jacob. "You're letting him get away with murder. The dogs took a beating for what he did, and our girls would have too." Mother was talking about the baby goats.

Father was silent for a long time. "Well, he works hard. I'd hate to lose him."

Mother snorted. "And I don't? Your oldest doesn't? What a thing to say!"

"Anyway. It's Sunday. Let's have peace." His big oil-stained hand slashed the air for emphasis.

Mother's chin wobbled, and she began crying. She pulled an embroidered floral handkerchief and dabbed at her eyes.

Wind whipped at the full skirt on the scare-a-crow in the garden and tugged at her "*babushka*". Her black drawn eyes on the flour sack that served as her face stared bleakly out across the garden she was to protect. Weakly, her arms stretched out as if pleading for mercy, but the grim red-lined mouth already seemed to know there was none. Dirt had caught in her plastic blue apron made from a tarp to rustle in the wind and scare birds and bunnies alike. Ironically, the bell-sleeved flowing pink and yellow flowered dress was one Mother dared not wear for fear of causing ripples in the church. How truly helpless she was, skewered into the dirt and kept helpless and dependent.

"Mom," Brenda-Jane piped up. "Can we have an English scare-a-crow next time?"

"Cuz it's no fun being German. Why have a sad scare-a-crow too? The English have all the fun." Mother made a sound into her snot rag that Brenda wasn't sure of and didn't answer.

The childless Friesens paid Mother and Father a visit, leaving the girls to entertain themselves while the sunflower seeds piled up on the brown and gold living room floor.

They played dodgeball on the lawn between the house and garden. Marlene and Brenda-Jane against Margaret. The canine unit watched from the lilac beset sidelines, while local gossip filtered through the opened screen window from the living room.

Things were going well until Margaret got the inspiration to replace the ball with Father's cowboy boots and do a sort of horizontal juggling act. The girls hurled them as hard as they could at each other, when suddenly, Margaret got a peculiar expression and winged a boot right at Brenda-Jane's face. The heel glanced off her nose, blood poured, and Marlene screamed.

Father and his visitor came running while Mother and her guest peered out of the window. "Take her in the house," he instructed Marlene regarding Brenda.

"And YOU!" He rained heavy slaps down on Margaret's head, face, and neck. "Vot rah-yeat-dee?"

(What is wrong with you?)

A low, wailing moan escaped Margaret as she scurried to the outhouse to hide her emotions.

"Not on the floor! NOT ON MY CLEAN FLOOR!" Mother yelled as blood dribbled down Brenda-Jane's cupped hands, dripped on her dress, and threatened to leave a trail across the sunflower seed shell-strewn surface.

"Here." Impatiently, Mother filed the foot bowl with water and carried it to the girl's bedroom. "Put you dress in there to soak when you are finished."

Brenda-Jane leaned over the sink and turned on the cold-water tap. Gingerly, she tipped her head to catch the cooling flow across her burning nose. Marlene watched wide-eyed and awestruck as crimson mingled with clear and ran pink down the drain.

From the angled archway of the living room, conversations between the visitors and hosts sounded like departure mixed in protest.

Once the company had left and Brenda-Jane's nosebleed subsided, Mother and Father gathered the three girls around the kitchen table for a tongue lashing.

"We are ashamed of you lot," Father began. Mother bustled around, sweeping, cleaning, wiping.

"Why couldn't you just play nicely? Are you trying to embarrass us and make us look bad?!"

Father's voice rose. "We can't even enjoy a visit with—"

"But, Dad, my nose could have been broken!" Brenda-Jane interjected.

"Ach!" Margaret scoffed. "I didn't hit you that hard, you big baby!"

"Shut up, you!" Mother snapped. "You could've done that and worse!"

"You girls are so terribly behaved we can't be proud of you. You keep this up, and the next time there's a funeral, we're gonna make you touch the dead."

That night, images of white-swaddled corpses creeping into her room and approaching her bed haunted Brenda-Jane. Then the recurring nightmare of getting caught in sticky sheets hanging from the beams downstairs in the playroom followed. The only light came from the wood room, and Margaret was silhouetted against it, gaping. A narrative note explained that once one touched the sheets, they would stick to you forever. Naturally, Benda Jane clasped the folds of one and drew it toward her face to inhale its sweet freshness.

Margaret gasped. "You'll never get rid of that!"

But Brenda pulled and pulled and ripped the sheet off. After all, causing Margaret to suck in her breath again.

Mother shook Brenda's shoulder gently. "Hey! Hey! Du driimst!" (You're dreaming.)

By the time she was fully awake, the hazy image of Mother in her long flowing granny nightgown with a drawstring and coded padlock at the bottom had dissolved into the hallway.

Fall came, school started again, and the ever-jovial Mr. Heinrichs picked them up in his musty old bus. Once again, they rode with the gang of Heinrichs children and the Penner cousins. The scent of homemade lye soap, stale linen, and wood smoke hovered over each navy-clad Penner.

Johan spied Brenda-Jane and leaned over to whisper, "Pap says we are getting our own school. Pray-vit shul." (Private school).

"How come?" Brenda was instantly curious.

He puffed up with self-righteous pride. "Ohhh." He paused meaningfully. "The public school is too worldly. We have to separate ourselves."

The new second grade teacher was a small, thin Chinese woman who came across as cold as her grimly decorated classroom. She herself wasn't much bigger than the students but, with her black hair cut severely short and face drawn into a tight frown, was plenty intimidating.

Miss Wang wore purple makeup like everyone else wore blue eyeliner, eyeshadow and pink lipstick and blush. All her face was white or painted a shade of purple. She walked with a yardstick, using it like a cane whenever she wasn't pointing at a child or rapping on a surface for attention and emphasis.

"When I point to sit! You sit! When I point to quiet! You quiet!" She was referring to four posters up on the wall above the turquoise chalkboard, drawn in black, blue, and brown marker on another white palette. "Quiet" was depicted with a stick child with a hand covering her mouth. "Sit" showed a side profile of a stick person sitting cross legged. "Attention" was replicated by a pair of wide eyes and tiny mouth line. Finally, "studying" was an open book that hid the twig pupil's face.

Brenda missed Ms. Whittingham. A long, drab school term stretched ahead of her like the elongated shadows on the farm every evening.

CHAPTER 67

Dreamsack

"WE MIGHT have Indian sommer yat." Mother spoke English in her heavy German accent, glancing at the warm fall evening just outside the kitchen window.

Jacob was also back in school and would only visit the farm on the weekends.

"Less blackened laundry for me." Mother snorted, setting a rhubarb pie on a wooden coaster for dessert.

Sometimes they ate raw sliced rhubarb dipped in sugar softened by sweetness. It puckered the victim's face like a drawstring bag.

Brenda-Jane was swept away by a wistful string of nostalgic thoughts from Ms. Whittingham's festive classroom, decorated with fuzzy Dr. Seuss creatures and shapes that spilled over the bulletin boards and onto the walls.

"Dreamsack," Mother wheedled. "What are you thinking about? Don't you like the new schoolbag I made?"

The said sack was a denim jeans makeover with the legs cut off a pair of father's old pants and the crotch sewn shut straight across the bottom. A metal zipper ran across the former waistband, and two denim straps allowed Brenda-Jane to carry it over her shoulder like Margaret's bag. Last year's green corduroy only had a hand grip handle sewn to it.

"Hey! I asked you a question," Mother insisted, still focused on Brenda-Jane. She had purchased two Holly Hobby sew on patches and hand-stitched them to the large pockets facing each other with their sunbonnet clad heads.

"Okay, I'll just take the bag back," Mother snapped.

"No! Mom! I like it! I was just thinking of school, that's all," Brenda-Jane argued. Mother's chiseled features relaxed. She even smiled.

Fall ripped by with the usual frenzy of soup bubbling, tomatoes stewing, and jars sealing in the canner on the stove. Father built a crow-scare-man out of rebar to stand beside the woman in the garden with his feet dangling off the ground. Every windy day, he danced, and Father imitated him until the lid on the soup pot rattled and Mother begged him to stop.

Frost fears came and every blanket, bedspread, and extra clothing articles from the box in the linen closet were dragged outside to cover the vegetation Mother was saving frantically. By morning, the yard sometimes looked like a second-hand store had been bombed and the carnage had all landed in Mother's garden.

Brenda-Jane tried to be invisible at school to avoid the scathing hissing tongue of Miss Wang. It worked most of the time. On some occasions, being quiet got the tutor on her case, and she involved the entire class in the discussion. "Why is Brenda so quiet?" Most days, Miss Wang was content to devour children in general.

Grandmother Gardener told Father and Mother not to cut Brenda-Jane's bangs nor call her by a hyphenated name anymore.

Usually, Grandmother's interference upset Mother to tears.

"She says you're all grown up now."

Snow fell early in the fall of 1983, and it kept falling like it was a popular tradition.

Brenda hung by her coat hook and waited for the other children to settle in the classroom before she entered as she always did. The hallway was deserted when her stomach rose to her throat and threatened to giraffe her neck.

The gray tile floor spun. She wasn't going to vomit and draw attention to herself—Ker-splatt! A volcano erupted inside her and spewed generously all over the hallway.

After that, everything around her was a blur. "Get the teacher!" someone hollered.

"The janitor!"

Brenda recognized Cousin Ernest's voice.

"Come with me." Purple nails dug into her arm. Miss Wang literally kept her at arm's length, all the way down the hallway to the office and its meager sick room.

"I'll call your parents," Miss Wang stated crisply. Her heels clip clopped away briskly, and Brenda weakly lifted the flannel Smurf printed blanket on the roll away cot and laid down. A thin white muslin curtain hung between her and the doorway, reminding her of the sheets in her recurring dream.

The ABC's on the sheet offered to dance a jig with the characters on the blanket like Father's garden dummies, so Brenda closed her eyes.

"Geez, she's burning up!" It was the secretary. The morning floated by in a haze whilst she waited for Father to come get her. Mother only drove as far as the homestead and didn't even write cheques. Sleep came easily despite her churning innards.

She dreamt Ms. Whittingham sat down at the foot of the bed and read *The Pokey Little Puppy* to her. Her curly black hair and turned-up bangs moved softly as she read with the usual vigor. Blue eyes sparkled like the Christmas tree the puppies helped decorate in the story. The slower spotted pup held a gold star in his mouth; he only came across while loitering on the journey. Now it would be perfect for the trimming of the berry-strung outdoor Tannenbaum.

"Branna." Father drew the curtain aside.

Weak and trembling like a baby kitten, Brenda followed Father to her cubby hole to retrieve her coat and bag. A dull burgundy dress-coat had replaced last year's brown robe length, and Brenda hated both.

The weekday Suburban sat running in the school's gravel parking lot. It took all she could do to muster the strength to climb up into it. Polka dots and fuzzy blobs of all colors encircled her.

Mother had chicken noodle soup and white flour buns on the table for lunch at home. She offered Brenda food but mercifully did not push it.

The patent couch in the parlor was draped in old leopard print flannel blankets. Brenda crawled under the red Hudson's Bay flannel with every joint on fire. Mother plunked an empty ice cream pail down beside her head on the floor. Her goose down pillow felt soft and cool. A work-worn hand hesitated on her forehead. A voice muttered a German epithet and footsteps scurried away. They returned, and a cold wet washcloth was laid across Brenda's forehead. Sleep followed, bringing nightmares of her being torn apart limb from limb, complete with real sensation.

"She is SICK," Mother's tone declared in the kitchen. Father wondered if they should make a trip to Eagle's Creek to the clinic there.

"Ersch mal zine." (Wait and see).

Marlene peered at Brenda curiously from time to time.

"You look awful," she ventured once but otherwise contented herself to mere staring and flipping the clammy washcloth over.

Despite her feverish, screaming, aching body, Brenda felt relieved to be pampered. That was the way the family was rude and abrasive until someone was sick. Rare kindness presented itself then, and it proved a soothing balm for the tattered soul.

The virus converted Brenda into a drum, beating her head into an aching pounding frenzy before veering off to each joint individually. The fiery searing pain crept over her limbs, threatening to tear them off and leave her incapacitated.

Father must have been somewhat touched by her emaciated stare because he got out his guitar and played songs of heaven. "How Beautiful Heaven Must Be" and "When We All Get to Heaven." Her ears roared and closed, distorting him.

In her feverish slumber, she overheard Mother begging him to stop.

"Let the child sleep!" Sleep was all she did for two days except for swallowing sips of water and gagging down Mother's offerings of cod liver oil.

Obligated by Mother's beseeching, Margaret brought homework and plunked it down on the two-tier laminated brown end table beside the davenport. Brenda's over sensitized ears made her startle.

"Oh c'mon, I barely set them down—" Margaret's voice trailed off as she stood gazing down at Brenda-Jane.

Her ears roared again, nearly drowning out the terse conversation between Margaret and Mother.

"That kid is sick! We could end up going in with her..."

"Going in" meant the great dreaded voyage into the nearby town for medical care.

"...looks as white as winter—"

Brenda drifted in and out of sleep where drums pounded, and horns blared in the head of a country kid who had barely ever witnessed a traffic jam nor band perform.

A fire had started from an electrical outlet in the Heinrichs living room. Rita, who was Brenda's age, had fled screaming into the falling snow, convinced hell had come for her personally. After all, Jacobson preached it every Sunday as did the Old Colony pastor and every devout Mennonite parent. Hell was used as a fearmongering threat to keep their subjects in line.

Poor Rita Heinrichs had frostbite on her feet and had to wear them bandaged to school. Her older brother's rubber boots were the only footwear that fit over the gauze and they were not being changed judging by the odor of dead animal. She finally unwrapped her "understanding," for gym class and released a stench and shards of dead skin intermingled with puss oozing scabs. That earned her the nickname "Rita Hindstinks," and a reaction from Miss Wang.

"That Miss Wang," Margaret emphasized, "blew up! She stomped up to Rita, ordered her to gather up her bandages and marched her to the office!"

"She was in trouble?" Brenda managed weakly. Mother had made her a cup of something awful under the guise of herbal tea, and Brenda was forcing herself to drink it.

"No…um…mmm." Margaret shook her head importantly. "Her sister, Anna, is in my class, and she told me all about it. Miss Wang called Mr. and Mrs. Heinrichs and cussed them out. Told them to get the girl to the doctor or she was reporting them!"

"I wish someone would report them for keeping their horses so skinny," Margaret mused. Marlene's eyes were enormous from her perch at Brenda's feet on the wide, flat armrest.

Brenda sipped the despicable drink from her propped position on an assortment of goose down pillows.

Gradually, between Mother's cups of steaming chicken in a mug soup and various herbal teas, Brenda felt better. She felt less like a brick lump and more like a stick of kindling.

First, she was well enough to sit up and watch the snow fall in pastel rings past the yard light outside and then recovered enough to breeze through the homework Margaret brought her.

One of Mother's concoctions was pink colored, spicy, and mixed with hot milk.

"It smells of heat liniment." Brenda shrank back and Mother's eyes shone dangerously dark.

"Just drink it!"

Margaret came home full of stories. "That silly Mrs. Redekopp tried to give homework today!"

"Ach!" Mother scoffed. "Die vite gowt bayta! Zie ass ein mannaneet von heah!" (She knows better, she is a local Mennonite).

"She's a substitute—"

"Who only got the job because her husband sits on the school board with the Shepnards," Mother interrupted.

Ernest and Susan Penner had started the commotion as soon as the homework assignment was mentioned.

"Ahem," Ernest had stumbled for words, "Vee don't take homework home. At home, work waits for us. Vee have chores." His German accent tinted his speech, and his face had flushed tomato rouge before he was finished.

"And?" Mother queried.

"Well, Mrs. Redekopp blew up about how she took her teacher aide course at home and became a career woman. She said if we wanted to be manure Sloppers and diaper washers all our lives, so be it. She couldn't do anything about that, but she would give zeroes if we didn't have the play read by tomorrow!"

Mother sneered and harrumphed, banging pots, running water and clattering dishes.

"Vall den!" She laid the verdict down in her thick accent. "Vee viii have to write deh school anodder ladder." Meaning she and Father would wage a war of printed words via their favorite weapon—pen and paper. It was a given, despite Butterhorn Community School being a public institution, that the Mennonite farming lifestyle be honored by the school curriculum. No one required a change of shorts and tank tops for gym, and no self-respecting educator sent homework to the barn loft.

Boys wore baseball caps to class, and the boot room reeked of thawing cow manure stuck to the bottom of boots. The wise wayfarer passed through quickly. That was simply the system.

Marlene found a loose corner of the sheets covering the chesterfield and pulled as hard as she could to wreak havoc on Brenda-Jane. A linen duel ensued. Pillows flew until one struck the glass door of the china shelf and rattled them both.

Mother came running, brandishing her butter block by the push handle and shouting, "Aha! Brenda-Jane! You must be feeling better. Grandma always said when a child got boisterous, they were over their sickness."

The summary was only partly true; both the virus and pillow fight had left her more winded than usual with no energy to speak of. Standing up while Mother changed the bedding on the settee proved quite a penalty.

Brenda caught sight of her reflection in the china cupboard doors and gawked at the gaunt holocaust survivor that mirrored her.

"There. I even ran the pillows in the dryer for twenty minutes." Mother smoothed the floral printed cotton sheet across the patent leather surface.

"Sometimes a fresh bed makes all the difference."

Sleep became Brenda's indoor sport, and she fast became a champion. Oh, how her body demanded sleep. Around the corner, just behind the wall that housed the entertainment cupboard, she sometimes caught whispers and snatches of conversations about her.

"Rheumatic fever" came across once. "Viral infection" and "should go in."

Father went off to work in the bush for Shepnard Logging as soon as the ground froze, leaving the barn chores for Mother and Margaret.

Brenda sometimes put on a stack of records while the house was empty of her kinfolk; Marlene tagged along with Mother and Margaret to slop the pigs and milk the cows. She favored instrumental music without anyone singing or narrating where one could just close their eyes and ride along to the tune!

Oddly, Mother said nothing when she re-entered the house and strains of "The Magic Organ," was still filtering through the speakers on the top shelf. Being sick had its perks, to be sure.

CHAPTER 68

Breakthrough!

A PANICKED PHONE call came one wintry afternoon: one long ring and two short. It was Grossmam, asking for Father's help. The cows had rushed for the ice hole to water and had broken through.

Mother bolted to action. Quickly, she gathered their snow suits and urged Marlene and Brenda to hurry and get dressed.

She drove tersely to the Senior Gardener farm, a little faster than usual, still painfully slow.

The Jerseys were white-eyed and bleating hoarsely while a frantic Uncle Daniel and Aunt Mary lassoed one by one and tied the rope to the saddle horn of the nearest Morgan twin. They pulled gallantly up the slope, sometimes slipping but struggling onward and upward.

"We're gonna lose'm!" shouted Uncle Daniel. The process was too slow only three cows were saved, still churned the icy water like a poor man's Jacuzzi.

Uncle Isbrandt's pickup rattled to a stop at the top of the hill.

"Give me a rope!" he yelled. "I'll pull them with my hitch!"

A rope flew to him. It circled and caught a flailing bovine around the neck. Swiftly, Isbrandt tied it to the ball hitch on his truck and put it in gear while the cow scrambled up the slippery bank. The rescued animals wasted no time racing to the open barn door for shelter and warmth.

Mother, Brenda, and Marlene took hold of the end of a rope and pulled. Mother's slender body bent into an arc like a willow sapling under the strain, but the cow worked with the agile woman, slipping and fighting to gain a foothold. The combined efforts at their end of the rope seemed to add the grain of strength that was needed for enough momentum.

Three cows fought valiantly in the Shreefah while the newly rescued were untied and the ropes adjusted. It was painful to move so slowly and observe the tedious rescue that screamed of needing swift resolution.

Grossmam stood in her skirt and boots, watching the watery rodeo and giving directions.

"Not so fast*!* Langsam! Mole langsam! (Slowly, now slowly)." The last three critters were roped to safety and pulled simultaneously out of their churning near-nemesis. Mother and Mary took one, Uncle Isbrandt's truck sputtered as it moved forward, and the stout horses sweated up the hill with last one.

"Hiyeh die alla?" (Do you have them all?) Grandmother queried from her pedestal on the crest of the rise.

Everyone within earshot glanced back furtively, but the water was slowing down and the gap in the ice empty.

"We'll take roll call in the barn!" Uncle Isbrandt joked, untying the soggy cow from his bumper.

That was a Gardener for you—tell a joke at the most inopportune moment.

"Nah!" Grandmother chided him. Humor was discouraged.

Despite the chilling ordeal, grins spread over the small crowd.

A heavy odor of wet dog hung in the aisle of the barn where the cows huddled together for warmth.

"Smells like beavers," Uncle Dan lamented. Nine rescued and dripping head of cattle.

"You did good," Grossmam praised the men. "Thank you all. How good of you. I'll put the coffee on. Batsy, you'll stay for coffee, yes?" Her reference to Mother's first name sounded stilted and odd.

Mother did not answer but remained stooped over in her navy-blue snow suit. Brenda and Marlene followed her to the Sunday Suburban the same color in silence.

"Mom, why are you walking funny?" Brenda dared ask.

"Arthritis" came through clenched teeth.

The journey home was slow. Mother slumped over the wheel in pinched-faced silence. She spent the day hunched over like a very old person, vociferously working, cleaning, and polishing in otherwise pained muteness.

Brenda went back to school, having missed three weeks.

Miss Wang rifled through the stack of her finished assignments and sniffed disdainfully.

"You may sit down" was all she said.

Miss Wang was evidently able to warm up to certain children; those who belonged to other teachers like the Redekopp twins, Abel and Annie. Mrs. Redekopp wasn't a real teacher; she was a mere teacher's assistant, but she put on airs like a Shepnard, and it drew respect and admiration from some. Others scoffed at her for working outside her home.

After lunch, Miss Wang handed out sugar cubes to every other student, skipping Rita Heinrichs and Brenda with a smirk and so on.

"What is your real name!" she hissed Friday afternoon, holding a paper with Brenda written on it, another with Brenda-Jane inscribed across the top of a math quiz.

"Class, we have a problem." She pointed her pointer at the "Quiet-or-I'll-Hiss-some-more," poster above them.

Everyone looked up from their textbooks and stared as Miss Wang's tiny heels clicked over to Brenda across the cold gray tiles.

"I am getting work handed in to me that says Brenda and work that says Brenda-Jane. Do we have a new student I don't know about?" Chuckles went around the room.

"Last year, she went by Brenda-Jane!" Annie Redekopp piped up importantly.

Brenda was mortified that her bottom lip began to quiver. She knew speaking would only release prohibited emotion.

"Let's have a vote," Miss Wang suggested cheerfully, walking to the chalkboard. She drew a Tchart with Brenda written on one side, Brenda-Jane on the other.

True to form as per Grossmam's wishes, the class voted Brenda.

"The idea." Mother got her dander up when Brenda got home from school and told the tale. "I will write that cow a letter she won't forget and send the principal and school board one too."

And God bless her, she did. Mother wrote a scathing letter on lined loose-leaf paper to the three entities that would have taken the chrome off a Chevy had it been held close enough. She wrote on block capitals.

Dear Miss Wang,

The day you rename my daughter will be a strange day indeed.

You overstepped the bounds yesterday and I will see about your job. You do nothing but pick on my child and now after a prolonged illness you do it again. I realize you are small, but I believe you understand me when I say: PICK ON YOUR OWN SIZE, not my daughter. Her name is Brenda-Jane Gardener which you already know if you would just read your information instead of belittling a kid. We, HER PARENTS have decided to shorten her name to Brenda which is our full right to do. Not yours. You owe the three of us an apology. We are a Mennonite community who doesn't like outsiders coming in as it is but your behavior is most deplorable,

> and I will see that it changes or your job
> will. Whichever comes first.

The three girls let out the breaths they had been holding while Mother read the letter out loud.

One could almost feel sorry for the imp-sized witch of the second grade.

Almost. Mother painstakingly rewrote the note twice to make copies.

Margaret delivered two of the letters to school, one for the wayward educator and principal, Shales. The other would be stamped and addressed to the head of the school board who lived in Hatchet Prairie.

What transpired next was somewhat of a mystery, but Miss Wang stomped around on her heels in sullen ornery silence that even the darling Redekopp urchins could not penetrate. Evidently, she got the message.

"I just don't find it that way at all. I just don't find it that way at all," Mother chanted, mimicking Principal Shales. "Of course, the schoolteachers all stick together! They are made of the same cloth!" "Moldy fortrel?" Margaret ventured, and they all laughed.

"No, I just don't find it that way!"

"Torn cotton?"

Whether Mr. Shales had spoken to the school frau or the acrimonious letter had fulfilled its purpose, Miss Wang did not call attention to Brenda or any other pupil again.

CHAPTER 69

The River

FATHER CAME home Friday nights reeking of sweat and sweetened tea. Mother flew to him and embraced him like he was the most loving, kind, considerate husband in the world, and the youngest girls followed suit. Margaret hung back and waited with a look of pure apprehension and tentative hope on her freckled face.

He beelined for the late supper Mother kept for him while Brenda snaffled his thermos of tea and drank it.

Mother babbled on and on, and he appeared to be listening as he shoveled forkful of chicken fried rice into his mouth. She paused and brought up the near drowning of Grosspabeh's cows.

"I think Daniel felt rather ashamed of himself, letting the cows all surge forward like that onto the ice. You can be sure he probably won't do that again."

Father chewed. Mother waited. Marlene stood by his elbow, blue eyes glowing.

"But I guess, once again, I didn't matter. I tried to help, strained my back, and heard her thank the boys for coming. Goodness sake—doesn't she get that her belief that womenfolk are nothing lowers her too? Oh, but then, again, deacon's wife. Uh huh." Mother rose to refill his plate while Father took a long slurp of coffee.

The room began to swim in front of Brenda's eyes. Straight lines wiggled. Margaret, from beside her, seemed to fog over and refocus. The yard light grew and shrank, Mother's face swam, and her voice echoed.

"I'm going to bed," Brenda announced to no one in particular. She thought she heard Mother agreeing behind her that indeed it was bedtime.

Somehow, Brenda got to bed. Nightmares plagued her fevered sleep. Rita Heinrichs chased her on bloody skinless feet that resembled chicken legs. All around the Gardener farm they zigged and zagged between outbuildings and outhouses where Father had kerplunked items anywhere on the farmyard as he saw fit.

Rita evaporated into the fog, and Grandfather's cows roared out of the stormy Shreefah and stampeded up the slopes to gouge her with their horns. The din was incredible; loud and riotous until it threatened to cause an explosion in her skull.

The boisterous night ended with the clamor of Corelle dinnerware and a sweet voice trilling; "I wanna go to heaven, when this life is o'er, I wanna be with Jesus, on eternity's shore ." Mother often sang that song, the chorus ending in, "Please, blessed Jesus, give Mother my crown."

Brenda's throat was on fire, and she was convinced the sandman had swapped sand for cotton and pumped her skull full to the brim with it.

Over oatmeal, Mother peered at Brenda, who struggled to swallow. Everything tasted like sawdust, the brown sugar and milk in the bowl made no difference.

"You have eggs on your throat," Mother remarked. "Dad!

"Look at those cheeks! She is never that color! We're gonna have to go in."

The snowy drive to Eagle's Creek was tedious. Father drove to the new All Saints of Mary Hospital a half-hour from Hatchet Prairie. It smelled of antiseptic chemicals and fluoride. Mother spoke to the blonde receptionist with dangling hoop earrings and a layered haircut behind the glass wall.

Brown, sack-like upholstered chairs with chrome legs lined the walls of the waiting room. A dark brown arborite coffee table covered in magazines stood stoic on its round chrome legs. A few native women sat waiting, plump and still.

Brenda was on fire one minute and freezing cold the next. Mother touched her forehead gingerly.

The doctor was a tall, thin man with dark hair whose face appeared to have fallen out of his hairline. His mouth seemed too big and wide for his otherwise narrow head.

Mother and Brenda followed the back of his white coat to a small examining room.

Dr. Reed told Mother, in his opinion, Brenda should be admitted to hospital.

"N-no." Mother shook her head. "We want to keep her home," came the carefully rehearsed phase the women passed around each other during Sunday afternoon gossip.

"Mennonites!" he muttered when they were still within earshot.

Brenda was reunited with her old pal the faux leather couch and a kindly mother that seemed foreign.

"I'll give you the red blanket this time," she soothed. "You like red, don't you? Anyway, it's already going gray outside with winter and all, why don't we jazz up the couch a little?" Brenda squirmed inside. The attentive compassion of her normally angry or lackadaisical mother prickled worse than the flannel Hudson's Bay blanket.

"I'll put on the record player and play the Derksen sisters that you like so much." Mother's voice trailed off as Brenda fell asleep.

The SEARS WISH book had come in the fall along with the beginning of a tepid school year and canning season.

Brenda spent several more weeks on the davenport, sleeping, sweating and, at times, delirious as fever throbbed in her ears while its roaring bedlam danced with mayhem. At times, a shadowy figure in a granny nightgown shook her awake and coaxed her to drink, draping a cold washcloth across her forehead.

Brenda studied the WISH BOOK, listened to records, and did homework in between flushed slumber and Sunday morning's in her head. She drank Mother's laced drinks without question and flipped the cloth on her forehead over when one side grew too warm.

Christmas was a month away, so Father's Sunday school class began practicing Saturday evenings in the oil-lantern-lit church. Grandfather and Grandmother unlocked the wooden building one night just to have the children go berserk, running along pews like heathens without a care.

This was the first and only time Brenda ever heard Grandfather yell.

"Children! This is God's house! Sit down!" Everyone shrank into their seats like a melting Disney cartoon character.

"That's better," he soothed.

Most of the pupils were memorizing High German Christmas carols from the gesangbuch (hymnbook), but Father always found a unique poem or song from other sources.

As soon as Brenda felt stronger, she joined her sisters in making a red and green paper chain to decorate the playroom with. She returned to school, turned in her "counting by hundreds, tens and ones" math homework and short stories, and practiced "Angels We Have Heard on High" with the class.

Miss Wang brought Mrs. Redekopp in to teach art and music, and good on her for it, because no one could picture her expressing herself in any way other than coldness and purple makeup.

The second-grade class rolled waxed string in more wax and glitter, creating lumpy, nostalgic candles for Christmas gifts for parents.

Mother made green velour dresses with ruffled skirts, ribbon-tied cuffs, and white lace trim. She caught a ride with the Benjamens to the school concert on a Wednesday evening and baked shortbread cookies.

On the Sunday morning of the church pageant, the Sunday school class filled the front two rows of the congregation. Grandfather's sapphire eyes twinkled like Santa Claus down at Brenda from his elevated seat with the leadership facing the church.

There was a grand repetition of "Dies Ist Die Nacht" (This Is the Night) and "Stille Nacht, Heilige Nacht," (Silent Night, Holy Night). Some sang in familial groups without accompaniment, of course, because instruments were considered worldly. Other siblings alternated reciting the verses and then chanting the chorus together.

Brenda felt weak and dizzy. The wood stove snapped and crackled merrily, sending sparks that stung her body all over from rows away. She slid past a sea of knees and staggered out to the Navy Suburban, opened the unlocked driver's door, and collapsed alongside the front seat. Tears poured out of her for no reason. Every reason. She cried and cried for how rotten she felt and that her recital was still upcoming. Tears like Jimmy Swaggart's river spilled on the faded blue upholstery until the door opened behind her. A gust of cold winter air mingled with her mother's voice.

"Oh, there you are. You'd better come on in it's almost your—" she hesitated upon seeing Brenda's tear-stained face.

"C'mon, the Heinrichs kids all got up and sang so beautifully, and the Zacherias girls couldn't sing without giggling. No one has a poem like yours. You'd better come."

Brenda knew the real mother was behind the tangent no matter how candy cane sweet at this moment.

Back in God's house, Brenda walked to the front and stood with Margaret and Marlene at the foot of the carved pulpit.

She barely heard Margaret's recital. Brenda-Jane fixed her gaze on a polished nail head in the varnished plywood floor and began "Die Weihnacht's Geschenk" (The Christmas Gift).

After the parishioners sang their two closing hymns, the Sunday school teachers were stationed at the end of the children's rows. They handed out brown paper bags full of peanuts, hard candy, a mandarin orange, and a small gift. This year, the girls received a small ceramic mug and saucer—doll sized, with tiny pink flowers painted around the edges.

Mercifully, Christmas holidays had begun leaving only the rehearsal at the family gathering before Brenda could rest listless days away.

"White as could be." Mother fretted over her.

"Ya!" Marlene chimed in, "Just like the hymn."

"And the Bible verse: through your sins be as scarlet, they shall be white as snow; though they be red like crimson, they shall be as wool." (Isaiah 1:18 KJV)

CHAPTER 70

Gathering at Grandmothers

GRANDMOTHER'S HOUSE teemed with her offspring, their spouses, and children as they did every Christmas, covering the vestibule floor in snowy footgear. The white-sided, tin-roofed house smelled of wood-smoke, home baking, and cow manure.

Not everyone attended the same church, and the clusters of seated gossips revealed denominations; the black kerchiefed Old Colony members sat in a stoic row along the bench underneath the window behind the table. The Old Order Mennonites sat at the ends of the table, babushkas and dresses color coordinated. Mother sat in that group nervously. Father's oldest brother had converted to Amish, so his wife and a string of white-capped daughters in long layered dresses sat by the wood stove. A few of the smaller girls darted around, zigzagging between bodies and chairs.

Aunt Mary had a boyfriend now, a young plaid-clad man with the majority of his thick brown hair combed over from a part on the side. He sat on proverbial tenterhooks in the square "great room," where the men conglomerated in no particular order. They were more or less dressed the same, dark dress pants and dark dress shirts. Any plaid worn was so dark it looked like a solid color. The Old Colony males wore suspenders and thick grey wool work socks like a gang.

Grandmother, Tante (Aunt) Zedah, and Mary, the oldest and youngest daughters, bustled around engrossed in food preparation for the first round of consumption by the men. The women would clean up and then reset the table and eat with their youngest children. Lastly, the remaining children would eat.

After the mountainous amounts of food had been consumed and vast total of dishes and put away from a single sink, the recitals began.

The Amish children—four boys and eight girls, sang "Silent Night" loudly. The Old Colony children—the Penners especially, chanted long, hushed renditions of High German hymns. They stood with their stockinged toes pointed outward. The stage was merely a spot on the yellow linoleum in front of the redwood pantry door beside the matching laundry chute cover.

Old Order Mennonites were quicker in recital and fancier in clothing. Making short work of their memorizations, the older children retreated to the basement, and the younger to the bus bench mounted to the hallway floor. A wooden crate underneath it held a miserly assortment of toys; a plastic doll whose tangled hair could no longer be combed out, a few blocks, wood slab ends, and the dreaded button necklace Aunt Susanna had made. Really, nothing to play with but mind games, and you had to make those yourself.

"That's wrong." Johan Penner sat spread eagled on the bench. "Necklaces are sin."

"It's ugly," Brenda retorted. "Then it's okay."

"Children!" Aunt Susanna waddled down the hallway in a billowing maternity dress and kerchief.

How she dwarfed her husband now, but evidently, he was into mountain climbing.

"Shall I get out Grossmam's button box?"

Buttons were the marbles of the day in Grandmam's drab household. Twelve red and a dozen black buttons promised a game of checkers on a bare patch of criss-crossing lines on the old linoleum. Connect the button pictures could be outlined on the indoor/outdoor carpeting the bench sat on.

"Vote braucht nate close dee?" (What did Santa Claus bring you?) Aunt Zedah asked any of her nieces and nephews within earshot. The same aunt who was married to the pastor of the strictest sect of Mennonites quizzed children about the "Ousta Hose" (Easter Bunny) at Easter gatherings.

As relatives departed, Grandmother and Grandfather pulled labeled brown bags from their post atop the large old deep freeze in the entryway and deposited them to the appropriated grandchild.

"Zay danke schon" (Say thank you), Aunt Tina prompted her string of children.

The loot for Uncle Jacob's Amish brood sure cleared a spot on the ancient appliance.

The contents of the brown paper bags were no mystery. They were similar to the Sunday school and public-school receptacles. Grandma's had the same telltale round bulge the mandarin oranges typically made.

"Of all the ideas—" Mother scoffed while prying the staples out of the bags in the car on the short distance home. "A preacher woman asking children about Santa Claus! Isn't that worldly? HAH!"

The children explored the contents of the lunch bags. The round object was a ball of rerolled yarn, three dusty rose yarn balls. Mother and Father's gifts were a pewter nutcracker and a set of dish towels.

"What?!" Mother gasped. "That cheap—" she left the sentence hang for Father's sake.

"Are Grandpa and Grandma poor?" Marlene piped up.

Mother snorted. "They are as rich as the Shepnards."

Brenda had been entertaining a notion, rerolling it in her mind until she saw Mother's disappointment with Grandmother.

"Mom—will you wrap one gift for us this year? Just one?"

A smile washed over Mother's tired face, and a rush of air escaped her in a silent chuckle.

"Oh—maybe. No promises!"

Between the couch and fevers, Brenda-Jane had perfected her Christmas list; a Barbie Doll and record player like Cousin Karla had with storybooks and matching records that read the book. She added the game "Operation," and a "Hook'n Latch" rug-making kit.

"Nothing with batteries, and no Barbie extras," Mother warned.

Mother's sewing machine hummed when her mouth didn't, and new flannel nightgowns were taking shape under her work-roughened hands. The new fabric smelled of vinegar and sported fluffy white sheep with pink ears, tails, hooves, and noses leaping across teal blue skies.

"You can pick out the buttons." Mother removed the pins from her mouth long enough to present several paper cards of plastic buttons. The assortment included plastic pink ribbons, white lambs, or blue orbs.

Brenda pounced on the ribbons. Marlene the lambs, leaving Margaret without options and looking crestfallen.

"Ach! Big girl!" Mother sneered. "You're big enough to sew your own clothes! Well, go then— get the button box. There's cards in there too."

Margaret's face flushed, and she looked close to tears, but she obliged Mother.

One could never have an awkward or emotional moment and then seek refuge someplace private to sort out those feelings. Oh no, the child attempting to slink away and save face was promptly ordered back to the group to meet the needs of the adult.

Brenda added "Twister" to her list. Mother and Father had a habit for buying joint gifts, especially for herself and Marlene. Brenda hated it. She wanted desperately to be her own person—to be individual.

Christmas was upon them, and the stage of "there's no money for presents this year" had passed to threats of "I'll send your gifts back!" over minor trouble. That was Mother. For larger infractions, it was "I'll tell Dad."

The weekly beatings started as soon as Father went to work in the bush. Saturday after lunch, he'd push back his plate and ask, "Well, how were the kids?" and for dessert, Mother would tell him. The list of misdemeanors made his face light up, and he'd smile pinkly. Then he'd line them all up starting with Margaret and screams of "NO!" and futile gestures of covering one's behind with the free arm would begin. Father always jerked one arm above the victim's head to keep them in place while he struck with his belted arm.

"*Mewl tow. Mewl tow* (mouth shut)." He demanded silence during a beating, or he'd threaten to thrash harder and repeat the process.

The churchless Benjamens lit up the big blue spruce tree in their yard, and so did the Henrys down the street by the "Penner Bridge."

Brenda was secretly glad to have the colorful Christmas tree next door, although she kept it to herself for safekeeping.

The flu flattened her against the black patent Davenport again, so she crocheted Grandma's yarn with her fingers and watched the snow fall outside. Northern lights danced with the yard lamp, swirling, whisking, and changing pastel spectrum. Brenda knew if she were outside, a soft audible tinkle would accompany the flowing skirts of the night sky.

Marlene got the flu also, so Brenda found herself back in her aged bed under a foreboding window much higher and less accessible. She had to stand and crane her neck to see the Benjamens' Christmas tree.

The farmhouse creaks and pops sounded like gunshots to the fevered brain.

Mother doted on Marlene, turning washcloths on the fevered brow and emptying the puke pot.

Brenda pretended to moan, so Mother dashed a hurried hand to her brow in passing. The sick and occasionally hurting stood a chance at being cared for at the Gardener household. Only then.

CHAPTER 71

Weak Nerves

CHRISTMAS EVE tradition hustled the children into the back bedroom to wait while Mother and. Father filled the bowl they'd set at the table. This year Tupperware was resumed after the previous year's "silver bowls." Father's was the largest, a green mixing bowl. Mother's orange cake mixes and nut reservoir sat at side by each above a chipped wooden bench across from Mother and Marlene's, a large brown basin next to Brenda's slightly smaller red cookie batter bowl.

True to her almost promise, Mother had wrapped one rectangular box for each daughter imprinted with Santa's countenance in betwixt red bows.

"It's ready," Mother's voice trilled down the corridor. The gifts were placed, nut bowls filled.

Father and Mother exchanged gifts too, usually a practical item. She took what of her child tax credit he hadn't stolen from her to purchase his expensive gifts, a table saw this yuletide occasion. Most of the toys, books, and games were funded with the change leftover from Father's "geschenk" or gift. He used farm credit or a near-maxed credit card to bless Mother in towels, casserole dishes, and kitchenware. Mother said so in her multiple pre-holiday tirades, "I'm the only one who makes Christmas happen around here."

The wrapped present was a Spirograph set. Brenda noticed there were no items from her wish list—nor anyone else's. A customary jigsaw puzzle, board game, and a box of chocolates sat at each place setting along with an item for each girls' hope chest; a set of glass tumblers painted on the side with wheat stalk designs.

"See?" Father beamed. "Isn't it better when Mom and Dad pick out your gifts than if you do?" They obediently chorused a yes.

"Veenachten" (Christmas) lingered on for a while; the peanuts and a hard candy bowls dwindled slowly, and the neighbors lit trees twinkled in the prairie winter darkness.

Brenda's birthday was coming up, and she badly wanted a little electric plastic sewing machine like Cousin Karla had.

"How come we don't know the Henry's?" Brenda laid the SEARS catalogue aside to ask Mother.

"Nah! Die zahn nicht fon unzeh yeahmint!" (They are not from our church) Mother exclaimed.

The couple lived obscured by mature tree foliage in their yard, separated by a church membership list. The Old Colony and Old Order Mennonites begrudgingly associated with each other—some fought against those associations. But to hobnob with an evangelical Mennonite member—no way. Such a connection could get you shunned after a good scolding from church leadership.

Once in a while, old Satan himself would bound out of the greenery of the Henry yard in the form of a giant St. Bernard dog and terrorize passersby.

It was rumored that the secretive household encompassed a "devil's box" or television set.

"Well, sure!" Mother or Father would remark dryly to the gossip. "The Evangelical Mennonites have what they call freedom."

Another story behooved that the couple had raised a half-dozen sons and hitched them all up to the plow when the one horse hurt himself too badly to pull.

"They believe in being 'saved,'" local gossips mocked. "As if you can ever be sure of heaven."

Mother busied herself selling eggs over the phone while Margaret and Marlene cut shapes out of construction paper. Everyone was preparing for Brenda's eighth birthday with the same zealousness that scripture verses were memorized, and church attended.

On the particular family member's birthday, everyone tiptoed around them, trying to be kinder than usual and make the day special. Mother made an angel food cake, homemade whipped cream, and stewed strawberries.

Last year's power outage candles were placed, lit, sang around, and blown out.

"Should we save Dad a piece of cake?" Mother purred, bringing out her pie-slice-shaped Tupperware dishes and lids.

"What about your bus driver?" Brenda agreed and watched Mother carefully cut and tuck them both into the fridge freezer ceremoniously.

Brenda waited for her gift eagerly, only pretending to be interested in the large bedecked card her sisters had given her.

Mother beamed as she awkwardly approached the table, brown eyes dancing, hands behind her back.

"Which hand?" she teased. Finally, Mother brought out a little Robin's egg blue sewing machine. It was out of the packaging, which meant Mother had achieved a discount by buying the display model.

The little machine had a foot pedal, presser foot, real needle, and everything Mother's had except reverse. The best gift of all presented itself when Father came home that weekend, and no one got told on or beaten.

Marlene clung to him more than usual and, by Sunday afternoon, cried uncontrollably while Mother and Father entertained guests in the front room.

"Vot ass lowce?" (What is loose; meaning what is wrong?) Margaret queried tenderly, stroking Marlene's hair.

She wept even more before emitting, "I want to die."

"Obah!" Margaret protested. "What makes you say such a thing?"

Marlene blubbered and cried, citing that she missed Father terribly when he was away working. After her sobs had subsided, faspa and the guests cleared away, Margaret had a meeting in the laundry room with Mother.

Brenda, sweeping sunflower seed shells off the living room floor, strained to hear. The meager assortment of words filtering through the sounds of brushing against the floor told her the conversation centered around Marlene.

Father was called into the session, and it was decided that Marlene would accompany him to camp and stay with Aunt Judy Gardener and her brood of children in their "bush cabin" while Father worked. At night, Marlene would sleep in Father's room.

Aunt Judy was married to Father's younger brother, Tobias Gardener, and was seemingly forever pregnant. Brenda envisioned her standing large at her cook stove in a straight maternity dress, unshaven legs swollen in her runny nylons. Her bush cabin windows boasted of red and white checked gingham curtains that matched the jaunty tablecloth lined with children coloring pictures.

"We must do this for her weak nerves," Mother whispered. "She's exactly like me."

Meanwhile at school, Brenda receded further into herself in an attempt to minimize trouble with the brittle teacher and her distant classmates. Weeks of seclusion due to her illness had only driven the wedge deeper between her and the rest of the world.

While Abel and Annie Redekopp lead all interactions and conducted the class participation under the glowing eye of Miss Wang, Brenda kept still. Remaining weak, pale, and listless in sequence of the virus that had ravaged her through and through, she offered no more communication than absolute necessity.

"Class," Miss Wang's dark eyes glittered like a serpents. "Have you ever noticed how Brenda never speaks in class nor runs in phys ed?"

Up to that point, Miss Wang had been a cold-hearted childless woman with no real skills relating to children except vast extremes. Now, she had graduated to a genuinely mirthless wizard tormenting Brenda.

Heat surged up from her stomach to her face, neck, ears. The class tittered.

"Say something," Annie hissed, flashing icy blue eyes at her.

Brenda tried to snicker along with the class, feigning she was in on the joke.

"It's not funny, Brenda," Abel warned.

"We are going to sit here and wait for Brenda to speak!" Miss Wang beaked triumphantly.

A thousand needles pried Brenda's skin open, prickling and burning. The room spun, expanded and shrank.

"I—," Brenda's mouth went as cotton polyester as the pajamas mother made last Christmas but didn't finish until her birthday.

Miss Wang raised greased pencil brows and mockingly leaned forward.

"Pardon me?" The class giggled again.

"I don't like you and I don't think you should be a teacher," Brenda rushed on. "You're mean and you pick on people."

The purple-lip stick mouth dropped open. A scattering of nervous titters rippled to the room's perimeter and flushed Miss Wang's face now. She slammed the storybook in her hands down to her knees and abruptly stood up, tenaciously stepping through squatting children who had gathered at her feet for a reading of *Black Beauty*.

Stomping out on her three quarter-inch pumps, Miss Wang left the classroom.

Annie glared at Brenda. "You've done it now. She's going to get the principal."

"Teacher's pet!" Brenda returned.

"Easy for you to say!"

"You're gonna be in trouble," Abel argued.

"I was already in trouble," Brenda retorted. "So what?"

Truth was, it felt good to return fire instead of forever swallowing it as if performing at a circus.

"Yah! You're gonna be in trouble!" one of the Redekopp followers chanted.

"You wish," Brenda shot back. Rita Heinrichs scooted over beside Brenda.

"My mom says teachers are mean when they have no kids of their own and that they should all have to have children before becoming teachers." She smelled of old muslin, moth balls, and sweaty socks, but Rita came to Brenda's rescue that day. Annie's mouth snapped shut.

CHAPTER 72

Outbursts

WHEN FATHER and Marlene came home Friday evening, Brenda and Marlene fought for a place on his knee. He sat one on each of his thighs and launched into a story.

"Girls, there was a little boy in the Bible times about your age whose Mother packed him a lunch and sent him to meet Jesus. When he found out Jesus and his disciples needed his lunch to help feed all their guests, he gave it up instantly.

"Now, girls," Father concluded gravely, "What would Jesus think of you two fighting over my lap?"

"Shhh—he's busy eating!" Marlene declared. Mother's face crumpled, and she hid her smile behind her large, work-roughened hand.

Margaret beamed but refrained from speaking.

"Every time you fight instead of sharing, you are going against Jesus. And God writes all these sins down in his book. One day, he will show us all the things we have done wrong."

Brenda slid from his lap. Crestfallen and condemned, she longed to skedaddle to sort out her feelings.

"Hah! Pouting!" Mother pointed out.

She was almost out of earshot, had almost made it, when Father's beefy arm snaked out and his finger and thumb closed on her ear.

"Hey, pouting is not allowed," he commanded.

Brenda squirmed as fire erupted around his grip. "I'm not!"

"Then why such attitude?" Mother interjected.

"It hurts!"

Mercifully, Father released her, and she could escape down the hallway to her room.

Saturday morning, Marlene was stationed to icing and began to drop the last of the shortbread cookies leftover from Christmas at the counter. Margaret bleated, "The more we get together," from the barn as Brenda got up.

"You're always the last one up, lazy girl," Mother complained. "Hurry up, go eat your breakfast, and then go dust the living room for me. I am behind on Saturday keeping."

"Zinult hullen" meant Saturday keeping or house cleaning and preparation for Sunday's company.

"I'll be checking your work." Mother carefully aimed her old black 126 camera at Marlene and took a picture, but she meant Brenda's work.

Brenda dusted the odd collection of mismatched second-hand pieces of furniture and around any plant perched on them. At the center of the entertainment unit, she got lost dusting in the china cupboard as she always did...the pink plastic swans with silk flowers growing out of their back were so pretty...floating on their pressboard brown pond. The small tin chest that resembled a medieval treasure trove sparkled red and gold faux jewel entrustment. A small group of Father's hand-carved horses stood ready to haul the chest full of jewelry, money, and sparkling finery.

Mother's plastic woven basket stood propped against the back wall of the cupboard, sporting a colorful floral stamp in its center.

Plastic flowers and ferns grew from a small white ceramic reservoir between the swans- "What is taking you so long?!" Mother shouted. Pots clanged, water ran, and dishes rattled.

"The floor needs to be washed and I can't do it all!"

Quickly, Brenda-Jane replaced the items in the china cupboard, forgetting their original order. She brushed her damp rag over the shelves where books didn't cover the space just as high-heeled footsteps briskly marched across the kitchen floor.

Mother's angry brown eyes darted everywhere.

"There! See! You only dusted the china cupboard. I can tell because everything's been moved. Now get moving and finish the rest so you can wash the floor."

A devious memory crossed Brenda's mind. If moving items meant she had cleaned… Quickly, she hurried to all the plants and lamps around the room, tweaking them just out of place. Since she was now deemed the deck scrubber not unlike a cartoon duck, she made good use of Mother's theory a second time and jarred the garbage cans slightly. By the time Mother's cauldron presented itself as a steaming old aluminum wash bucket with a strainer and the scent of Mr. Clean hung heavy in the air, Brenda had diminished her workspace slightly.

Father could not be appeased by a child's workmanship either, verbally etching the phrase, "Not good enough," on each laboring child's forehead for every effort and deed. The hot searing brand penetrated the skin and sank deep into the heart of a child, burning a path through to the spirit.

His favorite journey to failure for one of his offspring was to make a request like "Get me an eight-sixteenth wrench." And then come roaring, snorting, and stomping up behind the insufficiently informed and yell belittling insanities at them. "WHAT DO YOU MEAN YOU CAN'T FIND IT?!" That particular Saturday, he singled Brenda out. "Get me the bag from the laundry."

The laundry room was full of cloth bags of clothespins hung from the white paneled walls; brown paper bags full of dried dill stems stood on top of the dryer. A sack of grocery bags dangled from its hook under the raw wood windowsill.

Brenda stood pondering in front of the dryer for a moment too long.

Foot stomps pounded the floor. The stoves rattled, the house shook, and her right eardrum was blasted full of "I TOLD YOU THE BROWN PAPERBAG! CAN'T YOU EVER CATCH ON? I SAID —" His volume echoed and glanced off the walls of the tiny room.

Brenda's ears popped. A rushing noise of air moving filled her head, muzzling his anger.

Vibrations beneath her feet indicated the exit of the raging bull.

"You are going to have to start listening better!" Mother scolded. "You are not a godly child."

In her bed, Brenda took out her New Testament and read her favorite verse, Psalm 27:10, "Though my father and mother forsake me, the Lord will take me up."

Another tactic of Father and Mother was to bellow, "YOU'RE NOT A CHRISTIAN!" for miscellaneous demeanors, varied in kind.

Except for that one verse, God and Christianity appeared to be forever stacked against her. The crack of sunshine provided by the single piece of scripture, however, gave enough light to hint of a brighter view ahead. Brenda clung to that silver of illumination.

Father led the chores when he was home and Marlene and Brenda usually donned on their snowsuits to join him. Everyone had two sets of outdoor clothing and an ensemble for church and school. The impressionable wear hung upstairs on curved brass hooks behind the door of the white and gold porch. The barn clothes were downstairs by the cold storage room beside the entryway in the cement wall on primitive six-inch nails pounded into the nearly black paneling beside the heavy wooden door. A rectangle of orange indoor/outdoor carpeting was duct taped to the cold floor and a plywood shelter attached to two by four framework covered the cement steps that, commenced the path to the half-painted barn and well that flanked it.

Father's barn boasted electricity that flowed through the veins of the milk machine and chugged rhythmically on Bertha's udder. Margaret milked June, the red jersey, by hand while Father cut an alfalfa bale open for the horses outside.

Margaret tilted one of the pink teats, and a white stream arced through the air toward one of the barn cats, who leapt toward the treat with open-mouthed expertise.

"Why don't you just milk them all with machines?" Brenda wondered aloud of the four cows.

"Cuz. June's had trouble with Mastitis, and besides, we're not all as lazy as you!" Margaret's answer ended in a yell. The outburst upset June, who kicked at the pail that Margaret swiftly grasped and swung out of firing range.

Brenda reached above her for the set of "kickers," a pair of "cow cuffs," if you would; metal clasps that sat above the "knees" of the cow's hind legs to prevent kicking.

"Shvinn! Mal shvinn!" (Hurry! Hurry once!) Margaret hollered as Brenda tossed the shackles to her, knocking over the spade, pitchfork, and bench behind her.

"WHAT'S GOING ON HERE!" Father shouted in the doorway.

Cows mooed—all four in jagged sequence as Charlie and Skipper barged past Brenda to the opposing door to Father. Brenda tugged on the corner of the bench to right it while empty tins belched out the tools they'd stored, and the wooden seat caught a loose nail on the post beside it.

"I SAID CLEAN IT UP! Can you hear?!" Father kept yelling. Marlene safely sequestered in the chicken pen, gathered eggs and remained out of range.

"I AM!" Brenda hollered back. She managed to resurrect the fallen pew and replaced the tins on its rightness.

"YOU'RE NOT A CHRISTIAN!" Father damned her. "I CAN TELL BY THE WAY YOU ARE ANSWERING ME!"

Brenda broke inside. Tears and sobs streamed like milk from a beleaguered udder from her face. She spun on her booted heel and fled into the winter darkness outside, fully expecting to be ordered back for a thrashing.

She blundered off the packed path, and the snow rose in flurried arms to embrace her as she fell face down into it.

Brenda cried for all the unfairness of life as she understood it, the favoritism of Marlene, the cruelty of Margaret, and her parent's unkindness. For how she despised school and never having what other children had, always feeling somehow singled out, picked on, and materially without.

"Branna," Father sneered from the barn doorway. "Are you pretending?"

"YOU DON'T HAVE TO SAY ANYTHING TO ME!" she screamed at the be speckled night sky as tears melted the snow on her face while it, in turn, stung her cheeks.

Brenda was fast learning that when she spazzed, people backed off. Only then. She rolled over onto her back and faced the universe head-on, gazing at the twinkling specks against the velvet darkness between hiccups.

After her disintegration into the elements, Brenda erected herself to descend the rough cement steps back down to the basement.

Her arrival caught Mother en route to the cold room. Brenda kept her face averted, hoping for the customary negligence to avoid an explanation for her appearance.

"Did you fall in the snow?" The query proved her wishes to no avail.

Brenda only nodded, busying herself in the ridding of her barn clothes. Most of the outer chore wear was but a rung or two away from the classification of rags; the pockets and lining torn or worn from them. She hung her baggy handed-down snowsuit on its designated nail, mindless of its hollow leg dragging on the floor, sniffling as she went.

Mother halted by the dark walnut door laden with canned beets and pickled carrots.

"Are you feeling sick again?" The sudden unusual attentiveness prickled a warning across Brenda's skin. "It's cold outside." She excused herself, pulling her infernal tights up on the sojourn upstairs.

CHAPTER 73

Recurring Nightmare

THE TEMPERATURE of the prairie winter blew chills and loose snow across the farm, revving up for a blizzard. Wind tore at the tar-papered side of the house like a groom removing the bride's dress. The unfinished outer wall of the beige and burgundy abode faced the half-painted end of the nearly red barn in a bizarre dance of the incomplete.

"I almost needed a rope!" Father's footsteps and footsteps boomed simultaneously, referring to Pa Ingalls' method of leading himself to his barn in a blizzard.

"What's up with Brenda?" Mother asked in English, a sign of concern.

"Oh nothing, just a spell of self-pity." He dissolved worry and barn grime alike at the bathroom sink, spitting excess water unceremoniously.

Unconvinced, Mother emerged from under the kitchen sink bearing her ever-cure all, the brown glass bottle of Maltlevol.

Golden liquid from the bottle warmed the esophageal path clear down to Brenda's midriff and provided a burst of energy. Soon, she and Marlene had pushed their bedroom furniture around in a new dimension which resulted in Marlene's forefinger getting jammed between her wooden bed frame and the wall. She opened her mouth to emit a bellow from an oral width to rival Mother's mason canning jars.

Everyone thundered down the hall to investigate, Mother, Father, and Margaret.

"Why did you set this on?" Mother scolded Brenda. "A little too much vitamin yolk, I see. Turned you into a hyper-rectum."

The blizzard gusted in like there would never be springtime again, so Father added wood to the stoves; one in the porch and one beside the propane furnace downstairs. Fire snapped short quick retorts to Old Man Winter who only howled in defeat. Tonight, the house would be warm in spite of him and his sidekick, Jack Frost.

Saturday night was hymn sing night and sparsely peppered with the occasional bedtime story.

Brenda flanked Mother on the brown plaid settee and poked the bulging veins on her work-worn hands for sport.

"Your hands are ugly," she declared in the innocence of childhood honesty. Then cringed on the realization; that was the makings of a lashing of sort; either tongue or belt for rudeness to an elder.

Mother rose to retrieve a book of Uncle Arthur's bedtime Stories from the pressboard entertainment cupboard.

Father strummed his guitar impatiently.

"Wait, hold on a while," she urged, paging to a story. She read an anecdote of a woman endowed with badly scarred hands whose own daughter commented on their unsightliness. Upon learning how the scars came from a house fire and her mother's rescue of her, the youngster changed venue and exclaimed how beautiful the scarred hands were.

Margaret glared accusingly at Brenda, and Marlene mimicked her. Brenda glared back.

"There's a land that is fairer than day, and by faith we can see it afar, for the father waits over the way, to prepare us a dwelling place there…" Father sang baritone.

"In the sweet, by and by…" Mother's sweet trill joined in, distracted from the insult.

The girls followed. "We shall meet on that beautiful shore…in the sweet by and by, we shall meet on that beautiful shore."

Winter in Northern Alberta seemed a certain eternity whereas the afterlife of a Mennonite was not. Bright sunshine blinded the one who stepped out into the white cold and deep snow, the reflection of daylight brightened by a sea of glistening frost.

Miss Wang kept her distance from Brenda now, except for grading her stories.

"You will enter the contest with this one." She brandished Brenda's rendition of a child kidnapped to a better life. Every year, all the schools in the county district submitted poems, short stories, and descriptive essays to the creative writing contest. The three levels of winners all received a copy of the annual composition book along with an engraved plaque or medal.

Brenda dared not write her darkest memoirs of nightmares so ugly, so vivid and fearsome she felt no one else could ever know.

Or someone else already knew and meticulously maintained the dark secrets as well…one gray, hazy memory of being small, lying in a bed, and a white T-shirt stretched over a belly by her feet end was hurting her incredibly. Brenda screamed and cried for Mother to rescue her, but she didn't come running, although she was in the vicinity. Dimly, a sense of Mother's presence hung in the room, thinly veiled but well concealed just the same.

Brenda always woke up in a terrified sweat, heart racing and blood pounding in her ears like angry footsteps. The house lay undisturbed around her, the fire snapping merrily in the stove winter, and crickets rasping at gurgling frogs in the summertime. The nightmare stalked her without season.

The recurring horror picture strangled her, making breath difficult. Fear clutched at her throat so tightly Brenda was afraid to inhale or exhale, fearing the very motion would invite Big Belly and his sadistic game to return. Perhaps for self-preservation, the head of the perpetrator was cut off in the picture each time, making him a mysterious outsider and a more distant villain.

Deep down, however, far deeper than he had ever touched her…Brenda knew. Oh, she knew.

Whenever Mother made soup, she added everything conceivably edible, just shy of the neighbor's cat. The same went for her salads and berry soup recipe. Every scrap not given to the hogs was used up in cooking and baking. Used tea bags were cut apart to fertilize the house plants.

Plumi Moos (plumb soup) presented itself as an eatery nemesis to Brenda. A purple paste of milk, corn starch, sugar, and cinnamon were concocted in the bubbling cauldron on the green enamel stove. Next every dead piece of dried, shriveled-up fruit was thrown into the ghoulish liquid to complete the sweet slough age.

Plumi Moos, babbat (cake with cooked raisins in it), and rice pudding were few items Brenda detested ingesting at her mother's table. Of course, personal preference was to no avail. One ate what was provided—cleaned one's plate or got whipped for adding hardship to parents already financially hard done by.

CHAPTER 74

Death

THE PHONE clattered one wintry afternoon amongst the chaos of schoolbags and lunch kits on the kitchen table.

"I'll need the table soon," Mother warned on her way to pick up the black poly resin communicator as the children fulfilled their afternoon routine.

"Hello," she answered the two long rings in between the sequence before another duo of equal timing rang.

Mother listened while scholastic book orders fluttered to the brown arborite table, joining saran wrapped crusts from leftover lunch and hard covered homework.

"La hun dert" (The hundred), she exclaimed, her face blanching. It was a common expression of shock.

"Yes, I will call them," she agreed in a shocked undertone. "Okay. Thanks for phoning."

The conversation's hushed awe had quieted Margaret and Brenda's rummage regime and widened Marlene's bug eyes.

"Little Kyle Eckenswiller was thrown from their trike and killed." Mother anxiously rubbed her gnarly hands together. "His mother is Cousin Eva's sister, so Kyle is your second cousin, just like Jacob Gruenwald is your second cousin. The boys are first cousins. Oh, I've got to phone Grandma and tell her." She turned her apron tied back to them and carefully rotated the dial to place a call to Rosedale, Saskatchewan.

The shirttail relative of Gardeners via the Gruenwald side of the fence had joined his older brothers on the tripod mode of transportation to gather wood. Although the pathway en route the woodshed had lain packed from previous jaunts, a slip-swerve had jerked the trike, the hitched-on wagon, and cargo out of control. Kyle, thrown from the ATV, hit the frozen ground and broke his neck.

"He didn't suffer." Mother paced the length of the wall adjacent to the phone, lacing her fingers in the coiled black cord.

"Ahh…he'd be just a little younger than our Brenda. Yes. The Eckenswillers had him in April, we had Branna in February," Mother gossiped to Grandma Gruenwald.

The funeral was to be held at the English-speaking Evangelical Mennonite Church in town the following week.

In the days preceding the funeral, stories drifted Hatchet Prairie like gusts of winter wind, mingling with the snow drifts and the distinct chill of death.

One version of the circulating tales was of the three brothers utilizing a forbidden machine to make their chores easier. Another whisper hinted there had been roughhousing and horseplay, knocking young Kyle off the rack he'd been perched on.

The certainty of a manufactured casket, professionally prepared body, and English funeral was included in the ruminations.

Relentless rumors swept the prairie until one envisioned nothing but the corpses of deceased children in the blue cold of the endless season.

Both the city and town schools decreased their Canadian flags to half-mast and closed for the Thursday ceremony.

Funerals were a big event in Hatchet Prairie; a morbid social to-do that produced a mass turnout of the grimly fascinated.

The majority of Old Colony church members did not cross the threshold of other congregations, nor did, the Old Order Mennonites. Relatives of the deceased who held membership that were of an English denomination attended, and mother and father dared go.

Marlene and Brenda jostled each other in the backseat of the Sunday Suburban, each vying for elbow room in the spacious bench.

Brenda jabbed a quick shot to Marlene's ribcage, and on cue, Marlene expanded her jaws to release the art of blubbering for fame.

"BRENDA-JANE GARDENER! There are people burying their child today," and Mother's beady brown eyes flashed fire at her.

The Evangelical Mennonite's Church's polished pews filled fast. Bright green indoor/outdoor carpeting covered the floor, sprawling from the stairs flanking the pulpit, brightening the dullness of the somber affair. An enormous spray of wheat grasses narrowing to thick red roses, sunflowers, and blue daisies at its base sat in front of the bevel-edged pulpit. Curved benches were angle parted one at each side of the podium that rose above the aisle. A door on both the left and right of the front opened to emit an array of men in suits to line up facing the congregation before respectively sitting down simultaneously.

Colors exploded everywhere despite the numb occasion. Kerchiefs were sparse among the vivid crowd, and although most of the gathered wore an item of black in their ensemble, the assembly resembled mother's flowering garden in late spring.

Brenda was so preoccupied with gawking at the view she barely heard the sweet soft strains of the organ music being played by a young woman in a French braid.

Above, the half-dozen men to the right of the carved rostrum rose to announce the opening hymn, "Safe in the Arms of Jesus," his voice carrying through the microphone.

Brenda wiggled within her itchy woolen sweater, the motion catching Mother's fierce glare and hiss: "You're gonna catch it later."

At the ebbing of the last verse of the hymn, the hushed throng tuned a flurry of heads as the bereaved family walked in, the brothers carrying their sibling in a silvery-gray coffin. The Father led the mother to the front of the church.

As the melody of "Nearer My God to Thee" floated heavenward aided by the elaborate sound system, Brenda caught sight of Cousin Eva, her daughter Maria, and Jacob sitting across the way. Jacob met her gaze and pressed his lips together in a grim line at her.

The funeral at the Evangelical Mennonite Church seemed adversely jauntier than a regular service Sunday morning at the Old Order Church.

A handsome young man with a mid-part and feathered hair slicked back stepped up to the podium and addresses everyone joyously, as if having read Brenda's thoughts.

"My brothers and sister in the Lord," he gazed around the vast rectangular domain, eyes glistening under a thick layer of hair.

"We are here today not only to grieve the loss of Kyle Evan Eckenswiller but to rejoice in the memories of his short life and the life heaven has just gained at his arrival!" The effervescent speaker lifted his outstretched arms heavenward.

After the bright-eyed cheery preacher closed his spiel, he announced a forthcoming word from their bishop, Mr. Harold Redekopp. Grandfather to Abel and Annie Redekopp.

The looming, elderly man rose and gripped the edge of the pulpit like he wanted to rip it off and use it for firewood. Only this parish boasted an electric furnace in gentle sighs of warmth emitted by each register.

"Gott ha funs die chinyah bloss yeah-leet" (God has only lent the children to us), his voice boomed into the unnecessary microphone.

Beside her, given the sounds of air rushing from and getting sucked back, Brenda knew Mother was crying.

"And last week, God took one back," Bishop Redekopp resounded. "The Lord giveth and the Lord taketh away. Blessed be the name of the Lord. Shall we pray?"

After a prayer, the length of a dog-sled ride home including forty-one Lords, the sniffing congregation filed around the open casket and filtered out the nearest door into the fore bearing elements.

Seven-year-old Kyle lay nestled in silk, with his blue gray hands folded and holding a three-stem floral arrangement. A Smurf doll embraced the left side of his face, unsuccessfully hiding a blue bruise along his cheek.

Anyone stoic throughout the ceremony dissolved to tears at the sight of little Kyle in his coffin. All except Father.

The Gardeners didn't follow the procession to the windblown cemetery for the icy burial event. Father raced home, dry eyed and silent, to raid the medicine cupboard above the moss-colored fridge for antihistamines and vitamins.

"How come Dad never cries?" Brenda wondered aloud to Mother in the open bathroom, watching her splash her face with water.

"I-I don't know," Mother choked between handfuls of water. "Go do your puzzle with Marlene."

And once again, the summary of how emotions other than anger were handled at home. "Next please."

CHAPTER 75

Hoarfrost and Hormones

LOCAL TALK surrounding the youngster's death shifted to opinions of the service, the condition of the deceased, even the undertaker was dissected, in a manner of speaking.

"He can't have done a good job if the boy was blue," one mouth criticized over the "meagropen", a large lard filled kettle being stirred with a "reaholt" (stir stick). Lard wasn't by far the only thing being rotated in Father's garage at the junior Gardeners turn for hosting slaughtering.

Father had constructed the neatest meagropen out of a metal crude oil barrel by cutting it in half and welding the top and bottom bases together. The bottom half had a curved door on a metal hinge that opened to allow wood to be added to the fire inside it. Father had sunk an aluminum bathtub into the top to hold the lard for rendering over the fire.

Sawhorses held thick plywood slabs covered in vinyl tablecloths for the butcherers to work on.

"I couldn't stand that young guy." Mother was referring to the enthusiastic pastor. "He practically laughed the whole thing off!" That was the old Mennonite way of speaking. Religious matters were a long-faced, solemn affair. Piety was a somber thing.

"Nah, obah," clucked Mrs. Hoffman over her stirring paddle. This year, the Hoffmans had joined the three Gardener families at pig-butchering season; Senior Gardeners, Zeke and Elizabeth, Isbrandt and Betty, and the Hoffmans, who were members of the Old Colony Church.

Mother spied Brenda drinking in every word on her stool by the meat grinder, stainless steel and clean, ready to use.

"Go play with your cousins in the house. Come get us if there's any trouble. Hear?"

Once again, Brenda was dismissed from her mother's company at the first sign of any real emotion or anything real, period. Off she trotted to the house of bedlam, noise, and confusion where all the children were.

The parents, having left George and Margaret in charge of the younger children, clearly had a mile or so to climb before they reached the summit of good ideas.

Chaos escaped amok, younger siblings tormented older ones by many a pulled sash and torn collar as Margaret and George made eyes at each other and attempted to playhouse.

"Children! Play quietly!" George ordered in his best thirteen-year-old trying-to-be-father-voice.

The reprimand only served to delight the overly excited cousins more, and the group of Isbrandt Gardener offspring swallowed Brenda and Marlene like a total wave, surging over the couple on the couch. Margaret and George cowered and ducked as they were pummeled with pillows and clambered on mercilessly.

"Heah-op! Heah-op!" Margaret howled in vain. The tussling, wrestling, and bedlam continued until a bellow from a looming figure in the living room doorway halted the gang. Brenda knew without looking up who the enraged blast had come from. FATHER.

Uncle Isbrandt stood behind him.

"Shall I get out my belt?" Uncle demanded, stepping out from behind Father. "I'll go get Mary," Father stated grimly.

Uncle pulled up a homemade hand-covered vinyl stool and cleared his throat.

"You know children, mischief making is fun for a while, but don't forget what happened to the Eckenswiller boy. He and his brothers were told not to take the trike out that day, and they did anyway. Then they jostled and teased one another, and one fell to his death. Do you want that to happen here?"

"Well," Hendrix studied his brother Martin. "He has been getting on my nerves lately—"

"Children!" Uncle Isbrandt emphasized. "I am telling you a good story. One you can learn from. Those Eckenswillers they can't get their brother back. Wouldn't you rather have your siblings and get along with them than bury them?"

Through the frost clad window, Father's truck turned back in the yard with a figure in the far seat beside him.

Aunt Mary traipsed in as no-nonsense as she could muster for a gal that was chockfull of beans and a few extra marbles.

"Okay George, line up the younger kids for washing. Edith and Margaret, help me put supper on, the butcherers are hungry. Brenda and Marlene, go pick up the great room. Take your cousins with you."

The great room was the name for the living room at the growfash. (Gardener Grandparents).

Mother had prepared a feast of potato and egg salads, white and brown buns, and tomato vegetable soup with sliced sausage floating in the festive assortment of yellow beans, peas, carrots, potatoes, onions, and tomatoes. Mother's soups were both aromatic and attractive.

By suppertime, the adults brought "rab-shpa" (spareribs) they had cooked in the meagropen until the meat could easily be separated from the bone. The ribs had been salted as they cooled and tasted delicious with mustard, even when cold. They would become school lunchmeat for the following week.

"Yriven" (Cracklings), or fried pig fat, was also fried in the lard and then poured into containers through a colander to catch the cracklings. Brenda detested the greasy dish that so closely resembled raisins but growing up Mennonite meant you ate what landed on your plate.

After one had been berated by Mother's smoldering eyes and mouth to clean the platter, you knew what was expected of you at the dinner table. Bread was called "sups-ell" (soaker) or "ein supsell beat" (a soaking piece) and used to scrap up the remnants of food, gravy, and/or sauce like a sponge and eaten also.

Butchering time always provided a feast. The sediment at the bottom of the lard containers dubbed "griven shmalt" (crackling fat) could be spread on bread, lightly salted, and savored in absence of butter.

Mother's walnut arborite table yawned wide to encapsulate several more extensions, and stacking stools were added to the elongated table.

Mr. and Mrs. Hoffman had no children, so she remained slim unlike most Mennonite women and he droned on like a visiting minister with time on his hands.

"Well," Father declared, pushing back his plate. "I've come to the conclusion I'm retired." A story was forming to be sure.

"What makes you think like that?" Mr. Hoffman raised eyebrows over a worried forehead.

"Retired or retarded." Uncle Isbrandt snorted from behind his plate of potatoes, beets, and ribs.

"The government owns most of this property and the homestead, so I'm practically working for them, and as you know, most of their guys retire early." Father snicker laughed.

Mr. Hoffman frowned. "You need a son. A boy could help you turn this farm into a profit machine."

"You don't have any," Mother reminded him.

"No!' Mrs. Hoffman chuckled. "We don't have children, just chickens!"

After the "yriven shmalt" (crackling fat), had settled in its cooling reservoirs and the visiting butcherers had gone home, Mother and Father lingered in the garage, cleaning up the days labor. She, as usual, jawing at him for all she was worth and he, as usual, ignoring her as best he could.

Later that evening, Margaret, riddled with teenage hormones that her boy cousin had triggered, began chasing Benda around the kitchen table wearing a queer look on her face. The expression recoiled Brenda instantly. She recoiled from the glazed eyes, flushed delight, and peculiar smile Father often wore. Margaret flailed her arms wildly in an attempt to reach Brenda, grabbing air, making tickling, teasing motions. Marlene had gone to bed, Brenda remembered, diving under the table and promptly banging her head on the wooden bench upon landing.

Chairs scraped and moved. Margaret groped for Brenda's legs, bottom, and waistline.

"Leave me alone!" Brenda shouted. "Or I'll tell Mom and Dad!"

She dove again, shoving Father's chair away from its placid position. Stumbling toward the porch door, a step down, shoes on, forget the coat, slamming it behind her…

Brenda pitched forward into the darkness. Rounding the corner of the vestibule, her path illuminated dimly by the yard light, she bolted for the garage on the packed snow that springtime had begun to melt and now lay frozen in the night air beneath her rapid tread. Running, slipping, catching herself like a surfer, bursting into the garage fit to startle the deceased pork.

"What is loose!" Mother startled. "Look! No jacket! Haven't you been sick enough this past winter!"

Mother listened silently as Brenda rasped out the story, gathering bloody rags into a big aluminum bowl.

"Maybe she was feeling boy crazy," she said slowly. "I'll talk to her."

CHAPTER 76

On the Banks of the Shreefah

AFTER THE chasing incident in the kitchen, the contempt between Margaret and Brenda grew from a ditch width to a yawning chasm.

Spring blew in on the caps of snowless winds, bringing Jake Gruenwald and elevated stress to the Gardener farm.

Contention flared once more between the Shepnard and Gardener families, revealing itself in littered field driveways and a handmade sign on the Penner Bridge: "Shepnard Bridge."

Underneath the hand-painted lie, the solidified Shreefah thawed and began growling like a certain Troll awaiting Billy Goats.

Had the entitled and territorial Shepnards sincerely desired to be politically correct, they would have merely renamed the Shreefah (the German word for screaming, shreeyen, plus the Dutch word for river, reetah) "Grumble Creek," or "Die Grumzoyah," (the grumbler) for the way it groaned along its snaky journey.

The Penner boys made good on the hand they played to reciprocate the Shepnards move and not for the first time, editing it to read: "Shepnerds Leak."

On the bus, the Penner boys had once coolly eased off the Shepnard's move with the promise of violence behind the windbreaker at school. But now, they attended a spinster-taught private school, so the Gardener girls reaped the consequences of the newly lettered signage.

"You may have more money in the bank, but I throw bales around in my spare time," Margaret snarled at Billy and Henry Shepnard. "I'll throw you both to the ground like a straw bale to the cows if you don't take down that stupid sign of yours."

The pale, skinny Shepnard blanched behind his freckles and slid closer to his heavy-set brother.

Sadly, no one remembered the origin of the issue between the Shepnards and Gardeners. In a community of history and storytelling, where nicknames held as much importance as the anecdote behind them, no one knew why the two families despised each other.

Mother worked silently one Saturday while the girls blew the innards out of chicken eggs and collected them in a pastel Tupperware container so Mother could use them for baking. Brenda and Marlene had tapped the top of the egg with a nail to form a small opening and then repeated the action with the other end.

"Oh, I'm so frustrated." Mother sighed. That was their cue. Fix mother's feelings. The girls lowered their delicate palates. "What, Mom? What?" "Oh." Mother sighed.

Brenda picked up a Robin's egg blue wax crayon for the sky she'd start on her egg. A whole country scene was the goal, with grass and flowers at the bottom half. Later, she'd con Mother into placing the eggs into the heated oven briefly to melt the wax slightly to give the picture richer color.

"*Vote?*" (What?) Marlene repeated herself.

The tale of woe unwound and raveled up in the Easter craft project. Father had ensconced the farm deep in debt and was delving deeper at an upcoming appointment in Hydelan.

"The farm belongs to farm credit. At least, it will soon. I will leave and go home to my mother. Always wanted out of this miserable corner..."

Fear chilled Brenda in the heat of the baking, bubbling cook stove where she had stood waiting for the egg to "cure" in the tin plate mother had set it in.

"Dad is awful. Yes, Mother. Don't tell him I said so," Brenda soothed her. At that emission, a hiss-laugh escaped Mother's thin lips, revealing her splintered, yellow and gray teeth. Relief vied for a spot beside the fear previously encroaching on her expectation of a predictable life.

Outside, wind blew rivulets in the melting snow puddles and tapped the porch window with the branches of the lilac bush to remind them of springtime in Hatchet Prairie.

"Pretty soon the yard will turn into a big pile of loon-shit," Mother cursed.

Brenda and Marlene giggled, and Mother's features relaxed in a jack-a-lantern grin. "What would I do without my children."

When the appointment in Hydelan arrived, Mother and Father left a note on the kitchen table placing Margaret in charge. And charge she did.

"Let's surprise Mom by doing all the spring cleaning," she suggested.

Marlene, the ever-agreeable one, sprang her vote in with an enthusiastic; "yes. Lets!"

Working for Margaret proved to be as much enjoyment as being genetically connected to her. She boiled water and barked orders. "Wash the wall, do it right."

They scrubbed the white paneling walls in the kitchen, including the smudged black poly resin phone. The cupboards were washed down to their honey-colored, black-trimmed glory, the wallpapered walls with rusty condiments and recipes printed on them avoided.

After several hours of nagging, Brenda and Margaret's differences were stretched taut and looking for a place to happen when the ceramic eagle Brenda was dusting fell from its nest to the edge of the office desk.

"What have you done!" Margaret's face dropped all color and her eyes bulged. The tip of the bird's wing had broken off.

"I-I can glue it," Brenda stuttered.

"You are so evil! You are not a Christian!" Fury spat in all directions of Margaret. "You're the whole problem in this family! You are not a Christian! We would all be better off without you! Dad will beat you for this!"

Something in Brenda snapped and felt like a chintzy ornament breaking on housecleaning day. She had nothing left in her with which to endure another thrashing with ever again, she was sure. It could not happen.

Her bicycle rattled and slid over the frozen mud ruts of the dirt driveway, crunched on the snow lying beside it as she cut left for Penner's Bridge.

Gravel snapped and slid under her tires. In the distance, the Shreefah roared, beckoning her toward its murky hymn.

A half-mile from the beginning of her journey, Brenda expertly twirled her bicycle around to face home. The water level was a yard beneath the underbelly of the bridge, rushing past its tarred pillars.

The yellow bike clattered to the cement as she swung one leg over the metal railing. The water was so close, she could smell its muddy fishy odor. She leaned, dangling one arm and one leg over as far as she dared without letting go.

Mother and Father would be surprised when she wasn't present to take the beating for the busted ornament and other embellishments Margaret would have thrown at them. How sorry they would be for their favoritism of Marlene and belief in Margaret's deceptive saga.

Brenda stretched further, attempting to lose her balance. A car approached, so she scrambled to her feet to look nonchalant, one leg on either side of the aluminum railing as the Shepnard vehicle approached.

Forced smiles were exchanged as the navy-blue van rolled by with the Jacob Shepnard family in its confines. The gravel road led to a dead-end clearing of land that crept further and further east as the Shepnard machinery gnawed at it.

Brenda returned to her mission. Threw her left limbs over the guard. Slowly pulled her right leg over until her crouched body, feet on the concrete edge, dangled from her two fingers. Pain mingled with cold, forcing her trembling fingers to release. Another force picked her up and deposited her beside her bicycle. Shock petrified her for an instant. She had landed on her knees painlessly on the lightly graveled crossing.

Dazed, Brenda tried to move. Warmth penetrated the gray spring day and washed over her body. She realized only then how lightly dressed she was. How cold she'd been and, now, oddly basked in sunshine that seemed to shine straight on her.

She didn't see the Shepnard van again nor marker on the side of the road laying claim to the Penner structure. The gnarly ride home felt surreal and unfamiliar, somehow pleasant under the drab sky and early spring chill. Brenda wondered over the events of the ride and sudden change in its venue… Had the cold, black-robed giant above her less than affectionately known as God actually cared for her? Had he sent his angels to divert her intentions?

As awful as she thought her life was, an odd sensation of relief draped across her shoulders. When Mother and Father returned home to a flurry of tattling and proud exhibition of the spring cleaning, Brenda was oblivious.

Father heated up his glue gun and calmly reattached the eagle's wing tip, much to Margaret's chagrin.

"Marlene and I did it all ourselves, Brenda rode her bike." Margaret was still trying for trouble. She stared triumphantly over at Brenda, blue eyes glittering bewitchingly.

Mother appeared to be in her own world and didn't respond. Brenda escaped to her bed as soon as the supper was done and curled up with her library copy of Tom Sawyer.

CHAPTER 77

Rejection

A WARMING EARTH brought mud, shrieks from Mother to leave soiled boots at the door, and a visiting Jacob on most weekends.

Sunday visitors were forced to park their vehicles on the road and foot the sticky trail the driveway became that time of year.

Brenda retreated to her tree platform, when the socializing didn't bring children her age, with the book she had discovered under the sofa she'd spent winter on. It lifted to a secret storage compartment filled with old glossy cards from mother and father's courtship, seashells, and the book, *Lone Cowboy: The Life of Will James.*

"Bookworm," Mother teased her as Brenda passed her in the kitchen setting jellies in little crystal bowls in preparation for faspa.

With Father's Walkman around her head and Don Williams rendition of "Fairweather Friends" in her ears, Brenda clogged down the muddy clay path to the platform that hung tenaciously from four birch trees. A weathered ladder leaned a rung-ed path up to the oasis.

Sunday's company produced a young church couple and several knee-high offspring that played with the Fisher-Price school while the adults gossiped and dropped sunflower seed shells on the living room floor.

Faspa brought the usual discussion on its flat heels. "You have no boys," from the visiting farmer. George Heidelburg's three sons sat on a wobbly row on the wooden bench, jostling each another busily in their plaid and plain clothing.

"We have no girls," Susan Heidelburg chided her spouse gently, resting her hand on her pregnancy briefly.

"Actually, we do," Father beamed proudly. A story was in the forecast whenever he got that look.

He passed the plastic basket of buns to his guest.

"We borrowed from Elizabeth's cousin," Father joked.

"Oh?"

"Yes. Well, we just came back from Hydelan to borrow from farm credit and we figured, well, as long as we are borrowing..." By now, Father was snickering uproariously at his own cracks.

Mother's face smoldered. "Tell the truth if you're gonna tell stories."

The women lapsed into who they were both related to which made them second cousins. It was the begets chapter all over again.

Brenda detoured to the living room to sweep the mess off of the floor, knowing she would be told to do so anyhow. The plastic rocking horse grazed in a field of sunflower seed shells from his aluminum framed stature.

The message repositioned itself over and over, blazing a path of inferiority through heart and mind. A woman needed a man, and a family needed boys. Girls simply did not count on their own.

Capturing the husks in the green metal dustpan, Brenda deposited them into the pedal-operated kitchen garbage on her orange linoleum escape route. She would much rather be alone.

And when she decided to make a friend out of Annie Redekopp at school, things didn't go well.

Annie was at the top of the social food chain in second grade but hung out with Tina Harder, a hardcore product of Old Colony parents. Annie's parents lived like English people in Hatchet Prairie and attended the Evangelical Church.

Brenda thought she herself would blend into the middle of the two opposites nicely and accompanied them at lunch recess for a week.

Anne wore her ash blonde hair in a poker straight bangles bob or in pig tails. Her watery blue eyes sparkled and shone as she gossiped and told wild stories of her sophisticated home life. She was, however, as mother would put it, "Nothing to write home about."

After a week of connecting like south on South Pole magnets, Annie and Tina fell silent when Brenda approached them on the teeter-totters.

"Brenda," Annie blurted out. "Will you please just go play with someone else?" Mother snorted over her bread bowl when Brenda finished her story.

"It figures. Anna's mom is a Shepnard, and goodness only knows why they are too good for everyone—besides having money, that is."

CHAPTER 78

Seed Catalogues and Suffering Cats

FATHER HAD mounted an old metal-spoked wagon wheel on an axle sideways, welded it to a tractor tire rim, and the children had a merry go round. He attached four roughly cut boards to the spokes to serve as seats, and the Isbrandt Gardeners' shiny red go around from the hardware store couldn't hold a candle to it.

The Ford emblem showed white on the turquoise pickup box on skids that had been transformed into a sandbox years earlier. That was Father; he could create a masterpiece out of an ordinary object with a jackknife and a pair of pliers.

Rumors of farm credit bankruptcy drifted around Fieldarp. The Benjamen farm was informally listed as one of several in trouble.

Mother had made kringle with leftover pie dough, butter, cinnamon, and brown sugar rolled up and baked. The C-shaped pastry lay in its usual tin plate on the kitchen table, awaiting the hungry youngster. She was no slouch in creativity bred of sparsity either, churning forth delectable pastries on that baking day from mere ingredients like flour, eggs, and butter.

The seed catalogue had replaced the Christmas Wish Book with "radio" chattering on the counter behind it.

Every year, Mother urged the girls to choose a type of flower seed. Today, she flung the seed catalogue on the table between Brenda and Marlene, ensuing a tug of war.

"Girls!" Mother raised the knife she was working threateningly. They froze like Lot's wife. She dropped the weapon and burst out snickering. Mother laughed until they forced themselves to join with her. Ha-ha indeed.

Jacob began surfacing at the farm on weekends and staining every fabric surface he touched, much to Mother's annoyance. So naturally, the girls all caught colossal manure for making work for poor dear Mother in hopes that Jacob might catch the message. It resulted in Brenda having to wear the same dress to school all week and one she particularly despised; a blue cotton bedecked with dark blue roses.

"Brenda! You will wear it or you will be in Jacob's shorts! Nothing else!" Mother snarled before rupturing in a ball of mirth. Margaret leapt into the fray with a sputtering of raucous, joyous cackling.

Brenda slunk away from the platform with *The Lone Cowboy,* tucked under her arm. Reprieve would prove its expiry date when the next "You're not helping Mother" speech got peeled off the roll and doled out. For now, Brenda practiced her real lesson in life; retreat and avoid, especially the kitchen.

The honeyed cupboards framed a barrage of bad experiences awaiting in the kitchen. If Mother scrapped with a female relative, it was on the phone near the rising bread. If a fight broke out fit to rival a hockey game between Margaret and Brenda washing dishes, Mother swiftly kicked them both in the behind. Father beat them in the kitchen and told them to shut up at once despite the fiery burning pain that seared clear down to the spirit. No, the kitchen, in all its wallpapered finery, was a host for helleri and muchly to be avoided.

Career day arrived at the Butterhorn Junction School, and since Margaret's grade was in charge, she invited Father to represent mixed farmers. The representatives all had a booth and banner overhead stating their purpose. Each career monger offered engraved pens, stationary, and keychains.

The students of Butterhorn Junction put their parents and teachers to shame, namely the elementary students. Growing up Mennonite, everyone was poor or made like they were. Children received gifts at Christmas, Easter, and their birthdays Requests in between were met with "Vee han chine yalt" (we have no money), loud and clamorously in mid general store. The fair offered a chance to shop for free.

Naturally, the Shepnards were there in the satin bomber jackets embroidered and emblazoned with "SHAPNARD LOGGING." Mrs. John Shepnard wore her kerchief and dress with the coat largely beside Mr. Shepnard who towered above her. A comical pair they were, resembling the nursery rhyme of Jack Spratt.

After the younger grades and any Mennonite kid feeling both impoverished and opportunistic had made thorough asses of themselves gleaning trinkets off of the vendors, a cloud settled over the school. A stormy faced Mr. Shale positioned himself at the stern of the assembly.

"Students. Boys and girls of Butterhorn Junction." He paused. "I am deeply dismayed at what I saw happen at our career fair today." The lecture continued. "Ashamed of the greedy, rude behavior…" In conclusion, the entire school was assigned a writing assignment apologizing to the visitors for their greed.

Mr. Shale held himself in a quiet demeanor, never raising his voice. He finished off his spiel and dismissed them, striding away in his grey suit; a tall thin man built like a pencil. How could any other vocation other than school principal have suited him?

Brenda loved writing and tackled her project with vigor and gusto:

> "Dear Career Day Reps:
>
> I am truly sorry for my rude behavior at Career Day. I never saw so many lovely treats and trinkets in one place before except Christmas, so I went a little overboard. We were supposed to ask questions of which career we wanted, and the little gifts were so exciting that I never got asking any!
>
> In closing I want to say how sorry I am again and that I hope you will come

back to our school for the next career day if we have one. I promise I will ask questions and listen carefully to you.

Yours truly,
Brenda-Jane Gardener."

Miss Wang paused by Brenda's desk, reading over her shoulder.

"Oh. You could forget science, math, social," she said credulously. "Just write and do art. How about that?" she asked no one in particular, taking the loose leaf up to the front of the class and sticking it to her "egg-ceptional" Easter themed board.

The oriental teacher wrote a note of her own, targeting the parents of her pupils and sending a copy home with each one:

Dear Parents:

It is imperative that your child practices proper hygiene and cleanliness. Please ensure they change their clothes every other day and shower or bath several times a week, as my classroom slowly develops an odor that is unbearable by Friday.

I apologize for the topic of this notice. I trust you will understand and comply with me on this issue.

Sincerely, Miss Wang.

Mother read the photocopied letter and went ballistic. How dare that insolent teacher assume everyone had the same water supply? Did she want to pay the water bill?

The farm cistern only held so much and hot water cost more…

Brenda cringed at the thought of being forced to take another Pine-Sol sitz bath. Swiftly, she slipped outside to the platform.

Mr. Benjamen drove into the yard in his dilapidated pickup truck, sputtering and farting as it went. Although her distance kept their volume down, Brenda knew he and father would holler, "Hello, Zeke!" at each other as loud as friendliness allowed. Aside from being rueful namesakes, both men gestured a lot as they spoke.

The story that unfolded over a supper of flapjacks and homemade jam was the Benjamen farm was folding, and they were declaring bankruptcy before moving away.

"What's bankruptcy?" Brenda wondered aloud, rolling up her crepe.

"Shaw!" Mother shook her hand at Brenda, as if slapping her virtually for the distance between them.

"Bankruptcy is when you tell everyone you owe money that you can't pay and then everything you have debt on is taken away," Father explained somberly. "We could end up like the Benjamens the way things are going."

Even the pending financial collapse didn't hamper the spirit of the giggling gadabouts. Helen Benjamen sold liquid embroidery linens and markers, holding an inside garage sale when winter made a comeback with an April blizzard. The six Benjamen children that attended school sold plastic whistles for a nickel apiece, transforming the schoolyard into a chirp festival every recess. They also sold twenty-five cent harmonicas and little compasses on keychains for a dollar.

"Here." Father doled out a paper dollar and a quarter to each daughter. "Buy one of each of whatever they are selling this week. We have to support them."

"Dad!" Mother protested. "We need the money ourselves." But Father stayed firm in his philosophy to support those struggling as one would one day require the same.

Mother caught wind of the story of gluttony at the school career and trade fair from Margaret, triggering a pointing shadow over the house that wasn't leading the Israelites.

"The ideal acting like a bunch of greedy Mennonites! How shameful! How embarrassing for the rest of us!"

Brenda fidgeted with the gold printed pen that had her father's name on its pencil ridged side. It was coming, and to leave the kitchen now meant getting ordered to return accompanied by a slap in the face.

"Brenda was one of them." Margaret shot a gleeful glance behind her toward Brenda.

"It figures," Mother snarled. "That kid is like that. Always trouble. Rebellious. Now this."

And there it was. Mother had expressed her hate fix of the day, and Brenda would be free for a while. She tensed, still expecting violence for leaving to escape to her room.

Mercifully, it didn't follow her.

"And she's never in with the family," Mother added. "Always by herself."

Marlene looked up reproachfully toward Brenda from her hook and latch project. A spotted puppy's mugshot was slowly taking shape.

Brenda unearthed her "knit-wit kit" from last Christmas—her ball of dusty rose yarn—and set to work making a long-knitted chain she would skip rope with.

CHAPTER 79

A Nervous "Bakedown"

WHEN THE snow melted and springtime resumed, skipping ropes and hop-scotch games sprung across the sidewalks at school. Bright hair elastics laced with colored marbles were pulled out of hair to mark places in the chalk squares and prohibit them from being jumped on by one-legged contestants.

Friday evening, Father got out his accordion and played hymns on the raucous black resin instrument. With its ivory keys gleaming and pewter trimmed bellows, Brenda felt drawn to it and watched Father play as he sang, "Blest be the tie that binds our hearts in Christian love..." In the next room, Mother and Margaret bonded while fuming away.

"Suck up," Mother snarled loud enough for Brenda to hear. Obediently, Margaret tittered to placate her.

Marlene was curled up on the black settee where Brenda had spent the previous season, intently studying an Uncle Arthur's bedtime story book.

Father jammed where he usually did, by the office desk beside the heavy orange door that led to the dilapidated back deck.

"Don't switch yet," Brenda pleaded when her father made a motion to switch to his twelve-string guitar.

"Teacher's pet," echoed from the kitchen. Little did Mother realize Brenda had grown accustomed to the hatred, rejection, and contempt Mother shot her way.

The false accusations though, were much harder to swallow.

Mother held the firm philosophy that whenever something went wrong in the house, Brenda did it. If a vase broke, she was to blame should she be near enough to be considered a suspect. Usually, just her presence in the mere vicinity of the catastrophe (and mother) got her deemed guilty.

That night, because Mother was unequivocally peeved that Brenda had dared spend some time with Father, she found a bone to pick.

"Branna! You spilled heat liniment all over the bathroom sink! Come here and wipe this up! Now I say! Here! COME HERE!" Mother's voice got shriller and shriller, enough to rival a deer whistle.

"No, Mom, I didn't. I haven't—"

"ARE YOU MAKING ME A LIAR?!" Now, Mother was hysterical. "Huh? Huh? Answer me at once! Here! Come here!"

Brenda slowly forced herself into the firing range. The floor rag lay under a sink. Gingerly, she picked it up and clumsily dabbed at the pink smears and dribbles on the counter.

"Decently! Pour water and do it right! AND DON'T USE THE FLOOR RAG!" Mother huffed, panted, and wailed, jerking the grey cloth from Brenda and yanking a clean one off the linen shelf behind her.

"There! Fablingeddit chint! Dow mole riicht!" (German epithet cursing the object of wrath, child, do it right).

Brenda's chin wobbled, and she could not stop the tears from seeping from her eyelids.

"Are you crying?" Mother demanded. Brenda ignored her, wiping the false marble vanity top.

"Answer me!" Mother freaked.

From the background, Father called Mother. Over and over. She let out a burst of air and pivoted to go see to him.

Brenda smelled the lingering odor of stale coffee breath as she finished wiping the counter. She rinsed the rag, wrung it out and hung it over the bathtub edge. Coffee and heat liniment mingled odors as she tipped the green plastic basin within the sink to drain it.

Muffled voices releasing from the bedroom next door sounded like an argument.

Crying, Brenda buried herself under her bedcovers, face and all. Mother didn't do that to Marlene. In fact, for a woman who seemingly had only dislike for children, Mother had the capacity to dote on Marlene.

Heartbroken, Brenda sobbed herself to sleep and hardly noticed when Marlene kicked her bed leg en route to her own slumber.

She woke up to the soft sounds of someone crying and footsteps shuffling. Father supported Mother as they walked down the hall to the living room together. She was three handkerchiefs into the winds of another crying spell. Brenda knew her mother's spells well.

The next day brought tears and silence. Mother worked quietly, crying and sniffling.

Father had awkwardly slapped together some peanut butter-white bun sandwiches for their school lunches and left the house. The girls mutely ate cold cereal for breakfast, eyeing each other anxiously, knowing better than to speak. It was an intuition of pure necessity.

The school day breezed by, on its own volition, in a barrage of spelling quizzes, stickers, story writing, and learning string art.

Mr. Heinrichs jovially pulled the bus over to the bridge that was the senior Gardener's driveway The Gardeners hesitated, unsure of what was happening.

"Ya, your father called," Mr. Heinrichs explained. "Margaret, you and your sisters are to stay with your grandparents for a few days."

The aroma of fresh baking wafted through the screen door as they entered the vestibule without knocking. Grandma's rule was none of her family were to ever rap on her door. Strangers knocked; relatives entered already welcome.

"Chinya" (children), she announced brightly upon sighting them. "I got your mother's seed order in the post by accident. Look here," and she gestured toward an opened brown parcel.

"Who else would order as many flowers as vegetables?" Grandma shook her kerchiefed head and laughed that silvery titter of hers.

The package contained Margaret's Morning Glory seeds, Dahlia seeds for Brenda, and Marlene's order for sweet peas.

A lump of clay hung in Brenda's stomach like a tin pail dripping over a well. She felt sorry for Mother despite her constant mistreatment.

"Grandma," she piped up. "May I take some of these cookies to Mother?"

"You should!" Grossmam had rivaled any commercial bakery with an assortment of gingersnaps, chocolate chip and oatmeal raisin cookies cooling on every available surface.

CHAPTER 80

Lone Cowgirl

MOTHER STILL hardly spoke three days later when the girls returned home. Brenda presented her with an ice cream pail full of assorted cookies and a precariously repackaged seed order. There was a barely audible response that closely resembled a "huh."

A heavy cloak of sadness enshrouded the Gardener house despite the bright spring weather warming Fieldarp for planting season.

The Old Colony Mennonites had grouped with a few Old Order church members, formed a homemade school board complete with construction crew, and built their own school. They'd hired eighth-grade graduates to teach up to grade seven, and one day, the school bus and classrooms alike were emptied of their mustiest pupils. The smelliest, most manure and musty fabric clad students were gone.

For some reason, the more modern the Mennonite, the more changes of clothes, boots, and amounts of baths they had, and the opposite was also true.

The Old Odor—ahem—Old Order Mennonites left the school year incomplete at Butterhorn Junction to begin attending their group-erected clapboard, wood-shingled, one-room schoolhouse. Their school year would run according to planting and harvest season, ending in May and restarting in October. Males would once again be separated from females like they were in church, each half had a wood heating stove in their midst within the divided one room. Toilets were hewn holes in the handcrafted outhouses per gender; one on each side of the schoolhouse. All three buildings had been repainted an ashen shade of blue gray—the color of religion and death.

Brenda, for one, did not share the scoffing attitude of the general populace of Hatchet Prairie toward the Rosendarp Schule (Rose Village School), or the "Rosey Dork School," as Margaret and her friends had dubbed it. People scoffed that they had pulled up stake instead of stockings and interrupted the school term. Others pointed out the lack of accreditation of the "Rosey Village."

No, Brenda was greatly relieved of being delivered from her perverted cousin and all his lame come-ons. Heinrich couldn't bully her on the bus or at recess anymore, and Johan's plump advances and sick propositions would be limited to Sunday socials or gatherings.

"Dad thinks I am abusing you kids," Mother spoke up like a long silenced monk.

"What is that?" Marlene queried. But the emaciated figure at the counter had gone quiet again before the vibrating butter churn.

Brenda looked up the word in the Webster's dictionary. Anger flooded her. Who did Father think he was? How dare he?! Did he believe his leather belt rolled up into a halo? She packed her book by Will James, a handful of jam-jams, a mason jar of water, and a doll blanket and escaped to the platform.

She could relate to the solitary cowpoke and all his alone time in the Oregon Wilderness, accompanied only by an adoptive parent occasionally but mostly kept company by a pair of tame wolves.

The grader had passed through the area and disrupted all the smooth wheel marks on the road, making Brenda's loose yellow fenders rattle as she bicycled along.

A horse and buggy approached her from the Henry's treed lot. It was a sight to behoove and behold she did until Big Red clopped up to her towing Grosspabeh's red two-wheeled "Girling wagon," as he called it laughingly. It was basically a wooden Egyptian-style chariot painted red, the paint now peeling off it as it was harnessed to the Big Morgan, carrying Uncle Aaron and Tante Zonna. (Another version of Sarah) He was another one of Father's younger brothers, recently married and childless, having just returned to Fieldarp after his seasonal job at Hazel's Crossing ended.

"Is that fun?!" Brenda blurted out when she meant to say, "That looks fun!" The couple looked a little taken aback and a lot offended, but the trio had a brief chit-chattery before the buggy wobbled gamely into the Gardener yard.

Brenda felt her cheeks redden to rival the outlandish wagon over her blunder. She hoped Uncle Aaron would understand and make nothing of it. She was just a kid after all.

By the time she dilly-dallied on the smooth acid patch on Grandpa's field and watched the scarlet buggy wheel out of the driveway to continue its journey around the Fieldarp loop that was Grosspap's field, Brenda had a gnawing apprehension knot her stomach.

Sure enough, she turned in the yard. Father spotted her and bellowed, "Come here!"

"Brenda?" Margaret screeched. "You better get down here and explain why you said what you said to Uncle Ont!" (German for Aaron).

Wearily, she walked her bike to the barn to receive a tongue-lashing of a lifetime. Father yelled.

Margaret screeched and shrieked.

"You owe Uncle an apology for talking to him like that! How could you! How dare you!"

Brenda lost track of who was talking, and they coincided anyway. When the lashing screaming festival concluded, she walked her bike to the burgundy steps, crying silently.

Hot tears spilled over her defeated face as she quietly passed Mother in the kitchen, hoping to go her bed undetected.

"Hey?" Mother's footsteps quickened behind her. "What's wrong?"

Brenda stiffened, expecting blows to rain on her neck if she so much as spoke.

"What is it?" Mother seemed alarmed.

The unexpected kindness unleashed a dam inside of her, and Brenda broke open bawling, blubbering the whole story of her innocent slip up and how it had been maximized.

When Father and Margaret entered the porch laden with milk pails, they were greeted by an inflamed mother.

"You!" She slapped Margaret about the head and ears until she covered herself with her arms raised high and howled. Father looked aghast.

"Go to your room, Grandmother!" Mother called Margaret. "There are two parents that can deal with children. You don't need to interfere with anyone ever again!" Moaning, Margaret ran to her room and slammed her door.

An argument began between the adults that Mother fully intended on winning by the sounds of things. Brenda huddled under her blankets, hearing only pieces of the heated debate such as "AND YOU THINK I ABUSE THE CHILDREN?" and "EIGHT-YEAR-OLD KID, STILL INNOCENT!"

On and on they went, cream separator whirring, its parts clanging and bashing together afterward as Mother cleared them. All the while, she berated Father. "—think your family comes before everyone else. Even your own flesh and blood."

Father's voice got lower and lower until it disappeared altogether, drowned out and silenced by her relentless crescendo.

Marlene was asleep when a droop-shouldered man stumbled into their bedroom, and swiftly, Brenda pulled the cover higher and pretended to be asleep also. He stepped on the discarded clothing and walked up to Brenda's bed, head hanging.

"Ah, Branna?" he stuttered.

An eerie chill prickled all over her body as a memory flooded back. Branna, a man's voice breathed over and over as he stood over her. She was lying between some white walls, and he was hurting her, hurting her, HURTING HER. Brenda screamed and cried and cry-screamed, but Mother wouldn't rescue her, even though she sensed she was nearby.

She tensed under the cover, waiting for him to leave. For half an eternity, he stood there, just breathing. Finally, dejectedly, he turned on his heel and left.

What happened that day proved Brenda's burgeoning beliefs true. It proved safer to stay silent and solitary, especially when no one else cared for your safety. And that sometimes you had to play dead and just hope the bear called life would leave you alone.

She found the little red leather-bound testament on her nightstand concealed in an empty cookie tin. From the strand of light, the hall light provided, she read Matthew 18:2–4: "He called a little child to him and placed the child among them. And he said, 'Truly I say to you, unless you change and become like little children, you will never enter the kingdom of heaven. Therefore, whoever takes the lowly position of this child is the greatest in the kingdom of heaven."

The words both soothed and confused her broken little heart. If Jesus and God liked children so much, why was there forever a grownup beating on her for the childlike things she did. Still, a pinprick of light shone into her bleak life, promising more.

CHAPTER 81

Accused

THE BENJAMENS left their home in complete disarray when they moved, packing only what fit around the family in the former Penner van. The large vehicle rumbled into the Gardener yard and the giggling gadabouts rolled down what windows would roll to say goodbye.

"Don't be strangers now. We'll just be on the other side of Creek Landing," Zeke Benjamen boomed.

The Shepnard brothers had bought the dilapidated Timber-Benjamen farm and spared the upcoming bankruptcy.

"Of course," Mother scoffed. "Just because they can!" They all watched the van roll past the birch tree windbreaker. Jacob screwed up his bespectacled face, squinting thoughtfully.

"Is it just me or are those people just plain weird?"

Creek Landing sprawled on the other side of Butterhorn Junction. Zeke Benjamen's brother had a farm there he had given permission for the vagabond family to squat on.

Jacob followed Father like a creditor on debtor like Marlene did, and at the end of every month, the girls watched father hand him a twenty- and five-dollar bill, so evidently, it worked.

"This is for all your hard work," Father said as he passed the bills to Jacob.

The young lad's mouth hung open the first time he saw the money. His sister had-been married off at fourteen; as rumor had it, his mother couldn't afford to raise them, so she'd pawned off her daughter to a husband and Jacob to the farm.

Watching him clutch the money tight in his brown fist while running home, Mother turned, pinch-faced, toward father.

"You work your own daughter like a mule and don't say so much as thank you." Her voice became a sob. "I slave like nobody else I know and what do I get? More work!" She was crying full fledge now. "And you pay HIM when we feed and keep him?"

Father must have felt guilty, because he took everyone to Mary's diner for supper when Cousin Eva wasn't working- Saturday was her holy day. They ordered five plates of fish and chips and had vanilla ice cream for dessert.

"How's that?" he chanted all the way out of the parking lot. "How's that?"

"It's a start," Mother said dryly.

The empty Benjamen farm fascinated Brenda and far surpassed the platform she clung to when life's chaos got to be too much.

Lilac hedges grew wildly in once-manicured rows on the lawn. A tube swing hung slack and deflated from a birch tree branch on a single rope. Poppies grew among purple irises sporadically in the abandoned garden patch, among thickening "pig weed" that groped your ankle all the way down to the pond. The pond itself would be teeming with amphibious life; Brenda knew without drawing her hand through the tapioca-pudding texture of frog egg nests.

Colleen Timber's pale blonde complexion wafted to her mind and memory as Brenda picked a cheerful bouquet of red poppies, yellow goldenrod, and violet fireweed for Mother. She added white flowering chamomile as a lacey fringe around the entire bunch, threading in a few sprigs of white "vayzell kreet," (weasel weed) as mother called it.

Brenda rang the doorbell expertly on the burgundy deck and waited importantly for Mother to answer.

"For you!" Brenda thrust the bouquet into her surprised hands, "because you work so hard." Delight lifted Mother's tired features for a brief flickering of time.

"A florist." Mother beamed, accepting the gift. Then an invisible hand flicked a switch. Her countenance darkened.

"Nam ersht dot vayzell kreet doah reet" (Take the weasel weed out of it first), she commanded. "Duh vitz ack cone dot nicht fuhdreowen" (You know I cannot stand it).

"But it's lacey!" Brenda objected while her heart sank. She withdrew the frothy blooms from her mother's grasp.

Mother retreated to place the arrangement on the table, and the door with the false window grid slammed shut behind her.

On the road back to the Timber-Benjamen farm, a brown chrome less pickup slowed to an idling halt beside her. Grandpa Gardener.

"Hello, boy," he always called her that. In fact, he constantly switched the genders of his grand offspring to tease them.

"Hello, Grossmam," Brenda shot back. She surprised both, and a flash of fear jolted her even more. Grandfather merely chuckled as visions of getting reamed out in the barn for her retort momentarily robbed her of the present.

"You had thought about this," Grandpa's sapphire eyes sparkled. "What keeps you busy besides riding a bicycle?"

"That place," she inclined her head toward her destination.

"Oh?" Grandpa seemed to understand. "Are you farming it now?"

Brenda giggled. "Yes. Well, actually no. I just play there." Grandpa had a way of hugging you with words.

"And that works?" he questioned impishly. And so, Brenda found herself telling him about the rundown farm she explored a little further each day, listing the household items left by the Benjamens. Their conversation progressed as it always did, covering everything and nothing and all that lay in between.

A warm glow that always accompanied her around Grosspabeh stayed with her throughout that spring afternoon as she inhaled lilac trees and sifted household artifacts.

Brenda loved the old glass doorknobs in the house and dismantled one with a discarded butter knife. It shone once the cigarette ash, cooking grease, and dust was rinsed off in the frog pond, catching the sunlight brilliantly as she wedged it between her fingers.

At school the following week, Brenda wrote a story about an enchanted farm where a royal family lived in disguise, posing as ordinary farm people to protect their large fortune. Only Brenda herself had the unique privilege of socializing with the elite family as their private instructor for how to act ordinary. They, in turn, promised and paid in shares of their great jewel fortune which she kept at the farm to protect the identity of her friends and the treasure being pilfered by her unkind family. One day, a note materialized at the royal domain, indicating that Brenda was one of the distinguished household, having been grossly misplaced in a hospital conundrum. There it lay revealed on the faded burgundy step, the reason Brenda got along better with the belles than the beasts next door. She belonged at the fox farm, not the beating business.

Miss Wang read the story out loud to the second-grade class. Annie Redekop, usually at the center of attention, turned color and began whispering to all her classmates, one at a time, fervently. All but Brenda. An uncomfortable "too-warm," warmth rushed across Brenda's belly. Something bad was happening.

Abel's eyes grew wide before he blasted his sister's message, "You cheated! That's the story of Beauty and the Beast! Snow White! Cinderella! Whatever!"

"Class," Miss Wang queried. "Who here thinks Brenda cheated on her story?" Everyone raised their hands.

Tears rushed to the surface, unsteadying Brenda's chin. "Did you cheat on the story?" Miss Wang demanded.

Brenda rapidly lost the battle to tears but managed to speak. "I never cheat on stories," she choked out. "I don't have to."

The expression on Tina Harder's face softened. "Hey, she's right! Her stories are always good!"

Miss Wang threw the manuscript on her desk while a new whisper circulated the classroom. "I'm going to have to think about this."

It seemed the abuse and false accusations from home followed her around, shadowing her life at school.

Brenda spent the rest of the day reeling over how she lived her life as a punted football on the whims of other people, the result of other actions. It just wasn't fair.

A pair of baby doll shoes dragged home from school enough to catch Margaret's attention. "Vot ass louse?" (What is wrong?)

Father and Mother were seated at the table for a weekday faspa, supplementing his engorged belly, providing fodder for flushing later when mother vomited it all up to save her precious figure. It bewildered the local *frauen* (women) how mother stayed eighty-nine pounds with a dwindling supply of splintered, yellow-gray teeth.

Faspa drama unfurled around the raspberry jelly and brown bread. Mother and father loathed schoolteachers, so today's story piqued their interest greatly.

"That kid held a pen since before she could speak!" Mother blasted.

"Before she could walk," Father interjected.

"She has a pen! She has a PEN!" Mother mimicked an imaginary tattler. "Yes, I know," she answered herself, still mocking and miming.

Most matters of the conflictual nature were handled with a handwritten letter in a block alphabet by Mother or Father. Anytime an issue arose in the community, church, or school, Mother declared an ink war.

"Da failt ein ladder tuh shreeven" (They need a letter written to them), she'd practically shout.

A damning *brief* (letter) on loose-leaf formed against Miss Wang under Mother's flying hand in block letters.

> Miss Wang;
>
> We have-put up with your over strictness with some students and your laxness in regard to our daughter getting picked on by the entire class. You tell us our children stink and need to bath and change clothes more often. We put up with that too. But when my daughter is falsely accused of cheating in writing, which we know she excels at, it's your job to correct the other children. Not let them gang up on her!
>
> I want the story she wrote today marked as high as possible, or I will take this higher. Enough is enough. I will have your job taken from you if you can't smarten up! - Elizabeth Gardener. '

Neither Mother nor Father asked nor offered to read *The Enchanted Farm* and Brenda didn't offer to show it off.

"Tomorrow you'll hand it in, and she better mark it accordingly," a dangerous snarl edged mother's voice. "Let me know how it goes."

An ashen-faced Margaret pushed past her fear to present the letter to the second-grade schoolmarm before the morning's chalkboard chores.

Miss Wang read the letter while the pupils slowly trickled in. Her face reddened beneath her mulberry makeup. An aghast Margaret stood, waiting.

"Okay. Okay." The educator rubbed her mauve temples. "I'll give her an A. You'll see."

"NOW," Margaret demanded, blushing red with discomfort but wrestling the immediate devil rather than the one lurking at home. "She did not CHEAT!"

The world stopped and stared at the confrontation. Annie blushed. A few of her followers stepped away from her.

Sighing, the tiny oriental scrawled a large A on the top right-hand corner of the page. Satisfied, Margaret nodded and emitted the classroom.

Heavily, Miss Wang rose and trotted the paper over to Brenda's desk and dropped it like it was an offensive rag. Brenda ducked her head back into the chapter book she was reading, *Little House on the Prairie*, avoiding the tension and Annie Redekop's defeat around her.

CHAPTER 82

Bribery

ON SUNDAY, the Penners came socializing with the younger half of their dozen children, all smelling of woodstove and old mothballs.

The Penner offspring lined up shyly to square off with the Gardener children, who lost the battle of numbers instantaneously. Margaret, Susan, and Ernest quickly disappeared into the basement with Jacob Gruenwald to play hangman on the giant chalkboard.

Awkwardly, the younger generation left over filed into the living room behind the office desk. Private school had separated them where once they bussed and attended the same school together.

The adult gossip had only broached the weather—were they indeed getting rain? —when Mother sprang into action like a coiled snake, eyes flashing.

"Wallflower!" Mother hissed. Now Father looked uncomfortable.

"Go get out your last year's Christmas toys and play with your company! I am shaming myself over you!"

Marlene sat shyly alongside the cousins on the brown plaid couch, but as usual, Mother only saw opportunity to lash out at her favorite target.

"Dad! Do something about THAT kid!" she exclaimed, triggering an uneasy look on Aunt Zedah's face.

"Our children always want to come here," Aunt remarked.

Brenda forced herself to her feet, feeling the world had eyes on her. She pointed out the spring mounted rocking horse in the doorless closet and the toy bin beside it to the younger children.

Then she led the crowd into the kitchen ungainly for a session of coloring with wax crayons in yester year's Christmas books.

"And I am going to need the table for faspa!" Mother hollered.

My mother hates me, Brenda thought for the umpteenth time in her life. *I must be an awful person for my own mother to hate me.*

"Hey, who is the English boy?" Johan wanted to know. Even the Mennonite youngsters gossiped.

"That's our cousin from our mother's side. He's half-German," Brenda explained. "Half German, half-Indian." She wondered silently how humans could be halved.

Jacob didn't look particularly first nations; he could pass for a random English child with a tan.

"You have an Indian living with you?" Johan was credulous. "Does he steal? What color does he bleed if he cuts himself?"

After they finished coloring, Brenda led the group into their bedroom, trying not to be ill at ease with Johan, David, and Jacob Penner sitting on her bed. She had overheard Margaret's friends talking about women getting pregnant from a man lying on top of them in bed. This had eerie similarities, and the boys were her cousins to boot. She hoped whatever about them made babies didn't transfer to her bed clothes and then her. How would she explain that to her hateful mother?!

Quickly, Brenda engaged everyone in a game of Simon says, and the boys all ended up on Marlene's crackling, plastic-lined bed.

The Penner cousins were sensory-deprived; one could easily tell by the way they clung to your every word and parroted back verbatim. Every soul in that family stared at everyone else, not just the perverted boys. It was a home void of television, radio, board games, and most books.

Rain fell throughout faspa, turning the driveway to slick ick.

"Brenda is a horrible child," she heard Mother say to Aunt Zedah.

God bless "dey Pannasheh," (the Mrs. Penner) who rebutted Mother's pious siphoning with "Nah obah! Dot dahvayen nicht. Gott haf uns dee chinya bloss yeah leet!" (No, exclamation of protest, that isn't it. God has only lent us the children).

Which put Mother in fuming mode all throughout faspa, faspa cleanup, and after the large dark green van slipped and lurched out of sight.

Father burrowed deep into the medicine cabinet for his beloved antihistamines and, having gulped a few white and forest green oblong capsules, soon fell asleep sitting in the recliner.

Margaret dried the dishes, and Mother jabbered on about what a know-it-all Aunt Zedah was. Naturally, Margaret agreed with her, fashioning all kinds of arguments to suit and placate her. To appease and comfort her; the ONLY way to connect with mother.

"Susan is an all-visint (all knowing) too," Margaret stated eagerly.

Brenda slid away to the empty farm next door, oblivious to the mud and wet vines pulling and clinging on her rapid footsteps.

Water dripped off of every ivy, fern leaf, and Bluebell hanging its head, the only other sound being a Killdeer trilling like they always did after a rainfall. The silence, the dripping water, and "Deet! Deet! Deedlelah deedlelah!" soothed away the jagged teeth marks her mother had left on her spirit. Mayhem and misadventure ran amok as Brenda walked back home from her oasis.

"Branna!" Father yelled. "Where have you been! Don't always wander off like that!"

Doors slammed. The green and white picnic drink thermos dangled by its handle from Mother's free hand. The other carried a large cookie tin laden with pastries confined to the pyramid by saran wrap.

"We're going to wiener roast at Aunt Val's, and you made us late!" Mother screeched over the top of her burden. "You're never in with the family! Never in with the family!" Now she was chanting like a preacher.

Aunt Val had thrown a hasty party in honor of Uncle Corky's third, fourth, or fifth wedding, and of course, when the Gardeners arrived, there was the usual scene of debauchery. Uncle Levi and Uncle Hans were attempting to high kick each other while Uncle Bill, dark, mysterious, and handsome, made eyes at his wife, Aunt Valerie.

Long shadows lazed across the fabricated garden shed and watched the beer chugging grownups titter and make stories with overdone gestures.

An arm warmed the tops of her shoulders, and a body slid in beside her on the wooden beam she'd perched on. A scent of roses and bar soap and beer and cigarettes engulfed her.

"You look sad. Have your parents been beating you again?" a voice purred. Aunt Val in her store-bought polka dot dress shocked her; first with her closeness and then with the penetrating query.

Brenda nodded dumbly. She hadn't received a purple welt thrashing lately, but did she feel like she travelled through life with hurt feelings and bruises? Absolutely.

Did she relate those pains to her life givers?

Unequivocally, yes.

"Do they yell at you and say unkind things to you?" Aunt Val pressed on.

Brenda's bottom lip quivered. The gentle, tender voice purred on.

"Would you like me to talk to them?"

Brenda nodded again, hope springing up to defeat the lengthening shadows.

"Hey, Elizabeth!" Val hollered for all the background hootenanny to halt.

"This kid is giving you up! Says you beat on her and say nasty things. And I, for one, believe it and won't stand for it anymore!" she finished triumphantly.

Brenda's brief flicker of hope quenched. Now she'd be in even bigger trouble than ever previously.

Mother's face blanched. Father smiled like he always did when he was ill at ease…or about to whip his daughters all in a row.

On the trip home, Mother oddly had Brenda sit in front seat. Then, tucking Brenda's head under her arm like a football, she prattled on and on about how Brenda didn't mean to do what she did, right? Her and Father were good parents, weren't they?

"I wish you wouldn't drink with my brothers," Mother interrupted herself to eradicate and admonish Father. "It just encourages them. We should be the Christian example. Don't you think?"

Back to her true mission of the journey, other than to get home, Mother continued on. Aunt Val should be ashamed of her big mouth. Why couldn't she just have contented herself sucking on cigarettes? All their childhoods, Val had had a knack for getting Mother in trouble.

"I don't beat you, do I?" Mother squished Brenda's head against her bony torso. "I don't have to. You're always such a good girl."

This despotic affection was far worse than any physical altercation; an unfamiliar devil as it were. The worst part was the unspoken expectation of a specific response or else.

Brenda knew better that to squirm away and show her awkwardness, so she endured the grasp and nodded and shook her head obediently against Mother's abdomen.

Father turned on the eight-track, and the Chuck Wagon Gang obeyed in a rendition of "I'll Fly Away."

"Must you?" Mother interjected. He ignored her and flew along the gravel and dirt road still wet from rainfall.

It disappointed Brenda that the precipitation had been wasted on a Sunday. Rain on a holy day was lost on the strict religious regimes whereas the elements brought a break from endless chores for crafts on any other weekday. Then she wondered if God was mad at her for thinking such thoughts, and if rain was actually the tears of the Deity.

CHAPTER 83

Breaking Horses

THE LAST day of school loomed amid bare feet and dandelion fluff. Brenda liked the feel of her legs rubbing together under her dress in place of those wretched itchy tights whose crotch forever sagged.

Miss Wang and Brenda had developed a begrudging respect between them, like two south magnets held at bay of each other.

The librarian decided everyone should read over the summer, allowing two-chapter books to go home with each child. Brenda was all over it, watching the clock for reading period. She had her eye on *The Black Stallion* and *The Black Stallion Returns* and hoped to get to the two hardcover editions before anyone else did.

Jacob Gruenwald, the perfect city slicker and greenhorn to farming, paid dearly for his ignorance, minus the bliss.

When father brought all three horses out, Jacob wondered aloud where the bridle went or, in fact, what it was.

"That goes on the horse's tail," Margaret declared firmly.

Gingerly, he stood on tiptoe, squinted, and reached up to grasp Little Red's tail.

Father appeared with a hack more, having long since given up on putting a bit in the mouth of the stubborn beast.

"What are you doing?" he asked Jacob.

"Putting the bridle on. As soon as I can catch her tail—"

Father let out a hoot of laughter. "Then you've got the wrong end, son!

Mother had sliced watermelon and deep-fried biscuits floating in a vat of fat when the sky darkened.

"Ach!" she scoffed, busily rolling *roll kuchen* (roll cookies), expertly twisting them into the frying pot.

"Blasted rain. Now everything will stick to our boots and you kids will track it inside. You always do, it doesn't matter what I say!" To the visitors, she said; "That's clean mud! Bring your shoes in!"

She had relented on a pre-supper snack and given Marlene and Brenda a sliver of watermelon. Behind mothers back, they slid the rind in between their teeth and cheeks then tried not to laugh as they grinned green at each other.

Mother turned and caught sight of their grimaces and snickered.

"You kids!"

Margaret clattered into the porch like it was Christmas with her aluminum milk pails. Noisily pouring the milk into the cream separator void of her usual unmelodious racket, Mother seemed to sense something amiss. "What's wrong?"

"Dad has taken Jacob into the garage to build an airplane, and I am doing all the work! He used to take me to—" a sob escaped Margaret, interrupting her tale of woe and neglect.

"It figures!" Mother detonated. "I only agreed to take him on grounds that our children wouldn't suffer! There! See?"

By suppertime, both Margaret and Mother were sniffling and otherwise silent.

Rain pattered the roof of the farmhouse in a steady low rhythm that mingled with the snapping crackle of the stove in the porch.

Eating watermelon and then a "*roll kuchen*" (Roll cookie) posed an endless cycle. The watermelon juices were absorbed by the pastry; the fried biscuit although fluffy and delectable inside its crust, made one thirst for another slice.

Brenda observed her brawny brown second cousin sitting at fathers' elbow. His arrival had caused an entire shift of the family eating arrangement; Margaret down a seat from Father to insert Jacob. Brenda now beside Mother, and Marlene on the corner between her parents, leaving the sewing machine at the opposite end of Father.

After the children left the table, an argument unleashed betwixt the grownups. Brenda felt scared for her mother but dared not intervene. Images of her father's treatment of Little Red resisting the idea of bridling her flashed amid bolts of actual lightening...

Little Red hated a bit in her mouth, despised harnessing, and only barely tolerated the hack more and saddle. She had not been properly broken when Grandfather passed her onto Father. He had forcibly saddled and harnessed her and then mounted her, and the filly had promptly reared and bucked adversely. In a rage, Father had pulled the reins tight, forcing her head down into her neck while he sneered at her.

Breaking horses, unfortunately, among the much revered and respected Gardener family, was exactly how it sounded. Once a horse's spirit was broken, they no longer resisted man's imposition in the format of ropes and reins. Children were raised the same way horses were broken, but of course, no one knew different, and displaying one's emotional pain seemed unreasonable and unwelcome.

Father, convicted of his misdemeanor in parenting, included Margaret in the garage crafts the next day while the rain droned on. Brenda donned on her old green raincoat with wide white stripes along the wrists and bottom to include the shop shenanigans.

The 970 Case tractor parked inside made for limited space to play but lent an excellent climbing apparatus. Brenda braced her rubber soled feet on its faded orange body to crane her head into the attic of the structure.

"Don't fall," Father coaxed.

To her delight, a boxful of musty old Reader's Digests sat near the opening on a sloped pile of sawdust.

"Can I have those?" Brenda asked credulously. "Marlene and I can play library." She thought if she involved the favored child, the chances of a positive answer increased.

Father chuckled. "Well, come down off of there and I'll see what I can do."

Much more to Brenda's delight, the box of magazines was unscathed where the ever-present mice were concerned. They smelled of fuel, moth balls, and sawdust, but to Brenda, she discovered a bookworm's gold mine.

"Not upstairs! Not in my clean house!" Mother's shout greeted her upon entry of the white, gold, and honey colored porch with its braided twine rug.

"I can smell them from here! Get them downstairs!" Mother brandished her tea towel.

The boxed contents made a glorious addition to Marlene and Brenda's rainy-day play downstairs in the playroom. They wasted no time making library cards for the strip covered magazines. Brenda read the titles as best she could and explained their meaning to her sibling with help from the odd consultation with Mother.

Rainy days brought winter habits and hobbies from their hiding and made a toxic home cozy. Mother's sewing machine hummed over quilt patches, liquid embroidery covered the remainder of the kitchen table, and the shoemaker's elves couldn't have been more efficient.

Brenda joined her siblings in the embroidery activity for a while but grew weary of mother's instructions on how to shade things and her inability to do so.

"Look at Marlene, so talented," Mother praised the bug-eyed little imp. "She's so little and cute." Downstairs in the playroom-deep freeze-storage Jacob's sleeping quarters, Brenda found Father's accordion in its large case. Struggling, she pulled the twenty-five-pound 120 Bass piano accordion from its red velour resting place. Suddenly, she lay backward with the black ebony and ivory instrument on top of her as the wrestling champion.

Righting herself, Brenda knelt on the cold linoleum floor behind the machine and slid her left hand in the strap beside the buttons. Peering over it, she could just see the ivory keys. She pushed and pulled on the strapped side to force air movement. The apparatus barely budged. Then, by pressing a button, the bellows extended easier than they had. Brenda wiggled her fingers like Father did when he played. One, two, one, two. It worked.

Now the keyboard side… She had braced it with her free hand, but to play it, Brenda found she had to drag the cumbersome wind instrument onto her legs and, holding it sloped against her, could press the bass buttons and keys at the same time.

The living room boasted a pedestal organ with a heavy gunny sackcloth cover, the speaker beneath the keys. It had to warm up before anyone could play, and the audible hum of its efforts was ever present. Brenda could play "Mary Had A Little Lamb" and follow the alphabetical instructions in the Gaither hymnbook to play "Even So Lord Jesus Come." Father had purchased a larger organ at an auction with an electrical short in its circuit that sounded like popcorn popping in mid-strain. It sat up against the wall by Mother's deep freeze, ready to sputter and fart on rainy days.

"What's this?" Mother traipsed through the large room of multiple purposes, spotting Brenda.

"Look! I can play!" Brenda demonstrated.

"That kid has figured out the accordion," Mother told Father upstairs when he came in for supper, Jacob chattering at his elbow like a tamed squirrel. "Bran-NAH!"

he bellowed "Supper TIME!" "Come hear me play first!" she hollered.

Father's heavy steps *bah-boom, bah-boomed* down the hand-painted staircase.

Brenda squished and squashed the bellows back and forth, bass buttons up and down, and keyed in "Mary Had A Little Lamb" with pauses.

Father beamed. "Mein zeit" (My sakes), he said, and then, "Come up for supper."

After a meal of beef stew and buttermilk biscuits, the evening sun shone its slanted rays across the farmyard belatedly underneath a low hanging rainbow. Nostalgia lingered over the kitchen and those feasting within its orange expanses.

Even Jacob wrinkled his forehead, squinting toward the muslin-clad, be ruffled window that faced the garden. "Great. Back to work now," he muttered, grumbling and triggering a round of rueful smiles.

Made in United States
Troutdale, OR
11/10/2024

24627649R00297